Elena's Destiny

She pulled away, her dark blue eyes spitting scorn. 'You find it easy enough to insult me, my lord. Can you not find someone of your own rank to torment?'

He held out his hands in a mock attempt at appeasement. 'Insult you? I did not intend it as such. I was merely commenting on your sexual rapaciousness. You used to be so sweet, so innocent, Elena, but you have learnt much, I fancy. How many men have you welcomed to your bed since I relieved you of your maidenhead?'

She gasped and tried to pull away; but already his hands were moving upwards, cupping her small high breasts, twisting her nipples beneath the thin silk of her gown. She was on fire for him and he knew it. He pulled her roughly towards him and kissed her, his tongue plunging into her mouth, possessing it. She reached for his shoulders, pulling his head down towards hers, pressing her aching breasts against his hard chest. She clung to him desperately, not caring, not able to think. 'Dear God, Aimery,' she breathed. 'Why do you torment me like this?'

Elena's Destiny
Lisette Allen

BLACK LACE

Black Lace books contain sexual fantasies.
In real life, always practise safe sex.

This edition published in 2006

First published in 1997 by
Black Lace
Thames Wharf Studios
Rainville Road
London W6 9HA

Typeset by SetSystems Ltd, Saffron Walden, Essex
Printed and bound by Mackays of Chatham PLC

ISBN 0 352 33218 2
ISBN 9 780352 332189

Chapter One

In this year King William led an English and French host overseas, to conquer the province of Maine. The English laid it completely waste; they destroyed the vineyards, burnt down the towns, and completely devastated the countryside, and brought it all into subjection to William. Thereafter they returned home to England. (The Anglo-Saxon Chronicle, 1073.)

Henriette was making her way across the crowded banqueting hall with yet another jug of spiced wine when a man called out to her. 'Hey, sweetheart! Bring that wine over here, will you? And stop a while to serve it.'

Henriette giggled and patted her tumbling chestnut curls coyly as the burly soldier who'd just spoken relieved her of the heavy earthenware jug and pulled her on to his knee. Oh, she was enjoying playing at being a serving girl in Duke William's great stronghold of Rouen. Especially as the stern duke himself had been called away unexpectedly, and things were beginning to get rather out of hand.

She gazed happily round the disorderly gathering. All

1

the knights, squires and soldiers who'd been summoned to vow allegiance to Normandy this Eastertide seemed determined on having, one way or another, the time of their lives. The evening's feasting had been going on for hours; down in the kitchens the harassed cooks and scullions were weary with serving up the great silver dishes of venison, and spiced pork, and heron baked in chervil. Now, the food was almost finished. But the wine wasn't, and no-one seemed to have any intention of leaving. Least of all Henriette.

'You're a pretty lass,' murmured the soldier to her, running his hand covetously up and down her plump thigh as he settled her on his lap. 'New here, are you?'

'I've lived in Rouen all my life,' grinned Henriette, boldly gazing back into his hot black eyes. That was true, at least. But this handsome, brawny man-at-arms would never guess that she was in fact the daughter of a rich nobleman, whose mansion lay just inside the town's walls, and who would have had a violent fit of fury if he knew that his cherished only daughter was here dressed as a serving wench, in the very midst of all this boisterous feasting, instead of safely at home in her silk-curtained bed.

Even Henriette was beginning to find the noise somewhat deafening. In the huge, candlelit hall, where the smoke from the fire swirled up to the blackened rafters, there were over a hundred men, their appetite for food almost sated but their desire for wine and entertainment growing by the minute. All the gently bred womenfolk had retired long ago; and now there were only serving girls left, dressed like Henriette in rough serge gowns and linen aprons, running between the crowded trestles, laughing and trying to answer all the urgent cries for more ale, more wine.

Her soldier was talking army talk now with his drunken comrades, but he kept her firmly settled in his lap, and he was still managing to fondle her plump breasts through the coarse fabric of the gown she'd stolen from her maid before sneaking out of the house earlier that evening. As his thumb rasped her stiffening nipple, she felt delightful ripples of pleasure run through her body. She reached for the man's beaker of wine, and drank down several mouthfuls of the sweet, strong liquid; he grinned and refilled it for her. Henriette sighed happily. She'd never been to a feast such as this one before. How angry Duke William and his bishops would be if they heard of it.

Then Henriette twisted suddenly on the soldier's knee, because over in one corner, something new seemed to be happening. A group of rowdy young knights had swept a trestle table clear, knocking bread and wine and meatbones to the floor; an old lurcher hound who had been lying by the fire ambled over and began to devour them. A couple of slatternly maids, whom Henriette had seen working in the kitchens earlier, were laughing as three burly knights pulled a struggling young squire towards them. Henriette was intrigued, and excited. Something wicked was about to happen, she was sure, and she couldn't wait. 'What's going on?' she whispered in her soldier's ear. He grinned, his black eyes assessing her plump, flushed face.

'It's a seasonal sport, sweetheart,' he told her. 'Time for those young squires to prove their manhood. In public.'

'Oh!' Henriette was startled, and fascinated.

'Those wenches will help them along, don't worry. They've done this sort of thing before. See?'

Henriette wriggled on his lap, straining to see better over the sea of faces that filled the hall. The man gave a mock groan.

'Sweetheart, if you carry on moving around on top of me like that, then I swear I'll have to take you on the tabletop myself!'

Henriette blushed, then laughed. Perhaps that

3

wouldn't be such a bad idea. The soldier, who'd told her his name was Armand, was handsome enough, and his thumb was still rasping across her tight little nipples with delightful expertise. She felt warm and aroused. It was a long time – at least a month – since she'd had a good, stalwart man inside her. It was so difficult when her doting parents kept their precious daughter virtually under lock and key, and even more difficult since they'd announced her imminent betrothal to one of Duke William's most renowned knights. Not that she minded *that*. The thought of her betrothal sent shivers of delight up and down her spine.

If she craned her neck she could just see, through the swirling sea of faces, that the young squire had been encouraged to lay one of the kitchen sluts back across the table and was swiving her vigorously, pushing up her skirts round her waist and gripping her plump buttocks in order to penetrate her more fully. The older men were cheering him on drunkenly, passing loud comments on his technique and offering suggestions. Henriette gazed, rapt. She wished it was her lying there, feeling the young man's vigorous penis thrusting away inside her warm flesh. But then, after all, perhaps she could wait. She felt a fresh tingle of excitement as she remembered that tonight, the man she was going to marry was arriving in Rouen. That was why she had sneaked out here, to the Tower, this evening. Her father had promised her a meeting with her future bridegroom tomorrow, but Henriette was desperate to see him the moment he arrived, because she'd heard whispered rumours that he was the most dangerously attractive knight in all Duke William's domain.

Smiling dreamily to herself at the thought, she became aware that all the soldiers around her were raucously jeering and laying bets as another squire was pulled, bashful and protesting, towards the ceremonial table. 'I'll lay you five deniers this lad won't make it,' com-

4

mented Henriette's soldier Armand scornfully. 'Look at him. He's shaking with terror.'

'Ten deniers that he will,' drawled another man. 'If he doesn't, I'll go over and show him how to do it myself.'

The others laughed. Someone said, half enviously, 'Aye, you do that, Ralf. That would be a proper treat for the wenches, after having to make do with these puny puppies!'

By now, the older knights who'd organised the entertainment were pulling at the lacing of the reluctant squire's hose; and the two women were teasing him, thrusting their heavy breasts against his face, fumbling with his private parts. Henriette, a little bored with the youth's inadequacy, turned herself on Armand's knee to gaze at the man who had just wagered ten deniers. She knew that his name was Ralf, and that he was a knight from Normandy, who'd been rewarded with lands in England for his services to William after the conquest. Now he'd returned to Normandy, summoned to this great Easter gathering to swear fresh allegiance to his overlord. He was a good-looking man, she decided, a bit more refined than the others, with thick blond hair and keen, pale blue eyes that were only just starting to look hazed with drink. But his mouth, though beautiful, was somehow cruel. And then, even as she watched him surreptitiously and tried to imagine what he would be like in bed, she saw his pale gaze suddenly travel towards the open door that led to the upper chambers.

'Well,' Ralf said softly. 'So my lady wife condescends to join me at last.'

Henriette turned sharply to where he was looking and gazed in fascination. There, outlined against the doorway, her still figure illuminated by the dancing light of the candles on the walls, was the most beautiful woman Henriette had ever seen.

She was not tall, but she held herself almost regally. Her clinging gown, with its elegant narrow sleeves and flowing skirt that flared out from her slender hips, was of delicate green silk, and a long white kerchief covered most of her hair, though Henriette was able to glimpse that it was the colour of palest gold. Her face was a perfect oval, dominated by wide-set eyes of dark blue; and her gaze rested, expressionless, on Ralf.

Ralf banged on the table and beckoned her with his hand. She walked slowly towards him across the herb-strewn rushes; like a pure candle flame, thought Henriette wonderingly, amongst the noise and bawdiness of this riotous feast. Ralf grinned round at his comrades, who watched speechless as the lady approached. 'Isn't she a little beauty, now?' boasted Ralf. 'She's convent-bred, comrades – but she's long since forgotten her convent ways, I tell you!' Then he turned to his lady, who had drawn close and stopped. 'I sent for you some time ago. Why have you presumed to take so long?'

Henriette, like everyone else, strained to hear the lady's reply. When she spoke, it was in softly accented French that betrayed her English origins.

'My lord Ralf. You must understand that this is no place for me. With your permission, I shall now retire.'

Ralf grabbed her slender wrist and pulled her down beside him. She winced, but was silent. 'You have not my permission, lady Elena,' he replied silkily. 'You are my wife, and are sworn to obey me in all things. Sit here, with me.'

Henriette, spellbound, saw the beautiful English lady close her deep blue eyes in what looked very like despair. All the men at the table were silent too, watching her hungrily. One of Ralf's comrades licked his lips. 'She was a nun, you say, Ralf?'

Ralf grinned and stroked his lady's smooth white cheek. 'Aye,' he chuckled. 'A novice, at any rate. She never took her vows. Her English convent was burned down during the troubles in the north, three years ago. Just as well, because she's far too pretty to be a nun, isn't

6

she? Look at her creamy skin, her firm little breasts, her luscious sweet mouth . . .'

Around them the noise of the revellers ebbed and flowed like the roaring of the sea. Henriette's soldier was trying to fondle her again, but she ignored him and leant forward, anxious to catch every word. Another soldier was staring at Elena, before saying to Ralf, 'So. A sweet little virgin from a convent, eh? And you had her first?'

Ralf shook his blond head and poured himself more wine. 'No. This is the best of it, my comrades.' His hand moved round Elena's slender shoulders, stroking her possessively. 'My lovely young bride was in fact trained exceedingly well in the arts of love, by some foreign mercenary who took her captive after the burning of her convent. He used her for his entertainment for a few months, I gather, and taught her some delightful tricks. But then he left her. The novelty wore off for him, I suppose, as it does. Elena won't even tell me his name. Will you, sweeting?'

Henriette saw how the English lady gazed blindly ahead as Ralf fondled her. She hates her husband, thought Henriette suddenly, hates him! Oh, how she wished to fall in love with her own husband, the knight who was due to arrive here, in Rouen, tonight! Perhaps, she thought suddenly, the lady Elena was still in love with the foreign mercenary Ralf spoke of, the man who seduced her, and then cruelly abandoned her.

Ralf was toying with his wife's breasts, making the nipples stand out hard and tight against the silk of her gown. 'My lord.' The lady Elena's voice was scarcely a whisper. 'I implore you to let me leave this company.'

But Ralf only smiled. 'I thought you were enjoying yourself, my lady wife,' he murmured, still chafing her breasts with his thumb.

'She's a passionate wench, then, Ralf?' muttered another man, leaning drunkenly across the table to gaze at Elena. Ralf's pale blue eyes suddenly hardened.

'I thought so, once. She agreed to marry me quickly enough, didn't you, wench? And she'll do whatever I say – her foreign soldier taught her well. She has such pretty ways, with her mouth, her lips, her tongue. But I fear her little convent-bred heart is cold, cold as ice.' Ralf suddenly seemed very drunk. His hands were pulling at his wife's robes, fumbling at the lacings; at last he managed to pull her bodice apart, so that her small white breasts were exposed. Henriette felt her own excitement simmering at her loins; she heard the man whose knee she perched on growl deep in his throat, and felt his big hands stealing round her waist once more. Ralf, aware of his companions' fascination, pulled at his wife's taut pink nipples thoughtfully. Elena's face was white, desperate. 'Wouldn't you say,' murmured Ralf, 'that these ripe little beauties were begging for a man's touch, longing to be taken in a man's mouth? But she's no longer interested in such things, comrades. You can swive her till daybreak, and she'll not respond. Believe me, her blood is frozen in her veins.'

'Mayhap it's you!' called a fellow knight. 'Could be your lusty weapon's not stout enough for her, Ralf.'

Ralf, letting go of Elena, lurched across the table and gripped the man by the throat. An overturned goblet sent rivulets of red wine pouring across the table. 'Say that again if you dare!' he hissed. 'I've pleasured scores of willing women, and given them no cause for complaint.'

'Gently, gently, Ralf,' soothed another man, gazing longingly at Elena's naked breasts. 'Perhaps our friend Ivo has a point. Perhaps you ought to let someone else mount her, and then you could enjoy watching. A bit of variety might enliven the wench, and make her hotter for you.'

Ralf's eyes narrowed as he sagged back in his seat. Elena's head was bowed in silent suffering, her pale gold hair falling loosely from beneath her kerchief to curtain her cheeks, so Henriette could no longer see her beautiful face. 'You have a point,' scowled Ralf. 'Whatever the solution, I'm beginning to think I had a poor bargain of our marriage.'

So did the lady Elena, thought Henriette, stricken with curiosity over this gentle, lovely woman whose dark blue eyes were haunted by unhappiness. She wondered why her husband Ralf was so cruel to her. Oh, how she hoped her own husband-to-be would prove to be worthy.

They were all suddenly diverted by a huge bellow of laughter from the table over near the fire. The ritual humiliation of the young squires was proceeding apace. Yet another young squire, shy and embarrassed, was having difficulty in performing the allotted task. The women, laughing heartily, were taking it in turns to toy with his reluctant penis, competing in their efforts to coax it into hardness. Elena's torment was forgotten for the moment as Ralf, Ivo, Armand and the rest craned their necks or even stood up to see better across the noisy room. Elena sat very still, with her head bowed, as if wishing herself a hundred miles from here; but Henriette was glad to be in the midst of it all. She scrambled on to one of the benches with Armand's help, and laughed aloud to see everyone cheering noisily as the youth's pale, slender penis grew quiveringly erect at last.

One of the women, crowing in triumph, pushed her female companion aside and bent to lick the squire's genitals lasciviously with her darting tongue; the young man shuddered and cried out in rapture. Then the woman lay back on the trestle, her plump legs dangling apart, and rucked up her skirts temptingly. The youth dived for her with a groan of longing, fumbling with eager fingers at her exposed mound; the woman reached out to grasp his slender penis and, with a grin, coaxed him to enter her.

The youth was transfixed with pleasure. So was Henriette, who was leaning against the broad shoulders of her muscular admirer Armand and watching the crude coupling with radiant delight. She'd never seen anything like this in her father's banqueting chamber. The youth was starting to fumble at the doxy's heavy breasts, and began, tentatively, to thrust between her thighs. The older knights around him roared encouragement and banged their goblets on the table as his scrawny hips clenched with effort. Henriette licked her lips, feeling how her own nipples were hard with excitement, her secret flesh plump and slick between her thighs. She rubbed her legs together in agitation. And then Armand pulled her down suddenly into his lap again and murmured hotly in her ear.

'Like watching that sort of thing, do you, wench? Fancy a bit of sport yourself, eh?'

Henriette had fallen with a gasp into his arms. He kissed her, hard. Then his big, calloused hand cupped her breasts, chafing her stiffened nipples deliciously through the coarse fabric of her gown. At the same time his other hand slid down between her thighs, and his thick forefinger probed at the folds of her skirt and began to rub deliberately against her swollen mound, finding her delicate cleft and sliding up and down it, sending shivers to her very soul. Dear God, the soldier would feel how wet she was, how much she wanted him. As Armand's hot tongue roughly probed her mouth, she squirmed her hips with delight, and felt the outline of his strong, thick penis pressing hard against her from beneath his tunic. How she'd enjoy feeling that stout shaft jumping about inside her, thought Henriette rather dazedly.

The doxy who was sprawled on the table beneath the young squire was screaming out her delight now. Her bare legs were drawn high, and her fists thumped the table as the youth drove into her, faster and faster. His face was pink with pleasure, his bottom was jerking spasmodically; the men around him were banging their winecups in time to his feverish thrusts. The crowd had shifted slightly, and when Henriette's soldier stopped kissing her, she caught a tantalising glimpse of the youth's slender shaft diving in and out; then, just as he was about to reach his crisis, two laughing, burly knights wrenched him out of the woman, and his hot penis twitched across the woman's belly, his seed spurting frantically as he gasped out his pleasure. Henriette watched, transfixed with lust. At the same time her own grinning soldier pressed hard with his fingers against her cleft, rubbing her wet little nub of pleasure through the fabric of her gown while his other hand fondled her breast. Henriette caught her breath in rapture and spasmed desperately beneath his wickedly probing hand, clamping her lips shut to stifle her little moans as her secret, intense orgasm racked her body.

The soldier Armand laughed softly and nuzzled her soft cheek with his lips. 'Liked that, didn't you? But I'll wager you could do with more.' He took her small hand and shifted it so she could feel the hard thickness of his shaft stirring beneath his tunic. 'How about you and me finding a quiet place outside of here, sweetheart, so we can get things done properly?'

Henriette, who was only just starting to breathe again, grinned with delight. Oh, yes. She longed to feel his sturdy cock pleasuring her voluptuous wetness. But, just as she was drawing breath to reply, the big doors at the far end of the hall were flung open, and an icy draught of air blasted the room. Wreaths of smoke were driven from the great fire up into the soot-blackened rafters, and the candles in their iron sconces shivered and danced. A nervous silence gripped the hall. If this was the fearsome Duke of Normandy, returned a day early from his parley with the King of France, then his anger at these scenes of debauchery in the very heart of his

11

stronghold would indeed be something to daunt the stoutest soldier. The exhausted lad on the table pulled himself hastily from his doxy's arms and scuttled off into the shadows, pulling up his hose; the others slunk back to their seats. Someone coughed nervously. All eyes were turned towards the door, and the blackness that lay outside.

A man came in. The wintry sleet glittered on his thick, tawny hair, and on the long cloak of fine grey wool that covered his gleaming armour. Behind him were soldiers; a silent, formidable coterie of about a dozen men. Amongst their number was a foreigner with skin as black as night, with a curved sword pushed into his belt. Henriette watched, her eyes wide with excitement.

The leader of the men, tall and wide-shouldered, faced the silence contemptuously as his cold grey eyes swept the crowded hall. He took it all in; the drunken, cowering knights, the spilled wine, the sprawling, half-dressed doxies. Then he said, in a clear, chilling voice, 'I have come to Rouen to offer my sword to Duke William of Normandy. But I see – all too plainly – that he is not here.' His gaunt face twisted in scorn. Henriette noticed, with a sudden thumping of her heart, that a faded silver sword scar slashed his right cheek. 'Tell me,' he went on, 'have I come to the right place? Is this really the formidable Tower of Rouen, or is it some backstreet whorehouse?'

There was a breathless silence. Then the duke's seneschal, who'd been hiding in the kitchens away from the racket of the hall, came hurrying towards the newcomer, wringing his hands and grovelling out an apology. 'My lord! You are indeed welcome. The banquet is almost over, my lord; but there is another private chamber, down on the next floor, where you and your men can be served with food and wine in peace, while you rest, and recover yourselves after your journey.'

The seneschal's anxiety was genuine. For the last few

12

days, powerful stranger knights and barons had been arriving in Rouen with their retinues. They'd been summoned by William from his lands in England and Normandy, to vow their allegiance for a renewal of the campaign in Maine. They were influential men, and it was dangerous to offend them. Still wringing his hands, the seneschal led the tall, stern-faced knight and his followers through an inner doorway, towards the spiral stone staircase that led down to another, smaller banqueting chamber. Slowly everyone relaxed.

But not quite everyone, Henriette suddenly realised. Because the beautiful lady Elena was sitting as if frozen with shock, her hands pressed across her breasts, the colour draining from her face as she watched the scarred, handsome knight until he was gone from sight. 'No,' she was breathing, 'no, it cannot be . . .'

Henriette shrugged to herself. The English lady was obviously in a state of distress from her husband's cruel mockery. Henriette was becoming a bit bored with Elena, and was also finding herself rather jealous, because she was so beautiful. She herself was more interested in hearing what the others were saying about this intriguing new arrival, because a sudden wild hope had started to flicker in her mind.

'That man's nothing but a jumped-up mercenary from the looks of him,' Ralf was snorting contemptuously. 'He's obviously lived by his sword, and would change sides again as soon as some other lord offered him more gold than Duke William. Did you see the scar on his face? Wonder who he is?'

Ivo suddenly leant forward. 'I remember him,' he breathed. 'He's the Breton mercenary who fought at Hastings and saved Duke William's life. He was rewarded with a valuable fief in the north of England. But he fell out with William two winters ago. You remember the unrest in Flanders? The Flemish count

13

sent for aid from his ally, Duke William – but William offered to send only ten English knights, a pitiful force.'

The others nodded, murmuring. They were all soldiers. They remembered.

'Well,' continued Ivo, 'that Breton mercenary we've just seen, he argued with the duke, told him it was shameful to treat his ally Flanders thus. William was furious with him for being so outspoken. The scarred Breton mercenary stormed off, went with his own force to help the tiny contingent of Englishmen who fought for the count of Flanders. He was wounded and captured in the ensuing battle.'

'The Battle of Bavinchove?' put in another sombrely.

'Aye, the Battle of Bavinchove. Two years ago, in February. A disaster for the count of Flanders, and for those who supported him. William, meanwhile, still in high dudgeon, had stripped the Breton of all his English lands, as punishment for defying him. So he'd lost everything, along with his freedom.'

'But surely,' said Henriette, enthralled, 'William must have repented and paid for the brave knight's ransom?'

'No. You know our duke; his anger can last months, years, even, and he will never admit that he's wrong. The Breton was ransomed eventually by some friend of his, a rich French widow, whose name, like the Breton's, eludes me. Apparently she was his mistress. She tended him well, I believe, and by all accounts didn't want to let him go.' He grinned. 'They say that all the women go wild for the man, in spite of that ferocious scar.'

'Don't suppose they're looking at his face when he pleasures them,' sneered Ralf. 'Anyway, what's he doing here, in Rouen, if he's fallen out with Duke William?'

Ivo broke in. 'I think I know. Apparently, our fine duke has begun to experience a certain amount of remorse over the slaughter at Bavinchove. He's summoned the Breton back into the fold, has offered him

14

marriage with a young French heiress and the restoration of his English lands. In return for his sword, of course.'

Henriette's heart had started to thump so loudly she thought everyone must hear it. 'His name?' she whispered. 'Please. Doesn't anyone know his name?'

To her amazement, it was the lady Elena who answered her. Swiftly, silently, she'd got to her feet. Her small white hands were clasping her torn bodice together as she breathed, 'His name is Aimery. Aimery le Sabrenn.' Then she turned quickly, before Ralf could stop her, and hurried from the room.

Ivo thumped the table in drunken acknowledgement. 'God's wounds, but she's right – that's his name, I remember it now. Aimery le Sabrenn – that's Breton for Aimery the Swordsman.' He laughed coarsely. 'They say he was given the name on account of the long sword he wields, though I've heard that many a pretty wench has swooned over the way he wields his other, more private weapon.'

Henriette felt quite weak with excitement. She couldn't believe it, though it must be true. She'd come here tonight, full of trepidation, in order to catch a glimpse of her husband-to-be. Well, she'd had her glimpse, and it was more than enough. That beautiful, stern-faced knight, the man who had silenced the rowdy hall with one look, was in truth the man she had been waiting for all her life. Aimery le Sabrenn – her father had told her his name, weeks and weeks ago. Tomorrow she would meet him, at her father's house, for their betrothal. She could hardly wait. And the thought of their marriage night made her quite faint with anticipation. She must get home, immediately, and sneak back in through the servants' door, and prepare herself for meeting him in the morning.

Her soldier, who was still holding her on his lap, was starting to fondle her again. Henriette had forgotten about him.

"Tis my turn now, wench,' Armand was murmuring. 'How about a bit of attention for me? Let's go outside for a while. There are some sheds over behind the granary where we'll be nice and secret. I'll pleasure you nicely with my stout shaft – you must be as hungry for it as I am.'

Henriette remembered the feel of his swollen penis against her palm, and felt a stab of regret. Then she thought of Aimery le Sabrenn. 'Sorry,' she declared, planting a kiss on his weatherbeaten cheek, 'but I've got to go.' And, jumping up lightly before he could stop her, she ran towards the door and was soon lost to his sight.

'Damn,' muttered Armand angrily. 'Damn. I thought I was well set up there.'

'Plenty more where she came from,' said another soldier consolingly.

No. Armand shook his head. She was different, that wench. Lovely curling chestnut hair, soft and scented. Creamy skin and big brown eyes that danced with mischief. Plump, voluptuous breasts. She spoke and acted like a lady, except that she hadn't been a lady when he made her dance and moan secretly in his arms.

Armand sighed regretfully and, reaching for another jug of wine, decided to get drunk instead.

Chapter Two

*E*lena kneeled on the stoneflagged floor of the little chapel, high up on the fourth floor of Rouen's mighty tower. She could hear the gusts of chilly, sleet-laden wind hurling themselves against the thick stone walls, and she shivered, knowing that the air outside must be as cold as her heart.

'Please, God,' she prayed, 'oh please. Stop me loving him so much. Stop it hurting so much.'

She would have to get away from here, from Rouen, from Normandy. Tonight she would tell her husband Ralf – if he was in a fit state to listen to her – that she was leaving for England, on the morning tide.

She'd thought, at first, that she could learn to love Ralf. At least, she'd thought that she could endure her fate.

But the sight this evening of the only man she had ever loved storming his way into the banqueting hall, just as he'd once stormed his way into her heart, had shown her that even endurance was beyond her now. Everything about him tore at her soul. She was still hopelessly in love with Aimery le Sabrenn, the man who had seduced her and then gone back to his former mistress, Isobel de Morency.

17

This tower had become her prison. She had to escape.

Suddenly the door behind her began to creak open. For one wild moment Elena thought it might be Aimery, but of course it couldn't be, because he didn't even know she was here, in Rouen. And even if he did, why should he trouble to seek her out? Ralf's hateful friends had said that he was making some rich marriage to an eligible young heiress, at the bidding of Duke William. No doubt he and Isobel would break the girl's heart, just as they'd broken hers.

She turned round slowly. It was Ralf. He looked uncertain, hazy with drink; his thick blond hair was ruffled and untidy. She tried to remember why she'd once thought she could learn to love him. He moved towards her, frowning.

'You're my wife,' he muttered, 'my wife. You belong with me, in my bed. I won't have you skulking up here, amongst the crosses and candles, as if you were still back in your damned convent. Do you hear me?'

Elena shook herself free of his grip. A flush of rebellion warmed her delicate cheeks. 'I came here for sanctuary, my lord. Since you chose to abuse me, and humiliate me in front of your friends, I hoped that at least here I would be safe.'

He gripped her again, and this time she couldn't escape. 'So you say I humiliate you, do you?' he growled. 'By God, wench, it was I who lowered myself into marrying you. What are you? Just a base-born Saxon girl, abandoned as a babe at a convent; the debauched leavings of some nameless mercenary knight who took his fill of you then rode on his way. If I hadn't offered to marry you, where would you be now?' He sneered, cupping her face, twisting it up to meet his. 'You'd be earning your living on your back, in some poxy whore-house, that's where. And you wouldn't earn much, either, I can tell you!'

Elena gazed defiantly up at him, her blue eyes wide

18

with scorn. 'Then let me go. Let me depart, my lord. Let me go back to England, and find some convent that will take me in. I want nothing more.'

Ralf shuddered. He felt confused and tired. He wished he hadn't drunk so much wine. She was beautiful, his wife Elena. Sometimes he wished he'd never seen her, with her bewitching face, and her hair like pale spun gold, and her cold, cold heart. He'd thought that by following William's call to arms and bringing her here with him to Rouen, she would learn to be interested in him again. He was wrong. But he was damned if he would let her go.

The scorn in her eyes drove him wild, banishing any lingering feelings of tenderness. By God, she was beautiful, the bitch, and he'd arouse her to passion tonight if it was the last thing he did. Perhaps his friends had been right. *'Let someone else mount her,'* Ivo had said. *'Then at least you could enjoy watching.'*

'You're going nowhere, my sweet wife,' he snarled, 'except to my bed.' He gripped her hand; she stumbled after him, knowing she had no choice.

Their bedroom was a small, square chamber set in the deep thickness of the tower's stone walls, with just a single high, narrow window, and a heavy, barred door to secure it. A straw palliass on the floor and a wooden chest for linen were the only furnishings. Ralf and his wife were lucky to have that much, considering the crowds that filled Rouen this Eastertide. Slowly Elena followed Ralf inside, and he lit a wax candle in a bracket on the wall. Then, as the yellow flame washed the room with light, she recoiled and backed quickly towards the door.

'My lord,' she whispered through dry lips. 'I see you have company enough for tonight. I will find somewhere else to sleep.'

Ralf reached out to pull her back. His hand still fastened round her wrist, he turned to bolt the heavy door. 'Ah, but you are needed too. Stay and watch. You might just learn something.'

Elena leant against the roughly mortared wall, her heart thudding sickly against her chest. No. No, she would not endure it.

There was a man in their chamber: a rough-looking servant man, wearing a drab tunic and the leather apron of the kitchens. There were two women with him as well, two of the doxies the soldiers had been making free with down in the banqueting hall. The small chamber smelled overpoweringly of their cheap perfume, their unwashed bodies, the musky reek of their arousal. They'd hardly noticed Elena and Ralf coming in, because one of the sluts, the plump blonde one, was on her knees before the man, openly mouthing his phallus, which was hugely erect. Meaningfully licking her red lips, she was sucking and caressing at the straining shaft, and fondling the heavy sac of his testicles. The man shuddered with delight, then, catching sight of Elena, he grinned at her, his eyes roving over her body lasciviously. Elena, sickened, turned away; but Ralf grabbed her, forced her round.

'Watch this, my lady Elena,' he growled. 'You had some pretty tricks once, remember? I thought the sight of this might remind you. Watch Master Alain here. He's a favourite with all the women in the tower, and you can see why.'

The man Alain was beginning to thrust his stiff member rapturously into the blonde woman's mouth. The other, darker woman was leaning over them, watching avidly, taking Alain's free hand and putting it over her bare, heavy breasts. Her eyes gleamed greedily as she stared at the man's thick-veined shaft, which was glossy from the kneeling woman's encircling mouth as he pumped steadily in and out. Suddenly the watching woman sprang at her busy friend and pushed her aside. 'My turn! My turn now!'

20

The other woman howled with rage, and the two of them rolled on the floor, clawing and spitting at one another, their breasts bared, their hair flying. Then suddenly Alain was on the floor with them, wrestling the blonde woman to one side, furiously pushing up her ragged skirts as his big penis throbbed hungrily. The woman grabbed him. 'Oh, please,' she moaned. 'Take me now, Alain. I'm so wet for you.' She wrapped her legs round his stalwart hips, clawing with her fingers at his back, and he thrust himself into her with a grunt, pleasuring her with slow, deep strokes that made her cry aloud with rapture. The other woman had crawled into the corner and was watching, angry, defeated.

Ralf still held Elena tight, but his eyes were on the couple on the floor, and his expression was hot with lust. Elena watched them too, in despair. Dear God, she thought, Ralf, her husband, was wrong to think she was cold. She was on fire as she watched the crude mating going on in front of her. Her breasts ached and burned with desire, and her nipples pressed hungrily against her silk bodice. Her vagina pulsed tormentingly as she watched master Alain's thick penis burying itself again and again in the plump doxy's wetness, saw how his rough tongue rasped at her bared pink nipples. Then his big thumb moved to stroke at the woman's clitoris, and he began to thrust harder; and the woman started to cry out, in the opening throes of her climax. Elena closed her eyes. Her body was racked with torment, and it was Aimery she was thinking of, Aimery's devastating kiss she remembered, Aimery's strong yet skilful fingers stroking her body, while his burning shaft pulsed deep within her, driving her into undreamt-of ecstasy.

The dark-haired woman, watching jealously from her corner, had had enough of being a spectator. Suddenly she sprang across the room and flung herself in front of Ralf. Before he even realised what she intended, she was quickly untying the lacing of his hose, gasping in delight

21

as his hotly aroused penis sprang out. 'This one,' she crooned avidly, 'will do for me.' She began to run Ralf's swollen cock firmly across her bare breasts, muttering lewdly as the glossy knob caressed her engorged brown nipples. Ralf gasped and swore aloud. Then he grasped her by her loose hair, and threw back his head in a paroxysm of delight as the girl began to squeeze his hot shaft between her pillowy breasts; and Ralf, already excited beyond endurance, lost control and began to spurt fiercely across her plump bosom.

'That's what you like, isn't it, my lord?' murmured the girl happily. 'What a lovely cock you've got. And this is only the start.' Dreamily she used his still-throbbing penis to rub the sticky semen into her nipples, while Ralf panted and leant back against the wall in ecstasy.

Elena, seizing her chance, whirled round to pull open the door. Hearing Ralf's howl of rage as he realised what she was doing, she slammed the heavy door shut, and ran, twisting and turning down the endless passages.

There were sleeping bodies everywhere. All the guest chambers were occupied, so the lowliest inhabitants of the fortress of Rouen slept where they could, huddled in their cloaks on the stoneflagged halls and passages, snoring in wine-hazed oblivion. Driven blindly by her desire to get away from Ralf, Elena ran up a winding stone staircase and found herself suddenly out on the ramparts. The wind was cold on her burning cheeks. Gasping in great lungfuls of the clear fresh air, she gripped the encircling stone wall in an effort to steady her shaking body.

It was a long time since St Peter's bell had tolled vespers, and the city was asleep. All of Rouen lay spread out below her in the darkness, with its church towers, and the great mansions of the rich, and the hovels of the poor beyond the town walls, all glimmering faintly in the pale light of the cloud-obscured moon. The wide river was a black, glistening ribbon as it wound its way through the town towards the sea. High above her head, the proud leopard banners of Normandy beat and flapped against the grim turrets. Elena's hair whipped loosely about her face, and she closed her eyes, relishing the salt-laden wind, feeling the degrading heat of that hateful bedchamber being blown from her body.

Suddenly, she heard a sound: the sound of someone moving, near to her. Elena opened her eyes with a start. She wasn't alone. A man was watching her, with his back to the stone rampart; a man in a long grey cloak, which the wind wrapped sinuously around his tall, imposing figure. His narrow eyes glittered a pale silver grey in the darkness. She felt her heart stop.

Aimery.

Oh, he hadn't changed. Her heart, which felt as though a strong fist was squeezing it, was beginning to beat again, slowly, painfully, as she gazed up into that so-familiar face. He was just the same. How well she remembered those penetrating eyes, the hard, jutting cheekbones that stretched the smooth-shaven skin taut; the high-bridged, arrogant nose and the thin wide mouth lifted in a chilling smile by the long silver sword scar that split his right cheek.

He waited, assessing her carefully, with his arms folded across his chest. Then he drawled, in that low, cool voice she remembered so well, 'Is it a habit of yours, lady Elena, to wander the ramparts after midnight? Someone should tell your husband to take better care of you. You never know what harm might come to you.'

Elena swallowed down the aching dryness in her throat. 'I needed fresh air. I could not sleep.'

His mouth curved mockingly. 'Not tired of your husband already, surely? You've been married – how long? Just over a year, isn't it? I'd have thought you would still be in the throes of nuptial bliss. However, you tire of your men quickly, don't you, Elena? You certainly grew tired of waiting for me.'

23

Elena gazed up into his bleak grey eyes. Her heart was so painfully constricted she thought it would burst. 'I would have waited for ever,' she breathed at last. 'But they told me you were a prisoner, in a Flanders dungeon.'

His voice grated on the raw night air. 'Prisoners are set free. I was.'

Still holding his gaze, Elena said quietly, 'Yes, you were set free – by the lady Isobel. And then you proceeded to find solace in her arms. How is Isobel? So she won you back after all. How she must have enjoyed her triumph.'

Aimery's eyes narrowed to darkness. 'How did you know? About Isobel?'

His voice was tighter now, more dangerous. Elena felt suddenly heavy with tiredness, because he didn't even trouble to deny it. 'Didn't everybody know?' she whispered. 'I waited all through that long year, Aimery, for news of you. Then I heard that you were free. And that you had chosen to stay with Isobel de Morency, at her estate near Aumale. Her husband died, didn't he, leaving her a rich widow? How convenient that must have been for you. I'm surprised you didn't marry her. But now, they say, you have an even richer prospect ahead of you: a beautiful young heiress whom Duke William is dangling before you. What does Isobel think about your forthcoming marriage? Is she angry? Or will she help you with the girl's education, my lord Aimery, as she once helped you with mine?'

'Blood of Christ,' breathed Aimery. His eyes flashed suddenly, dangerously, like glittering steel; then his face was an impassive mask again. 'You taunt me with my disloyalty, Elena. But what of yours? I know something of Ralf; we once served in the Vexin together, though he will not remember me. Why did you marry him?'

The wind curled round the open battlements, and Elena couldn't stop shivering. 'I had nowhere to live, nobody to turn to, nothing. After you'd gone, the king put your estates in the hands of cruel reeves, who would have sold me on, or worse. Can't you imagine? Ralf was passing through, with a band of soldiers who were on their way from York to Lincoln. They stayed several nights at Thoresfield, and Ralf noticed me. He was kind to me.'

Aimery's eyes burned with scorn. 'Him? From what I've heard, he's a weak, drunken lecher.'

'No!' She was desperate now. 'He was good to me. Who else would have had me? He offered to marry me. He said he loved me.'

'And do you love him?' He gripped her trembling body by the shoulders and shook her. 'Do you?'

'Yes. I love him!' She shouted it out in despair, because at his merest touch the familiar, overwhelming longing was sweeping through her. 'He's my husband. I love Ralf!'

Suddenly he was kissing her to drown her words, pressing his mouth hungrily over hers, devouring her soft lips as he pulled her against his hard body; and as his tongue deliberately thrust and probed, Elena felt all the hidden passion, all the hopeless yearning of the past two years, consuming her flesh like fire. His hand was on her breast, stroking, caressing the taut skin until she gasped. His finger and thumb were squeezing her thrusting nipple through the fine silk of her gown, and she was crying out his name as the fierce cords of longing knotted in her belly. He was whispering in her ear; the sound of his husky voice ravished her senses, but his words chilled her blood.

'Your husband Ralf puts the word around that you are cold, lady, cold as ice. But I think not.' He twisted her tender nipple softly and she cried out, her body arching helplessly towards him, her thighs open, throbbing with torment. Aimery smiled chillingly down at her as the wind ruffled his thick, tawny hair. 'Have you been taunting him, little Elena, with your beautiful, passionate body? Taunting him and deceiving him, just as you deceived me?'

She cried out, 'No! I loved you, Aimery. I waited for you.'

'And I wonder just how many men pleasured this fair flesh in the waiting?' he murmured. His hand was sliding lower now, across the smooth-fitting silk that was taut across her flat belly. Then Elena gave a little cry of despair as his fingers suddenly sank, hard and demanding, into the softness at the joining of her thighs. He would be able to feel how wet, how slippery she was through the flimsy fabric of her gown. She wanted to die of shame. His face was set and grim as he continued to callously fondle her. 'You deceived me once into thinking you were innocent and virginal, just as you deceived your husband. I almost feel sorry for him. How many others, Elena? *How many others?'*

Suddenly he hitched up the flaring skirts of her gown, running his calloused swordsman's hands over the white, smooth flesh of her thighs above her silk stockings. Then his strong fingers were delving into her, probing her wetness. Elena leant back against the high parapet, helpless to resist, as his thumb found and relentlessly caressed her swollen little ridge of pleasure. Her loins clenched and tightened into aching need. She cried out as he slid her small white breasts from her bodice and suckled them one by one, his mouth drawing on the tight crests, his tongue wickedly swirling them. He lifted his head. His dark eyes gleamed like those of some predator.

'How many others have ridden you, sweet Elena, since I last pleasured your wanton body? How many others have savoured these exquisite breasts, tasted your lovely mouth, driven themselves into this lush, melting flesh?' And his fingers slid high up into the liquid warmth of

26

her sex, in, out, in a devastating simulation of intercourse.

'Leave me,' she whispered. 'Dear God, Aimery. Leave me alone.'

He drew away briefly, and Elena had to force herself not to cry out for him. But it was not his intention to leave her. Instead, he took her gently by her shoulders and kissed her with lips that were almost tender. *No*, she told herself. It could not be tenderness. He was mocking her, devising some fresh cruelty for her.

Then she gasped aloud, because he was pressing her close, thrusting gently at her trapped body with his hips, and she suddenly felt the velvety smooth head of his rigid penis stroking at her melting flesh. She shook with desire, and tried to draw away. This was madness. But the feeling of the swollen glans nudging at her honeyed entrance was so exquisite that she couldn't speak, couldn't move. He kissed her lips, and she responded with all the pent-up passion of her longing for him as his tongue thrust and probed. She reached up to his wide shoulders, pulling his head down to meet hers. And then she felt him thrust more strongly, felt his hot, iron-hard shaft slide up into her flesh, and she cried aloud beneath his kiss as he sent wave after wave of incredible pleasure flooding through her with each purposeful stroke. She clenched herself around him, moving with him, her feet almost lifted from the ground by the power of him. She was gasping aloud; her blood was on fire, her pulse a violent hammering of desire as he plunged up into her melting softness, again and again.

He paused to gaze down at her, his penis a throbbing rod at the very heart of her. She was overwhelmed by the sudden blaze of passion she saw in his sombre face. 'Oh, Aimery,' she whispered, reaching up to touch first his lips, then the thin line of the scar on his cheek. 'Dear God, Aimery. Don't stop.'

He thrust harder then, his mouth a compressed line,

his eyes narrow slits as he ravished her again and again, holding her slender body tightly in his arms as she arched against him, her face dazed with pleasure. The root of his thick shaft was rubbing forcefully now against her swollen clitoris; she clenched her inner muscles desperately around it as he bent his head to suckle her burning breasts. As his teeth fastened gently round her straining nipple she suddenly gave a long, whimpering cry and started to move frantically against him. 'Oh, Aimery. Oh, dear sweet Christ . . .'

Relentlessly he continued to pleasure her, his massive penis driving into her pulsing womb as the tension inside her climaxed, and broke, and steadily released itself in a rapturous unfolding of sensation. His lips continued to draw on her nipples; his hips continued to steadily thrust as she cried out again and again in the extremity of her ecstasy. Then he began to drive faster, fiercer; Elena could see how his teeth were gritted in his shadowy face as his loins tightened and at last he reached his own harsh release deep within her.

Her back was chafed from the stone wall behind her, her silk gown ruined. Aimery was breathing hard, still holding her tightly, and she buried her face against his chest. Those excruciating waves of pleasure had drained all the strength from her body. Oh, Aimery.

At last she lifted her face, knowing her lips were bruised from his kisses, her blue eyes dazed with long-ing. 'I must go, Aimery. This should never have happened.'

She wanted him to hold her again, to kiss her and tell her that he would never let her go. But he listened to her, and his face tightened, and his hypnotic silver eyes narrowed almost to blackness as he let his hands fall to his sides.

'You're right. You'd better go back to your husband.' He drew his grey cloak around his shoulders. 'Tell him he's mistaken in you, just as I once was. Was it so hard to wait for me, Elena?'

His casual words lashed her. 'Oh, I waited for you, Aimery,' she whispered. 'I would have waited for ever. Even when they told me you were a prisoner, with no freedom in sight. But I gave up hope when I heard you'd gone to Isobel.'

'So ready to believe the worst of me,' he gritted.

'What else *could* I believe?' she cried out, desperately smoothing down her rumpled gown, backing away from him as she did so. 'Do you deny that she paid your ransom? That you went to her, stayed with her?'

Tiredly he shook his head. Elena went on, almost wildly, 'And now you're to be married, to a beautiful young heiress. No doubt all your English lands will be restored to you as well, now that you're back in William's favour. What a prosperous match for you, Aimery. How well you've done for yourself. What does the lady Isobel think of it all? Your poor young bride; I almost feel sorry for the girl. Will Isobel destroy her, as she's always sought to destroy me?'

Down below, in the darkness of the sleeping town of Rouen, the church bell of St Peter's sonorously tolled midnight. The wind stirred up from the Seine, bringing the salt scent of the sea. Heavy black night-clouds scudded across the moon, and ragged stars glimmered forlornly overhead. Aimery said, at last, 'I could tell you what really happened. But you've already made up your mind, haven't you?' He moved towards the stairs. 'You'd better get back to your husband before you cause more trouble, Elena. And I need some sleep.'

Elena laughed bitterly. 'You'll not even find floor space in the Tower of Rouen tonight. Unless you find yourself room in some fine lady's bed.'

He said flatly, 'I've been invited to spend the night in the mansion of Henri of Sizerne. His daughter is to be my wife.'

'My God, I pity her.' And with that, Elena turned and ran down the stairs, leaving him gazing silently after her.

She found Ralf asleep, alone on the pallet in their tiny chamber. But the sickly, cloying scent of the two women remained. Elena lay down beside him, easing the rough wool blanket over herself, careful not to touch him, weighed down by hopelessness.

Her past had come back to haunt her. Almost three years ago, her convent in the north of England had been raided by Aimery le Sabrenn's soldiers during the dreadful harrying of the north. She'd become Aimery's serf, and he'd captured her heart, and enslaved her body. He'd vowed his love for her, and rejected his cruel, capricious mistress, Isobel de Morency. Or so Elena had thought.

When Aimery had been called away to fight for his king, Elena had waited desperately for news, always believing that he would come back to her as soon as he could. Even when she'd heard he'd been captured at the disastrous battle of Bavinchove, she still tried to hope, not to give way to despair. At least he was alive. But then she'd heard the news that he had been freed through the intervention of the beautiful, scheming widow Isobel, and that he was once more enslaved by her, the two of them living in luxurious isolation on one of her husband's estates near Aumale.

Elena remembered little of the time after that. She and the other serfs were treated roughly by the new reeve, appointed by the king in Aimery's prolonged absence. Then she'd caught the attention of a travelling Norman knight, Ralf, who had a small fief of his own in the south, near Chichester. He had fallen in love with her, and asked her to marry him.

Elena had hoped, desperately, that she could learn to love her husband. At first, she'd climaxed in his arms by

30

remembering Aimery. But Ralf was not Aimery; he was selfish, and weak, and after several months of his crude, perfunctory lovemaking, Elena could hardly bear him to touch her.

And now Aimery was back in her life, and her body was as traitorous with longing as ever. She hated Aimery for what he had done to her tonight, rousing her body so expertly, so casually. She hated him, but she hadn't been able to tell him to stop. The feelings were too sweet, the desire too strong. She shuddered with arousal even now at the memory of his tongue on her breasts, his silken penis endlessly pleasuring her into that excruciating state of bliss that she never failed to reach in his arms.

Beside her, Ralf stirred. His hand stretched out in his sleep, instinctively seeking Elena, pulling her possessively towards him.

Elena lay rigid in his arms, her mind in torment. With Aimery's arrival at Rouen, her life here was no longer endurable. She had to get away from this place somehow; away from Ralf, and most of all, away from Aimery le Sabrenn.

31

Chapter Three

*A*imery stayed alone up on the ramparts until a sudden burst of sleet brought him to his senses. Pulling his cloak around himself, he went to find his servant Hamet, who had been attending to the billeting of Aimery's soldiers in the thatched barracks within the courtyard. Together, the two men passed through the postern gate and rode away from the grim Tower of Rouen, through the silent streets of the town, towards the prosperous district where Henri of Sizerne's large mansion was situated.

Hamet, glancing at his master's face, realised that something was wrong; but the devoted Saracen knew Aimery too well to ask what had happened. Busy with his tasks, Hamet had not seen Elena, otherwise he might perhaps had guessed. Instead he said, in his rich, softly musical voice,

'The hour is late, lord Aimery. Will the lord of Sizerne not have gone to his bed?'

Aimery laughed shortly. 'I was told to arrive whenever it pleased me. After all, lord Henri will have heard that I'm completely reinstated in Duke William's favour.

Rich as he is already, he'll be hoping, no doubt, that he and his daughter will share in my good fortune.'

'She is pretty, this daughter of his?'

Aimery shrugged, holding his reins in one hand. 'I don't know, and I'm not sure that I care. She's certainly likely to inherit a fortune – she's her father's only legitimate child.'

Hamet nodded, thinking to himself that no doubt the girl would be a plain, pious virgin. He wondered what she would make of the formidable Aimery le Sabrenn.

They soon reached the courtyard of the substantial beamed and plastered town house, which was screened from the Street of the Cutlers by a gated palisade and winter-bare plane trees. A bevy of manservants with lanterns came hurrying out at their approach. Henri of Sizerne himself followed more slowly in their wake, clad in a rich, ermine-lined cloak. Lame from years of campaigning – for which he was now too old – he brushed aside Aimery's brief apology for the lateness of the hour.

'No trouble, no trouble at all. Delighted to have you here. Duke William's tower is packed from wall to wall, they say – his enemies in Maine must be quaking at the thought of the renewal of his campaign. Your soldiers have all found billets? Good, good. You and your manservant – ' he glanced a little uncertainly at the dusky figure of Hamet – 'are most welcome to our hospitality. Tomorrow, we will talk properly. You were at the battle of Bavinchove, were you not? A bad business, that. Even worse that Fitzosbern, one of William's most trusted lieutenants, should have lost his life there.'

'That was why I went to fight,' said Aimery, handing over his horse to a groom. 'I knew that Fitzosbern was pledged to fight for Flanders, with a lamentable lack of support from William. My lord Fitzosbern was an honourable man. I fought under him at York. He deserved better.'

'And so you told Duke William,' marvelled Henri of

33

Sizerne, fingering his grizzled beard. 'They say that he raged at your insolence for three days and nights. He stripped you of your English lands on account of that, didn't he?'

Aimery bowed his head in acknowledgement.

'Well,' sighed Henri, 'at least Duke William has relented now. And they say he has secretly never forgiven himself for not sending his friend Fitzosbern more help. But I prattle on. Come in, come in.'

In the upper chamber they drank wine, a good claret brought to them by Henri's plump wife, dame Jeanne, who watched Aimery for a while with a kind of startled fascination before making her excuses and leaving the men to talk. Henri was just a little put out by the presence of Hamet, who melted discreetly into the shadows in the corner of the room, but seemed determined not to retire until his master did. They talked politely over their wine of old campaigns, and of the current enterprise against Maine, which William had long disputed with his rival the Count of Anjou. Then Henri, once more stroking his greying beard, coughed and changed the subject.

'You'll meet my daughter tomorrow, my little Henriette. She's but a young lass, hasn't seen much of the world. Her mother dotes on her, with her being our only one. I suppose we've both spoilt her, over-protected her, you know?'

He broke off, suddenly a little embarrassed. There was something formidable about this Aimery le Sabrenn, who was an undeniably handsome man, in spite of that terrible scar. And Henri had heard the rumours about how women found him irresistible. Why, even his comfortable, middle-aged wife, dame Jeanne, had simpered and blushed like a young girl when the Breton had greeted her.

There'd been rumours, too, that after his release from imprisonment he'd spent some time with the lady Isobel

34

de Morency. A beautiful green-eyed witch, that one. Henri had met her once. She'd led her old husband a merry dance. He felt his own ageing loins twitch unexpectedly at the memory of Isobel's tantalising loveliness. They said she knew how to capture a man's heart and body, how to make him her slave for life. They also said that this Breton here, the man who was going to marry his daughter, was the only one Isobel had ever really longed for.

'Well,' Henri went on rather awkwardly as all this flashed through his mind. 'What I'm trying to say is, you'll treat our precious daughter with care? She knows little of men and their ways, you know? Oh, she's happy enough to be wed, but – damn me, how can I put it? You'll break her in gently? You're a mature man, with a man's experience, a man's needs, and my Henriette – well, she's only a girl, and she might be frightened at first by your husbandly demands of her.'

Aimery smiled gravely, and Henri felt reassured. They said the Breton was a man of honour. After all, he'd lost everything, nearly his life as well, when he'd ridden in defiance of the king to support his old comrade Fitzosbern at Bavinchove.

'Be easy, my lord,' said Aimery quietly. 'I will treat your daughter with the utmost respect. I will demand nothing of her that she does not freely wish to give.'

Henri nodded, well satisfied, and poured them both a final goblet of wine. The black servant, Hamet, did not drink. A strange heathen habit, thought Henri, not to touch wine.

Aimery was wearied to the bone when at last Henri summoned a heavy-eyed but deferential manservant to show him to the guest chamber. Henri had assumed that Hamet would sleep in the servants' quarters, but Aimery insisted, politely yet firmly, that his manservant stay close to him. Fussing, Henri arranged for a palliasse to

35

be laid in the passageway outside Aimery's door; and Aimery, having lit a single candle from the glowing embers in the grate, shut the door of his chamber at last, and prepared for bed.

His quarters could have been a cow shed that night for all he cared. On campaign, he was used to sleeping on the ground, with his men, beneath the stars. He was the illegitimate son of a poor Breton knight and a scullery maid, and to him this luxury was oppressive. He could have done without the fire in the grate, and the big, curtained bed in the corner looked almost suffocating. But it was somewhere to sleep, which was all he wanted at the moment. Quickly he shrugged off all his clothes except the long linen shirt he wore beneath his armour. His sword he caressed and laid on the floor by the bed. Then he blew out the candle.

Tomorrow, he would meet his future wife. From Henri of Sizerne's anxious words, he assumed she would be virginal and devout. So much the better. He would be relieved of the burden of constantly bedding her if she had no taste for carnal sports. He ran his hand tiredly through his thick, tawny hair, hoping that sleep would drive from his mind the dark torment of his encounter with Elena. Then he climbed into the bed.

He sprang to the ground, a harsh oath on his lips. There was someone already in the bed – someone soft, and warm, and female. For a brief moment, he'd felt silky, scented skin pressed against his body.

'Your pardon,' he grated out. 'I think a mistake has been made.'

And then, a cajoling, husky girl's voice whispered, 'Oh, please, my lord, don't go! If you only knew how much I've been longing for you to arrive!'

Aimery's hand was on his sword. 'In the devil's name, who are you?'

'My name, my lord, is Henriette.'

Aimery groaned aloud. This was the last, the very last

thing he wanted; this silly young virgin, his bride-to-be, bent on some teasing adolescent dalliance. But then, the careful words of dismissal he was preparing died on his lips, because Henriette of Sizerne had crawled out from between the linen sheets and was kneeling up on the bed, a wicked smile on her lips. She was quite naked; her slender yet voluptuous body glowed golden in the dying light of the fire. Her curling chestnut hair lay in silky swathes round her shoulders, enticingly framing her large, pouting breasts. She murmured happily as she reached to caress his cheek, and noted how his eyes were already fastened on her magnificent brown-nippled bosom. Carefully she pulled up his linen shirt, then bent her head and took his phallus in her mouth.

Aimery groaned again. Dear God, but she knew what she was doing. Quickly, inevitably, he surged into hardness as her lips and tongue played over the taut skin of his manhood. Her wicked little fingers tickled at his bulky testicles, cupping, tormenting. With an effort, he pulled himself away. His penis, wet from her tongue, quivered angrily as he gripped her head and held her firmly, his fingers entwining in her soft hair. She looked up, stricken.

'My lord Aimery. You do not like me?'

He glanced grimly down at his massive erection. 'I would clearly be lying if I tried to say that. But you are Henriette of Sizerne? We are to be betrothed. Such games, demoiselle, must wait for our wedding night.'

'Oh, nonsense!' Her brown eyes gleamed. 'I've waited for someone like you for years.'

'Then another month of waiting, lady, will not harm you.'

'It will drive me mad. Oh, how lovely you are. How big, how strong your cock is, my lord.'

He remembered, with difficulty, what her father had said, because she was stroking the surging length of his penis with her fingers, making little crooning noises in the back of her throat. Her large breasts were jutting ripely, with long brown nipples that looked as if they ached to be kissed. As she knelt, her thighs parted, so he could see the silky, reddish-brown fur that covered her sweet little mound, allowing him just a glimpse of the moist coral flesh that peeped out from beneath. Aimery said carefully,

'The pleasures of love have to be learnt, fair lady. Best to take time, for you to enjoy it all to the full. You will take more pleasure in such things when we have more time, more privacy.'

'I've learned everything I need to know, believe me,' she laughed. Trying a different approach, she began slowly to play with herself, drawing her forefinger down into her secret cleft and rubbing, slowly, up and down. Aimery could hear the wet slipperiness of her. He closed his eyes briefly as his penis swelled and throbbed.

'You are a virgin,' he began gently, but she interrupted him, laughing.

'I? Oh, no! No maid in Rouen is a virgin, my lord, unless she is too hideous for a man to contemplate. I began to learn about love years ago. The priest who was supposed to give me lessons was young and handsome, and I got him to tutor me in a different kind of knowledge. He used to stare at me longingly, when he thought I wasn't looking. His name was Julien. One day I noticed how Julien's long serge gown was twitching at his loins, and I reached to touch it, and realised it was his lovely hard cock, jumping about, wanting me. I rubbed him, and watched his semen spurt, and it was the most exciting thing I'd ever seen. He used to groan and say I would drive him to hell, but it seemed like heaven to me, to play with that throbbing shaft of flesh.' She smiled dreamily, her finger pressing harder, speeding up as she rubbed herself. 'But he refused to teach me any more, even though I begged him. And I think he would have been a disappointment; his prick was so small and stubby, and he hardly lasted any time at all, especially if I showed him my breasts while I caressed him. He used to love kissing them, and his mouth was all hot and wet.' She shivered with excitement at the memory.

'Then, when I was older, my father hired a stalwart new groom called Manot. He was better. I used to hide in the stables, and watch him pleasuring the maidservants. They loved him, because his weapon was so huge; they used to argue over who could get the most of his length inside them. On the first night I went to him, he was nervous with me, scared of getting into trouble. But he pleasured me well, getting me all wet and ready first before he slid himself gently into me.' She paused, licking her lips, gazing hungrily at Aimery's swollen shaft. 'Then he swived me thoroughly, and I almost fainted with pleasure. He was not handsome, but his prick was big and dark, and his balls were heavy, and covered with black hairs. He loved me to take them in my mouth, and lick at them. It thrilled him that I, a fine lady, should take pleasure in such things. But then, he began to slyly ask me for gifts, and money. He would mock me, showing me his huge weapon, then rubbing it himself very slowly and telling me I wasn't getting any of it until I brought him gold. So I told my father that Manot had tried to kiss me one night. He was flogged, then branded and banished.'

She shrugged at the memory, her finger absently caressing her protruding clitoris. Aimery could see it clearly now, because her folded labia had parted to reveal the glistening pearl of flesh. Her brown nipples stood out hard and proud from their dusky areolae, and her full breasts were flushed with excitement. 'There have been others,' she went on thoughtfully. 'I learnt different things. I like to be licked. Don't you?' Aimery was speechless. She said suddenly, anxiously, 'You don't mind? About me not being a virgin? My friends say that experienced men like you are bored by virgins, because they have no fire, no life in them.'

Aimery suddenly thought of Elena, who was never far from his thoughts anyway. He remembered taking her virginity that first night in his castle, almost three years ago. He remembered how she trembled with love for him as he first penetrated her, remembered her soft, startled cries of pleasure as he slowly, carefully pleasured her until she shimmered into ecstasy. He closed his eyes, banishing the image as Henriette went on anxiously,

'I'll be true to you, my lord, of course I will. I've been waiting and dreaming for someone like you. When my father told me I was to be married to you, I couldn't believe it. I'd heard of you, you see.' And, moistening her lips hungrily, she gazed at Aimery's long jutting penis. He looked at her voluptuous body and said slowly,

'Lady, I think we will suit one another very well.'

She caught her breath with pleasure. Swaying towards him she touched his scar, and wrapped her arms around his neck. 'Oh, Aimery. Dear God, Aimery. How I've been longing for a real man, a man like you. Fuck me. Fuck me, please . . .'

She kissed him, her tongue flicking hungrily into his mouth. Twining herself around him, feeling his hot shaft pressing against her belly, she pulled him back on to the bed, moaning as she wrapped her eager legs around his thighs. Aimery's rampant penis thudded blindly at her moist petals of flesh, then found its home and plunged up to the hilt in her silken inner warmth. Squealing with delight, Henriette thrust her breasts up into his mouth and arched against him as his thick shaft drove into her, again and again. She made him pause, once, while she looked down to see where his dark, glistening root penetrated her sex; then she began to whimper and writhe against him as he took her to the brink and held her there, in seemingly endless rapture, as her orgasm throbbed through her.

Afterwards, when he'd reached his own powerful climax, she held him in her arms, stroking his muscled body dreamily, tracing the paths of old battle scars with her fingers. There was one newer than the rest: a long, ugly red mark along the side of his stomach. The skin was still stretched and shiny around it. She caught her breath. 'That blade must have nearly killed you.'

Aimery replied, 'Almost. It was the wound I got at Bavinchove.'

'And then you were a prisoner of Robert the Frisian for many months. I know all about you, you see. But you survived, for me.' She sighed dreamily, her hand travelling down to toy with his phallus. 'Your body is truly wonderful, Aimery le Sabrenn. They said you were a magnificent lover, and now I know it's true. Tell me, what were you thinking of when you were at the very height of your pleasure just now? Were you thinking of me?'

Aimery smiled tiredly. He knew what to say. 'Who could help it, demoiselle?' After all, he couldn't exactly tell this wanton, voluptuous girl that he'd actually been thinking all the time of a slender Saxon maid, with pale golden hair and blue eyes that became dark with passion; who trembled like quicksilver at his touch and haunted his every moment, asleep or awake. He closed his eyes briefly, and Henriette pulled suddenly away from him.

'Oh, you must be so tired! You look exhausted – how long is it since you slept?'

'Longer than I care to remember. My men and I have ridden thirty leagues to be here.'

'Thirty leagues – to be with me?' Henriette was entranced at the thought. Aimery didn't bother to deny it, because he just wanted to sleep. She curled up dreamily in his arms, and was still gazing into his gaunt, scarred face as he fell asleep at last.

* * *

41

Henriette was far too excited to sleep. She couldn't believe her luck. Aimery was going to be hers, all hers. How envious her friends would be. Tomorrow she would be able to tell them every detail about his hard-muscled soldier's body, his firm mouth, his strong but sensitive fingers; and oh, how she would enjoy telling them about his lovely, massive cock. She shivered in fresh delight as she remembered the feel of his virile weapon jerking inside her again and again as he climaxed. She knelt up naked on the bed, her heavy breasts swaying as she pulled back the sheet and gazed longingly down at Aimery's sleeping phallus, still substantial even in its softness, with the heavy, silken pouch of his balls nestling between his iron hard thighs.

She would have to run back to her own chamber before dawn, before the first cock crow roused the servants out of their beds. But she would wake him first, to have a taste of his lovely body again. What did he really like? she wondered. How could she truly enslave him and make him hers? Henriette was under no illusions. A man like Aimery le Sabrenn would always have women after him. And now that he was back in the Duke of Normandy's favour there would be many campaigns and much travelling. She wanted to be sure he would always come back to her, Henriette. She fondled her long brown nipples thoughtfully as she gazed down at him, feeling them harden like pebbles as she anticipated their next delicious session.

Suddenly, she froze. There'd been a soft creaking noise, just outside the door. She panicked. Her mother, or father? One of the servants? No, ridiculous. It was the dead of night. But someone had moved out there. Who could it possibly be?

Then she remembered.

Aimery had brought his black manservant with him, a burly, silent figure with a sinister-looking curved sword in his belt. Henriette had been peeping from her bedroom window, watching as they rode into the courtyard of her father's house. And, when it was time to retire, Aimery had posted the man outside his door. One of the servants had brought him a soft feather palliasse, but the manservant had spurned it, saying in his deep, sing-song voice that he was used to sleeping in his cloak, on the floor.

Henriette stayed immobile, her hands still on her breasts, thinking hard. Well, he wasn't asleep now. She could still hear soft sounds outside. They were rhythmic, somehow disturbing.

Swiftly she reached for the loose silk robe in which she'd crept along to this chamber earlier. Then she sprang for the door, pulling it wide open. She'd guessed right. A shaft of moonlight pierced the wooden shutter on the landing, revealing to her the dusky manservant, who was kneeling upright facing the door, his black eyes hazed with guilt as he stared bashfully at Henriette. His hand was still on his throbbing penis; his fingers were motionless now, but they'd obviously been busy. His cock reared into the air, huge, dark, trembling with excitement. It was beaded with a drop of dewy moisture, exuding slowly from the tiny mouth at its tip. He looked at her silently, waiting for her reaction.

Henriette felt dizzy with anticipation. My God. The man was vastly over-endowed. Her brain worked quickly, even as her body churned with excitement at the thought of that enormous member slipping up into her own private parts. This servant of Aimery's could prove useful.

She let her silk robe fall apart a little, revealing the abundant ripeness of her breasts. The Saracen frowned in anguish. His big black penis jerked and trembled in his motionless hand.

'You're rather wicked, aren't you?' she breathed, leaning over him. 'Were you spying on us?'

She knew there were plenty of cracks between the

43

planks in the door. She'd used them herself. When she was younger, before the days of the young priest, she'd watched her father's randy steward busying himself in this very chamber with a giggling young maidservant. Henriette had been shocked at first, but then she'd been fascinated, and started to play with herself as she watched. She'd had a sweet, secret little orgasm as she saw the girl taking the man's funny, swollen thing deep in her mouth. She'd thought it hideous, but at the same time wildly exciting.

The big Saracen was looking wretched. 'I heard strange noises, my lady. I thought my master might be in danger. He has enemies, you see. So – I looked . . .'

'And you couldn't take your eyes off my breasts,' thought Henriette smugly. In fact, he still couldn't. Aloud, she said sternly, 'I should report you to your master for this.'

'No. Please.'

'But I might, just might be merciful,' went on Henriette, 'if you're co-operative.' Tentatively she touched his glossy black member. It jerked upwards hungrily; the man moaned. Henriette was already very aroused. His loose open-necked tunic, which he wore belted round his waist, had fallen apart to reveal his muscle-packed ebony body. Beneath his straining cock she could see his big, semen-filled balls. He wasn't as beautiful as Aimery; nobody could be. But oh, he was certainly tantalising. He could provide a welcome diversion in the future, when her husband Aimery was away.

'We'll come to an agreement,' she said thoughtfully. 'Your master and I are to be married. You know that?' She licked her finger and ran it down his velvety shaft. He shuddered and nodded. 'And I want to keep him,' went on Henriette softly. 'I want to know everything he likes. You understand? For example – does he like *this*?'

She leant forward suddenly, letting her pendulous breasts dangle over the tip of his rampant cock. He groaned. 'Yes. Yes . . .'

Henriette pulled herself up. Then she reached to take his penis deliberately in her hands, rubbing slowly up and down, feeling how the mighty shaft throbbed with power. 'What else does he like?' she whispered enticingly. 'You and he must have shared many adventures. Tell me.'

The Saracen shrugged helplessly. She could see beads of sweat on his broad brow. 'My lord Aimery likes beautiful women, lady, as beautiful as you. And he likes what most men like –'

'This?'

Hamet had broken off as Henriette bent to swirl the tip of his cock with her tongue. He groaned rapturously as her warm lips slid over his flesh, up and down, catching the fleshy rim of the glans.

'Ah, yes.' His voice was hoarse.

'And this?' She flicked with her tongue along the taut, velvety skin of his balls; he shuddered and clenched his big fists.

'Who would not? Lady, you are truly exquisite.'

Henriette lifted her head. Her cheeks were flushed, her lips swollen with passion. 'I know I am beautiful, but so are many women. You must tell me some secrets, the secrets that will win my lord's heart.'

Hamet was in utter torment now, his powerful cock swelling with angry life, desperate for release. 'Lady, there is one thing. No matter how beautiful the woman, my lord Aimery cannot bear to be trapped. You understand? You must know that many women have loved him.'

'Oh, yes,' sighed Henriette. 'And who could blame them?'

'But he himself has no room in his heart for love. These women, they make the mistake of trying to trap him, to cling to him. Towards such women, he rapidly becomes cold. Keep your distance, lady, if you would keep him. Tantalise him, tease him with little games to keep him guessing. And then, only then, give him what he wants.'

Henriette frowned, pushing back her tumbling chestnut locks from her warm cheeks. Little games. But who would teach her? How could she learn about all the pleasures that men loved? Oh, she'd learnt as much as she could of the bawdy goings-on between the servants. And her own experience was considerable, if crude. But there must be more, so much more, that a man of Aimery's refined tastes would expect.

'How can I find out everything?' she murmured aloud. 'How can I become the most desirable woman that Aimery le Sabrenn has ever met?'

Hamet hesitated. To encourage him, Henriette began to rub slowly, luxuriously at his straining penis. It felt smooth and velvety in her hands. Hamet trembled.

'There is one person,' he blurted out, 'who would tell you. This lady is so beautiful, so skilled in the arts of love that men fall at her feet. And if a man's appetites seem jaded, she devises little entertainments to rekindle his ardour.'

Henriette's brown eyes gleamed. 'Her name?' she breathed; and when Hamet hesitated yet again, she wrapped her fingers round his thick cock and began to pleasure him with her fist, pulling the foreskin up and down the iron-hard core, harder and harder until the swollen glans was protruding angrily. Hamet began to shudder at the onslaught of pleasure.

'Her name,' he gasped out, 'is the lady Isobel de Morency.'

Henriette nodded intently. Isobel de Morency. *'I will find her,'* she vowed silently. *'I will find her, and learn from her.'* Aloud, she murmured coyly, 'Do you like me doing this, Saracen? Would the lady Isobel approve of me doing this to you?'

'Yes,' he gasped. Almost beside himself, he grabbed

for her naked breasts, his black fingers fastening round the creamy flesh, his eyes glazed with passion.

Henriette rubbed harder at his cock, though she was distracted by the hot way he was pawing at her bosom. Some other time, perhaps, she would enjoy him properly. But there wasn't time now, because he was almost there. His big penis was jerking of its own accord into her hand. At last he gave a low cry, and flung back his head, and she watched in fascination, still gripping him hard, as the clear creamy liquid started to spurt from the black velvety tip of his cock. His fingers squeezed and pulled on her nipples as his body tensed and spasmed; she'd thought herself sated with Aimery, but she was so excited by what was happening now that she felt the fresh longing coursing through her.

He must have known. As soon as he was capable of movement, he bent before her to pull her thighs roughly apart; then he thrust out his powerful tongue and lapped at her, circling her clitoris, diving into her hungry vagina. Henriette whimpered with ecstasy, pushing herself on to his lovely strong tongue, climaxing wetly against his face. His black hands continued to play with her distended nipples until the last throbbing of pleasure had faded sweetly away.

His dark face was wet from her body's juices. He looked as if he wanted to take her in his arms, to kiss her. No doubt, with a little encouragement, they would soon be able to start all over again. But Henriette, suddenly frightened in case she was discovered, extracted herself from his tempting embrace and hurried back to her own room. Well, she'd certainly had some memorable company tonight. First the soldier in duke William's hall, then the beautiful lord Aimery, and now his rather delicious black servant Hamet. What a feast of pleasure.

And Hamet had given her some good advice. 'Keep your distance,' the burly manservant had said. So she wouldn't let Aimery find her in his bed when he awoke in the morning. She'd strive to be cool and sophisticated, and infinitely desirable. *'He himself has no room in his heart for love . . .'*

Why not? She would certainly do her best to make him love her, Henriette. She would learn everything she could. And in the meantime, she reckoned she had a useful secret ally, Hamet, whose big dusky body had intrigued her. She couldn't ever love him as she loved Aimery, but his big tongue had been a pleasant distraction, and his penis would be even more entertaining.

But first, she had to make sure of Aimery. Hamet had said that the mysterious lady Isobel would help her, because she knew what every man longed for. Henriette was intrigued by the sound of the lady Isobel. Snuggling down between her cool linen sheets, her body still awash with excitement, she resolved to find her. As soon as possible.

Chapter Four

*I*sobel was staying with a friend that night, a minor
Norman lordling who held a stronghold in the fertile
valley of the river Avre, some seven leagues from
L'Aigle. She was only resting there for one night, because
she was on her way north, to Rouen, with all speed.

There were some hours to go before dawn brought the
start of another day of travelling. She couldn't sleep. The
cold wind moaned outside the narrow window of her
bedchamber, sending little flurries of sleet rattling
against the shutter. Hard to believe it was supposed to
be spring. She tossed and turned a while longer beneath
the fur coverlet of her bed, then she pulled herself up
and called out angrily, 'Alys. Are you there, Alys?'

Her maid, who'd been fast asleep in the adjoining
room, took some moments to answer her summons. In
that time Isobel had risen, and pulled on a fine blue
woollen gown over her silk chemise, and brushed her
long, silky black hair. The log fire was still glowing in
the hearth, thank heaven, lending some warmth to the
chilly room. As Alys stumbled in, bleary-eyed from lack
of sleep, Isobel regarded her unkempt figure with contempt. Dear God, Alys was ugly. But she was a loyal

servant, who knew her mistress's needs only too well. And Alys's eager, pathetic hunger for sex made her amusing, if nothing else. She'd been with Isobel for some years now, more years than Isobel cared to remember.

'Fetch me wine, Alys,' she said curtly. 'I can't sleep.' Alys hurried over to the table by the door and poured a glass of deep-ruby wine from a silver decanter while Isobel wandered over to the window. 'Look out here, Alys,' she commanded.

Alys, rubbing the sleep from her pockmarked face with her free hand, hurried to where Isobel was holding aside the hide shutter. She handed Isobel the wine and gazed out into the blackness. The wind stung her cheeks, making her shiver.

'I see nothing, mistress,' she muttered, wishing she was back in her bed again.

'Out there,' rapped Isobel sharply. 'Beyond the lantern light. That soldier on guard duty. He's wandered away from the others – do you see him now?' Alys nodded, just making out the shadowy outline of a lounging soldier leaning against the wall. In these marcher lands between France and Normandy, everyone of any substance had soldiers on guard, in case of attack. It was every man for himself, and the peasants had to manage as best they could. If there were raids, they were lucky to make it to the shelter of the nearest donjon, from where they could gaze out and see their miserable crops and livestock being put to the flame by some rival baron.

'I see the soldier, mistress,' said Alys sullenly.

'Then go out and fetch him,' rapped Isobel. 'He'll be glad to get in from the cold.'

'Bring him up here? Now?' Alys was incredulous.

'Didn't I just say so, you fool?' Isobel sipped her wine and began to pace the room impatiently, her fine woollen robe trailing on the rush matting. 'Go, and quickly, or you'll face a flogging tomorrow!'

Alys hurried off, and Isobel paused by the fire, watching the glow of the embers through the delicate glass goblet, deep in thought.

In a few days, if all went well, she and her entourage would reach Rouen. It seemed as if the whole world were travelling to Rouen; the Eastertide summons of the powerful Duke of Normandy was not lightly ignored. She was travelling there, not to offer fealty to Duke William, but to reclaim homage that was due to her, Isobel.

No-one spurned Isobel of Morency. No-one. She put down her glass and gazed thoughtfully into the polished bronze mirror that hung on the wall. She was still beautiful. Her ivory skin was flawless as ever, her lips as enticingly, richly red; her thickly lashed green eyes, which lifted slightly at the outer corners, gleamed with promise, and her long glossy hair, black as a raven's wing, was as yet untouched by grey. Beneath her gown her breasts were firm and high, and her tiny waist would still fit a man's handspan. Yet the only man she'd ever truly desired had left her.

The door opened, creaking in the silence of the castle. Alys stood there, with the young soldier behind her. Isobel surveyed him slowly, then said, 'You may go now, Alys.' Alys's plain face fell with disappointment. She left, closing the door behind her, and the young soldier stood there looking bashful, overawed.

Isobel poured herself more wine, and gazed at him as she drank. He was just as she remembered him from this afternoon: not tall, but sturdy and strongly made. The muscles of his shoulders and upper arms, hardened by daily sword practice, bulged enticingly beneath his leather tunic. She sipped her wine, and said,

'I saw you this afternoon, soldier. You were pleasuring a kitchen wench behind the granary.' He opened his mouth to protest. She said sharply, 'Don't even trouble to deny it. You were on duty, weren't you? Just as you are now. Shall I report you, soldier?'

He started forward. 'No. Please, my lady. I'll be flogged for it. It was just a bit of harmless fun, my lady. That wench from the kitchens was begging for it.'

'You have a high opinion of yourself,' breathed Isobel. 'Show me.'

He paled. 'My lady?'

'Show me.' She laughed scornfully. 'I want to see this incredible weapon of yours that has girls pleading for a taste of it. Go on. Uncover yourself.'

'My lady. If I'm caught . . .'

'If I report you for this afternoon, you'll be flogged anyway,' she retorted silkily.

Stunned, he began to remove his soldier's apparel. He unbelted his leather tunic, and lifted it over his head, ruffling his cropped nut-brown hair. Then he pulled off the coarse linen undergarment he wore next to his skin. His body was stocky and hairy; the brown silky pelt that matted his chest and belly grew even more densely around his penis. What she could see of his manly weapon showed promise, reflected Isobel, even though at the moment it dangled limply between his thighs. She would soon alter that.

'You look,' she grinned, 'about as much use as a corpse. Let's see if you can do better, shall we?' And, with exquisite grace, she shrugged her fine gown to the ground, then pulled her silk chemise from her shoulders so the upper part of her body was completely exposed. The soldier gasped, and flushed a deep red. His hot eyes fastened hungrily on Isobel's small but voluptuous breasts. She began to caress them herself with her fingers, gazing at him all the while, pulling out her long coral nipples and feeling a pleasurable surge of arousal at the pit of her belly as she did so. The soldier's heavy phallus thickened, jerking into life. Isobel laughed as it rose to attention, jutting eagerly from the man's hairy loins. Better than she had thought – much better. No wonder the serving wench had been whimpering so happily as he drove it up her this afternoon. 'Not bad,' she murmured approvingly. 'Now, let's see how you perform, shall we?'

The man leapt towards her, hands outstretched greedily towards her breasts, heavy penis swaying. She struck him hard on the cheek and he fell back, stunned. 'Insolent cur,' she hissed, 'to think you can pleasure the lady of Morency! How dare you be so presumptuous?'

The man staggered back towards the door, his cheek reddened from the blow. 'My lady – I thought you said –'

'I wanted to see you perform,' she said icily. 'But not with me, I assure you. Alys!'

Alys came in immediately. Isobel knew, of course, that her maid had been listening and watching through a crack in the door. Her plain, pinched face was flushed with excitement. 'Take her,' said Isobel curtly to the naked soldier. 'Do it well, and I won't report you. If you fail to entertain me, I'll see that you are flogged.'

Alys was used to her mistress's ways. Her drab eyes lit up with excitement. Totally ignoring the crestfallen expression on the face of the soldier, she dropped to her hands and knees on the floor, pulling up her skirts to offer her skinny rump to the naked man. She knew that Isobel liked to watch men pleasuring her like this; it gave her mistress a better view of their lively cocks. And Isobel looked happy enough now. Easing herself back into her gown, the lady of Morency reclined on the bed's luxurious coverlet of miniver and vair and watched as the soldier knelt behind Alys and began to probe with his meaty shaft between the woman's skinny thighs. Alys whimpered with excitement.

Isobel watched thoughtfully. She was in need of a man, just as much as Alys. The trouble was that only one man would do for her. Aimery le Sabrenn had left her nearly a year ago, telling her coldly that he was never coming back; and she wouldn't believe it,

53

wouldn't accept it. That was why she was travelling to Rouen. She had her own plans to get him back.

The soldier was arched powerfully over Alys's crouching figure, rubbing his jutting prick in the copious juices that flowed from Alys's hungry sex. He had a big grin on his face; evidently his disappointment over Isobel was forgotten. He drew back, shuddering with pleasure, his penis glistening; and then, as Isobel watched, he gripped the serving maid's scrawny buttocks with his hands and began to push his red, throbbing weapon into her puckered arsehole. Alys cried out with shock, and the soldier pushed again. 'Easy now, my beauty. Gently does it.' Alys gasped again, holding herself very still. And then the soldier pushed anew, and the tip of his swollen penis slipped suddenly through the tight, fleshy ring of the woman's anus.

Isobel laughed. Not many people called Alys a beauty, but she had her uses. The soldier was gradually easing his entire cock into Alys's clenching rear passage, thrusting inch by inch. Isobel watched its swollen length almost disappear, then slowly emerge, eager, ready for more. She licked her lips, feeling suddenly extremely aroused. Alys was breathing hard, throwing back her head, making strange guttural little sounds in her throat as the man ravished her. Isobel imagined what it would feel like to have that thick penis penetrating her own forbidden passage, bringing her heavy, dark pleasure. She soothed her breasts with one hand, and with the other reached under her full skirts to stroke at the hot little pearl of her clitoris. She was slippery and wet with longing. Oh, Aimery.

There was no-one else to match him. She'd known him since he was a handsome but penniless young mercenary, who'd been employed by her foolish old husband to defend his property against lawless neighbours. Isobel had crept out to him one night, craving his beautiful soldier's body; and Aimery had ravished her on the floor of the armoury, awakening her to exquisite heights of pleasure. Isobel, no stranger to illicit love, had been enraptured by the Breton. She'd followed him to England, and seen him grow rich in the favour of Duke William. Then she'd lost him for a while, to that foolish, virginal little Saxon called Elena, who'd somehow managed to win him off her. Isobel's heart still grew cold at the memory.

But then he'd come back to France, to war, and he'd been captured by his enemies. In rescuing him, Isobel had found power again. He'd been severely wounded just before his capture, and the ugly gash down the side of his abdomen had been badly tended by his captors. She sometimes wondered if they'd ill-treated him deliberately, had taken pleasure in his pain. At any rate, after nine gruelling months of imprisonment he'd been wasted and ill.

Isobel had travelled up to Flanders to secure his release from Robert the Frisian. She'd been shocked by Aimery's state, and quickly realised that the long winter journey back south to her dead husband's castle of Morency would of a certainty kill the Breton. Instead she took him to the safety of another, nearer fief which was part of her dead husband's legacy: a small estate near Aumale, to the north of Rouen, so remote that not even his faithful servant Hamet could track him down. There, she had tended him through a dreadful fever that all but consumed him. Isobel had been frightened for him. He seemed to hardly know who she was; he dwelt in a world of his own, filled with battles, and dungeons, and nightmare dreams. Isobel cared for him, and waited.

One night, she'd heard him crying out, and she'd hurried along the passage to his chamber to find him tossing and turning on his sickbed. He was completely naked. The sword gash so close to his belly had healed now, but was an ugly red that showed up the perfection of the rest of his sinewed body. His eyes were closed as he muttered and turned his head; his smoothly muscled chest was coated with sweat; and from his loins his penis jutted in rampant erection, making her heart stop. Isobel had gone silently towards him. She'd swept back his long tawny hair from his gaunt face, gazing with hunger at his achingly familiar features that were emphasized by his illness. Then she'd caressed his deliciously velvety cock, her fingers trembling with joy. He wanted her. Even in his fever, he wanted her, knew she was there.

'Aimery. My darling,' she'd whispered. She'd been so slick and wet for him that she had to have him immediately. Quickly she climbed on to the bed and straddled him. Then she'd taken his huge penis reverently in her hands, and bent to lick it. He'd moaned aloud, and she'd moved her supple body to slide herself rapturously on to him, wondering how much more of him she could take inside her, delirious with joy because he was hers again, and he was just as wonderful as she remembered.

It hadn't taken her long. Passionately she'd ridden up and down on his hard, throbbing cock, playing dementedly with her own naked breasts, burning with a fever of her own. She remembered it now, the feeling of him plunging deep inside her, the exquisite sensation as the root of his shaft rubbed relentlessly against her throbbing flesh.

Her memories were interrupted by other, more pressing matters as she suddenly realised that on the floor before her, the soldier and Alys were frantically working towards a mutual climax, both of them grunting with pleasure. The soldier, his head thrown back, was pumping vigorously between Alys's buttocks. Isobel could see the slippery length of his penis driving in and out, could see the clenched tightness of his balls as he exploded hotly within her. Alys was crying out happily, her hips writhing against him as she too was engulfed with degrading pleasure. Isobel's green eyes glazed; her finger rubbed hotly against her swollen cleft as she remembered how Aimery's wonderful cock had pounded into her that night, again and again, while her noisy orgasm had washed through her and she'd covered his fevered face with kisses.

She knuckled her soaking clitoris and orgasmed again, now, imagining that Aimery was inside her, filling her with his wonderful hard shaft. Oh, Aimery. Dear God, but the pleasure with him that night had been intense.

She shuddered as the last of her climax rippled through her, and opened her eyes. The soldier was pulling his cock out of Alys's backside at last. The maidservant was still crooning softly with pleasure, her ugly face quite flushed. Suddenly Isobel wanted them out of here. Pulling her gown across her own heated body, she called out, 'You may leave now. Both of you.'

The soldier, glad of the pleasure and gladder still to have escaped a flogging for neglecting his official duties, pulled his clothes on hurriedly and left the room. Alys followed, still dazed after the vigorous coupling.

When they'd gone, Isobel lay back on the bed and closed her eyes, remembering again. She'd gone to sleep that night in Aimery's arms, after bathing his forehead and easing cool water down his throat until his fever had turned into a deep, heavy slumber. When he awoke, she promised herself, he would remember everything she had done for him, and turn to her with love.

She would never forget his expression that next morning, when he awoke and found her lying beside him. His fever had completely gone. His grey eyes were cold and hard.

'Why are you here?' he'd said through gritted teeth.

Isobel had been frightened, but she'd reached out to stroke his cheek, so that he could see her pretty, uptilted breasts as the morning rays of the sun stole across the bed. 'Don't you remember?' she whispered enticingly. 'Last night, my lord Aimery, you must have had pleasant dreams indeed.'

The scar on his cheek had twisted his mouth into a grimace. 'I lay with you?'

'Is that so terrible?' Isobel still tried to smile, though inside she had gone cold. 'You have been here in Aumale for well over a month, my lord. I saved you from the Flanders prison where you would have died, paid a king's ransom to Robert the Frisian for you. You have been very sick. I have nursed you, cossetted you like a babe. Is it any wonder I require a little recompense?'

He dragged himself to his feet and stood on the other side of the bed, pulling on his clothes. Isobel started to tremble.

'I will pay you back,' he'd said in a cold, harsh voice. The scar on his cheek stood out, a white stark seam. 'I have nothing in the world at the moment, but I will pay you back, with money. For your care and attention, lady Isobel, you have my thanks. I owe you nothing more. My stay here is at an end.'

She'd run after him then, forgetting herself, twining her naked body around him at the door of the chamber. 'Aimery! We could be happy here, you and I. My husband is dead – I have all his lands, all his money. Stay with me, my lord!'

He'd put her from him, his eyes as dark as slate. 'You and I were finished a long time ago, Isobel. I thank you for your attention, but I want no more from you.'

Her green eyes had blazed into hatred then. 'It's that Saxon girl, isn't it? That stupid little Saxon slut from the convent. You're going back to her, aren't you?'

'Yes,' he'd replied simply.

After that she'd screamed and raged, but he'd ignored her and left. In fact, he would have set off from Aumale on foot, but Isobel, sick with disappointment, had made him take one of her horses. He agreed to, but only on condition that he returned it to her as soon as he had one of his own. She'd watched him go from a high window, hating Elena with all her heart.

She often wondered just how far he'd got on his solitary journey to England before he heard that the blonde little Saxon slut had married someone else in his absence. Isobel was hugely, joyfully happy when she heard the news. So Aimery's precious Elena hadn't troubled to wait for him after all. No doubt the messages that she, Isobel, had sent back to England, claiming that Aimery le Sabrenn was living happily and in full health with his beloved lady of Morency at a secret retreat and would do so for the foreseeable future, had helped to encourage Elena into marriage with someone else.

She, Isobel, was prepared to wait for Aimery for ever. That was why she was on her way to Rouen now, with all haste. She'd heard that Aimery had been reinstated in Duke William's favour, and had been offered marriage to a rich young heiress.

This piece of news scarcely troubled Isobel at all. She would soon deal with the young heiress. Innocent, trembling virgins were not Aimery's style. Elena had been the exception, and she was well out of the way now, at home in England with her husband.

Isobel had laid her plans to reclaim Aimery, and the thought of meeting him at Rouen filled her with excitement. He would feel differently towards her now that Elena had betrayed him. He would appreciate Isobel's worth. He would reject the stupid little bride Duke William had picked for him, and turn to her, Isobel, instead.

Isobel suddenly realised that dawn was beginning to lighten the blackness of the sky over to the east. She had scarcely slept, but her consuming desire to reach Rouen would give her all the energy she needed for the hard day's ride ahead. Scorning a covered cart or a litter, she travelled on horseback, at the forefront of her little convoy. Already eager to be on her way, she called impatiently for Alys to fetch her warm water for bathing.

Alys took some time, and when she eventually came

with jug and basin, Isobel scolded her roundly for her tardiness. But Alys didn't seem to notice. She looked excited and anxious.

'My lady,' she blurted out, 'you remember the lady Elena, from the English convent?'

Isobel stiffened. Then she placed her hands in the warm water, letting it trickle over her white fingers. 'Vaguely,' she replied with a dismissive shrug. 'She was of no consequence. She married some lowly knight in England, and is no doubt living in some cold, draughty hall with him.'

'No!' said Alys excitedly. 'No, my lady. I've been listening just now to the gossip in the kitchens. She's at Rouen, my lady. They say she's the most beautiful woman there – everyone is talking about her.'

Isobel had gone very still. Then she turned to take the towel from Alys, and there was a chilling smile on her face.

'Really, Alys?' she said softly. 'Well, her insipid looks always did have some admirers. And she's at Rouen, you say?'

Alys nodded breathlessly. Isobel's green eyes glittered, and she turned to her mirror and started to brush her long dark hair slowly.

'How very interesting it will be,' she murmured, 'to meet with Elena again.'

Chapter Five

*T*he clarion cry of a trumpet split the clear blue sky, and for a few moments the clear notes hung shimmering above the gaudy tents and pavilions that filled the meadows below Rouen's high tower. Bright pennons streamed in the gusty April breeze; pages and men-at-arms strode purposefully about their tasks, and anxious grooms gentled the warlike destriers whose great hooves trampled the green turf.

Duke William of Normandy had returned from his latest parley with the foxy Philip of France, only to be greeted by the news that his enemy Fulk of Anjou – probably with Philip's secret backing – was raiding once more into the disputed territory of Maine. William, blazing with rage, was preparing a fresh army to travel south, to confront Fulk in his lair. And his knights, scenting imminent battle, crowded the dusty tiltyards of Rouen to practise their warlike skills, while a throng of spectators watched, entranced, from the sidelines.

'Look at that,' breathed the Norman knight Ralf, gazing enviously as an armed horseman on a great black horse pranced to and fro in front of the quintain. 'What would I give for a mount like that? You saw him centre the quintain with his lance, three times in succession? A hit, every time. Never misses.'

The horseman was Aimery le Sabrenn. The person Ralf addressed was Elena, who stood silently at her husband's side amongst the other knights and their ladies of the Norman court. The white veil that covered her hair and shoulders lifted gently in the April breeze; she smoothed it with her hands, and Ralf's golden ring shone on her finger.

She too was gazing at the Breton, like most of the other women there. He'd pushed back his helm, and his thick, tawny hair glinted in the bright afternoon sun. His lean body, clad in sinuous chain mail, seemed to move as one with the powerful black charger he rode. As he wheeled to ride for the quintain one last time, Elena's eyes lingered almost despairingly on his familiar, hard-boned face, adorned by the terrible white scar.

She wished she could stop watching him. She wished she could stop dreaming about him. Last night, she'd dreamt she was back in Aimery's dark castle of Thoresfield, set amidst the wild, bleak forests of northern England. In her dream, she was his prisoner; he'd chained her slender wrists high to the damp stone walls of the dungeon, and then he'd slowly pulled her silken gown apart with strong, sure fingers, leaving her naked and on fire. As he'd bent his tawny head to suckle her soft pink nipples one by one, they'd burnt and hardened in his exquisite mouth. She'd moaned softly, pressing her loins towards him, her thighs parted in longing as the chains round her wrists raised her body taut. Her delicate sex, naked beneath its covering of soft blonde down, pouted crimson and wet, demanding his attention. He'd cupped her there, caressing her swollen heart of pleasure with the ball of his thumb, gliding in her honeyed moisture until the exquisite sensation was a bright pain of need. Then he'd released his throbbing manhood from the constraint of his clothing, and cupped her hips, and eased the hard length of his shaft up inside her, inch by beautiful inch, as she moaned and gasped her pleasure.

In her dream, he brought her almost to the brink, his silken penis gliding within her, rousing her to undreamt-of heights as he fingered her hardened nipples. And then, he left her. His smile was coldly devastating as he vanished from her dream; her sex was quivering, aching with bruised emptiness.

'*Aimery. Please . . .*' In her sleep, Elena had bitten back a sob of despair, and as she awoke her fingers had already found the wet slickness between her legs, rubbing herself quickly to an empty but searing release. All day, she was haunted by the memory of Aimery's cold smile as he left her crying out for him.

It was almost a week since Aimery had erupted into the banquet, and back into her life. Since then, she'd worked silently, almost feverishly, to get together her small store of money and possessions, and find some way to get away from here and back to England. It was difficult, because as Ralf's wife she was supposed to possess nothing of her own, but she thought she had almost enough. She kept her secret pouch of coins hidden, in case Ralf should suspect.

She'd prayed that she would see no more of Aimery after their bitter reunion that night on the battlements. After all, wasn't he lodging at the mansion of Henri of Sizerne, father of his bride-to-be? But she'd forgotten that Aimery would be spending most of his time in the company of his liege lord, the Duke of Normandy. And Ralf, by some cruel twist of fate, seemed to seek out Aimery at every opportunity, as if he was besotted by the tall, grim Breton knight. Why? wondered Elena desperately. Ralf didn't guess, surely, that Aimery had been his wife's lover? Or that the Breton had pleasured Elena cruelly, magnificently, that night on the battlements?

63

Certainly, Ralf could have devised no worse torment for his wife. During the last few days he'd followed Aimery everywhere, whether invited or not; he rode hawking with Aimery and his retinue to the woods beyond St Sever, and followed Aimery's men eagerly as they took their bows down to the misty riverside early each morning after snipe and nesting mallard. Aimery's cold, scarcely concealed scorn for Ralf, and utter indifference to Elena, seemed to do nothing to dampen Ralf's hero-worship of the Breton.

In a way, Aimery's coldness towards her helped to preserve Elena's outward defences. But inwardly, she was suffering beyond endurance. Even the lascivious ladies of the court added to her torment, for Aimery was their latest darling.

'They say the Breton is magnificently endowed,' breathed one. 'And that he has the stamina to go on for ever, until his bedmate is exhausted with pleasure. Oh, what would I give to have him for one night in my bed, instead of my fat, indolent husband.'

'I would be happy just to lie there and gaze at him – for a while, anyway,' sighed another wistfully. 'I think he must be the most beautiful man I've ever seen in my life, in spite of that terrible scar.'

'I wouldn't waste precious time gazing at him,' laughed the first woman. 'I'd take his lusty cock in my mouth, and lick his balls, and watch his lovely face tighten with pleasure as I sucked the last drop of juice from him. There must be something special about these Bretons. Remember how the duke's wife Matilda was secretly obsessed with her handsome young squire from Brittany, Samson? But he's nothing compared to Aimery le Sabrenn.'

The memory of their hungry gossip tormented Elena as she stood beside her husband, gazing at the prancing knights waiting to take their turn at the quintain. She could bear no more of this. She had two gold pieces and

64

twenty deniers saved in her hiding place, and she prayed that it was enough to pay a sailing master to take her back to England.

Just then a fresh breeze stirred the bright pennants, and the sunlight glinted on the stone bulwarks of Rouen's great tower, distracting her. She saw that Aimery had ridden successfully down the lists for the last time and caught the quintain dead centre, his supple body hardly shifting in the high-cantled saddle. There was a burst of admiring applause from the other knights who circled around, awaiting their turn, and the young squires who were gathered further down the field gazed in rapture at the Breton's prowess. Ralf leant on the wooden rail that enclosed the tiltyard and called out,

'Aimery! A handsome tilt there, my lord. You certainly show the rest of them how to do it.'

Aimery, riding slowly past the spectators towards the grooms who waited to take his horse, looked across at Ralf. He nodded his head to him curtly, and his steel grey eyes flickered, just for a moment, over Elena. Elena shivered as if his gaze was a knife blade slicing through her vulnerable flesh.

It was not only Aimery who haunted her. Isobel obsessed her thoughts too. She knew it was but a fancy, yet she had the feeling that the beautiful lady of Morency was not far away, and that any day now, she would be here, at Rouen, gazing mockingly at Elena with her slanting green eyes as she took her place at Aimery's side.

Ralf was still shaking his head in admiration as Aimery rode on past them. 'My God,' he said raptly, 'but there's no-one to beat the Breton in the art of war. I shall ask Duke William if I can be in Aimery's company when we ride south for Maine.'

It was the turning point for Elena. This was too much for anyone to bear. She turned to face Ralf and said quietly, 'My lord. I must inform you that I will not be coming with you to Maine. I have been making enquiries, and I have been offered a passage home to England within the next few days. I am resolved to accept it.'

He confronted her sharply, his fair hair ruffling in the breeze, his pale blue eyes narrowed in sulky anger. 'Oh, no, my lady. You're coming with me. It will be a fine summer's jaunt, this campaign. Many of the knights are taking their ladies with them; William has commanded it, because he is weary of the cuckolding that goes on when his men are away at war. You and the others will be settled comfortably in some secure castle, while we drive Fulk of Anjou from Maine's borders. There will be hunting, hawking, feasting. Of course you're coming. That was what we decided.'

She shook her head, her blue eyes dark and increasingly stubborn. She said, 'I have been offered a passage to England on the next fair tide. I said I would give the shipmaster my answer today, and now I am decided.'

'And how are you paying this shipmaster?' he sneered. 'How? You have no money. Answer me!'

'That is my business. I will settle the matter myself.'

'You're not going back to England. Do you hear me? You're coming with me, to Maine!' He gripped her arm, hurting her. She whipped herself free.

'You would take me with you by force, my lord?' she asked scornfully.

He was silent, his eyes slitting into impotent anger. He knew only too well that to force her would make him a laughing stock amongst his companions. Elena watched him struggling for words; then she turned away from him and drew her long mantle over her shoulders.

'I shall send a message to the shipmaster and tell him that I will sail for England with him on the next tide,' she breathed. 'Do not humiliate yourself further by trying to stop me, Ralf.'

* * *

66

The Tower of Rouen was dark and cool after the brightness of the river meadows as Elena hurried inside. She had lied to Ralf. She had made no arrangements. She didn't even know how much to offer the stern-looking sailors down by the riverside. But she was resolved to fetch her money, and go down there now, to beg for a passage home. The thought of travelling to Maine in the company of Ralf and Aimery was too much for her to bear.

She hurried to the women's bower, a little-used room on the first floor where she had hidden her precious purse beneath the loose fabric of an old tapestry-covered settle. This room was one place where Ralf could not follow her, could not spy on her, for it was forbidden to men. She sank to her knees to reach for her purse of coins.

But it was not there. Her heart started to thump slowly, painfully. She looked again, but her money had gone.

She sank on to a cushioned seat in the window embrasure and gave way briefly to despair. All her money, gone. And it was no good raising the alarm; Ralf would punish her for the mere possession of money of her own. How would she escape now from the trap that was closing around her?

She spun round as the door to the chamber slowly opened, catching her unawares. At first, she couldn't believe that it was Aimery standing there, out of his armour now, clad in a long tunic that was girdled at his narrow waist, and deer-skin boots that were still dusty from the stables. Then the slow throb of warning developed into an insistent ache at the pit of her stomach as she gazed at his tall, wide-shouldered figure. Her heart was also beating in panic, because she remembered what had happened the last time she was alone with him.

She drew herself up and said, with an effort at calm disdain, 'This bower is for the ladies of the court only, my lord. You intrude. Or were you looking for someone?'

'Yes,' he replied softly. 'You.' He came in, then turned and shut the door, deliberately dropping the bar across it to secure it. 'Your husband tells me that you do not travel with us to Maine. That you return to England instead. Why?'

She had backed up without realising it until she was against the window embrasure. She was trembling, but strove to keep her voice calm. 'Perhaps because the prospective company does not please me, my lord.'

'Ah,' he drawled. He fingered his lean jaw thoughtfully. 'I wondered if perhaps you grew tired of your husband, and wished yourself away from him. In England, after all, you could soon get some fresh young knight to warm your bed.'

Elena paled. 'You insult me, Aimery,' she whispered. 'The other night, you took advantage of my distress, and of our previous intimacy. Be assured that I have no desire for such an encounter again – with anyone, let alone you.'

His dangerous silver eyes suddenly blazed with light above his hard, jutting cheekbones; his strong, sensual mouth, so cruelly twisted by the long white scar that slashed his cheek, was compressed in a thin, intimidating line. Then, suddenly, his expression curled into a chilling smile as he moved slowly across the room towards her. Her blood churning darkly, Elena felt her breasts ache with longing, felt her nipples grow tight and tender.

'Really?' he said softly. 'You look ripe and ready this very minute, lady Elena. Your lovely face is quite flushed, and your pulse is racing, is it not?' He was close to her now. He reached out his hand to stroke her breast through the thin fabric of her gown, and Elena leant back against the wall for support as the familiar tremors of desire coursed through her. He was hateful, and yet she wanted him so badly that her insides were melting with

68

lust. She ached for his hand to move lower, to caress between her thighs and feel her lushness opening for him. She hated herself for the way he made her feel.

She pulled away, her dark blue eyes spitting scorn. 'You find it easy enough to insult me, my lord. Can you not find someone of your own rank to torment?'

He held out his hands in a mock attempt at appeasement. 'Insult you? I did not intend it as such. I was merely commenting on your sexual rapaciousness. You used to be so sweet, so innocent, Elena, but you have learnt much, I fancy. How many men have you welcomed to your bed since I relieved you of your maidenhead?'

She gasped and tried to pull away; but already his hands were moving upwards, cupping her small high breasts, twisting her nipples beneath the thin silk of her gown. She was on fire for him and he knew it. He pulled her roughly towards him and kissed her, his tongue plunging into her mouth, possessing it. She reached for his shoulders, pulling his head down towards hers, pressing her aching breasts against his hard chest. She clung to him desperately, not caring, not able to think. 'Dear God, Aimery,' she breathed. 'Why do you torment me like this?'

There was a big carved settle, covered with a rug, set before the fire. With a low oath, Aimery picked her up in his arms and moved swiftly across the room to lay her down on it. She clung to him still, breathing his name. He pushed up her gown to her hips and knelt between her parted thighs, running his fingers urgently through the soft blonde down at their joining, playing with the pink, pouting lips of her sex. She moaned and quivered at his touch, the tremors running hotly through her. Her little bud of pleasure swelled tormentingly as he laid it bare. Sweet heaven, she no longer cared that the silvery moisture of her arousal was glistening on her thighs. She needed him, now.

His dark face was intent as he loosened his own clothing and his rigid member sprang free. With a low cry, she reached to touch the hot, velvety rod. Then he was finding his way to her heart, rubbing with his phallus against her parted labia, sliding inwards, filling her aching emptiness. His hands found her breasts, stroking the tingling peaks, and he began to move faster, driving his hard penis into her, again and again. She arched against him and began to utter little moans of excruciating pleasure as her climax swept through her. 'Ah, *caran*,' he moaned. 'You say I torment you. But that is nothing to the way you ensnare me . . .' And then he drove himself hard into her, his teeth clenched; she could feel his shaft leaping, exploding deep within her as he kissed her, his strong mouth moving with deliberate passion over hers.

They lay entwined, sweat-sheened, breathing slowly, deeply. Elena closed her eyes, feeling his arms around her, never wanting this moment to stop. He had called her *caran*. His beloved.

And then his fingers, which were gently entwined with hers, found her wedding band. He let his hand rest for one moment on the coldness of the gold. Then he drew himself up, his eyes hooded and unreadable, and said to her, 'Well. You've become a passionate little doxy since we first met, haven't you? Marriage must suit you.'

Elena covered her breasts as the coldness of his words stabbed through her. As he got slowly to his feet, he carried on, almost conversationally, 'You really should accompany Ralf on this forthcoming campaign, you know. We could enjoy some sport together, you and I. After all, now that you are married, things are so much easier. And Ralf doesn't exactly guard you well, does he?'

Elena swallowed hard on the sudden, dry ache that almost stopped her throat. For one moment, she'd thought that Aimery still loved her, still felt some tenderness for her. What a fool she was. She got to her feet to face him, and said tightly,

'I told you. I leave shortly for England.' *Somehow*, she promised herself. *Somehow, I will find a way . . .*

His gaze was unreadable as he looked down at her. Then he shrugged. 'I thought you told me you loved your husband,' he said. 'If you were as devoted as you claim, then you'd stay by Ralf's side wherever William's orders took him. Wasn't that why you came to Rouen in the first place? Or was it just to find new adventures, new lovers?'

Elena said in a low voice, 'You find pleasure in insulting me. I see no point in prolonging this conversation. If you will excuse me, I –'

She was interrupted by a sudden knocking at the door, a man's harsh voice, rasping out, 'I seek the lord Aimery le Sabrenn. Is he there?'

Aimery moved slowly towards the barred door, smoothing down his clothing as he did so. He opened it, saying calmly, 'I am here. Who wants me?'

'The duke himself, sire!' stammered the man, who had glimpsed Elena standing frozen by the window. 'He demands your presence now, in the hall.'

'Very well. Go – I will follow.' The man hurried off; Aimery turned to Elena. 'Come. I will return you to your husband, to whom you claim to be so devoted.'

'I will stay here,' she said, backing away from him.

'You will come with me, Elena!' He added, in a softer voice, 'That man saw us together, closeted in here. We must pretend that we were just talking, that we are friends. Otherwise the gossips will make much of it. Come.'

He was right, so she went with him. But surely, people would know, could see what had just taken place between them. Sweet heaven, how quickly she had given in to him; he had only to touch her and she was his. How shameless he must think her. Oh, if only she could

71

get away from here. The loss of her money stabbed at her yet again.

The hall was crowded as they entered. William was on the raised dais at the far end of the room, apparently holding audience with someone who knelt before him, hidden from view. His lords and bishops were gathered around, serious, intent as they listened. A matter of some importance, then.

The crowd parted as Aimery moved with long, graceful strides towards the duke. William saw him, and broke off in what he was saying.

'Aimery!' His stern face relaxed in welcome. 'Come to my side, my lord, and listen. This is a sad tale we have here; one of my loyal subjects tells me that her estate is being harassed by robbers. I am prepared to send her aid, but she specifically asks for your help, my lord. She says you owe her for some service she rendered you in the past.'

He stood up and reached for the hand of the lady whom Elena could now see was kneeling before him, and drew her to her feet. Elena, who had moved silently to Ralf's side amidst the onlookers, felt herself stop breathing. She saw a beautiful, heart-shaped face, with slanting green eyes and full red lips. The woman's hair, coiled at the nape of her neck, was dark and gleaming beneath her almost transparent silk veil. She turned to gaze at Aimery with the triumph in her eyes scarcely concealed. 'My lord,' she whispered. 'You are pleased to see me, I hope?'

Isobel was back.

Isobel had not been happy to see Aimery come into the hall with Elena at his side. The old, bitter jealousy seared her heart. But then she observed that Elena, though still as hatefully lovely as ever, looked tired and distressed; her dark blue eyes were shadowed with unhappiness, and her face was pale.

Perhaps she and Aimery had quarrelled. Perhaps Elena had pleaded for Aimery to come to her bed, and he had refused. At any rate, the little Saxon slut Elena had gone to stand at another man's side. That, presumably, was her husband. He looked handsome, and lecherous, and weak; and he hadn't been able to take his eyes off Isobel since the moment she walked in. Isobel's imagination stirred interestingly. There could be some sport to be had there.

As for Aimery, he was as magnificent as ever, in that long grey tunic that emphasized his powerful shoulders and lean hips. He looked restored to full health; his skin was golden from the sun, his powerful body honed with exercise. She felt a little pulse flicker excitingly between her thighs as she gazed up at him. The journey from Morency had been long and tedious. She had found some entertainment on the way by bedding a young esquire with a lusty penis, who was utterly besotted by her beauty; but she was tired of the lad now, and needed a real man's body – preferably Aimery's. If he was surprised to see her here at Rouen, he hid it well.

She noticed that Duke William had indicated the carved chair at his right hand side for Aimery le Sabrenn. So the Breton was truly back in favour. All the better for her plan.

'Lady Isobel,' the duke was saying, his normally stern voice full of compassion, 'perhaps you would tell the lord Aimery your story?'

Isobel, kneeling once more in supplication on the steps before the dais, moistened her lips and gazed up sadly at the duke. Then she turned her emerald gaze on Aimery. She saw his beautiful grey eyes harden for an instant, as if in warning, but he said nothing. Dear God, how she wanted him. He belonged to her, since the night she'd seduced him, a young, penniless mercenary, in her elderly husband's castle all those years ago. She would get him back.

'My lord Aimery,' she began in her low, spellbinding voice. 'I have been telling Duke William that I have ridden here to beg his aid. My home, the castle of Morency, where I lived in such happiness with my gentle husband before his death –' she let her eyes fill, just for a moment, with tears – 'is now beleaguered. There are brigands living in the forest of Belleme nearby, and they harass my villagers, steal my crops at night, and attack the honest travellers passing through my lands. Since my husband died, I am alone. I have come to implore help from the duke, and to beg for the services of one of his most renowned knights. You, Aimery le Sabrenn.'

Aimery's eyes narrowed. He said, 'Lady, I am promised to the duke for his forthcoming campaign against Fulk of Anjou.'

Isobel's voice throbbed with passion. 'My lord. You owe me a favour, I think. Must I remind you?'

Aimery said flatly, 'Perhaps you better had. I seem to have forgotten.'

Isobel drew a deep breath. 'Two years ago, my lord, you were wounded and taken prisoner by your enemies. You languished in Flanders for many months, in danger of your life. It was I who found you; I who paid your ransom; I who nursed you gradually back to health –'

William leant forward, frowning, his leonine head jutting from his short neck, his tanned face grained and leathery from many hard campaigns. 'Aye, and it is a story I shall not forget, since, to my shame, it was I who should have saved you from such a fate, Aimery le Sabrenn! I owe the gracious lady of Morency a great debt for her services to you; and I wish to repay her by offering you to her in service, to secure her estate from the brigands who encircle it.'

Aimery said to him carefully, 'My lord Duke. How can I go to Morency? Soon, you depart for Maine with your army; and I am bound to you in fealty.'

Isobel held her breath. Then William laughed, and

clapped Aimery's shoulder, and said, 'Then you shall fulfil your oath to me, as well as your debt to this beautiful lady. The castle of Morency lies on the borders of Normandy and Maine. Aimery, you will set out with a chosen band of men, to make safe this lady's lands. The lady Isobel will travel with you – you can set out as soon as she is rested. And then, your task completed, you will move on, to join my army in the marcher lands north of le Mans. We will save some of the sport of battle for you, never fear.'

Aimery was quite still. Isobel waited, in anguish. Then the Breton said, at last, 'My lord Duke, if that is your will, then of course I shall obey you.'

'And repay your debt to the lady,' said the king jovially.

Aimery, looking straight at Isobel, said, 'She could have had the price of the ransom many times over, in gold, my lord Duke. But she did not want that, I think.'

'No,' breathed Isobel, gazing back at him. 'I did not want that, my lord.'

She felt a great, surging sense of joy. Aimery had been ordered to accompany her, to her castle in Morency, and stay with her until the castle was secure. A journey of perhaps fourteen days and nights, or more, with her lord at her side. Then who knew how long he would stay in her isolated stronghold deep in the forests of Belleme? It would soon be summer, and the brigands from the forest would be lively, audacious. Oh, it would give her long enough to reclaim him, to make the Breton all hers again.

William was bidding her rise and stand by his side. She did so gracefully, her long green gown rustling as it clung in swathes to her slender figure. She kept her dark lashes demurely lowered, but allowed herself a long, sweeping glance at the assembled crowd, wondering if Aimery's heiress bride was somewhere here. If so, she ought to be weeping, because Aimery would have

75

forgotten all about her by the time he saw the Tower of Rouen again.

Isobel saw that Elena was still there, standing motionless beside her husband. Surely there was nothing between her and Aimery now? Isobel knew from her spies that Aimery had been devastated on learning the news of Elena's marriage. He had turned back to the shores of France, to hire himself out in the mercenary wars that fermented constantly in the Vexin. And the Saxon girl was still at her husband's side. Isobel let out a small sigh of relief. Surely Aimery would have nothing but contempt for her now.

William was speaking again, his voice full of authority as he explained Aimery's quest to the gathered assembly. 'The mission carries little danger,' he was saying. 'The land between here and Morency is at peace, apart from the outlaws who plague the forests. But, remembering the fate of Fitzosbern, I would wish for more company for my knight Aimery, as well as his own retainers. Several of the stalwart knights gathered here today, together with their men-at-arms, would make a formidable array. And, like Aimery, you could move onwards to join my main army once the lady Isobel is secure.'

Isobel watched, interested. Most of the men's eyes were fastened on her hungrily, but they said nothing, probably because they were afraid of losing rank and importance if they were not constantly at their duke's side.

And then, to Isobel's amazement, Elena's husband stepped forward. He'd hardly been able to take his eyes off Isobel since she entered the hall. 'My lord Duke,' he said eagerly. 'Let me offer my services to the lady Isobel! I will gladly ride at lord Aimery's side and defend her lands from the brigands who trouble it!'

William rasped his chin with his thumb thoughtfully. 'An interesting proposition. You have several men-at-arms, don't you, my lord Ralf? And other retainers?

76

Together with Aimery's men, that would make a suitable number. And your wife –' his face lit up in a smile – 'your lovely young wife, Elena, can go with you. You have not been married long, and it seems a shame to separate you. She shall accompany you, as my wife accompanies me on my campaigns, and she will also be a travelling companion for the lady Isobel. Isobel too has lived in England – the two women will have much in common.'

Isobel's green eyes darkened. Oh, no. Not what she'd planned. But still, neither had Elena, to judge by the stricken whiteness of her face. Suddenly, Isobel wanted to laugh.

Did the duke realise what he had done? Place the two bitter rivals for Aimery's love in the same travelling company as the man they both adored, and send them on a journey of some thirty leagues, in enforced companionship?

Isobel turned to the duke and curtsied low. 'I thank you, my lord,' she murmured.

It should prove an interesting journey, at any event. She was sure – quite sure – that she would triumph easily over Elena. And maybe have some sport with Ralf into the bargain.

Chapter Six

Ralf was simmering with irritation. Ever since the duke's command three days ago that he and his party should accompany Aimery le Sabrenn south to Morency, his wife Elena had seemed quite distracted.

'I cannot accompany you. I will not,' she had insisted stubbornly, almost desperately, that night when they were private at last in their small bedchamber.

Ralf shrugged. 'You must. No-one defies an order of the duke's.'

'Then I shan't ask his permission – I shall just leave! I shall sail on the morrow with the first ship that departs for England.'

'You will find,' said Ralf, swiftly unbuckling his sword belt as he prepared to undress for bed, 'that the sea captains of Rouen will be most unwilling to defy the duke's wishes. You will find yourself unwelcome on any ship, my lady. I shall see to it personally.'

Elena gazed at her husband, her breasts beneath her gown rising and falling in distress, her dark blue eyes shadowed with some sort of dread. Ralf almost felt sorry for her.

'What ails you?' he said curtly as he eased his black

velvet tunic over his head. 'This journey to Morency should be a pleasant diversion. We will have every comfort we require on our way, and the lord Aimery will be a fine travelling companion.' And so will the lady Isobel, he added happily to himself. He remembered the way her green, slanting eyes had appraised him earlier in the hall, and he felt a pleasurable thrill of anticipation.

Elena said, almost desperately, 'My lord Ralf, I find the company of both of them uncongenial.'

'Why, in God's name?' Ralf was pulling off his long leather boots. 'Most women seem to find the Breton quite irresistible, despite that ferocious scar. Who knows? His presence might even spark some fire beneath that icy exterior of yours.' He laughed, finding the thought improbable. There could never be anything between a man like Aimery le Sabrenn and his convent-bred wife. Anyway, Aimery would be marrying that spirited little armful, Henriette de Sizerne, very soon, so his mind would be full of her. A thought suddenly struck him; he paused in his undressing and laughed aloud.

'By the way, I've heard that Aimery and the intriguing Isobel were once lovers. Henriette won't be at all pleased by her betrothed's departure in Isobel's company, will she? There may well be some sport between the two of them. This journey is bound to rekindle old flames.'

Elena was standing very still, her eyes dark pools of anguish. Then she stepped forward and said, her voice tremulous with passion,

'My lord Ralf, I beg you to grant me this one favour. Allow me to depart for England, to await your return there. And afterwards, when you return to me, I swear that I will serve you, always, in whatever you desire.'

Ralf was silent for a moment, gazing at her. Dear God, but she was stubborn. And she was as beautiful, as desirable as any woman at court.

'You talk of serving me,' he said thoughtfully. 'Well, you can serve me now, and then I will pay some attention to your request. Undress yourself, my lady wife.'

Slowly, not looking at him, she unlaced her gown. It slipped from her creamy shoulders. He gazed hungrily on her high, lovely breasts, with their little tips of rose, and caught his breath. His phallus throbbed and grew; she saw it, and her cheeks flushed with colour.

'Come here,' he grated. 'Let me touch you.'

He ran his palms roughly across her nipples, his face tightening as the dark buds hardened in instinctive response. His penis jerked hungrily towards her. 'Oh, but you're beautiful,' he muttered, still hotly caressing her breasts. 'Show me exactly how you will serve me, my sweet wife. Take me. Take me, in your mouth . . .'

Obediently, her face quite expressionless, she sank to her knees and took his straining member between her soft lips. Her eyelashes fluttered shut: carefully she moved to and fro, sucking, caressing the sensitive ridge of his glans with her tongue, pulling him sweetly into the moist warmth of her velvety mouth. Ralf groaned, his hips clenching, and began to thrust. Dear God, but her mercenary lover, whoever he was, had trained her well in these delightful sports. Almost on the brink, he grasped her hand and pushed it against his tightening balls. 'Show me your little tricks, lady wife.' Obediently she caressed his scrotum and ran her fingers further, up behind the crease of his bottom cheeks, as her mouth continued to slide up and down his straining shaft. The tip of one finger found the tight collar of his anus. With a groan Ralf began to spurt into her mouth as she thrust her finger inside and the dark pleasure flooded his senses. She swallowed, again and again, sending rippling sensations of bliss through his exploding cock; and he plunged hard into her until he was spent.

She waited till he had finished, then slowly got to her feet. 'I pleased you, my lord?'

'Yes. Oh, yes.'

'Then – you will let me go to England?'

'Sweet Christ; enough of this foolish talk,' rasped Ralf. 'I can't let you go. Don't you understand that no-one countermands an order given by the duke himself? You will come with me to Morency.'

For a moment his wife looked so stricken that he felt sorry for her. He almost wished that he hadn't stolen that little purse of money she was secretly saving for her journey. He'd known it was there all along, because he'd followed her once to the ladies' bower and saw her hide it there.

He took her in his arms, stroking her soft breasts with his hand. He felt sleepy now, and content. 'Look,' he said. 'You've got to come with me. But we'll fare all right together, you and I. You'll see.' He drew her down beside him on the mattress and was soon asleep, not realising that Elena lay awake beside him until dawn, staring into the blackness.

Ralf went down to the stables the next morning, to check over his horses before the long journey to Morency. Duke William had promised the travelling party that they would have ample changes of mount at his strongholds along the way, but Ralf still hoped to take his favourite destrier. He'd brought the stallion out into the sunny cobbled courtyard beside the stables, soothing the battle horse's flanks and consulting with his groom, when he heard a low, silken voice behind him.

He turned quickly and saw Isobel, mounted on a prancing chestnut mare. The hot sun sparkled on her gleaming black hair, and lent warmth to her flawless ivory skin. She wore a dark blue mantle of finest wool that clung to her sinuous figure. With one hand, she held the reins expertly. On her other, leather-gloved wrist was a hooded merlin.

'Well, lord Ralf,' she said, her eyes sparkling, 'I hear we are to be travelling companions. I am glad to know I

81

shall have you at my side, to protect me from my enemies.'

Ralf bowed his head, his heart thumping against his ribs. 'My lady. Consider me yours.'

She gazed down at him from her saddle. Was he mistaken, or did he see a glint of mocking laughter in those wonderful green eyes?

'I shall,' she said. 'Oh, believe me, I shall.' She ran the tip of her tongue very lightly over her full red lips. Ralf caught his breath, aware that his member was rearing into hardness beneath his long tunic. He gazed at her, his mind filled with a vision of that dancing tongue working over his throbbing shaft. She was openly laughing now. She must know, this beautiful witch, what she was doing to him.

The hooded merlin on her wrist suddenly stirred restlessly, its bells tinkling. Isobel frowned in irritation and tightened its leash mercilessly. Ralf, watching, said, 'Careful, my lady. The bonds may distress it.'

She eased back the bird's leather hood. Its piercing yellow eyes darted and glowed like fire. 'Then,' she said softly, 'it will enjoy its freedom all the more when it comes. After all, what is pleasure without a little pain?'

Her last word was almost a whisper. The rest of her party was gathering, ready to move on to the woods beyond St Sever where good hunting was to be found. She wheeled her horse expertly away, leaving Ralf gazing after her, blinking into the sunlight, quite entranced.

Isobel, politely declining the sparse, cramped quarters that were offered to her and her retinue in the over-crowded Tower of Rouen, stayed instead with an old friend in one of the fine timber manses that lay just within the town's walls, close by St Peter's cathedral. There, she rested in preparation for the return journey to Morency, and considered her plans.

So far, everything was going well, better than she had dared to hope. The duke himself had commanded Aimery to follow her. It would not take her long to entrap him in her wiles again. And the presence of the Saxon girl Elena would add a certain spice to the challenge, especially as her weak, flaunting husband, Ralf, was already half-besotted with Isobel.

Alys had been in earlier, to pile more logs on the grate in Isobel's private chamber. The night had turned suddenly cold, and the wind was chilling, a reminder that summer was not here yet. Isobel was glad of the thick tapestries hanging round the walls, and the shutters at the window that kept out the cold night air. A few more days to rest herself, to recover her beauty, and then the journey south would begin, with her lord Aimery at her side.

She would make him her slave again. She remembered, longingly, how once he had worshipped her with his beautiful soldier's body. When he was but a lowly mercenary, and she was the wife of a great lord, he'd been captivated by her. She remembered how she'd come to him, in the darkness of the night, to the guardhouse of her husband's castle. Silently, his strange silver-grey eyes burning with passion, he'd undressed her; then he'd bent his head to take each of her ripe breasts in his mouth, worshipping her. Gasping with the dark, forbidden pleasure, she'd run her hands over his rippling, battle-hardened torso, thrilling to his scarred male beauty. Swiftly he'd laid her down, and when Isobel caught sight for the first time of his throbbing phallus, she'd cried out softly with longing, and rubbed herself against him, desperate for his embrace. Slowly, deliberately, the handsome Breton mercenary had impaled her, easing the whole of his beautiful iron-hard length into her quivering hips. She'd clung to him, drowning in pleasure, gazing up into his darkly brooding face as the cataclysmic pleasure engulfed her and left her weak and sated.

She'd lost him, to Elena. How she'd hated the blonde, virgin Saxon girl, who'd entranced Aimery with her simpering innocence. But now, it seemed, Elena had lost him too. Aimery was on the verge of betrothal to a young heiress, but Isobel wasn't worried about her either.

Isobel hadn't seen Henriette yet. No doubt the girl was being kept cloistered at home by her doting parents, where she would be dreaming of lying in the arms of her husband-to-be.

She, Isobel, would make sure that the girl never got any further than dreaming. She would cast her spells on Aimery as they travelled south, and make the elusive Breton all hers again, as he was before. How she hungered for him now. Her loins melted at the memory of his rigid shaft, pleasuring her purposefully until she was brimming with rapture.

She gazed at herself in her bronze mirror. Her cheeks were tinged with colour, her lips slightly swollen; her nipples tingled enticingly. Just the thought of the Breton aroused her to wantonness, as ever. Yet she would have to play her game with care, and not repel him with her ardour.

There was always Hamet, of course; a delicious bonus whenever Aimery was around. She smiled softly into the mirror, seeing how the firelight cast a burnished sheen on her glossy black hair. Hamet was besotted with Isobel, and no doubt she could use the burly Saracen to discreetly ease her sexual torment on the journey. He was not Aimery. But he was massively endowed; his dusky shaft was eager and willing, and stout enough to ease the inner lusts of the most rapacious of women, time and time again. She smiled, remembering. How Hamet used to love it when Isobel climbed astride him, poising her slender white hips above his loins and easing her sex slowly down the glistening pole of his lengthy

84

black cock, while he pawed and suckled hungrily at her dangling breasts. Isobel used to slide frenetically up and down his dark shaft, climaxing with little moans; then she would quickly pull herself off him before he had time to spend himself, and torment him with her fingers and lips, cupping his heavy balls and teasing his great cock with her tongue, until his penis started to explode with pleasure, and he shot his sperm all over her stomach and breasts, his dark face slack with bliss . . .

Her sex was wet and swollen even now as she remembered how she sometimes used to take the two magnificent men at once. She liked to have Hamet thrusting into her mouth, while Aimery pleasured her slowly, magnificently from behind. Sweet heaven, but she longed for them both now. Biting on her soft lower lip, she went rapidly to her oak travelling chest, and searched quickly for the polished box that contained her secret possession, her carved ivory treasure that was shaped like a man's erect appendage. She needed it now, needed its long, hard thickness to ease the longing within. She sucked at the rounded tip of the creamy ivory shaft, her eyes closed in anticipation of pleasure, her breasts aching with need.

There was a knock at the door. Dizzy with disappointment, Isobel thrust the big ivory phallus quickly back into the chest. It could not be her elderly hosts, for they always retired early.

It was Alys. Her pinched, pockmarked face was surly as she muttered, 'A visitor for you, my lady. A girl – well-born, to judge by her high-and-mighty manners. She won't tell me her name, but she says it is most urgent. She says that no-one but you can help her.'

Isobel frowned in irritation. But her anger was mingled with puzzlement, and curiosity. Why should a solitary, well-born girl be seeking an audience with her, Isobel de Morency, at this time of night? 'Show her up,' she said sharply.

When the girl came in, she looked almost breathless with excitement. She gazed raptly round the room, taking everything in: the log fire in the grate, the fine tapestry hangings, the fur-covered bed. Then she swept to a low curtsey before Isobel. 'My lady,' she breathed. 'Thank you for agreeing to speak to me. I am desperate. And there is no-one else, you see, who can help me.'

Isobel assessed her quickly. She was well-spoken, no doubt highly born, as Alys had said. But she contrived to hide the fact by covering herself in a drab old cloak that was swathed round her head and body. Even so, Isobel could see that she had a merry, mischievous countenance, with tumbling chestnut curls and dancing brown eyes.

'I am intrigued,' said Isobel dryly, 'as to how I can assist you.'

The girl threw back her cloak and dropped to her knees. Her figure was slender yet curvaceous beneath her plain grey gown. She was indeed a tempting little beauty.

'I want you,' breathed the girl, 'to tell me how to capture a man's heart. Someone – I cannot say who – told me, lady Isobel, that you know all the wiles to enslave a man's heart and mind, to make him yours for ever. Please – oh please – tell me.'

'And what do I get for my reward?' said Isobel slowly.

The girl looked at her imploringly. 'My lady. I would not insult you by offering you gold, for I know you to be wealthy already. But I would offer you my eternal loyalty and gratitude.'

'Are you going to tell me who you are?'

The girl coloured. 'No. My mission is secret, you see. And the man I wish to enslave – he is well-known, and would be angry with me if he knew I was consulting you. But I must – oh, I must have his love!'

Isobel walked slowly across the room towards the fire, then turned. 'You sound as if you should be consulting some woman of magic, paying her to cast her spells on this man you are so besotted with.'

'No!' The girl's response was firm. 'No, my lady. I know that I have the magic here, within my own body. I know that men find me attractive – I know that *he* finds me attractive.'

'You have bedded him already?' queried Isobel sharply.

The girl coloured, but her brown eyes were joyful. 'Yes. And he was everything I've ever dreamed of.'

Isobel was feeling a slow, burning throb of jealousy. What had first been an inkling of suspicion was now becoming a certainty. This girl could be none other than Henriette of Sizerne, Aimery's bride to be. She could have no idea that Isobel and Aimery knew one another well. The girl obviously had even less idea that Aimery would soon be leaving Rouen, to travel with Isobel to Morency; from whence, if Isobel's plans went aright, he would not be coming back.

And she had come to her, Isobel, to ask for advice on how to capture Aimery's heart. Isobel's lip curled in scorn. Well. She would have a little sport with the girl. And teach her that no-one, no-one, would succeed in taking Aimery away from Isobel of Morency.

She called Alys to fetch some sweet wine. The girl drank thirstily, from nervousness and excitement. Isobel poured her some more of the powerful liquor and watched her downing that as well. The girl's cheeks became slightly flushed, and she began to relax. Isobel smiled at her kindly, and gestured to the girl to sit beside her, on the cushion-covered chest that lay at the foot of the bed.

'Well, my dear,' Isobel said silkily, 'I will not pry. But firstly I must know just a little about you. Tell me. How much experience have you had of men?'

By the time Henriette had finished eagerly telling her about the young priest, Julien, and Manot, and the various other men who'd pleasured her willing flesh, Isobel was feeling quite thoroughly aroused again herself.

'You must think back on all this,' she said kindly, 'and recall to yourself when these men are at their most vulnerable. When they would forget everything except the overwhelming need to take you in their arms.'

'They adore my breasts,' Henriette said proudly. 'The young priest used to grow hot with arousal every time he looked on them; he would ejaculate at a touch, such was his excitement. And Manot – oh, he loved to rub his big cock between them, and spurt over my nipples.'

'And the man whose adoration you crave? Did he too like your breasts?'

Henriette frowned. 'He was aroused by them, certainly. But – he has not been back to see me since that first night. He tells me we must wait, for our marriage. But I cannot wait. I fear that other women are bound to covet him, and oh, I want him all for myself, so badly, you cannot imagine.'

Oh, yes, I can, thought Isobel. Aloud, she said in the same kindly voice, 'Show me your body, my dear. Then I can see for myself how best you can show it to advantage.'

Henriette looked anxious, just for one moment. But the strong wine was doing its work, and her body was already heated from the rich warmth of the log fire. Almost defiantly, the girl pulled her gown and chemise over her head, and stood proudly before Isobel, wearing nothing but her silk stockings, which were gartered with ribbons just above her knees.

She is indeed a juicy prize, thought Isobel, with her young, creamy body and her full but firm breasts adorned with striking dark brown nipples. The chestnut curls ran riot round her pudenda, but even so Isobel could glimpse the sensuality of her glistening nether

88

lips. Isobel felt an answering stab of arousal as she gazed on the girl's blatant sexuality.

'Play with yourself,' she said softly. 'Show me how you satisfy yourself when you lie in bed at night longing for this man.'

Henriette coloured with shyness, but only for a moment. Then she began to touch herself, cupping and holding her heavy breasts, pulling at the long brown teats, her face growing dreamy with longing. Between her slightly parted thighs, Isobel could see the moist coral flesh of her sex.

'More,' said Isobel softly. 'Let me see more.'

Biting her lip, the girl reached down and began to stroke at herself, rubbing her finger slowly between her labia. Her nipples strained and darkened, and her eyes began to close. Quietly Isobel got up from the chest and opened it to withdraw the ivory phallus. The girl, who was breathing heavily with lust as she rubbed herself, heard something and opened her eyes. She gasped with shock when she saw the massive ivory phallus, carved with cunning protuberances to enhance enjoyment.

'Do not be alarmed,' said Isobel silkily. 'I want you to lie back on my bed, my dear, and open yourself to me. I am going to probe you with this instrument of love, to examine your responses, and offer you advice. Lie down, and trust me.'

Henriette, wide-eyed, desperate with lust, scrambled to do as she was told. Gently Isobel raised the girl's knees and parted her stockinged thighs. She smiled inwardly as she saw her wanton, lustful flesh, the lips already parted and pouting in invitation. Slowly she poured some scented oil from a little glass phial into the palm of her hand, and rubbed the ivory phallus. Then she carefully positioned its blunt, heavy head, and started to slide it sweetly into the girl's vagina.

Henriette reared with pleasure at the cold, satisfying hardness.

'Lie still. Feel it within you,' soothed Isobel. 'Grip it deep within your womb, and let your muscles tense and relax, as if you were playing with your lover's penis. Play with your breasts, pull on their lovely crests. Lick your lips in welcome and move your hips slowly, sinuously against the ivory cock – oh, is that not good?'

'Yes,' gasped the girl. 'Oh, yes . . .'

She was writhing greedily now as Isobel drove the ivory penis in and out, pulling at her soaking flesh lips with each movement. The pale pearl of her clitoris protruded eagerly from its little hood, glistening with longing. One touch, one little touch there, and she would be consumed by waves of pleasure.

Isobel slowly withdrew the phallus, and gazed thoughtfully at the glistening love juices that adorned its formidable length. The girl almost groaned with disappointment. 'I beg you. Do not stop,' she whispered, rubbing her thighs together in a vain attempt to comfort her empty vagina.

Isobel positioned the phallus and eased it inside her, just a fraction, teasing Henriette with the fat, blunt head. Every time the girl arched her hips to take it in, Isobel pulled it back. The girl's face was hot and flushed as she begged wordlessly for consummation. Isobel said at last, 'I shall give you what you want in one moment. But first, tell me. Who told you to come to me?'

The girl, her thighs splayed wide to reveal her unfurled coral sex, gazed at the long ivory phallus with anguish in her eyes. 'I cannot tell you, my lady. It is a secret.'

Thoughtfully Isobel ringed her forefinger and thumb and ran them slowly up and down the oiled phallus. The girl looked desperate. 'Who told you?' repeated Isobel softly.

'Hamet,' the girl blurted out in despair. 'Hamet the Saracen.'

Isobel nodded. Just as she'd guessed. 'And have you

had your way yet with Hamet, you little slut? Has the Saracen pleasured you yet with his juicy black cock?'

The girl rolled her head from side to side, her lips pressed tightly shut. Gently Isobel reached to rub the tip of the cold ivory shaft along the side of her straining clitoris. The girl arched and moaned, on the brink. 'No! No, he hasn't! But I have pleasured him. I have taken his great cock in my hand, and stroked his balls, and been coated with his plenteous seed as he spurted between my fingers, again and again . . .'

'He has given you no pleasure in return?'

'Yes – with his tongue. He licked me, lapped me like a thirsty animal at water, brought me to my crisis by thrusting his stiffened tongue inside me, again and again – oh, please, my lady, I can bear no more –'

'We are almost there. But first, you must tell me the name of the man you wish to enslave.' She eased the fat ivory shaft just inside the girl's pouting sex, stretching her, increasing the pulsating tension on her yearning clitoris. 'His name,' she repeated softly.

'Aimery. Aimery le Sabrenn. He is to be my husband – and I wish him to love me, only me.'

Slowly Isobel began to drive the thick phallus into the girl's throbbing vagina. 'Aimery,' she murmured. 'A man worth fighting for indeed. Imagine this is Aimery le Sabrenn's lovely strong penis driving into your sweet flesh. Imagine his tongue licking your breasts, his hard body arching over you, his mighty cock dancing, exploding with fierce rapture deep within you . . .'

In, out, went the long, slippery phallus. Henriette gasped and drummed her clenched fists against the bed, then began to climax with high, whimpering little cries. Isobel continued to ravish her writhing loins coolly, deliberately, until at last the girl fell back on the fur-covered bed, sweat sheened and sated, her ripe breasts flushed with ecstasy.

Isobel, putting the phallus aside, went to pour herself

91

more wine. She also refilled the girl's goblet, and waited with it at her side, until she had recovered her senses.

Then she said, 'I have sad tidings for you, Henriette of Sizerne. You won't see Aimery le Sabrenn for many months. You see, he will shortly be accompanying me to my castle of Morency.'

The girl pulled herself up, her eyes wide, uncomprehending. 'So you know the lord Aimery? But why? Why is he going with *you*?'

Isobel was confirmed in her guess that the girl knew nothing of her former relationship with the Breton. Good. Better to keep her ignorant of that, or she might begin to suspect Isobel's motives.

'The Duke of Normandy himself has commanded it,' she said. 'You see, my castle, which lies in the marcher lands between Normandy and Maine, is beleaguered by brigands. Aimery will bring soldiers to destroy them.'

'But he will then return to me?' said the girl hopefully.

Not if I can help it, thought Isobel. But aloud she said in a caring, supportive voice, 'Of course, my dear. Especially if you convince him that you are capable of the sort of wild, wanton behaviour you have displayed to me tonight.'

The girl gazed at her eagerly, folding her arms across her naked breasts. 'He likes his women to be wanton and eager?'

'Oh, yes. The Breton lord positively craves the kind of behaviour you have described. A soldier's life is hard and often degrading, and he requires corresponding qualities in his women. You must adore him openly, at every opportunity. Hover at his side, listen to his every word and touch his arm constantly when you are with him in public. In private, worship him with your body. Kiss him, display your lovely breasts to him, offer to take his manhood in your mouth. If he is weary, or temporarily sated, then tell him stories. Tell him about your past exploits, just as you've told me tonight. And, for a special treat, display your various talents to him. Invite one of his servants – Hamet, or one of his grooms, or a lowly soldier, anyone, as long as he is well-endowed – up into your chamber. Then invite the lord Aimery to watch as you are serviced by your guest. Make your behaviour lewd, enticing. Be insatiable, always eager for more. The lord Aimery will worship you for it.'

Henriette listened, entranced. 'Oh, I will, I will. I will make him adore me.' Her face fell. 'But he is leaving, you say. Very soon.'

'In a few days or so,' said Isobel casually. 'Time enough, my dear, for you to ensure that he is yours for ever.'

The girl jumped to her feet, her eyes alight with eagerness, and began to dress herself rapidly, slipping on her silk chemise and her long woollen gown. 'Yes, indeed! Oh, lady Isobel, how can I ever thank you enough?'

'Just follow my instructions,' said Isobel kindly, showing the girl to the door. 'Remember, now. Make your behaviour, in private, as lewd and enticing as possible. The lord Aimery will adore you, and will not be able to wait to get back to you.'

The girl reverently kissed Isobel's hand, then wrapped her mantle round herself and ran down the stairs. Isobel paced her chamber slowly, a little smile on her face.

A few days. Time enough for the stupid little slut to display her brazen wares to the lord Aimery and put him off her for good. Isobel sipped her wine with relish.

Hopefully, Henriette would realise too late that if there was one thing Aimery could not bear, it was women who were too clinging, too possessive. And if they were openly sluttish, and copulated with his servants – well, he would take them once, perhaps, for the brief pleasure of it. More often, he would offer them to the rapacious Hamet, and watch impassively, then go and take his own refined pleasure with someone more tantalising, more alluring.

If Henriette proceeded as Isobel had instructed, there was a good chance that Aimery le Sabrenn would never want to see the little slut again, let alone marry her.

A few days later, Henriette of Sizerne was pacing the floor of her candlelit bedchamber, feeling increasingly desperate. The hour was late. Tomorrow, Aimery was leaving, to travel south in the lady Isobel's company. And she had had no chance whatsoever to be alone with him, to display her passionate love for him, in the ways that the kind lady Isobel had suggested. Whenever Aimery visited her father, she tried her best to edge close to him, to put her hand on his arm and smile up at him adoringly, but he merely looked cool and impatient, and more impossibly desirable than ever. Earlier that evening, Henriette had managed to persuade her father to take her to the Tower of Rouen, to an assembly that the duke was holding. Henriette had looked round desperately for Aimery, and found him quickly. He was so easy to pick out, with his tall, wide-shouldered figure, and that beautiful, chillingly scarred face. She frowned a little as she saw that he was talking in a corner with the Saxon lady Elena, Ralf's wife, the woman who had been so humiliated by her husband on the unforgettable night that Aimery had arrived in Rouen.

Neither of them looked pleased to see her. Aimery looked stern; he was talking in a low, harsh voice, and his eyes were hard as flint. Elena was looking pale and distressed. She was saying, urgently, 'If you had any pity in you, my lord, any charity at all, you would order my husband to send me back to England –'

Aimery was drawling, sardonically, 'You would disobey the duke's command, to join my party and provide female company for the lady Isobel? Not a wise move, I think. You will come with us, lady Elena. After all, we might enjoy each other's company, just as we used to, while you play the part of devoted wife.'

Henriette saw Elena step back as if he'd struck her. 'I do not deserve that, my lord,' she whispered.

Aimery folded his arms across his chest and stared down at her. 'Don't you? But I thought I spoke nothing but the truth. You are always telling me how much you love your husband, the estimable Ralf. If you are as devoted as you claim, then you would have no doubts about coming on this jaunt to Morency.'

That was when Henriette, frowning at what she had just heard and not understanding a word of it, bounced up to them, and put her hand possessively on Aimery's arm. Then she said sweetly,

'Excuse me, lady Elena. You do not mind if I have a little private conversation with my future husband?'

Elena had looked dazed. 'No,' she whispered, 'no, of course not. There is nothing further for the lord Aimery and I to discuss.' Then she left quickly, disappearing amongst the crowds that thronged the duke's great hall, and Henriette had the uncomfortable feeling that Aimery, who looked angry, would have gone after her, had not Henriette clung to his arm. They talked as if they knew one another well. Why? What was Ralf's wife to him? And why was Elena so desperate not to go on this journey to Maine?

'My lord Aimery,' she pouted up at him. 'You do not resent spending a few moments with me, I trust? Soon we are to be parted for a while, and I wish, so much, for us to have sweet memories of one another.'

He gazed down at her, still looking distracted. Henriette thought, with a little fluttering at her heart, that he really was the most beautiful, the most devastating man she had ever seen. She remembered that first night he arrived in Rouen, when she'd accosted him in his bed-chamber, and he'd pleasured her so wonderfully that since then she'd constantly ached with wanting him again.

He said, flatly, 'I am a soldier, my lady, pledged to the service of the Duke of Normandy. We will often be parted, unfortunately.'

'Then come to me tonight,' pleaded Henriette. 'Please, my lord. My maidservant will let you in by the back stairs.' Suddenly she remembered what Isobel had told her, about whetting Aimery's appetite with tempting entertainments. 'My maid is very comely,' she whispered. 'And she loves to debase herself with one of the servants, a lusty youth called Hubert. I have watched them often. If you wish, my lord, I will summon them to entertain us. We will have sport watching them, and fine wine to drink. Then you and I can plight our love for one another.'

He almost pulled himself away from her. Was it Henriette's imagination, or did she see a flicker of scorn in his silver-grey eyes?

'Lady Henriette,' he said, 'tomorrow my men and I set off on a long, hazardous journey. Tonight I have much to do – orders to give, supplies to be gathered together, horses to be prepared. You will forgive me if I decline your invitation.'

'Please come,' she begged. 'If only for a while.'

He said curtly, 'Lady, you must excuse me. I think the duke is looking for me.'

Henriette had watched him go, the tears pricking her eyes. She didn't understand. Isobel had said that Aimery loved such diversions as the one she had offered him, that they were the one way to his heart. But he had scornfully declined her invitation.

Now, up in her lonely chamber, she came to her inevitable decision.

Aimery was leaving Rouen. Very well, then. She would follow him, and prove her love for him.

Chapter Seven

*T*he sun shone brightly down from a cloudless blue sky as Aimery le Sabrenn led his cavalcade of fifty men and all their retinue southwards into the lush valley of the Risle. They'd been on the road for ten days now, and each day the lovely Normandy countryside seemed to unfold yet more of its early summer ripeness to them. Tender young vineyards clung to the gentle green hills; flowers starred the lush meadows where black and white cattle grazed, and the woodlands were bronze with the unfurling foliage of oak and beech.

Aimery rode at the head of his men, with Hamet at his side, forever watchful. They moved with all the accompanying sounds of a marching military column: creaking leather, jangling bits, and the metallic slither of armour proclaimed their progress. Even in this seemingly peaceful landscape, they were nevertheless only twenty leagues from Normandy's troubled borders, and were prepared for fighting. Aimery constantly sent scouting parties ahead, and there were yet more of his soldiers at the rear of the convoy, guarding the slow-moving baggage wagons that were laden with corn and wine, and tents for the soldiers. There were women in the carts too, lowly servants who were there to prepare and cook the soldiers' food as they journeyed south, and who saw to their other needs at night.

The lady Isobel rode in the middle of the convoy on a spirited bay mare, having scornfully declined Aimery's offer of a carriage at the very start of the journey. 'What, and be jolted to death in some clumsy contraption that is little better than an ox-cart? Oh, no, my lord!'

Isobel was a skilled rider. Ralf was constantly complimenting her, and showing her further tricks of horsemanship. Isobel praised Ralf in turn for his own fine riding, and he blushed with pleasure.

Elena rode silently at her husband's side, gazing at the beauty of the countryside with unseeing eyes. She, like Isobel, had declined Aimery's suggestion that she rode in one of the baggage carts, where the grumbling Alys had settled herself. At Elena's refusal, Aimery had frowned down at her from the high saddle of his restless black horse.

'It is thirty leagues to Morency,' he drawled, his grey eyes assessing her slender, vulnerable figure. 'You will be exhausted, making such a journey on horseback.'

Elena's blue eyes flashed defiance. 'Your logic seems somewhat faulty, my lord,' she said with quiet scorn. 'If you cast your mind back, you will recall that I had no desire to make this journey in the first place, on horseback or otherwise. So will you let me travel to England, as I requested?'

He compressed his lips into a thin line. 'It is the duke's will that you travel to Morency,' he said. 'Besides, I thought you were averse to being separated from your husband?'

To that, as ever, there was no argument. He was right; hadn't she defiantly told him how much she loved Ralf at their last smouldering encounter? Whether he believed her, she doubted, but it was certainly her only defence against the Breton now.

With his usual precise efficiency, Aimery moved away to find her a placid, easy-paced palfrey to ride, and assigned a young Norman squire, Gilles, to attend to her and her horse. The gently bred Gilles, who worshipped Aimery and hoped one day to become a knight like him, attended Elena assiduously. Aimery, in appointing him, had presumably anticipated that Ralf would have little time to attend to his bride. But Elena, weary of Aimery's taunts, had determined to play the role of demure, devoted wife to stubborn perfection. Ralf, flattered but somewhat bemused, was pleased by her apparent docility, but found himself constantly distracted by the beautiful, vivacious lady of Morency, his eyes straying again and again to her sleek figure.

Isobel said nothing at all to Elena, unless she was forced to. It was as if she had decided not even to acknowledge that she and Elena had ever met, let alone once fought bitterly over Aimery le Sabrenn. Elena, who hated the scheming temptress with all her heart, was happy to comply with her decision. Hamet, too, treated Elena with cool disdain. Aimery, meanwhile, continued to lead the convoy with relentless, impartial authority. If he was cold and brusque with Elena, then he was so with everyone, even Isobel. Not that the fact gave Elena much comfort. Her throat was dry and her eyes were aching because of the constant dust from the rutted track, but she would die rather than let the Breton know what an effort her endurance cost her.

Then, one day when they had paused in their journey to rest the horses from the powerful midday heat, Elena saw Isobel with Hamet.

Elena had wandered off into the cool shade of the beech trees while Aimery's men watered the horses, bringing leather buckets up from the slow-flowing river. As she walked slowly across the leaf-strewn carpet of the dappled forest, feeling the stiffness from the saddle gradually leaving her chafed limbs, she suddenly heard sounds, strange yet familiar sounds that brought the warm colour to her cheeks. She'd stopped just in time, at the edge of a little clearing. There she saw Isobel pleasuring Hamet.

The burly Saracen was lying on his back on the soft undergrowth, moaning softly in his outlandish native tongue, and Isobel was riding him, her gown pulled up so he could fondle her breasts, her stockinged thighs spread wide across his loins. Rhythmically she rose and fell, her head thrown back in delight, her eyes closed, while little soft, mewling sounds came from the back of her throat as she impaled herself on Hamet's mighty weapon.

Elena remembered how formidable the Saracen's dark penis was in arousal. Her own pulse racing, she gazed, unable to move, as Isobel lifted herself up on the Saracen's dusky great pole, then shuddered her way down on to it again, her face rapt with pleasure. Hamet was reaching feverishly to pull at her rosy teats, his own face alight with adoration. Isobel was riding him faster and faster, almost at the point of no return, the soft pink lips of her sex glistening with excitement as they sheathed the Saracen's mighty black phallus. Then she reached her crisis, dancing wildly astride him, while Hamet thrust dementedly into her, spurting his hot release inside her womb for what seemed an eternity.

Elena, her own desire throbbing darkly, slipped away and made her way back to the others, the shame warm on her cheeks. Isobel had not changed at all. She was as lustful, as feral as ever. Did Aimery know? Probably. After all, Elena knew that Isobel used to enjoy taking them both together, the Breton and his servant, arousing them tormentingly with her exquisitely sensual body.

Ralf caught sight of her as she returned to the river bank where they were all gathered. He'd been drinking unwatered wine: he was still holding the leather wineskin, though it looked almost empty. His handsome face was flushed in the noonday sun.

'My beautiful little wife,' he slurred as he saw Elena. 'Come here, to me.'

Gilles, the esquire, moved quickly away, and one or two of the other soldiers looked at Ralf with distaste; but Ralf ignored them as he pulled Elena into his arms and kissed her. She submitted, but her face was very pale when at last he released her mouth. 'You will ride at my side this afternoon,' he instructed her. 'You understand? You will keep me company, sweet wife.'

He was still holding her, still pawing her openly. Elena said in a low, urgent voice, conscious of the soldiers watching, 'My lord. You have drunk too much wine. Let me go.'

Suddenly his face went dark with anger, and he pulled her closer. 'How dare you criticise me?' he breathed. 'You humiliate me, wife. I almost regret not letting you go back to England, as you wanted. I should have let you keep your stupid little purse of gold –'

Elena froze. 'My – my *money*? You *knew* about it?'

Ralf realised he'd made a mistake. But he took refuge in sneering, 'Of course I took it. You have no right to any possessions of your own. You are my wife, remember?'

Elena cried out and began to struggle wildly in his grip. But then a shadow fell across them, and Elena realised that Aimery was there. Gilles, who was standing behind him, must have slipped off to warn him. Aimery said, in a low voice resonant with menace, 'I suggest, lord Ralf, that you cool yourself in the river, as the horses have done. Wine and the midday sun do not go well together.'

Ralf's face flushed. His arm was round Elena's waist now; he was fondling her openly, caressing her breasts through her gown. 'I was simply expressing a desire for my wife's company, my lord,' he said, his words still thick from the wine. 'Isn't she a tempting little morsel,

101

now, this Saxon wench? Wouldn't you like to try her out for yourself, Aimery le Sabrenn? Sometimes, she seems cold and reluctant, but it's all a pretence, you know. Really, she's a hot little bitch, can't wait for me to get it up her. Try her – try her for yourself –'

He broke off as Aimery, in one swift movement, seized a leather bucket of water that had been brought for the horses and threw it over him. Ralf staggered at the shock, shaken and angry, with water streaming from his face and hair to his shoulders, but he took one look at Aimery and did not dare to say anything. He slunk away, towards the horses.

Aimery and Elena were alone. Aimery said flatly to her, 'You may travel at the rear, with the wagons, if you wish. At least you would be spared such degrading scenes.'

Elena lifted her head proudly, though her eyes were still dark with humiliation. 'You forget you are talking about my husband, lord Aimery.'

He gazed into her face and said, almost bitterly, 'Of course. And you love him, don't you? How could I have forgotten that?'

All of the soldiers seemed to have melted away, leaving them alone. But then, suddenly, Isobel was there, back from the woods, her face glowing with satisfaction. 'Well, my lord Aimery,' she said, carefully positioning herself so that he had to turn away from Elena, 'are we all suitably refreshed and ready to continue?'

Aimery gazed at her gleaming eyes, her reddened lips. Hamet was back too, and could be seen silently saddling up Isobel's bay mare.

'It seems like it,' said Aimery, and moved away towards his men, already issuing commands.

Elena turned her back on them all in despair, the sickening truth about the loss of her purse almost forgotten in her sudden, heart-wrenching longing for Aimery.

102

Oh, why had she ever thought that she could compete with Isobel for the Breton's dark love?

Every night they stayed at some stronghold or castle belonging to one of Duke William's loyal vassals. By the evening of the twelfth day of their journey, they were approaching L'Aigle, and their route required them to ford the broad river, where it spread out into rock-strewn shallows. The sun, though starting to sink in the sky, was still warm; its golden rays danced on the broken surface of the water as Aimery's convoy prepared to cross.

Since his humiliation at Aimery's hands, Ralf was tersely dismissive of his wife, ignoring her most of the time and choosing instead to ride with the ever-sparkling Isobel. Elena, scarcely able to bring herself to speak to Ralf after his admission about her money, yet still forced to play the part of devoted, submissive wife, was rescued from her loneliness by Gilles, the esquire Aimery had ordered to look after her. Gilles told her of his childhood in Caen, and his rigorous training as a squire. It was his most ardent wish to travel to England as a soldier of Duke William, and he was eager to learn the Saxon language. Elena found him quick to learn, and she took more pleasure than she'd expected in speaking to him in her native tongue. She was grateful for his respectful but entertaining company, and now, as they prepared to cross the river, it was Gilles who was at Elena's side, holding her palfrey's reins. Aimery and his knights on horseback lined the passage in case of mishap, their big mounts hock deep in the water. Gilles glanced a little apprehensively at the far bank. It seemed a long way off.

'The word for *river* in your native language, my lady?' he enquired.

Elena translated for him willingly, grateful for his kind courtesies, his gentle companionship.

Gilles's eager young horse stumbled slightly on a

submerged rock, but he righted it quickly. 'And the words for *falling in?*' he grinned ruefully.

Elena told him, laughing. His company made her lonely journey so much easier to bear. He was young and handsomely made, with long brown hair and hazel eyes. He had stripped to his breeches and boots for the crossing, and his supple body, with the powerful muscles rippling beneath his bronzed skin, stirred her with some indefinable longing. He made her think of what Aimery must have been like ten years ago, unscarred by life and love.

And then, Aimery rode up to them just as Gilles was leading Elena's palfrey up from the river. They were still smiling together, but Aimery's cold, silky voice broke into their companionship.

'I entrusted the lady Elena to you, Gilles. Take care that your efforts to amuse her do not lead you both into danger. I saw how your horse stumbled back there. It was clumsily managed.'

Gilles bowed his head, his smooth, sun-browned cheeks flushed with shame. 'You are right, lord Aimery,' he murmured. 'It will not happen again.'

'Take care that it does not,' said Aimery.

Gilles rode away in mortified silence. Elena turned swiftly to Aimery.

'Is it your wish to humiliate me at every turn?' she breathed. 'Once more, my lord, you make a spectacle of me.'

'Perhaps because Gilles, like Ralf, is not taking sufficient care of you.'

Elena rose hotly to the young squire's defence. 'You are unfair, my lord Aimery. Gilles is most assiduous in his care for me.'

Aimery's gaze burnt into her, sending a leap of sheer physical longing scorching through her flesh. 'I am glad to hear it, demoiselle,' he said softly. 'I hope you do not encourage him too much in his attentions.'

104

'And why should you care?'

He paused, his strange silver-grey eyes assessing her. Then he said flatly, 'I do not like to see my men distracted from their duties.'

Elena felt a strange constriction round her heart. It could not be, surely, that Aimery was jealous of Gilles? But she was aware of that dangerous little pulse of hope flickering still as he slowly turned away from her and wheeled forwards to take his place at the head of the convoy.

And then, urging on her own weary palfrey, Elena saw Isobel gazing at her with such hate in her eyes that she went quite cold. Why should Isobel hate her so, when she'd won? She'd got Aimery, hadn't she, the only prize that mattered?

Or had she? Certainly, Aimery spent little time openly with Isobel as they travelled. Elena had assumed that this was a deliberate device to deceive his men as to the true nature of his relationship with Isobel.

But what if things really were over between them? Was that why Isobel was taking consolation with Hamet? Elena tried not to hope, but nevertheless she felt a resurgence of impossible, searing desire for Aimery le Sabrenn.

They reached L'Aigle at last, a strong castle perched on its crag like the eyrie of the eagle after which it had been named. L'Aigle was small and shabby compared to Duke William's tower, but nevertheless it offered them more comfort than they had known since leaving Rouen, and they stayed there for two days and nights, safe in the green, rolling country of the Ouche, with its fertile wooded valleys and silver trout streams.

On the first night, Elena had the chance to bathe and to wash her hair with sweet-scented soap. Afterwards she was invited to the first-floor solar by the chatelaine's wife, Briot, who had once spent some time in England

and was anxious to relive her memories with Elena. The lady Briot had left her, just for a while, to make sure that all was well with provisions for their guests, and Elena waited for her, gazing out through the little window of the solar as the sun set over the pale green beech forests that lay all around the little town. Elena was grateful for the peace, the sense of refuge. Not that Ralf troubled her much, now. She'd confronted him again, about the theft of her purse, and he'd defended himself surlily, repeating again that as his wife she had no right to any money of her own. Elena, remembering anew how close she had been to securing a passage to England, could hardly bring herself to speak to him. At night, he was usually filled with wine by the time he came to her bed, and as she always feigned sleep, he would just tumble into the space beside her and fall into a deep slumber.

The door to the bower opened, just a little, and the candles on the wall flickered in the draught. Elena, thinking it to be Briot returning, stood up in deference to the lady of the castle. But then, she froze as she heard Isobel's all-too familiar voice just outside the door.

'You will come to tell me, Alys, when the water is heated? I swear, I am covered with dust from top to toe; I must bathe.' She gave a little, languorous yawn. 'For now, I will take my rest in here. I am so weary of these nights without sleep, Alys. I am tempted, you know, to tell the lord Aimery that I cannot come to his bed tonight. He is so rapacious, Alys, he gives me no rest. He says he hungers madly for me all day, and so must have me in his arms all night to slake his lust . . .'

Elena heard Alys murmuring something in reply. Then she heard Isobel's laugh, low and husky. 'And he is such a man, Alys. So vigorous, so well-endowed. His lovely long cock is so lusty, and he will pleasure me for hours with it if I wish. How can I turn such a man away? As I said, I will rest in here while you prepare my bath. Use

106

that little phial of sandalwood oil to perfume the water. Come and tell me when everything is ready.'

'Very well, madame,' Elena heard Alys say tonelessly, and the servant's footsteps pattered away.

For Elena, there was no escape. Isobel came in, and saw Elena standing tensely by the darkening window, her face all but drained of colour. The lady of Morency pulled up in mock surprise.

'Well,' said Isobel. 'I did not expect to see you in here. How are you enjoying our journey, little Elena?'

Elena slowly faced up to her hated rival. 'I think you know, lady Isobel, that I would rather be anywhere else but here.'

Isobel laughed, her green eyes gleaming with triumph. 'Come, come. Surely you are not still sulking about losing the delicious Breton to me, when you have such a fine young husband at your side? You should give Ralf a chance, Elena. He would enliven your nights if you would let him. But he says that you are frigid, Elena. That is not what I remember.'

'You forget that my husband also seems to have fallen under your spell, Isobel. You must be busy indeed, with Aimery, and Hamet, and Ralf all clamouring for your attention.'

'Oh, dear,' laughed Isobel, sliding softly into a cushioned window seat, her green silk gown rustling around her. 'So you are still after the lord Aimery? Give up, my dear. He will never be yours. He finds your blonde innocence insipid, your lack of experience tedious. He told me so himself, only last night, just at a most delicious moment, when I was pleasuring him in one of his favourite ways...' She leant forward conspiratorially. 'You see, I had taken his manhood between my lips – no easy task, for you know how big, how strong his penis is. And he is so desperate for me, he finds it hard to restrain himself – he has to pretend constantly to his men, you see, that there is nothing between us.

107

Anyway, he was sliding his strong shaft into my throat, trying not to stifle me with his power, while I licked and teased with my tongue, just as he loves. At the same time, I was pulling with my hands at his lovely tight bottom cheeks, easing them apart. Slowly I slid my finger into the little crack of his delicious arse, and I moved it in, out, in, out, exactly as he craves it – oh, my dear, he was in ecstasy! He grabbed my breasts, thrust his wonderful cock again and again in my mouth, while I drove my finger firmly into his pulsing secret place. His bottom cheeks clenched to the hardness of iron. Then he began at last to spend himself, filling my mouth with his hot seed, and his face was dark with pleasure as he pumped himself into me. And he takes so long to be sated. You know yourself of his strength, his stamina, as his semen spurts on and on deliciously . . .'

She broke off, because Elena had rushed from the room. She slammed the door of the bower shut behind her, and leant against it, struggling for breath.

Foolish, naive, innocent, Isobel had called her. Indeed she was, to have allowed her hopes to be raised, to thus lay herself open to this new, unbelievable pain.

Blindly she hurried through the corridors and stairways of the great castle, searching instinctively for the fresh night air to cool her burning cheeks, and to ease away Isobel's hateful taunts.

Gilles was just crossing the stableyard when he saw her. All the rest of Aimery's men were gathering in the great hall for the evening meal, but he'd been to tend to the horses, and was late. It was dark now, but still warm. Lanterns had been hung around the stone walls of the stables, their yellow light pale in comparison with the hundreds of silvery stars that pierced the black velvet of the night sky.

He pulled up when he saw Elena standing there. She looked so beautiful, so unhappy. Gilles worshipped

Ralf's wife. He would do anything for her. Most of all he would like to kill Ralf for his treatment of her. And then take Elena to his own bed.

In your dreams, he told himself bitterly as he put down the leather harness he was carrying and went up to her quietly, his soft leather boots making scarcely any sound on the cobbled courtyard. 'Lady Elena,' he said, 'is anything wrong?'

She gazed up at his familiar face, trying to shrug and smile, but he could see that her eyes were filled with desperate hurt.

'Oh, Gilles,' she said, 'everything's wrong, I think.'

He saw the tears brimming slowly at the corners of her wonderful blue eyes, saw how the curve of her mouth trembled even as she tried to smile. With a soft oath, he moved towards her and took her in his arms, kissing the tears away. She went very still; he could feel her trembling against his body. Ardently he kissed her forehead, her cheek, her lips, and as his mouth found hers, he realised, with a jolt, that she was responding with desperate passion. His tongue moved slowly, strongly between her parted lips. She seemed to shudder with longing, reaching out to clasp at his wide shoulders, and whispering, 'Gilles, help me. I need you.'

He felt his penis burning and hardening beneath his tunic; and her tongue, caressing him back, told him that she was in as much need as he. Swiftly he lifted her in his arms and took her into one of the empty stables, where the air was scented with the warm fragrance of horses and hay. As he lowered her to her feet, she leant back against the wall, still gazing up at him: he kissed her again deeply as she moved her slender body longingly against his. He could see the hardness of her nipples beneath her silken gown. His phallus reared into erection.

Quickly, in the shadows, he unlaced her so that her gown fell to her feet. Then he slipped her chemise from her shoulders, gazing at her lovely rose-tipped breasts as he did so. She whimpered softly as he bent his head to lick deliberately at her stiffened teats, pushing them to and fro with his tongue. Desperately she clung to his shoulders while Gilles dealt quickly with his own clothing, his handsome face dark with passion as his phallus sprang free at last.

Already, there was a dewy tear of desire on the glans of his swollen member as it jerked up at her from the pouch of his heavy testicles. She seemed to give a little shudder as she gazed at it, and Gilles, quite distracted with passion, said, 'Lady Elena. I mean you no dishonour, I swear. But all these long days, in your sweet company, I have worshipped you, burned for you. This is like a dream.'

She took his warm brown hands again and rubbed his calloused horseman's fingers across her taut nipples, still gazing at his quivering penis. 'No dream,' she whispered. 'Do it, then, Gilles. Oh, God. Do you not realise that I burn too?'

He gazed down at the softly furred little mound at the base of her belly, where the pink sex lips peeped out longingly from beneath the silky golden down. Then he took her up against the wall, easing his stiffened shaft up into her tender sex and sliding himself into her softness with a slow, delicious strength that almost lifted her from her feet. At the same time he bent to take her breasts adoringly into his mouth, drawing them one by one between his lips, teasing the hard pink nipples with his white teeth. Elena clasped his shoulders desperately, crying out her searing pleasure as his lengthy penis drove up into her again and again. He could feel her vagina rippling fervently round his cock as her ecstasy engulfed her; shuddering, he clenched his hips and jerked furiously inside her womb. Just as the sweet release was about to flood through his body, he pulled himself out of her, and spent himself between her thighs;

desperately he pumped his engorged penis to and fro against her flesh as the hot, sticky liquid spurted in stream after stream, to trickle down her warm skin. His passion exhausted at last, he covered her exquisite face with kisses.

'Lady,' he breathed at last. 'I wish you nothing but joy and love. I am your servant always. You must know that I burn for you, night and day. If you ever need me again, I will come to you. Meanwhile, rest assured that I shall breathe nothing of this to anyone, on my honour.'

Elena touched his cheek, her blue eyes molten with repleteness. 'My thanks to you, Gilles,' she whispered. 'I shall remember.'

He found clean linen cloths to wipe his offering from her thighs. Then he took her hand and kissed it in silent homage. Without speaking, he helped her to clothe herself again, and watched as she hurried away across the deserted courtyard, back to the hall.

Elena, still dazed by what she had let the young squire do to her, her body still throbbing from his ardent lovemaking, knew that she must enter the dining hall, to take her place at her husband's side, before anyone should suspect anything. She prayed that Ralf would be well into his wine by now, and would not notice that his wife's cheeks were still aglow, her lips still swollen with passion.

But Aimery noticed.

She saw him the minute she entered the hall. He was talking to Isobel. Elena felt the familiar, aching torment return as badly as ever when she saw the lady of Morency rest her jewelled white hand possessively on Aimery's sinewed forearm, and gaze up into his stern scarred face as she asked him something.

But the Breton commander turned away from Isobel and walked slowly across the rush-strewn floor towards Elena, barring her passage to her seat. Elena, her heart thudding, caught a brief glimpse of Isobel's glance of hate. Aimery's scarred face was chilling as he appraised her loosened hair, her creased clothes.

'Secret assignations, lady Elena?' he murmured mockingly.

Elena, wildly confused by his physical nearness as always, folded her arms defensively across her breasts. 'I needed fresh air,' she said defiantly. 'The evening is sultry, and the heat is stifling inside the castle.'

Aimery reached out to touch her lips. They tingled and throbbed under the casual caress of his lean finger. 'And you are cooler now?' he said.

'I thank you, my lord, yes!'

He nodded thoughtfully and moved away

But he left her burning with longing for him. Gilles had been a pleasant distraction; his handsome young body had eased her physical torment. But it was still Aimery le Sabrenn, Isobel's cynical lover, who held her in thrall.

She must brace herself to endure their approaching arrival at the castle of Morency, where Isobel would no doubt spare no trouble to show everyone, especially Elena, that the lord Aimery was well and truly hers.

Later that night Ralf, who was hazy with the good red wine provided by the Lord of L'Aigle, brooded over the banqueting table, even though most of his fellow soldiers had left. Elena had retired. It was no good thinking of joining her, because she would only feign sleep. He was angry with her, because she humiliated him at every turn with her coldness.

He was regretting now telling her that she must accompany him. He regretted stealing her stupid little purse of money, and spending it in a whorehouse in the stews of Rouen the night before they set off for Maine. Even more, he regretted letting slip that he'd been responsible for its loss.

Elena's presence tormented him. Her beauty still stirred him, but her coolness was an insult to his manhood; his manhood that raged constantly in the lady Isobel's presence. Isobel's subtle hints, her provocative sensuality, the deliberate cruelty that he sensed beneath her polished surface, aroused him wildly. Perhaps at the castle of Morency, he could translate her veiled promises into exquisite, lusty action.

His heart juddered as Alys, Isobel's ugly, pockmarked servant whom he found quite repulsive, came silently up to him. 'My lord,' she said in a surly voice. 'My mistress would see you, in private.'

Ralf almost stumbled to his feet in his haste, knocking the remains of a loaf to the rush-strewn floor. Finally Isobel had recognised his worth, had acknowledged her need for him. He followed eagerly as Alys led him along a stone passageway to the deserted armoury. Alys's candle flickered on the dank stone walls as they passed locked wooden doors and shadowy vaults. At last she opened a door and led him in. The door shut behind him and, in the radiant candlelight, Ralf saw Isobel.

His pulse raced. She looked even more exquisite than ever. A long white veil skimmed her raven hair and slender shoulders. Her gown was of dark madder rose, girdled with a silver chain. The ugly Alys hovered still by the door, and Ralf wished she would go, so they could be alone. A low fire burnt in the grate to counteract the chill of the windowless stone chamber; there was a table with two chairs, and a flagon of wine.

'My lady,' breathed Ralf, and sank to his knees.

Isobel smiled. 'Lord Ralf. I think we understand well what we want from one another, do we not?'

His throat was quite dry. 'Oh, Isobel. If you knew how I worshipped you . . .'

Her fingers tapped idly on the oak table. 'Yes, yes. You are prepared to do exactly as I say? To follow my instructions implicitly?'

'Oh, yes. I am yours to command.'

Isobel snapped her fingers to Alys, who brought her a folded piece of black silk. Ralf's heart began to thud as Isobel moved to tie the silk around his eyes, blindfolding him. 'You will learn,' she whispered in her low, spell-binding voice, 'that I prefer to take my pleasures discreetly. I permit no man to witness me in the extremity of my pleasure.'

Ralf's phallus leapt and hardened at the thought of the beautiful lady Isobel in such a state. Then he remembered the repulsive servant. 'But Alys? You surely do not permit her to see you, to see us?'

'Alys has gone,' said Isobel. 'Did you not hear the door close behind her? Now we are alone, Ralf. Alone . . .' He felt her hand sink to his groin, kneading his hardened genitals. He groaned softly as the clever fingers dealt with his clothing and pulled out his quivering erection. He reached for Isobel, to hold her close; he felt a swift, painful squeeze on his rampant cock.

'You do nothing – nothing at all – unless I command it,' said Isobel sharply. 'You understand?'

Understand? Oh, yes. He worshipped her. Blindly he nodded, feeling her caress his scrotum until his penis throbbed with dark excitement. She was doing something else now, pulling his hands behind his back, tying them loosely at the wrists with a cord. Then she pushed him to his knees. He stumbled, struggling for balance, his penis straining into the empty air.

He heard a soft rustle of silk and smelt the faint, musky perfume of female arousal. He could hear her breathing, close to his face.

'Lean forward, Ralf,' she murmured. 'Put out your tongue. A little further.'

Ralf gasped with astonishment as his tongue encountered naked female flesh. His cock shuddered into fresh arousal as he felt the furry mat of pubic hair, the plump folds of a woman's pudenda, the startling little ridge of

114

her clitoris. Isobel was breathing heavily now, running her hands through his hair. 'Pleasure me,' she was urging. 'Pleasure me, lord Ralf, with your lovely tongue. Lick me with it, drive it into me. Ah, yes . . .'

Ralf needed no encouragement. Vigorously he ran his tongue up and down the hot cleft, tasting the moist secretions there. He caressed the surprisingly long stem of the erect pleasure bud, hearing Isobel gasp with excitement as he did so. Then he slid his mouth down the juicy folds and found the pulsing entrance to her hungry love channel. He drove in, stiffening his tongue deliberately, pleasuring her slowly with it and thrusting the tip deep inside her, until he began to feel her body gather, and tremble, on the very brink of explosion.

His penis quivered and strained. He wished his hands weren't tied behind his back, so he could caress Isobel's wonderful breasts. He wanted to bring her to such a pinnacle of exquisite joy that she would look at no-one else. Sometimes he saw her watching Aimery the Breton. Well, he would make her forget Aimery. Fiercely he mouthed her, sucking her clitoris, driving his tongue deep within her juicy hotness, until he felt her clamp her loins against him, and shudder into an excruciating, lengthy orgasm, crying out hoarsely and pulling at his hair in her pleasure.

Ralf frowned suddenly as he listened to those delirious little cries. Something was wrong. That was not Isobel's voice, surely?

He blinked, dazed, as the blindfold was removed from his face. The first thing he saw was the sprawled figure of the servant Alys. Her bodice was open to reveal her scrawny breasts. Her skirts were up to her waist, her legs still agape, her ugly face dazed with pleasure. Her dark pink sex was wide open and still wet from his tongue; she was moaning softly to herself, and fingering her own nipples as her orgasm slowly faded.

Behind him, Isobel said softly, 'Well done, Ralf.'

He whipped round, conscious of his tormented penis still throbbing hungrily. 'You said that Alys had left the room.'

She shrugged coldly. 'What does it matter? Those who wish to give pleasure to me must give pleasure to my servant too. They must obey my every command.'

He groaned as he saw her eyes assessing his straining cock. 'My lady. Please. It is you that I want. Can you not see how I burn for you?'

'If you wish to take your pleasure, then take it with Alys,' she said shortly.

He saw how Alys's dull little eyes almost sparkled as they fastened on his swollen shaft. He moved back in revulsion.

'That, or nothing,' Isobel snapped. 'You have not proved yourself worthy of me yet, lord Ralf.'

With a groan, unable to contain himself any more, Ralf lunged towards Alys's open, waiting sex. His bound hands made him awkward; his hips writhed frantically as he struggled to slide his powerfully throbbing member into her still-pulsing love channel. Alys reached with a grin to help him, grabbing his cock and pushing it into herself. 'This way, my lord,' she laughed. Then she mewed with fresh pleasure as he penetrated her, and he felt her body jerking in renewed orgasm as she bucked against him. Hotly he spent his seed, breathing raggedly as his penis thrust to and fro.

At last, exhausted and degraded, he drew himself away, his spent cock dangling heavily between his thighs. Alys got lazily to her feet, smoothing down her skirts and fastening her bodice, her pale eyes blazing with pleasure. Isobel calmly unfastened the bonds that tied Ralf's wrists. 'You have done well, Ralf,' she said. 'You have shown your devotion to me, and proved that you perform stalwartly. You will come to me again when next I summon you?'

Ralf rubbed his numbed wrists, gazing into her

116

bewitching green eyes. Dear God, but she was an enchantress, and he wanted her badly even now, with the seed but freshly spilled from his body. 'Yes,' he groaned. 'You will send for me again soon?'

'Perhaps,' she smiled. 'You may go now. And if you breathe one word of this to anyone, you will regret it.' He staggered away, dazed and entranced, longing for more.

Chapter Eight

*H*amet the Saracen was weary. Two days out of L'Aigle, the weather had changed for the worse. The afternoon brought low, ominous thunderclouds sweeping up from the west, and soon afterwards the lowering heavens had opened, drenching Aimery le Sabrenn's convoy with heavy, relentless rain. Soon, the fresh horses they'd acquired at L'Aigle were fetlock-deep in mud, while the heavily laden baggage wagons slithered and stuck in the quagmired track.

There had been no chance of them reaching the settlement of Longny au Perche by dusk as planned. Instead, Aimery had sent his scouts scouring the empty countryside for shelter, before darkness engulfed them, and the best they could do was this remote, bare little monastery in the depths of a marshy forest. The stern abbot had been far from pleased to see them, and the monks seemed reluctant to produce any food for the new arrivals.

Hamet would have sworn they had plenty of good victuals secreted somewhere – fish or mallard from the marshy ponds, or plump capons dressed with sweet Normandy butter. The monks looked plump and well fed, and not the type to live on bean pottage. But they were unwilling to feed their unexpected guests, so supplies had to be brought in from the wagons, and they supped on hard rye bread and cheese, with a little salted meat simmered in a broth.

Hamet knew that Aimery wondered if this monastery, on the uncharted borders of the great forest of Perche, was in fact under the influence of the notorious Rotrou of Mortagne, who swore nominal allegiance to William of Normandy but had a long history of treachery and intrigue with his enemies. Be that as it may, they had no choice but to shelter here for the night.

The chapel bell tolled compline, and he heard the monks' thin, reedy voices rise in plainsong. There would be little enough entertainment for the soldiers tonight, in this grim place. Perhaps it was just as well, because they had need of haste. A saddle-weary messenger had tracked them down early that morning with news that brigands had attacked the castle of Morency four days ago. They had been repelled by Isobel's loyal steward, Hugh de Brosny, but they burnt crops and homesteads as they fled.

Isobel had paled as she heard the news. Aimery had said curtly to the messenger, 'Return to Hugh de Brosny. Tell him we make all possible speed.'

But speed was impossible in this wet, muddy weather, thought Hamet sourly, longing suddenly for the warm sun of his Sicilian home. He and some of the men-at-arms were struggling to fix a wheel that had come loose from a wagon: four of them held the frame up, with much muscle-straining effort, while two others attempted to prise on the mended wheel. They worked by the dim light of lanterns, in the monastery's old barn, to give them some shelter from the weather. Outside, the rain still poured down in the blackness.

'It's no good,' grunted one of the men, a brawny

119

sergeant. 'We need some sort of lever. Don't suppose these mean-faced monks have anything we can use?'

'I'll go and see if I can persuade them,' said Hamet grimly, and braced himself against the sweeping rain outside.

A flash of movement in the blackness caught his eye. Earlier they'd unloaded some of the provisions from the broken cart into a lean-to shed alongside the stables. Someone was there, in the darkness, rummaging in one of the sacks. After food, no doubt. Hamet strode across the yard and plucked up the slight figure by the shoulders of his rainsodden tunic, so he dangled helplessly. It was one of the young squires, his cheeks bulging from the smoked sausage he'd just been cramming into his mouth.

'Well,' murmured Hamet dangerously. 'They aren't feeding you enough, lad. Is that right?'

'We had naught but bread and hard cheese for supper,' replied the youth defiantly. 'So I thought I'd help myself.'

'Did you, indeed? Even though the lord Aimery himself thought bread and cheese sufficient?'

The lad hesitated. 'He's used to such rations. He's a soldier.'

'And don't you want to be one some day?'

The young squire hesitated.

'Don't you?'

'I – I'm not sure –'

'Then I'd better beat you black and blue till you decide either to become a proper soldier, and live off rations like your betters, or run off home to your wet-nurse,' roared Hamet. Swinging the lad round, he began to spank his surprisingly plump buttocks with the palm of his hand. The boy dangled and squirmed. Then Hamet realised, suddenly, that instead of squealing with pain, he was laughing. Hamet stopped.

'Oh, master Hamet,' gasped the boy rather breath-

120

lessly. 'Don't stop now, please. I was enjoying that. Weren't you?'

Hamet's big hand froze in mid-air. The lad had been relishing it, wanted more. Unexpectedly he felt a swelling, a tugging at his groin as his lusty penis responded accordingly. This was a lithe, pretty youth, with pert little buttocks, who was no doubt well used to being approached by soldiers who had a taste for such things. Hamet himself, when younger, had not been averse to enjoying the firm beauty of a comely soldierly comrade occasionally. But he had not indulged in such activities for a long time, because they brought back dark, shameful memories.

During the harsh time of his captivity in the dungeons of Messina, from whence Aimery had rescued him, Hamet's guards had made sport of his lusty cock and its readiness for arousal. One of his chief captors, a slim, sly-faced Moor with a taste for all kinds of debauchery, had enjoyed putting Hamet in chains, securing the burly Saracen on all fours so that his men could take it in turns to pull his buttocks apart and mount him. The slim Moor had loved to take Hamet himself, as a final act in these night-time degradations, gasping and moaning as he slid his own slender weapon deep into Hamet's secret passage. Hamet used to feel his own excitement mount despairingly as he felt the hard penetration. Sometimes one of the other soldiers would slide beneath him, fondling his mighty black penis even as his chief captor ravished him. The dark, heavy pleasure of his shame would engulf Hamet as he groaned and helplessly spurted his lascivious seed, and the spectators would cheer and applaud before thinking of fresh torments. From such degradation, Aimery rescued him. But sometimes the sordid memories of his captivity came back to haunt him. And though he found his pleasure mainly with women now, there was something wickedly tantalising about this little vagabond.

The youth, damn him, was bending over with his back to him, and pulling down his breeches. In the darkness, Hamet could see the glistening whiteness of his smooth buttocks, marked with dusky redness where Hamet had spanked him. Hamet swallowed hard as his phallus swelled relentlessly. Little devil, he should beat him properly, with a whip.

The youth twisted round, and grinned merrily. 'Don't you recognise me yet, master Hamet?' And as Hamet watched, open-mouthed, the youth pulled apart his shirt to reveal plump, swelling breasts. He grinned a merry grin, and Hamet saw the lovely brown eyes, and cropped chestnut curls, and realised.

Henriette. Henriette of Sizerne.

Hamet let out a long, low oath, in the language of his own country. Henriette pouted. 'Don't be disappointed, Hamet, please. I'm longing for it, just as much as you are.' She fondled Hamet's massive erection through his breeches, with tender hands. 'Oh, dear God,' she breathed. 'Yes, I really am longing for it.'

And she bent over again, on all fours in the dusky shadows of the thatched shelter, and lifted her bare bottom to him. Still Hamet hesitated. Then Henriette turned round and said, 'You can take my bottom hole if you like. One of Aimery's soldiers took me like that, the other night. He was rather drunk, and in the darkness he thought I was a lad, you see. At first, I thought it would never go in. But then he spat on his cock, and rubbed and stretched me deliciously with his fingers, and it slid up me so wickedly, I loved it.'

Hamet said grimly, because his erection was raging at his loins, 'This way first, my fine lady.' And then he mounted her, sliding his pulsing glans between her thighs and finding the wet juiciness of her vagina.

She didn't take long. 'Oh, that's good, Hamet. Slide it into me, all the way.' Grimly he ravished her from behind, his heavy balls slapping against her tight little bottom, his dark cock sliding relentlessly in and out. She cried out happily as he reached to fondle her dangling breasts; and he drove himself in, faster and faster until she whimpered aloud in the throes of her climax. Then he pulled himself out, rubbing his twitching shaft across her buttocks, moaning softly in his own language as his copious seed gouted forth and was smeared all over her white skin.

Afterwards, she rolled over in the hay and lay on her back with her head pillowed against her arms, gazing at him raptly. 'Oh, Hamet. That was so good. Aren't you truly pleased to see me?'

Hamet, buckling on his sword belt again, was grim faced. 'I would lie if I denied that I enjoyed your company, lady. But why are you here? And in such a disguise?'

'I had to follow Aimery. I love him, you see. But he wouldn't let me travel with him, even though I am to be his bride, and so I decided to come like this, in disguise. Now that we are almost at Morency, he cannot possibly send me home. Besides, my lord Aimery will be so glad to see me.'

Hamet groaned inwardly. He had his doubts about that. The lord Aimery already had more than enough to contend with. Obviously this brazen, enticing little minx had no idea that the lady Isobel was desperate to keep Aimery for herself. Or that the Saxon lady Elena – whom Hamet ignored with cold disdain, because she had betrayed his master by marrying the weakling Ralf – was also once passionately involved with the scarred Breton.

He sighed. 'Lady Henriette. The lord Aimery is a soldier, first and foremost. Believe me, he will not be pleased to see you, his future bride, travelling with such lack of dignity amongst his soldiers. If you wish it, I will quietly arrange for you to stay here at the monastery. Aimery need never know. Then a discreet message will be sent to your father, who must be beside himself with worry, so that an escort can be sent to take you back to Rouen.'

'No!' Henriette was on her feet, adamant. 'I must stay with Aimery. You must take me to him now, or – or I will tell everyone that you seduced me, thinking me to be a boy, and took me against my will.'

Hamet shrugged resignedly. 'Very well. I will take you to the lord Aimery.'

He felt sorry for Henriette. She was a sweet little wanton, with engaging looks and courageous impulsiveness. He would be happy to pleasure her plump flesh again, at any time, in any way.

But in spite of her wantonness she was a complete innocent compared to those around her. She was no match for the likes of Aimery le Sabrenn and Isobel de Morency. And he feared that she might be badly hurt by the time she discovered that for herself.

'Henriette is *here*, you say?' Aimery le Sabrenn was incredulous as he listened to Hamet in the small, bare guest chamber that the monks had provided for him. He was still dressed in the long leather gambeson that he travelled in. The scar was livid on his lean cheek, a sign that he was in a dangerous mood.

'Indeed, my lord.' Hamet's voice was resigned rather than apologetic. 'Apparently she's travelled with us, in disguise – she's been with us ever since we left Rouen. She wishes to speak with you, my lord. She is in the women's chamber at present, dressing herself in more appropriate attire.'

Aimery's eyes narrowed into steely slits. 'Show her to me. She must be told that on no account can she continue with us to Morency.'

Hamet bowed his head. 'So I told her, my lord. I will fetch her to you.'

When he had gone, Aimery paced the flagstones of his narrow room in mounting concern.

It was bad enough to be making this journey anyway, to be temporarily stranded in the dubious territory of Rotrou of Mortagne, without further complications being added. Already, he was not happy with the company he was in, and Henriette's presence would not help.

His own men were no trouble. He had fought side by side with them for many years. He trusted them, and in return they followed him without question. But Ralf, with his drinking and his roving eyes, was weak and untrustworthy, and would be unsound in battle. Aimery despised him. And Isobel grew increasingly possessive as they approached her home, reminding him all the time of the old ties that lay between them.

As for Elena, Aimery would have wished that she, of all people, was not here in their company. Her vulnerable, exquisite beauty, which had once reminded him of a pure flame burning in darkness, continued to haunt him. He had to remind himself constantly that she had betrayed him, and would no doubt do so again.

Also, though he had not mentioned this to Hamet, he felt increasingly uneasy about their mission to Morency, which had seemed so straightforward at first. Isobel had told him, when he questioned her, just a few more details about the raids by brigands that she had complained of to Duke William, but her manner was vague and imprecise.

'But your own garrison under Hugh de Brosny is well armed, Isobel,' Aimery pointed out. 'And you have gold enough to purchase more soldiers should you want them. Surely your own men can chase these wretches back into the forest, and rout them from their lairs?' He remembered dealing with the Saxon rebels who once threatened his English castle at Thoresfield. Their clumsy weapons and foolhardy courage had been no match for Norman steel.

'Oh, no!' Isobel had said quickly. 'I need more formidable support, my lord. Hence my mission to Rouen, to ask Duke William for aid. I could not believe my good fortune that you yourself happened to be there at that time.'

Aimery said, 'Have you never suspected that Fulk of Anjou might be behind these raids? After all, his lands adjoin yours to the south.'

Her incredible green eyes widened in surprise. 'Fulk? Oh, no, my lord. How could that be? If Fulk desired Morency, then he would send an army, and take it within days.'

Exactly, thought Aimery to himself. And that was just what he was afraid of. His intuition, infallible through many years of warfare, told him that he was being led into a trap. Though of whose making, he was not yet quite sure.

The feeling of being entrapped increased as Hamet came in leading Henriette behind him. She stood there looking demure and bashful in her over-large borrowed gown and her startlingly cropped chestnut hair, but her eyes sparkled with lust as she gazed at Aimery.

'My lord,' she murmured. 'How glad I am to see you again.'

Her short curls were curiously enticing, and he saw that she had reddened her plump lips with salve, which she was now moistening with the tip of her pointed little tongue. Dear Christ, but she was a tormenting minx. Even in his cold anger, he felt his loins ache as he gazed down at her. 'Henriette,' he said at last, 'you should not be here. A convoy of soldiers is no fit company for a lady.'

'Isobel is here,' she flashed back. 'And the lady Elena.'

'Isobel is here of necessity, because we escort her back to her home,' he said flatly. 'And Elena travels with her husband, Ralf. As I said – this is no place for you. We

126

must devise some way to get you back to Rouen, as soon as possible.'

'No!' She flung herself forward and knelt at his feet. 'No, Aimery! My place is with you. Oh, please, my lord.' Aimery tried to raise her, but she clung to his booted legs. 'I will bring you such pleasure at night,' she went on wildly. 'I will do anything – anything you wish. Only a short while ago, I allowed your servant Hamet to pleasure me out in the yard. We could do it again, here, and you could watch if you wished. I know you would enjoy it.' She was reaching to stroke Aimery's thighs. Hamet looked away, embarrassed. 'I could take your lovely cock in my mouth,' she went on wildly, 'while Hamet took me from behind. Wouldn't you like that? I've heard that you enjoy all kinds of wicked entertainments. Believe me, my lord, I shall be only too willing to do whatever you wish.'

Her voice died away at last as she realised that Aimery was looking down at her with cold scorn written across his face. Her heart sank. Isobel couldn't have been wrong, could she? Isobel had told her that Aimery loved his women to degrade themselves, to beg openly for pleasure.

Hamet stood in the shadows, silent and grim faced. Aimery turned to him. 'Hamet,' he said, 'the lady Henriette cannot stay with our party. Make enquiries. See if there is some private place near this monastery, where she can remain in safety until we can arrange to send her home.'

Henriette burst out, 'You can't send me away. I am to be your wife.'

Aimery said coldly, 'Demoiselle, your behaviour displeases me. I would not expect my wife to couple with my servant, and then offer to do it again in front of me. If we are to be married, then I would require you to restrain your fervour for licentiousness. You will return to Rouen.'

127

Hamet led the stricken Henriette from the room, leaving Aimery feeling more and more that he was being led into some unseen trap.

Henriette was perplexed, and bitterly unhappy. Everything had gone wrong. Why was Aimery not pleased to see her? Why was he not enthralled when she did as Isobel suggested and offered to participate in lewd sports for his entertainment?

She longed for him with a stubborn, burning desire that had only been temporarily soothed by Hamet's virile shaft. It was Aimery she wanted, with his stern, scarred face, and his powerful soldier's body, and his wonderful weapon of love that had given her such devastating pleasure on that first night they met.

She was wet and hungry for him now, set on fire by that lean, handsome face, so tantalisingly disfigured by the cruel scar. They'd put her in a forbidding guest chamber of her own that was little more than a cell, with a narrow bed and bare flint walls. How dare they treat her like this? She would go and find Aimery now, to protest, were it not that she was afraid of facing his stern rebuff once more.

Aimery had said she was to stay here, at this bleak monastery in the middle of nowhere, until a message could be got to her father to send an escort to bring her home. Her eyes narrowed in calculation. She would see about that. She would have to ensure that her stay here at the monastery would be very brief – no more than one night, in fact. She would also have to arrange matters so that Aimery would be forced to take her with him on the morrow, whether he liked it or not, because there would be nowhere else for her to go.

She opened the door and wandered petulantly along the stoneflagged corridor. Everywhere was dark and silent. To be incarcerated in this dreadful place, if only for a few days, would be like living in a tomb. Restlessly

128

she wandered along the echoing passageways, past the empty refectory, the cloisters, the little chapel. She thought she saw a glimmer of light from beneath the chapel door, and quietly opened the door.

There was a monk kneeling before the altar, and the single candle glimmered beside him. He looked shy and earnest. Although he was draped in the long loose habit of the Benedictines, she could see that he was well-built and young, and his face beneath the tonsured hair was pleasingly handsome. He reminded her suddenly of the young priest, Julien, who had introduced her to the surprising mysteries of a man's body. He turned suddenly, springing to his feet as Henriette walked slowly towards him.

'You are looking for something, demoiselle?' he said quickly. 'Perhaps I can help you.'

Henriette had sidled very close, with a little smile on her red lips. 'Yes,' she said archly. 'I think perhaps you can.'

'I am only a novice,' he blurted, suddenly wary. 'Perhaps you would rather speak to the abbot, or one of the older monks.'

'Oh, no.' Henriette reached out to touch his groin through the coarse serge of his gown. As the young man gasped and went pale, she slowly lifted up his heavy skirts, revealing a pair of brawny legs covered with rough dark hairs. He stood there frozen while her hand travelled purposefully up his thigh and fastened round his long, loosely hanging penis. 'You will serve my purpose perfectly, believe me.'

Alys was creeping back to the dreary outhouse that she shared with the other female servants. The monastery buildings were dark and silent: it was long past compline, the last service of the day, and everyone was asleep, except for those who were lucky enough to be spending the secret hours of the night in carnal pleasures.

Alys, her pocked face still twisted in envy, had just come from the stables, where she'd been watching from the shadows as the Norman knight Ralf pleasured a doxy he'd brought in from the settlement of little hovels that lay in the shadow of the monastery. How Alys envied the girl as the man's weapon rammed into her. She'd twisted and squealed in pleasure, then gone quite still as her climax overwhelmed her. 'Oh,' she'd breathed at last. 'Oh, my lord ...' And she'd let out a great sigh that was almost a groan, and her body shook with passion as the gasping Ralf sank himself deep within her.

Alys felt her own scrawny breasts tingling, her vagina pulsing hungrily at the sight and sounds. She would have to hurry back to her own solitary pallet, and satisfy herself quickly, silently. It was many days now since the handsome lord Ralf had unwittingly pleasured her with his eager tongue. It wasn't often that her capricious mistress Isobel allowed her such fine sport, and she knew that she would have to live on the memory of that for some time to come.

As she passed the little chapel, from where the bell tolled out the services that ruled the monks' days and nights, she stopped, because she thought she heard something unexpected. Surely, that was the sound of a girl's low, merry laugh? Frowning, Alys tiptoed to the door, which was just ajar, and gazed in.

There was a single candle burning on the altar, casting a pool of light in the darkness. Apart from the altar the chapel was bare, with just a few wooden benches resting on the stone flagged floor. Alys screwed up her eyes narrowly, accustoming them to the flickering candle-light, the moving shadows. There were several men in there, moving softly in the shadows beneath the high, arched window. Again, she heard the sound of the girl's mischievous giggle.

It was the girl, the lady Henriette! She was crouching

over one of the young monks, engaged in devilry, while the two other monks watched in fascination, and no wonder. Henriette had pulled the man's robe up to his waist, and was sucking his engorged cock, letting her ripe lips swirl wetly over its rigid length. The man was beside himself with pleasure, groaning softly. Alys could see his hairy balls tightening as he prepared to spill his seed. And the girl, Henriette, was glancing over her shoulder to the others, and whispering enticingly, 'Take me. Take me, one of you, while your friend spurts his seed in my mouth.'

One of the monks, who was small and dark haired with a youthfully chubby face, sank down behind her with a rapturous sigh. Quickly he pulled up Henriette's skirts, grinning with delight at the sight of her plump bottom cheeks. Then he reached swiftly for his own stubby, fat little cock and ran it along the cleft of her buttocks, finally homing in on her tight little anal crevice.

Henriette gave a squeal of happiness and lifted her head, just a little, from her task. 'Oh, yes. I like that. Is that how you pleasure one another, here in the monastery? Yes, stick your stiff cock up my arse. That's right.'

The young monk below her cried out in desperation, the swollen purple glans of his penis straining for her velvety suction again. The novice who had crouched behind her was easing his thick shaft joyfully into the tight little ring of Henriette's anus, gasping out his pleasure as he felt her sphincter muscles grip him. And the third monk, unable to bear his own deprivation, had pulled up his own robe and was masturbating furiously, his fist jerking at his throbbing shaft as he slid the foreskin up and down.

The man on the floor began then to ejaculate into Henriette's mouth, his seed spilling rapturously from his pulsing rod. Behind her, the young monk who was ravishing her anus was thrusting powerfully towards his own climax, his face dark with excitement as he gripped

Henriette's plump buttocks and rocked himself to and fro on his knees. And the third monk was reaching his extremity too. As his fist pounded away at his meaty cock, his face went slack, and his semen spurted at last from his body, landing on Henriette's quivering buttocks in silvery strands. Henriette whimpered in ecstasy and started to cry out her own release.

And Alys, watching from the darkness by the door in bitter envy, rubbed quickly at her own heated sex through her gown, pressing hard with her knuckles into her moist cleft and stimulating her yearning clitoris until she too shook with intense, silent release. Oh, if only she were pretty like Henriette. If only she could have three lovely, stalwart young men paying homage to her body, pleasuring her, shedding their seed in her so wickedly.

Slowly her orgasm washed away, leaving her drained and discontented. Then she gazed in disbelief. The girl seemed ready for yet more. She had rolled back, and was sitting on the flagged floor beneath the altar with her hands wrapped around her knees. And she was gesticulating, explaining something, laughing.

Alys frowned, her jealousy giving way to anger. She was not without a certain sense of duty. She knew that she must tell someone what was happening, or this girl, who was to be lord Aimery's wife, would have the whole monastery in an uproar. Alys, to whom eavesdropping was a way of life, knew that the abbot was already unkindly disposed to this convoy of soldiers who had arrived so unexpectedly in his territory. And the abbot fell under the jurisdiction of the lord Rotrou, whose loyalty to Duke William was debatable. An incident like this could lead to bloodshed.

But who should she tell? If she told her mistress Isobel, then Isobel would probably just laugh, and encourage the wayward Henriette in yet more of her debauchery. She ought to tell the lord Aimery, but she was afraid of him, even though she lusted after him too, like every other woman she knew. And Aimery would be coldly angry to hear of such antics. Didn't that little fool Henriette realise that the Breton lord was repelled by such avid, undiscriminating lust? His tastes were darkly, deliciously refined, as Alys knew, from spying on her lucky, lucky mistress Isobel in the past. Even now, Alys shivered with longing at the thought of the handsome Breton in action.

The girl Henriette was leaning forward, caressing another of the young monks, encouraging his flaccid penis into life again. She had to be stopped. But how?

Suddenly, Alys thought of the lady Elena. Though she had not dared to speak to her on this ill-fated journey, she secretly respected and admired Elena, who had always been kind to Alys. It was Alys's opinion that Elena had been badly treated by Isobel and Aimery, and now, it seemed, she fared no better at the hands of her husband Ralf.

Well, Ralf would be preoccupied for some time yet, it seemed. Alys decided she would run to find Elena, and tell her. She would know what to do about the young minx Henriette.

Elena was asleep when Alys began her low but urgent knocking at her door. Earlier, Gilles had accompanied her to the door of the little room she'd been allocated, and asked her, quietly, if there was anything he could do for her.

She'd seen the longing burning in his eyes, but she'd shaken her head, seeing how his shoulders drooped in silent despair. 'Gilles,' she said quietly, 'it would not be fair for me to use you in the way you wish.'

'My lady, I am yours. You may do as you wish with me.'

But she sent him away.

She knew that Aimery spent his nights with Isobel, but when sleep claimed her, her mind played cruel tricks on her, because it was Aimery she dreamt of. She dreamt that he was kissing her, as he'd kissed her that first time, pushing her tremulous, virginal hands downwards to touch his erect phallus. 'Feel me, *caran*,' he'd murmured, his voice tense with passion. 'Feel what you do to me.' Then, in her dream, he'd started to kiss her innocent, pouting breasts, and she'd cried out in incredulous pleasure as his silky hard penis began to penetrate her melting flesh.

The knocking at the door of her bleak little chamber woke her, and she felt dazed with disappointment as the sweet illusion of her dream faded, leaving her cold and alone. It couldn't be Ralf, anyway. He slept separately from her now, not even troubling to keep up the pretence of their marriage. By the light of a rush dip that still flickered faintly on the stone window ledge, Elena got up quickly, pulling a woollen mantle over her white shift and slipping on her little leather shoes before opening the door. 'Alys,' she breathed. 'What is it?'

Once, Alys had been kind to Elena and had helped her to escape from Isobel's retribution. But Alys was still Isobel's servant, and Elena knew she should not trust her.

'Lady Elena, you must do something quickly,' whispered Alys frantically. 'It is Henriette. The girl is wickedly seducing half the young novices – she must be stopped, before they are discovered.'

'Why tell me? What can I do?' said Elena. She knew Henriette was here – everyone had heard of her unexpected appearance in their midst. And she had heard rumours that the young heiress was prone to scandalous behaviour. But what business was it of hers?

'You can tell the lord Aimery. He will know what must be done. After all, Henriette is to be his bride.' Alys said these words with scorn. 'I dare not disturb him myself, but he will listen to you.'

Elena doubted that very much. She couldn't believe

what Alys was asking her to do. 'How can I disturb him?' she said in a low voice. 'When he will be in the arms of your mistress Isobel? How can I possibly break in on them, Alys?'

Alys shook her head, bewildered. 'No. Isobel is not with him. He sleeps alone, as always. You must go to him.'

Elena felt dazed. 'But Isobel is with him every night. I know it, Alys. I heard the two of you talking, that night at L'Aigle.'

Alys blushed and hung her head. 'I had forgotten that,' she muttered. 'It was all a lie. Isobel told me I had to stand there, outside the door with her, while she boasted of the lord Aimery's lewd demands on her. She knew you were in the room, and would be forced to hear every word. She was incredibly jealous of you that day, because the lord Aimery had been paying you so much attention. But he has not slept with her once since she came to Rouen.'

Elena took a deep breath. *Not once.* Yet again, it seemed, Isobel's cruel deceits had made her suffer. She struggled to absorb the impact of what Alys had just said, while Alys grabbed her by the arm, begging, Please. You must tell the lord Aimery, now. The girl is quite shameless. If the abbot finds out, then the whole place will be in uproar. Already we are not welcome here, and we are in uncertain territory. I will take you to his room.'

Elena took a deep breath to steady herself. 'I think I would rather confront a wolf in his lair, Alys,' she said quietly.

'Please. I beg you.'

Elena bowed her head. Picking up the rush dip to light their way, she said at last, 'Very well. You had better take me to Aimery.'

Chapter Nine

Swiftly they passed through the dark and silent corri‑
dors of the monastery. It was Alys who knocked on
the door of Aimery's chamber, and it was barely a
moment before Hamet opened it. If the big Saracen had
been asleep, then he evidently slept fully dressed, with
his curved sword at his side, in order to guard the
Breton his master with his own life if need be. His face
was set and grim as he recognised Elena, with her
woollen mantle drawn tightly over her long white chem‑
ise, and her pale gold hair falling loosely round her
shoulders. Alys, frightened now, scurried off into the
shadows.

'What do you want?' said Hamet flatly.

Elena knew that Hamet had no time for her, but his
outright antipathy dismayed her. She said, as steadily as
she could,

'I must speak to your master.'

'At this hour?' His foreign voice was cold and richly
scornful. 'I think not, lady Elena. You hope to tempt him
once more with your wiles? You have done him enough
harm already.'

The colour burned in Elena's cheeks at his vile impli‑

cation that it was she who had betrayed Aimery. 'No. How can you even think it?'

And then Aimery was there, pushing Hamet aside. His thick tawny hair was ragged from sleep, otherwise he was alert, breathtakingly masculine. The soft woollen tunic he wore skimmed the breadth of his powerful shoulders, to be clinched at his narrow waist by a leather belt from which his sword hung in readiness. His silver-grey eyes glittered in hard mockery as he assessed Elena's unbraided hair, her loose mantle pulled hastily over her shift.

He ran his hand back through his hair, unwittingly emphasizing his starkly chiselled features. 'Well, Elena,' he said softly. 'I dare not presume on the rather obvious appearance of this midnight call. Or dare I? Has young Gilles failed to give satisfaction? Your wifely devotion to Ralf, which you were always telling me about, didn't last very long, did it?'

Elena realised she should have expected this, but she still felt sick. He knew. Of course he knew. Didn't Aimery know everything? He had to, as master of this convoy. 'This is not the time or the place for your insults, my lord,' she said with quiet despair. 'I have come to tell you that you must come with me, quickly, before your wife-to-be sets the whole monastery in turmoil.'

'Henriette?' His eyes narrowed in disbelief; but then he spun round sharply to issue some low words of warning to Hamet. Then he beckoned to Elena to lead the way, and followed her swiftly to the chapel, asking no more questions. It was as if he had guessed already.

She heard him utter a low, bitter oath under his breath as he quietly pushed open the door of the little chapel. Elena wanted to go – this was no place for her – but he seized her wrist and drew her relentlessly inside with him. Elena had hoped that Henriette might have finished her lewd business and departed, but no, she was as busily engaged as ever. Too busy by far to even notice that Aimery and Elena had entered the dimly lit room.

She was watching her companions, a pleasurable little smile on her lips. Two of the young novices were on the floor beside her: one was on all fours, his gown rucked up round his buttocks, while the other was kneeling behind him, pleasuring him lewdly with his shaft, his face slack with bliss as he thrust into the man's tight bottom hole. Henriette was gazing, entranced.

'Oh,' she was murmuring. 'I've always wanted to see that. Is this how you take your pleasure, here, locked away in your lonely monastery? It looks exquisite; so tight and lovely.' She glanced up at the third monk, who was watching, rapt. 'Why don't you join them?'

He seemed to sag at the shoulders. 'My lady. I would do so willingly. But my passion is all spent, I fear. I can do no more for the moment.'

'Oh, shame,' said Henriette, her face gleaming with mischief as she cast her eyes around the altar. 'Then use *this* instead.' And, from an open chest beside the altar, she pulled out a thick wax candle. 'Pleasure your friend with this, if you cannot manage it yourself. I want to see him squirm with delight. Pleasure him, I say, or I will tell the lord abbot of your wicked games.'

Biting his lip in shame, but unable to take his eyes off the copulating pair before him, the young monk sank to his knees and sought his friend's puckered anus with the smooth candle end. It was difficult, because the eager novice was pumping so enthusiastically between the other man's bottom cheeks; but he slowed down, as if realising what was being attempted, and eased himself back on to the firmly held candle. 'Ah!' He gave a great sigh of pleasure as the wax stem penetrated his forbidden entrance, pushing himself more firmly on to it. Then he gripped his kneeling companion's buttocks and thrust furiously, his stiff cock diving in and out, his face dark with passion as the excruciating pleasure overwhelmed him. Then Henriette had darted to reach for the loins of the man who was being so darkly pleasured, fondling his erect penis and rubbing with sperm-slippery fingers as the man's shaft began to twitch and jerk, sending gouts of creamy liquid across the flagged stone floor.

Aimery said tersely to Elena, 'Wait here.' Then he began to move forward slowly, his face tight and set, until one by one the members of the little tableau before the altar saw him. Elena waited by the door, hating this, wishing she could go. The monks cowered back in panic, whimpering, when they saw him. Henriette's eyes widened in shock. Then she pulled herself to her feet and said enticingly, 'Welcome, my lord Aimery. You have come to join us? We can offer you fine sport, as you see.'

Aimery smiled. The white-ridged scar lifted the corner of his mouth, and his eyes glittered like cold slate.

Henriette did not know him well enough to be afraid of that smile. 'Yes, come and join us, my lord,' she repeated happily. 'The night's entertainment is only just beginning.'

Aimery had whipped out his sword. He raised it and pointed it, one by one, at the cowering monks. 'For you, it is over,' he gritted out. 'Get out of here. And if you whisper one word to anyone of what has happened, now or at any time, I will come back here to seek you out and silence you more effectively. You understand?'

They stammered and nodded and hurried blindly for the door, not even seeing Elena in the shadows. Then Henriette, pouting sulkily, began to paw at Aimery's chest.

'That was ill-done, my lord,' she complained. 'We were having such fun. Just the sort of fun you enjoy.' She ran her finger down his lean cheek, lingering over his scar. Aimery took her hand away and held it in a vice of iron.

'You endanger us all, demoiselle, with your games.

139

The abbot here is no friend to our party. Any word of this in his ear, and he will call on the Lord of Mortagne and his men to punish us all. Get to your room, and stay there till you are summoned. We depart at daybreak.'

'Then – you won't leave me here, as you planned?' breathed Henriette, her brown eyes alight.

'Sweet God, how can I?' he grated bitterly. 'You'd have them all in turmoil within a day. No – you will have to come with us to Morency, and we will find some way of getting you home from there. But one more hint of trouble, demoiselle, and I will beat you soundly, and lock you away.'

She pouted sulkily. 'You wouldn't dare. I am Henriette of Sizerne,' she said. 'And you are nothing but a base-born mercenary, raised high by your sword –'

She broke off then, because for Aimery it was enough. Elena watched, a pulse pounding in her throat, as the coldly angry Breton gripped Henriette by the shoulders and shook her as if she were some disobedient child putting herself into danger. Henriette gasped at first, but then she gazed defiantly up at him. 'Now drive your lovely big cock into me, my lord,' she murmured. 'Stick it right up me, and pleasure me. That's what you really want, isn't it? That's what all this is about?'

For answer, Aimery pushed her away so that she lost her balance and almost fell. 'Go,' he said flatly. 'I am weary of your tricks, demoiselle.'

She opened her mouth to protest, but something in his face warned her otherwise. She turned to go with a scornful little shrug, but she pulled up with a start as she saw Elena by the door and her eyes burned bitterly.

'Was it *you* who told him?' she whispered scornfully. 'Spying, and playing with yourself as you watched us? I won't forget. You're my enemy, aren't you?'

Elena said quietly, 'I think you are your own worst enemy, lady Henriette.'

Henriette flounced off to her room. Elena waited, as

Aimery had commanded her, trying desperately to control the blood that raced in her veins. The degrading sights she had witnessed had set her body on fire. In her loins a throbbing pulse beat constantly, a mixture of pleasure and pain. As Aimery walked slowly back to her, she tried desperately to pull herself together, so he wouldn't guess how her senses were betraying her.

Then Aimery was beside her, saying tiredly, 'I am sorry that you had to witness all that. But I am grateful for your message, otherwise the trouble could have been much worse. Why did you want to help me?'

She gazed up into his silver-grey eyes, saw the familiar harsh, jutting cheekbones, the wide thin mouth lifted chillingly by the cruel white scar, and she wanted him so badly that it hurt. She said, quietly, 'Perhaps my desire was not so much to help you, my lord, as to save us all from being slaughtered. I was aware that the abbot is no friend to you, and could summon powerful friends to destroy us.'

He nodded, tiredly running his hand through his thick hair. 'That is true. Rotrou of Mortagne would gladly attack us on the grounds of sacrilege. We shall have to take the lady Henriette with us to Morency. Isobel will not be pleased.'

Isobel's name sliced like a knife through Elena's weariness. 'So Isobel objects to your marriage?' she said scornfully. 'I'm surprised – I wouldn't have thought such a little matter would worry her. Nothing else seems to.'

He gripped her shoulders, sending tremors of desire rippling through her as his eyes locked with hers. 'Isobel is nothing to me,' he said urgently. 'I have told you that.'

She wished she could believe him. She could feel the heat of his hands on her shoulders, the warmth of his hard, sinewy body so close to hers. Dear God, she felt so weak with longing. She said, 'And I am nothing to you either. You have made that plain enough, my lord.'

'Blood of Christ, Elena.' His oath shook her to her core.

'First you torment me with your so-called love for the weakling Ralf. Then you take the boy Gilles to your bed. Is there no end to your games, lady?'

She pulled away from him, her blue eyes wide and aching with despair. '*My* games? Oh, Aimery. I pleaded with you not to bring me on this journey. I would have gone down on my knees before you, to avoid this suffering, this humiliation.'

He caught her round her tiny waist, steadying her because she was trembling so hard. 'Who makes you suffer? Who humiliates you?'

'You do, my lord. You do.'

'How? I have scarcely spoken to you since we left Rouen, since you made it so plain you wanted nothing to do with me.'

'You don't need to speak to me,' she said in a low voice. 'Your very presence destroys my reasoning, my lord.'

His hands were running up and down her back, sending impossible shafts of longing burning through her. She was molten with desire for him. His low, passionate voice sent wicked tendrils of arousal curling up and down her very spine as he breathed, 'So you find me cruel. How do you find your squire Gilles? Is he tender and sweet? Does he kiss you softly and call you pretty names as he pleasures you? Do you tell Ralf, your husband whom you assure me you love, all about him at night, and laugh together at the boy's passion for you?'

She was almost on the verge of tears, fighting to free herself. 'How dare you? Between Ralf and me, there is nothing, as you must surely know.'

'Ah. So we are beginning to get the truth, are we? Are you admitting to me at last that your much-professed love for your husband is an empty lie?'

She continued to struggle, fighting for breath. 'I did love him. I did! Oh, not as I loved you, Aimery. But you

142

left me, for Isobel. Between you, you almost destroyed me.'

'So you no longer love Ralf. And Gilles has taken your husband's place in your bed?'

'At least Gilles is kind to me.'

'Ah. Kindness,' he breathed. Passion glinted in his hard eyes like sparks of gold. He was kneading her small breasts, pulling mockingly at the hard little nipples. 'Is it kindness that you want, little Elena? Or is it this? And this?'

He pulled her roughly against him and kissed her hard. His tongue thrust strongly between her lips, probing in an erotic simulation of intercourse as his fingers continued to torment her aching breasts. She could feel the hard pressure at his groin forcing itself against her belly; the heat of him burnt her. 'Aimery,' she gasped. 'Stop.'

'You said you loved me,' he said roughly, drawing his mouth away to leave her lips bruised and swollen. 'Blood of Christ, Elena, when did you stop loving me? When?'

She shook her head blindly. 'I never stopped loving you, Aimery. God help me for it.'

There was a moment's tense silence. His eyes seared into her. Then he whispered, 'You're right. The chapel is no place for this. Come.'

He pulled her up into his arms, and carried her swiftly to his room. There was no sign of Hamet. He laid Elena on the bed and undressed her rapidly, his lean, sunburnt hands caressing every inch of her trembling flesh as he did so. He ran his fingers softly through her long fair hair, and the intensity in his scarred, chiselled face made her churn with helpless, hopeless love. She was whimpering, crying out his name as his warm mouth touched her lips, her nipples, her stomach. Soon, the passion would overwhelm her completely, and she would be lost. Desperately she pulled herself away.

'Aimery. Why are you doing this to me?'

He gazed down at her, his face hard with passion in the light of the moon that crept through the little window. 'Because you haunt me, Elena. I want you night and day. It is purgatory to me, to see you with your weak husband, to see you laughing with Gilles. I want to love you, need to love you. *Caran*, let me . . .'

Caran. The Breton for beloved. The name he used to use, when she thought he was all hers.

She could not have stopped him, even if she'd wanted to. Already his hand was rubbing softly between her legs, coaxing the sweet, honeyed folds apart, and she opened herself to him, moaning softly at the back of her throat. He'd already drawn off his tunic, his boots and his hose, and she caught her breath at his magnificent male beauty. His naked body was sinewed and brown, marked by pale sword scars. She thought she glimpsed a new scar, angrily puckered alongside his abdomen. She reached to touch it, her fingers soft with concern, but he said abruptly, 'It is nothing,' and turned that side away from her.

She drank in the sight of him, everything. His shoulders were broad and heavily muscled, his stomach taut and lean; and at his narrow hips, his pulsing manhood jerked hungrily towards her from its cradle of soft dark hair, enticing her with its glorious promise of pleasure.

With a low cry of need, Elena reached to pull him to her. He continued to coax her relentlessly, teasing her, stroking her soaking cleft with his fingers until she was in flames of longing for him, her loins rubbing against his hand like an animal on heat. Then he cupped her slender hips, raising her with his hands, and with gritted teeth began to ease his long, pulsing phallus into her silken love-passage. She cried out, clenching her inner muscles around him, shivering with bliss as he filled her. He soothed her gently with his kisses as he stroked

144

his way inside her, fulfilling her beyond even her dreams with his glorious length of hard male muscle.

There was no-one else like Aimery, she acknowledged despairingly as the searing waves of pleasure began to mount. And for her, there never would be. He kissed her breasts, drawing them one by one into his mouth, circling her nipples with his abrasive tongue. Then, as he arched above her and drove the full length of his magnificent penis deeply between her splayed thighs, his thumb found its way to the burning ridge of her clitoris; and he stroked it, sliding in her wetness, driving his thick shaft ever deeper into her until she was delirious with passion.

She clung to his strong shoulders, her hips quivering against his, her climax splintering through her as his consuming kisses devoured her lips, her throat, her breasts. She felt him thrusting hard within her, driving himself to his own ecstasy at her very heart. And then at last they were both still, and she lay sweat sheened in his heavily muscled arms, powerless to move until her pulse began to steady.

She heard someone moving softly outside the door, and it brought her to her senses. She tensed against Aimery's body, but he tightened his hold on her, and said softly, 'It's only Hamet. He'd gone to check the watch. He'll be making his bed up outside the door.'

She shivered. 'Hamet hates me, doesn't he? Why?'

He drew himself up a little to gaze down at her, and her heart leapt with painful longing again as she saw the incredible tenderness in his silver-grey eyes.

He said, 'Hamet vowed long ago to serve me to the death and protect me from my enemies. He thinks that you betrayed me, and cannot forgive you for it.'

'How? How can he think that?'

He stroked her cheek lightly with his fingers. His grey eyes were opaque as he replied without emotion, 'Hamet was with me when I first heard the news that you were

145

married, *caran*. He thinks you did me wrong. It will take time for him to be reconciled to you.'

Elena pulled herself up to face him, her eyes wide and haunted. 'Always, you blame me. But you were with Isobel when I married Ralf. You chose not to return to me, Aimery.'

'I had no choice,' he replied gravely. 'But enough of this, *caran*. You look white with tiredness. Sleep, and we will talk of this tomorrow.'

She lay back with a little sigh, and he kissed her, and she fell asleep, cradled close against his body.

The following morning at dawn, fresh messengers arrived from Isobel's castle of Morency to urge Aimery's party to make all speed. Hugh de Brosny, the steward, had received intelligence that the brigands were gathering in large numbers in the woods, driving all honest folk from their homes, and he feared an imminent attack.

Elena was still asleep when she heard the horn braying out the alarm to Aimery's men at dawn. She struggled to rouse herself, aware immediately that Aimery had gone from the bed. The cold chill of fear stabbed her heart. She pulled on her shift and mantle quickly, and gazed out of the tiny window set in the bare walls of Aimery's chamber.

Aimery's men were gathering in the monastery courtyard, already fully armed, the lily pennant of Normandy streaming above their heads as their horses pranced, eager to move on. Yet there was no sign of the baggage wagons, or of Isobel and her retinue.

For a moment, she wondered if Aimery had already left, without wanting to speak to her. But then the door opened quietly, and Aimery came in. He was fully clad in the sinuous chain-link armour he wore for battle. His face was alert and purposeful, but his grey eyes softened as he looked on Elena, standing alone by the window.

'*Caran*,' he murmured, moving to take her in his arms.

'Once more we must part. I have to ride with my men for Morency, because there is trouble there. You and the others will follow on with the wagons, at a gentler pace. All should be settled by the time you arrive. Then you and I can settle our future.'

Once more, the horn brayed its summons. How Elena hated that sound. He kissed her tenderly. 'God go with you, Elena.'

'And you,' she said, gazing up at him, bereft that they were to be parted once more. 'And you, my lord.'

She watched him ride away, the coldness of premonition that she would never see him again gathering in her heart.

Isobel found their progress during the last stages of the journey irksomely slow without Aimery there to drive their company onwards. Their depleted group now consisted of Isobel, Henriette and Elena, their various servants, and the men who handled the slow baggage wagons, together with a small escort of well-armed soldiers to safeguard them on their way to Morency.

Hamet, Ralf and Gilles had gone ahead with Aimery. Isobel swiftly took charge.

She had quickly realised that Elena had spent the night at the monastery in Aimery's bed, and anger burned inside her. She knew because she'd woken when Alys returned, and threatened her quaking servant with vile punishment unless she told her exactly what had happened. Isobel had laughed scornfully at the tale of Henriette and the three novices. How avidly the plump little heiress had taken Isobel's advice. And she was following it well enough to put the lord Aimery off even wanting to take her for a mistress, let alone marry her.

But then her expression had darkened as Elena came into Alys's tale. Pushing the frightened Alys to one side, Isobel had quickly dressed and stolen to the chapel to see what was happening.

She'd been just in time to see Aimery sweep the insipid Saxon girl up in his arms, and carry her purposefully to his room.

Isobel had been so passionate with fury that she'd been quite unable to sleep for the rest of that night. She contemplated telling Henriette, telling Ralf even, about his wife's debauchery with the Breton.

But then the urgent summons came from Morency at dawn, forestalling her plans. At least it meant that Aimery and Elena were, for the moment, separated. And it gave Isobel a few days to take some action, before the lovers were reunited.

It was late in the afternoon on the second day of their journey southwards from the monastery when Isobel at last managed to get Elena on her own. Henriette was a nuisance, riding constantly at Isobel's side, chattering and gossiping incessantly about Rouen and her future marriage, presumably quite unaware still of the failure of her campaign to capture Aimery's heart. It was also quite obvious that she still did not realise that Isobel had a prior claim on the Breton, or that Elena too was competing for his love.

'I've been doing just as you said,' Henriette whispered earnestly to Isobel when they were out of earshot of the rest of the party. 'I've been driving Aimery quite wild with my wanton behaviour. That night at the monastery, he took me by the shoulders and shook me, and his eyes were dark with lust.'

'And did he sleep with you after that?' enquired Isobel politely.

Henriette frowned. 'No. But that is all part of the plan you suggested, is it not? He'll pretend to be angry at my wanton ways, but secretly he'll want me more than ever. Won't he?'

If you believe that, you'll believe anything, thought

Isobel, but aloud, she said, 'Of course. He will be desperate for you, lady Henriette.'

'Anyway,' said Henriette a little sullenly, 'Elena spoilt everything that night at the monastery. She was in the chapel as well, you see, so he could not give way publicly to his desire for me, even though he was longing to ravish me then and there. She looks so virginal, so pure, doesn't she? Her husband Ralf complains she is cold in bed, and I can well believe it.'

Then don't, thought Isobel, in silence. Unfortunately, for the time being at any rate, the Saxon Elena seemed to have found the way to the Breton's cold heart in a way Henriette never would. Gazing suddenly at Elena, who was riding ahead in her accustomed solitude, Isobel urged her spirited mare forwards and reined in at Elena's side, easing her mount into a walk that matched the pace of the Saxon girl's palfrey.

'My dear Elena,' she said, 'at last we have a chance to talk to one another properly. We have all been so preoccupied since Rouen, have we not?'

Elena gazed at her. 'Have we?' she said. Isobel hated her for her pale, exquisite beauty, her flawless skin, her silken blonde hair and sultry blue eyes. The fact that Elena was several years younger than herself, and had no need of artful aids to enhance her beauty, rankled like poison in Isobel's soul.

'Well, yes,' she pressed on cheerfully. 'You must be missing your husband, Elena, and young Gilles. Or – do you miss the lord Aimery more? Surely you aren't going to tell me that *you* haven't been busy?'

That got through to her. Elena's soft cheeks were tinged with rosiness as she replied, in a low voice, 'You lied to me, Isobel. You told me that you spent every night in Aimery's bed. That was untrue. I have no desire to listen to your lies any further.'

Isobel bit her lip angrily, her green eyes flashing with annoyance. Then she let an expression of concern settle across her own perfect, heart-shaped features. 'Oh, my dear. That was only out of concern for you. I was so afraid, you see, that you still loved Aimery, and that you might get hurt. But I knew that if I tried to warn you, you would not believe me. After all, we did not part last time on the best of terms, did we?'

That was true. Almost three years ago, as part of a last, desperate attempt to get rid of her rival in their battle for Aimery's love, Isobel had sold Elena into serfdom. Aimery had rescued Elena, and banished Isobel.

Elena said scornfully, 'You must think me witless. I cannot believe you have my welfare at heart any more now than you did then.'

'Oh, but things have changed. You see, you gave up on Aimery, did you not? You realised he would not come back to you, and you married Ralf. But as for me, well, I am so sure of Aimery that I can afford to let him go, at least for a while, knowing that afterwards he will come back to me, all the more in need of what only I can offer. I am his for life, and both of us know it. Why, I can even afford to let him marry that foolish little creature, Henriette of Sizerne.'

Elena drew her horse round to face Isobel, and her blue eyes burnt. 'You lie again. Aimery is yours no longer. He has not slept with you since you came to Rouen to summon him so deviously. He does not want you.'

'Damn Alys,' Isobel thought. She must have passed on that information to Elena. She would beat her soundly tonight for her disloyalty. But aloud, outwardly serene, she said, 'But that, of course, is part of our plan. You see, Henri of Sizerne is a powerful man. He knows that Aimery and I have long been lovers – though fortunately his daughter does not – and he expressed private concerns to Aimery about the two of us going on this journey together. He warned Aimery that if he should hear any reports about Aimery betraying his precious daughter by sleeping with me, then he would have the wedding called off. And Aimery wants this marriage, very much. It will give him considerable wealth and power to add to his prestige as a knight. With such advantages, no doubt Duke William will raise him again, to who knows what heights? So, you see, Aimery and I decided that a little forbearance for a few weeks was not too high a price to pay. After all, once Aimery is married to that silly little slut Henriette, he can incarcerate her in the country somewhere and do what he wants – with me.'

Elena was gazing at her, shaking her head. 'No,' she said. 'I still do not believe that he loves you.'

Their horses had stopped; they were alone. The others had moved on, and the jangle of bits and the creak of leather harness was fading away.

Isobel put her head on one side and threw her enemy a mocking glance. 'Why don't you believe it? Because the Breton pleasured you with his rather delicious cock that night at the monastery? He made Gilles and Ralf appear somewhat inadequate in that department, I assume – his physique is magnificent, is it not? Ah, see how that brings a blush to your pretty cheeks! So you've started making romantic plans again, have you, Elena? Well, don't. Because that is what I have come to warn you about. You haven't forgotten, surely, that Aimery hates all Saxon women, and is sworn to lifelong revenge against them, for what happened to his brother?'

She saw Elena go white. Good. The girl hadn't forgotten. 'No,' she whispered. 'That is over. He told me so.'

'Did he indeed?' Isobel laughed. 'Oh, no. It is not over. You remember the tale, don't you? It was a beautiful Saxon girl, Madelin, who seduced both Aimery and his brother, manipulating them both with her wiles. She betrayed the two of them into the hands of the Saxon rebels. Aimery's brother died in agony at the hands of

151

his captors. Aimery escaped, but not before Madelin had split his face with a Saxon sword, and scarred him for life. It was then that he made a vow to humiliate and destroy every Saxon girl that he encountered. You remember?'

Elena remembered. How could she forget? That was why she was taken a prisoner to Aimery's dark castle of Thoresfield, in the bleak northern wilds of England. There, he had tormented her, roused her to forbidden ecstasy, then finally to love.

'You think you were different, don't you?' went on Isobel silkily. 'Well, they have all thought that. What use would his revenge be, if you did not believe that he really loved you? Believe me, Elena. It is only when you think you are truly his that he will reject you and make you suffer. You thought he loved you before – you grew over-confident of his love – so he left you, until you despaired and married Ralf. Now you have presented yourself to him again, and offered him your undeniably tempting body, so he has decided to toy with you for a while, and make you trust him once more. Be careful, Elena. Because this time, when he turns on you, it could very well destroy you.'

'No,' said Elena, but Isobel, seeing that her hands were trembling on the reins, pressed on.

'Ah, but the Breton is cruel, and scarred in his very soul. I am the only one who has ever been able to master him. That is why he will always be mine. Keep away from him, my dear, before he destroys you utterly.'

Elena whirled her horse away. 'I tell you, I do not believe you, Isobel. You have lied to me so often.'

Isobel urged her horse after her, laying a hand on Elena's reins, her green eyes glittering with spite.

'And Aimery has deceived you so often before. How many months did you spend waiting for him, hungering for him, before you gave up and married Ralf? All that time, he and I were making sport in my secluded fortress

152

near Aumale. Oh, we had many fine diversions, I tell you, and he did not think of you once. For example, I had several plump little serving wenches, who were well-trained to serve the lord Aimery in whatever way he wished. Two in particular he loved; I have them waiting for him at Morency. And there was a strapping if elderly serving-man from the Auvergne, whose body was grizzled with grey hairs, but who had a pizzle like a bull; the girls adored him, crude though he was. Aimery loved to watch as he pleasured my girls one by one with his long, gnarled cock. As I said, this servant was old and stooped, but his toothless gums would open in a wide grin as he thrust merrily away at my lovely girls. And then, with the chamber still reeking of sex, Aimery would take me, and ravish me, and swear that he was mine for ever. Sometimes, when the girls were still there, watching and breathless with lust, I would tie Aimery to the wall with fine silken cords and whip him tenderly, and then I would send one of the girls to him, to suck his penis until he groaned out his desperate release. You can imagine it, can't you? And there you were, shy little Elena, for all those months, sitting patiently waiting for your Breton lover, who never came back to you.'

With a little cry of revulsion, Elena whipped up her horse and cantered away out of earshot. She could not, would not believe it all! Isobel was lying again. Aimery loved her even though she was a Saxon; she knew it. Only two nights ago she had slept in his bed, with his arms round her, as he murmured words of passion against her cheek. She had to fight Isobel, and refuse to listen to her until they got to Morency and Aimery could prove his love for himself. But she still felt sick with shock at Isobel's sordid tale, because it was true, that once Isobel and Aimery had taken their pleasure in such things.

* * *

Isobel, watching her ride off, smiled and rode on to rejoin the others.

She could tell that the Saxon girl was badly shaken, and the shock she had received might just be enough to shatter the rebuilding of her relationship with Aimery. Elena, in spite of her denials to Isobel, would regard Aimery with fresh mistrust when they were reunited at Morency, and her lack of faith in him would anger the harsh-tempered Breton, and turn his heart against her once more.

Isobel's next task now was to deal with Alys, and her mouth thinned as she urged her horse forward to search the company for her surly, pockmarked servant, who had betrayed her yet again.

Alys, however, was a minor problem. Isobel's face grew serene as she reflected that everything else was falling rather deliciously into place. And at Morency itself, Isobel had yet another breathtaking scheme arranged which would, she hoped, bring her complete victory over those who tried to steal Aimery le Sabrenn away from her.

Elena was startled when Alys came desperately in search of her that evening. It was dusk, and they were still a league or more from the nearest settlement. It was too far to travel in unknown territory in the dark, and the lady Henriette was complaining vociferously, letting everyone know that she had had enough travelling for the day. So the captain in charge of the soldiers gave orders that the leather tents they carried in the baggage carts for times such as this should be put up for the women, while the soldiers would sleep in the open on beds of bracken, taking it in turns to keep watch during the warm night.

Elena had one of the small tents to herself. She was brushing her hair slowly by the soft light of a glimmering lantern when Alys, who had been waiting for a moment to catch her on her own, came silently in through the tent flap. Alys's face was red from weeping, and her hair was lank and distraught. Elena whipped round to face her, her eyes wide with questions, remembering the last time Alys had come to her, in the monastery.

'Alys,' she breathed. 'What is it?'

Alys sat down suddenly on the little wooden chest that contained Elena's possessions. 'It is too much,' she blurted out. 'I hate Isobel, hate her.'

Elena was silent for a moment. After all, she had reasons to hate Isobel too. Then she said, 'Do you wish to tell me about it, Alys?'

Alys rubbed the tears from her eyes and swallowed hard. Then she whispered hoarsely, 'She punished me. For telling you that she and the lord Aimery have not slept together. While the rest of you were riding ahead, late this afternoon, she called me aside, and asked me if I wished to be pleasured by one of the soldiers. His name is Moldo. She must have seen me watching him – he is very handsome, lady Elena, with dark, flashing eyes and brown skin and a finely built body. So of course I said yes. She told me to strip, and Moldo came to me. But he beat my naked buttocks with a leather whip, while Isobel watched. She told Moldo that I hungered after his fine body, and Moldo laughed, and said – and said that there were not enough gold coins in Isobel's purse to persuade him to pleasure an ugly wretch like me . . .' Her voice broke off, and she fiercely dashed the fresh tears from her eyes.

'I would have run, then,' she went on, 'but that witch Isobel commanded me to stay, or I would be punished again. She told me I had to watch, while Moldo pleasured her. And he did. He held her up against the stout, smooth trunk of a tree, and he lifted her skirts, and pulled out his stiffened penis, and ravished her tirelessly with that mighty weapon until I was faint with envy. How Isobel quivered and moaned as he impaled her. Then, when they had quite finished, she threw my clothes at me, and told me to go and hide my ugly face, because it was spoiling their pleasure.'

Alys drew a ragged breath, struggling to calm herself, and went on, in a steadier voice that was full of scorn, 'They are still there in the woods, rutting like animals as darkness falls. The last I saw, Isobel had bent to suck Moldo's eager cock. So I have come here to tell you the rest of it.'

Elena said quietly, 'I think I know enough of Isobel's nature, Alys. There is no need to tell me any more.'

'But there is. You will understand when I tell you. You see, this is a quite different kind of wickedness. The lady Isobel plans some hideous mischief at Morency.'

Elena felt suddenly cold. 'What do you mean?'

'Oh, I am not sure exactly. But I want you to know that there is danger there. You must tell the lord Aimery. He will listen to you – he did last time.'

Elena was aware of a pulsing of fear at her heart. 'What danger, Alys? What must I tell him?'

Alys leant forward in the shadows of the little tent, her voice fearful as she whispered, 'I tell you, I do not know exactly. But I do know that this winter past, Isobel has held secret meetings with Fulk of Anjou. They are plotting something, together.'

Fulk of Anjou. Elena drew in a sharp breath. Duke William's enemy. Aimery's enemy. Her mind raced wildly. Aimery would have reached Morency by now, with his men. Not far from Fulk's territories, but many, many leagues from the aid of the duke and his loyal barons.

'Alys,' she said urgently. 'You must find out more. If there is treachery planned at Morency, then Aimery must know of it. His life might be in danger.'

Just then, they heard the sound of muffled voices, and heavy footsteps close to the tent. They went by, but Alys, panic-stricken, flew to the tent-flap and peeped out.

'Dear God. If the lady Isobel finds me here, talking with you again, then she will flay me alive for her amusement. I must go.' She started out, into the darkness. But then she turned, one last time. 'Remember,' she whispered. 'Tell the lord Aimery that there is danger for him at Morency.'

Elena waited until her footsteps faded away. Then she sat on her little wooden chest, feeling sick with tension.

They were not far from Morency now, where dark treachery lurked. Aimery must be warned. Pray God she would not be too late.

Chapter Ten

Ralf was far from happy. He'd expected this sojourn at Morency with Aimery le Sabrenn to be a pleasant summer's entertainment. He'd anticipated good wine, plentiful food and some excellent hunting in the forest nearby, enlivened by the occasional stimulating foray to rout out a few of the pesky brigands who troubled Isobel's lands like flies in the summer heat. And he'd expected the company of Isobel herself: Isobel, with her beautiful yet cruel face and slanting green eyes, her luscious body beckoning him, her husky voice telling him to do wicked, wicked things.

He grew hard just thinking about her. But Isobel was not here yet. They had been at Morency a week, having ridden at a hard campaigners' pace under the irritatingly firm leadership of the Breton. On arrival at the small donjon of Morency, built on its rounded hill overlooking the green forest that stretched to the distant borders of trouble-torn Maine, Ralf had prepared to relax, and await the arrival of Isobel.

But Aimery le Sabrenn had other ideas. He set them to work.

A flanking party was sent out first into the forest, to

scour out the brigands. Hugh de Brosny, the nervous, somewhat shifty steward of the place, told Aimery of their suspected hiding places. But the soldiers found nothing: only some hacked-out clearings, and doused fires, and burnt hovels where the brigands had recently raided.

Then Aimery gave his orders. The stronghold of Morency, he said, was dangerously unfortified; a mere rabble of armed peasantry would be able to capture it if they had surprise on their side. He pointed out the shallow, stagnant moat that a man could wade across, the broken-down palisade, the mossy wooden roof to the donjon that fire-arrows could turn into a death trap. From dawn till dusk, his men and Hugh's existing garrison were set to work.

First the moat was dug out – a slimy, filthy task because of the rubbish that had accumulated over the years – and a nearby stream was diverted to fill it. The donjon was freshly roofed with stone, and the broken palisade was repaired with sharpened stakes of timber hewn from the surrounding forest. There was no rest, even for knights like Ralf. They were all roused by a clarion call at prime, then they were ordered to the stables to see to their horses. After that they drilled and schooled their powerful destriers on the hastily enclosed parade ground just beyond the palisade until the sun was high and merciless in the summer sky. After a brief noonday repast of bread and cheese with watery ale, it was time for weapons exercises, for knights and men-at-arms alike: they were ordered into ranks for sword practice, and archery with heavy yew bows, until the strongest men's sinews protested and the sweat trickled down their grimy, sunburnt faces. Only Aimery and his ever-watchful black servant Hamet seemed cool and tireless, though they worked as hard as any, and Aimery, damn him, was effortlessly the best at any martial sport he took part in.

Meanwhile, Ralf watched in astonishment as the castle's lowly servants were ordered to put all weapons to the grindstone. Bowyers and fletchers worked to replenish Morency's warped, dusty supplies of bowstaves and arrows. Horses were re-shod, and armour burnished till it gleamed. Sixty days' rations, of wheat, oil, dried meat and wine, were meticulously gathered together and secured in a granary, while the castle's old, dried-up well was cleared for use.

Why, in God's name? thought Ralf grumpily as he hoisted the last sacks of wheat into the granary. They were only here to frighten off a few lawless, poorly armed outlaws. Why all this, as if preparing for battle with Fulk of Anjou himself? Ralf laughed to himself at the idea, because Fulk, William of Normandy's troublesome enemy, was far away beyond the horizon, stirring up strife in neighbouring Maine. He asked Aimery once why they were going to all this trouble to fortify such an insignificant spot, and Aimery gave him a short, empty reply.

The Breton was strict, too, as if they were already under martial law. He allowed no slacking, no thievery. Two men had been flogged already for raiding the wine cellars one night. And, to do him justice, the Breton worked harder than anyone. He seemed everywhere at once, from dawn till dusk, quite tireless, and missing nothing.

There was no hint of the lazy debauchery Ralf had hoped for. There was plentiful food and wine at night in the hall of the donjon, and their accommodation, if somewhat cramped, was clean and pleasant, with fresh rushes strewed every morning, and brocaded hangings softening the bare flint walls. Their evening meals were frequently supplemented by fresh venison from their hunting expeditions, and the casked wines in the cellars, hoarded by Isobel's dead husband, were excellent.

But Isobel was not here. In fact there were few women

here, except for the lowly serving maids, and the wenches who'd travelled with the soldiers to cook and tend to their needs. Ralf took a young, willing lass to his bed, but he dreamt of Isobel.

One night he dreamt that Isobel had blindfolded him once more, and had bound his hands behind his back. Then she knelt to play with his already aroused penis, stroking it meltingly with little licks of her darting pink tongue, swirling her lips across it and sucking wickedly round the sensitive glans until his darkly veined phallus was rigid and straining. His hips arched longingly in his sleep, and his erect shaft pressed hungrily against the plump buttocks of the girl who shared his bed. With a drowsy murmur of pleasure, she turned to him. 'Ready again, my lord? My, but you're a greedy one and no mistake.' Sleepily she crouched over him, her body all warm from slumber, and sucked his rampant cock until he jerked his seed into her lush mouth. Afterwards, he fondled her heavy breasts and still longed for Isobel.

Then, one night, Aimery sent a message to say that he would not be back till daybreak. He had taken Hamet and some of his chief soldiers to dine at the stronghold of a minor neighbouring landholder some three leagues distant, who had invited him to visit. There, they would discuss their plans to join with Duke William's army in Maine later that summer once Morency was secure.

In his absence, Ralf and his companions, who were equally restless under the iron hand of the Breton, engaged in debauchery. Hugh de Brosny made weak protests, but was over-ruled. The wine cellars were ransacked, and strong ale flowed. Musicians were found, who played merrily on their lutes and rebecs. The serving wenches were given wine too, and they lolled happily on the welcoming laps of the drunken knights and men-at-arms, kissing them and letting their breasts be openly fondled. Some of the women danced lewdly to the music, baring their breasts and legs as they cavorted around the trestle tables of the hall. One of them, young and nimble and pretty, did cartwheels, and the men roared with pleasure at the brief glimpse of her furred little mound between her thighs as her full skirt tumbled back to her waist.

It was not long before more lascivious entertainments were on everyone's mind. Ralf, his fair, handsome face flushed with wine, remembered something his bed companion had told him about one of Isobel's stable lads, whose name was Pierre.

'He's almost a simpleton, and is unable to utter a word,' she giggled coyly. 'But he's good with the horses. And oh, he's got a prick like a horse – I saw him once, at Eastertide, when three of the kitchen girls were tormenting him. They were daring one another to take his mighty weapon between their legs. One of them managed it at last, by making him lie on his back on the stable floor. All three of them helped to get his great penis nice and ready by covering it with their saliva – oh, how he shuddered at that – until his stiffened flesh was dark red with angry desire, and the great knob on the end was swollen and glistening from their tongues. Then one of the girls slipped astride him and played with herself to open her love passage, rubbing at her plump cleft, spreading her love juices and drawing them out. At last she crouched over the groaning lad Pierre and eased his quivering great prick into herself, while the other girls watched, breathless with excitement. I watched too, from the shadows. Oh, how I envied her as I saw that great gnarled shaft pushing its way into her inch by inch. She gasped and moaned and danced about on top of him, so we could all see his stiff prick plunging in and out of her. Then she began to cry out, her face pink with lust as she took her pleasure. At last she pulled herself off him, before he'd finished, and the poor lad lay there, his eyes glazed, as his massive penis twitched and spurted his seed across the straw of the stables. How I would love to see him again, and take him myself.'

Ralf remembered all this now, as the feasting grew more riotous and the men around him grew hotly, silently lustful as they gazed on the lewdly dancing girls.

He called one of the manservants over to his table. 'You know Pierre the stable lad?' he said curtly. The man nodded, his eyes widening a little in question.

'Aye, sir. He's been in the lady Isobel's service for several years – came back from England with her three years ago.'

'Then fetch him,' said Ralf.

Pierre was big, strong yet clumsy, with shaggy brown hair that fell to his shoulders and dull brown eyes that blinked dazedly as he was led into the candlelit hall. His rough tunic was still dusty and covered with straw from the stables, and his brawny thighs were clad in cross-gartered leggings. For a moment the music, the crowds, the noise, seemed to daunt him. Then he saw the girls with their clothing pulled away from their bare breasts, and he grinned slowly. 'Pierre,' the girls cried, their hair tumbling round their faces, their eyes shining with lust. 'Oh, sweet Pierre. Come here, to us.'

'Yes, and show us what you've got, Pierre,' giggled one of the prettiest of the wenches, skipping forward and openly fondling his groin.

Ralf and his companions poured themselves more wine, and leant back in pleasurable anticipation. This was more like it.

Pierre was soon disrobed of his crude leggings. His tunic was short, and barely covered his penis, which dangled heavily between his hairy thighs. He grinned round happily at them all as the girls gathered and crooned hungrily at it. It was indeed a mighty weapon, thought Ralf with reluctant admiration. As the girls played with it, it swelled and grew alarmingly, almost like another limb. It was so long and heavy that it sloped down a little, even in full erection. The girls pretended to back away from it in mock dismay.

'Take your pick, stout Pierre,' called out Ralf. 'A denier for you, lad, if you choose a willing wench and pleasure her here, in front of us.'

Pierre understood that all right. His dull brown eyes lighting up, he picked a pretty blonde girl and motioned her to the ground, on all fours. Giggling, she lifted her bottom to him, licking her lips in anticipation of the delights to come. Pierre's tongue too was hanging out as he lifted her skirts, gazed at her white bottom, then knelt and plunged his massive erection between her thighs, rubbing himself rapturously in the silky wetness there. As the girl wriggled about excitedly, he homed in on her pulsing vagina and sank himself slowly into her sweet softness.

The girl went rigid with delight as his thick shaft impaled her, still with half of it to go. Then she began to rock herself gently back against him, moaning with pleasure. 'Oh, oh . . .'

Pierre grasped her bottom, grinning, and began to thrust harder. With each thrust, he withdrew his massive penis almost to the hilt, so his rapt audience could see the incredible length of his veined shaft, and the tight, straining bulk of his balls. Ralf, his throat dry with desire, his own member rapidly swelling into hardness, poured himself more wine, but never took his pale blue eyes from the lewd scene being enacted before him. Everyone else was watching too, spellbound.

The girl began to climax noisily as she clenched herself around Pierre's vigorous rod. Pierre, wildly excited by her jerking body, started to thrust more and more fiercely and finally collapsed over her sated body as his great penis jerked and spasmed inside her for what seemed an eternity. Everyone watched in reverent silence, savouring every moment.

Then, suddenly, Ralf thought that he heard the jarring

clatter of horses' hooves in the courtyard outside. No. Impossible. Everyone was in here; the gates were closed. A moment later he thought he heard voices shouting in warning, and he shook his head, his senses blurred with the heavy wine. He must be imagining it, surely.

But dear God, that was the sound of a war horn, calling the alarm. The others heard it too, those who were not senseless with drink, and they leapt to their feet. Ralf ran for the door, his hand on his sword. Aimery had left him in charge. If this were an attack, and their enemies had found them like this, drunk and enervated with lechery, then the Breton would have him flayed alive.

He scrambled down the wooden steps that led into the ward, feeling almost deafened by the sound of shouting, of clashing armour. The night seemed alive with men and horses swirling agitatedly around the courtyard, their big hooves drumming the beaten earth floor, as several of the men-at-arms struggled to heave the big gates shut by the light of the wavering lanterns. Ralf struggled through the melée, his sword in his hand, the wine fumes in his head being rapidly dispelled by panic. Then he saw – Isobel.

He heaved a huge sigh of relief. So that was the reason for all this apparent turmoil. No attackers – just Isobel and the rest of the convoy, the baggage carts and the guards, arrived at Morency at last.

Isobel was dismounting from her mare, looking weary and shaken. Ralf ran up to her and held her reins steady.

'My lady,' he breathed raptly, excited as ever by the sight of her beauty. 'So you have had a safe journey. Welcome to Morency.'

She gazed at him dazedly, as if not even realising who he was. 'Safe? Hardly that. We barely escaped with our lives.'

Ralf went cold. 'Brigands?' he snarled. 'By God, my

lady, I shall take my men out now, to follow them and kill them. Their impudence exceeds all bounds.'

Then he broke off at the sound of a familiar, drawling voice behind him. 'Not brigands, Ralf, but Fulk of Anjou's men. With Fulk himself at their head. They encircle us even as we speak. We are under siege.'

Ralf whipped round to see Aimery the Breton, in full armour, looking tired and dangerous. He had blood on his sword hand.

'My lord?' he stuttered. 'Fulk of Anjou? And you were with Isobel? I do not understand.'

Aimery had dismounted. The strong, high gates were being bolted shut with a heavy beam of timber that Aimery himself had ordered to be made on their arrival here. The archers, under Hamet's command, were leaping to the battlements, and the armoury was being rapidly emptied of swords and shields. Aimery said curtly, 'My business was finished earlier than expected. I was riding back with my men to Morency when we came across Isobel's party, being pursued through the forest by some outriders from Fulk's army. We were able to fight them off, and bring our convoy here to safety before Anjou's main force closed in on us. But where were your guards, Ralf? Where were your watchmen? Fulk of Anjou himself could have ridden straight in here and you would not have known. Would you?'

His harsh voice ripped into Ralf, even amongst the surrounding din. Ralf stammered, 'We were ready, my lord, I assure you. And at least it seems that no-one has been hurt . . .'

Aimery stepped back, silently clearing the way as a litter borne by two men was brought carefully from one of the baggage wagons towards the castle's keep. On it lay a young woman. Her eyes were closed, the lids blue-veined against the whiteness of her face. Her long fair hair lay like strands of spun gold around her head and shoulders. She had been covered with a grey wool cloak – Ralf dimly recognised it as Aimery's.

'You are wrong again, Ralf,' said Aimery softly, dangerously. 'Your wife, the lady Elena, has been sorely injured.'

Ralf gasped and leapt forward as the news sunk home. But Aimery, barring his way, continued, 'Stay away. There is nothing you can do; she will not recognise you. I will make sure she is in good hands, believe me.' And he spoke urgently to the men who carried the litter, giving curt commands, and watching as Elena was borne away with the utmost care into the castle. Only then did Aimery turn back to the stunned Ralf.

'As I said, we are besieged,' he continued with a note of scorn in his voice. 'If you climb to the battlements, you will see that Anjou's men surround us. This was carefully planned.'

Ralf bowed his head, suddenly frightened, the wine gripping at his innards. This was real. This wasn't some summer tourney, with mock fights followed by jollity and feasting. This was war, and Aimery's men were isolated in semi-hostile countryside, where the neighbouring barons owed little loyalty to Duke William, and Maine's troubled borders were less than five leagues away.

He felt himself pale. Aimery watched him, the scorn glittering openly in his hard grey eyes. 'Don't look so frightened,' he said. 'They won't attack tonight, and risk death from our archers. More likely they will try to starve us out. And we have provisions for sixty days, remember? All the same, we need to set a watch on the ramparts, night and day. Since you failed to look after the castle in my absence, you can make up for your lack of soldierly vigilance by arranging for guards to be posted for the remainder of the night – and you can take up position with them yourself. You will be relieved at dawn.'

Ralf, still dizzy with an excess of wine, quailed at the thought of the long night's vigil. 'But my wife?' he said quickly. 'I should be at Elena's side, surely.'

'Such compassion,' drawled Aimery. 'Your wife may be unconscious for some time. She was struck a blow to the head in the fighting, and fell from her horse. I have already told you that I will ensure she has the best of care. There is nothing you can do for her. Take your men to the ramparts.'

Ralf turned sulkily to do as he was bid.

Only then did he remember how the Breton's cold eyes had seemed to momentarily blaze with tender passion as he gazed on the unconscious Elena. He frowned, then shrugged. He must have imagined it. The arrogant Breton showed warmth to no-one – not even to the tempting little armful Henriette, his future bride, who was hovering anxiously at Isobel's side. Sulkily, his fear somewhat abated by the sight of Aimery's competent bowmen, led by Hamet, already circling the battlements, he went to set up the night watch.

Later that night, when the sky was at its very blackest, at that moment just before dawn started to creep with grey fingers across the eastern horizon, Aimery was still awake, gaunt from his efforts to see that the small, isolated stronghold of Morency would stand some sort of chance against the might of Count Fulk of Anjou. Henriette had been troublesome, because she was frightened, and refused to leave his side. He'd left her at last in Hamet's charge. The big, calm Saracen, with his soothing voice, seemed somehow able to placate the wilful heiress into a semblance of peace. And Elena too was in good hands, being tended in a private chamber by an old goodwife with considerable healing skills, who'd clucked in pity over the pale, motionless Saxon lady. 'Rest assured, my lord,' she'd said, 'I'll care for her well. A blow to the head, was it? I'll watch her night and day, and let you know the minute there's any change.'

'Be sure that you do,' said Aimery quietly, casting one last glance at Elena's pale, fragile face, seeing the dark shadows like bruises beneath her closed eyelids.

Then he went to see Isobel.

Isobel too was wide awake, despite the lateness of the hour. She'd had Alys bring her wine, and a selection of choice cold food: richly spiced venison left over from the evening meal, which she knew Aimery loved, and soft manchet bread, and a dish of sweet little grapes coated with honey. She'd bathed herself in water perfumed with sandalwood, and brushed her long dark hair until it gleamed like a raven's wing, falling in loose tresses to her shoulders. Then she changed into a white silk chemise and a long, clinging gown of emerald green that enhanced her vivid, dark-lashed eyes. Her slender waist was encircled by a green girdle threaded with gold, whose ends hung to her dainty red shoes of softest kid leather. She gazed at herself in the bronze mirror with some satisfaction, and brushed the faintest hint of blue shadow into the arch of her brows. Then she blackened her lashes, and tinted her lips a delicate hue of rose to bring colour to her face, which was pale with excitement.

She poured herself a goblet of rich white wine and felt her pulses throbbing with anticipation as she paced her small but luxuriously furnished room. Outside, the spine-tingling sounds of Aimery's men preparing for war stirred her blood. She thought of Fulk's silent army, with lances and helms gleaming in the moonlight, gathered around the castle walls.

She was back at Morency, her home. Aimery was here, with her. All her carefully laid plans were going so, so well, but within the next few crucial hours, she would know for certain whether or not Aimery le Sabrenn was truly hers again.

He came to her in the early hours of the morning, just before dawn, and when she saw him standing there in the doorway, with his powerful frame outlined by the flickering tallow candle that glowed in the passage behind him, Isobel could hardly speak for excitement.

'Come in, my lord,' she said, as calmly as she could, and turned towards the small oak table where the refreshments waited. 'May I offer you wine?'

For answer, he pushed the door shut with his booted foot, and drew the bolt across it. Then he crossed the rush matting towards her and grasped her wrists, pinning her back against the wall so the tapestries that hung there abraded her shoulders.

'I don't want wine,' he said flatly. 'But I want an explanation, Isobel. What game are you playing now, that endangers all our lives?'

Isobel shivered with arousal as she gazed up into his hard-chiselled face, conscious of his powerful body, hard and heavily muscled beneath his long soldier's tunic, as he pinned her to the wall.

She moved lasciviously, her breasts starting to peak against the silk of her chemise. 'I do not understand you, lord Aimery,' she gasped. 'You offered to accompany me here to fight against brigands, did you not?'

'Offered? I was forced,' he said. 'And those brigands were paid to do their business by Fulk of Anjou, as well you knew.'

'No. I swear I knew nothing of Fulk's designs on Morency. How could you even think it?'

For answer, he lifted her imprisoned arms slowly above her head, stretching her supple body taut, so that her hard-tipped breasts jutted towards him from beneath her gown. She ran her little tongue across her white teeth in excitement.

'I think you did know, lady,' he drawled slowly. 'You see, Hamet and I captured some of your so-called brigands in the woods the other day. We made them talk. They told us they were actually trained soldiers, sent here by Fulk of Anjou to harry Morency's lands and draw Duke William's men to its aid. Why, I wonder, go to such trouble when Count Fulk could have taken this weak place so easily, without any need for strategy, at any time in the last few years?'

'I do not know,' she cried as his fingers bit into the soft flesh of her forearms. Oh, she loved him when he was like this. Stern, angry, his narrow eyes ablaze. She could see the sinews of his arms and shoulders standing out like whipcords beneath his tunic as he gripped her tighter. 'Please, lord Aimery,' she whispered, her green eyes sparkling. 'You are hurting me . . .'

'And you love that, Isobel, don't you?' he murmured. 'Very well then. I can see that I shall have to persuade you to tell me the truth.'

'Oh please,' whispered Isobel, feeling the thrill of desire rippling through her sensitive breasts down to the aching tightness at her loins. They had played these games before. 'Please . . .'

The game began. He unbuckled his leather belt deliberately from his lean hips. Then, gazing all the time into Isobel's desire-hazed green eyes, he bound the supple dark leather round her wrists and lifted them up, securing the big buckle to one of the wooden hooks fixed high to the wall, from which Isobel's precious tapestries hung. Isobel was breathing hard, her eyes half-shut now. Once she was pinioned, lifted almost on tiptoe, Aimery leant forward to kiss her harshly, his strong mouth fastening on her already parted lips, his tongue jabbing, probing. She arched her hips towards him, her mouth clinging desperately to his kiss, her upstretched arms straining at their bonds. Deliberately the Breton drew away and with strong fingers, slowly pulled off her jewelled girdle and ripped her emerald-green gown in two from the neck downwards. It slithered to the ground at her feet. Then he tore at her silk chemise, just enough to expose her breasts; they were full and white, with red-tinted crests that strained towards him.

'You have painted your nipples, Isobel,' Aimery said silkily, caressing them with his thumb until they stood out like hard stalks. 'Why? Were you expecting me?'

'I hoped, my lord,' she breathed. 'As I have hoped these weeks past that you would come to me again.'

He pulled away the rest of her chemise. She stood there naked and powerless, her white silk stockings that were ribbon-gartered at the thigh only emphasizing the vulnerable flesh of her loins and stomach. He gazed down thoughtfully at the dark, luxuriant curls that concealed the core of her femininity. He could smell the musky fragrance of her arousal. 'And meanwhile,' he said, reaching down to grip with his hand at the hot mound at the joining of her thighs, 'you have enjoyed yourself with Hamet, have you not? You always did enjoy being pleasured by my stalwart servant, didn't you?'

'He is but a shadow of you, my lord,' she breathed, writhing herself against his hand, longing for his masterly fingers to explore her melting sex. 'Oh, Aimery. How I have missed you.'

'You have been playing games, Isobel,' he said softly, his thumb parting her pulsing folds at last and rasping with delicious skill at her engorged clitoris. She was wet with longing; the ball of his thumb slid softly in her juices. Her breasts swelled and throbbed, her nipples straining angrily as she longed for his cruel, sensual mouth to soothe their blissful agony. 'Tell me what you have been plotting,' he went on. 'Tell me exactly what you have planned with Fulk of Anjou.'

'Fulk is Duke William's enemy, my lord,' she snapped back angrily. 'Why should I be in league with him?'

'Because he has offered you something, I would guess. Something you want very badly. What, I wonder? Money? Lands? You have those already in plenty.

172

Power? Perhaps.' He laughed. 'Fulk has offered himself to you?'

'No!' Isobel was panting, desperate as his fingers continued to slide skilfully in the unfolding petals of her sex. The juices of her arousal were trickling now in silvery threads down the softness of her inner thigh. 'He is a scented, effeminate weakling compared to you, my lord.'

'I had heard that he preferred pretty young men,' agreed Aimery thoughtfully. 'But there must be something going on, Isobel. You see, I have been told by my informers that you and Fulk were in secret communication with one another before you set off on your mission to Rouen with colourful tales of brigands.'

Isobel flushed, her wrists straining against the bonds that held them high above her head, her suspended body ripe and open with longing. She could see the hard stirring of Aimery's phallus against his clothing. Dear God, if he didn't penetrate her soon with his magnificent weapon, then she would die of need.

'I will not tell you,' she snapped.

'Then there is something to tell? Good. We are getting somewhere.' Slowly he moved away from her and worked at the lacings of his hose. She gasped aloud as his phallus sprang free, already proudly erect. Isobel flushed again, and caught her lower lip between her teeth. Sweet heaven, but she had blissful memories of riding that magnificent shaft of flesh. Her loins quivered and clenched, releasing a fresh flood of longing in her womb.

Aimery laughed and moved nearer, his heavy member swaying. Gripping his penis by its thick stem, he rubbed its velvety head between Isobel's nether lips, sliding it up and down her soaking cleft in open provocation. She gasped aloud, closing her eyes, and tried to move towards him, to guide him into the aching emptiness between her legs, but her bonds restrained her cruelly.

'Please, Aimery. Please, my lord. Drive yourself into me. Let me feel your hard shaft easing my torment. I will tell you anything.'

He let himself slide a little way inside her, and she gasped with excruciating pleasure and began to thrust herself desperately against him, trying to sheathe him inside the melting mouth of her vagina. He drew away, the blunt tip of his lengthy phallus glistening with her juices.

'Tell me,' he repeated coldly. The scar on his chiselled face was a thin white line as he stretched out his hands to graze her burning nipples. 'Tell me about Fulk of Anjou.'

Isobel cried out as the fierce pleasure shafts shot from her breasts to her loins. It was as if a cord was tightening, drawing her into a secret vortex of mingled pain and delight. 'Fulk came to me in the winter,' she choked out at last. 'He – he wants to make Morency his – *oh!*'

'Then,' said Aimery le Sabrenn, still stroking her breasts cruelly, rolling the turgid nipples between her finger and thumb until she was hovering on the very brink of searing release, 'why did he not just take it, weak and undefended as it was?'

'Because – because he wanted more. He wants more than anything to humiliate Duke William, his arch enemy. He pleaded with me to entice some of William's foremost knights here first. Then he could be sure that, when he at last laid siege to Morency, it would be well defended, and William would be forced to send more men, an army, to attack Fulk and raise the siege.'

'A risky business.' Aimery's erection was still throbbing, and Isobel could hardly take her eyes from it. She licked her dry lips.

'You had better tell me the rest of this plan,' he said.

Isobel took a deep, ragged breath. 'Once we are under siege, we wait for Duke William to send an army to our relief,' she whispered. 'Then, I am to persuade the

174

commander of the castle – you, my lord – to open the castle gates, and to ride out – to join Fulk's army. You will then, all of you, turn on William's approaching men, and with your combined might and the advantage of surprise, defeat them and kill them. A mighty victory for Fulk.'

Aimery registered no surprise. It was as if he had already guessed. 'You play deep games, Isobel. You are sworn vassal to William of Normandy.'

She licked her lips. 'So are you, my lord. But you must know that Fulk has an ancient claim to the suzerainty of Maine, which was acknowledged in the past by Duke William himself, until it suited him otherwise. Aimery, if you join with me in this – if you will send a desperate message to Duke William for aid, then keep up the pretence of the siege, and join Fulk to turn on the relieving army when it arrives – then there will be rich rewards for you. Fulk has told me he will offer you Morency, together with more estates and lands, so that you have a fief stretching all the way to Maine's border. In return you must swear loyalty to Count Fulk, and marry me.'

Aimery listened. He was very still. 'And if I refuse?'

She whispered, 'You cannot refuse, my lord. Fulk's army is gathered at the castle walls. Just remember – he will reward you well.'

Her heart pounded with longing as he gazed silently down at her, his sensual mouth that could bring such pleasure lifted in a cruel smile by the savage scar.

'An interesting proposition,' he said softly. 'And, of course, I must accept. I am a mercenary, after all, on sale to the highest bidder.'

Isobel gave a little sob of relief. 'Then take me, my lord. Oh, take me.'

She writhed in her bonds, her slender thighs wide apart, exposing her glistening coral sex in wanton invitation.

175

Slowly, Aimery reached to cup her buttocks, and eased his rigid penis into her.

She shuddered with speechless delight as she felt the Breton's magnificent shaft impale her steadily over and over again. She gazed down, panting with lust at the sight of the exquisite length of his cock sliding into her greedy sex. She clutched at him with her inner muscles, sobbing with loss each time he withdrew, only to sigh again with bliss as he penetrated her once more. This was why no other man could slake her appetites. Aimery was cool, powerful; he could sustain his virile powers for ever, until a woman was exhausted with dizzy pleasure.

She rubbed against him as the root of his penis thudded against her swollen clitoris, drawing in harsh, gasping breaths as his hands tormented her thrusting nipples into sweet pain. And then he began to ravish her with harder, faster strokes. She gasped out, her cheeks flushed with longing, and ecstasy started to throb through her as his mouth came down on hers. His penis continued to pleasure her with devastating strength, and she leapt in her bonds as her crisis flooded through her captive body.

He drove himself to his own climax deep within her, silently, powerfully. She sagged back, her face glazed with pleasure as she felt his shaft spasm again and again inside her loins. Afterwards, he loosened the belt around her wrists in silence, and she leant back weakly against the wall. She longed to cling to him, to press her breasts against his lovely battle-scarred body and run her hands across his muscled shoulders. But she knew Aimery, and knew that he would not want that.

'So am I to tell Fulk that you accept his bargain?' she whispered, rubbing her chafed wrists.

He looked down at her with those chilling grey eyes. 'Yes,' he said. 'But say nothing to anybody else within this castle. None of the soldiers must know, or they

176

would openly rebel against such apparent treachery. I will have a message sent to Duke William, begging for aid – presumably Count Fulk will tell his men to turn a blind eye to a horseman slipping out through Morency's gates one night. Then, when the relieving army arrives, I shall speak to my men. I will give instructions that we are to ride out and join with Fulk's men to attack and destroy those who have come to our aid.'

Isobel sighed happily. 'Then Morency – and I – will be yours, my lord. But even if you send your messenger to William as soon as possible, it could be days, weeks, before William's army arrives. In the meantime, you and I – we shall enjoy ourselves? As we have done so often before?'

He hardly glanced at her as he buckled on his belt. 'If you can devise ways to pass the nights in diversions, so be it,' he said. 'But spare me from the attentions of Henriette of Sizerne, will you?'

Isobel sighed rapturously. He loved her. He wanted her. Henriette, Elena, all the other women who had tried to tempt him in the past – they were nothing to him. She felt the joy of it overwhelming her. Her plan had worked. She would let Fulk know as soon as possible.

It was some months since Count Fulk, in persuading her to this act of treachery, had struggled to find the one thing that would tempt the lady of Morency.

'There must be something,' he had urged. 'Something that you want more than anything on earth.'

Her green eyes had slanted covetously, and she'd whispered, 'Give me Aimery le Sabrenn, and I will help you take Morency and inflict a crippling humiliation on Duke William's knights.'

'You shall have him,' Fulk had said.

Now, Aimery was turning to go. Isobel was disappointed; she didn't want him to leave so soon. 'Stay, my lord,' she said quickly. 'I have refreshment for you here: venison, white bread, fine wine. Stay and eat.'

'I must go,' he said expressionlessly. 'The watch changes at dawn. I need to be there.'

She pouted seductively. 'But you know they won't attack you now, my lord. Rest easy.'

Aimery said, 'Old habits die hard. And we must keep up the pretence of hostilities, so my men don't suspect. They would see your scheme as treachery.'

'But you don't?'

'I told you,' he said. 'I am a mercenary. And mercenaries always sell themselves to the highest bidder.'

She touched his arm suddenly, still anxious to detain him. 'My lord,' she said eagerly. 'I have had an idea. For our entertainment one night. You knew, of course, that the young squire Gilles has been pleasuring the lady Elena all the way from Rouen?'

He went still. 'I knew.'

'Then let us punish him, my lord. He is a handsome, well-built youth, and we could have some sport. Shall I make preparations? I have several beautiful maidservants who would help us.'

He shrugged. 'Why not?'

Then he left her, and walked out along the castle's ramparts. All around, as far as the encircling forest, Fulk of Anjou's men had set up their tents and their horse lines. Pennants fluttered wraithlike in the breeze that preceded the dawn; lanterns glittered forlornly through the darkness. He looked, assessing their strength with practised eyes.

Then he moved on, to the little room where the old crone Mathilde watched over Elena. A single candle burned dimly by the bed. The crone was dozing in a chair, but she was instantly alert the minute he came in. She was used to his visits.

'My lord,' she whispered. 'Less than an hour ago she stirred and breathed your name. She seemed agitated, was rambling on about something she must tell you, some tale of treachery. I would have called you, my lord,

178

but they said you were with the lady Isobel. I slipped a little healing elixir between her lips, my lord, and now she sleeps.'

Aimery gazed down at Elena's long lashes sweeping her pale cheeks and touched one finger to her golden hair, lifting one soft tendril and letting it fall again. Then he looked back at the old woman.

'Make sure she rests. Do not let anyone else speak to her,' he said.

After that he went to inspect Ralf's guard, and to prepare for the tasks that the long day would bring.

Chapter Eleven

*F*or many days, Elena lay in the dark twilight world between unconsciousness and waking. She was aware of unknown people moving silently, carefully in and out of her little candlelit chamber. An old woman sat constantly beside her, who cooled her brow with soothing cloths that were fragrant with lavender, and eased strange-tasting potions between her lips. They tasted bitter, like the herbal medicines Sister Winifred used to prepare in the infirmary of the little convent where she grew up. Sometimes the old woman muttered to herself with her eyes closed, as if in prayer, but to Elena it sounded more like incantations, muttered spells.

She knew that she had to see Aimery, to tell him something, but her brow ached so tightly when she tried to remember it all that she grew fevered again and the old crone Mathilde gave her medicine to make her sleep.

She woke once, in the middle of the night. Old Mathilde was lying in the corner, on the pallet she used for her rest, but she was not asleep, and neither was she alone. A stalwart young serving man seemed to be crouching over her in the shadows, and through the tangle of limbs and clothing that was too dark for her to discern, Elena felt a wrenching pang of arousal leap through her own prostrate body as she realised that the serving man was pleasuring the old woman silently. She could see his penis, lengthy and rigid, as it plunged between the woman's thighs; Mathilde was stifling little moans of pleasure as he stooped above her. He looked somehow familiar, his intent face stirring unwanted memories, and Elena closed her eyes to try to shut out the feral sounds of their copulation.

In the morning Elena, still disturbed by what she'd thought she'd seen, decided that it must have been a dream, a product of her illness and the strange medicines the woman gave her.

Occasionally Ralf came in. He seemed agitated and cross as he questioned the old woman about his wife's condition, as if he was angry with Elena for being in this plight. Elena, her eyes closed as she feigned sleep, wished that he would leave, and in fact he never stayed long.

Once Aimery came, and she longed to speak to him, to tell him that he was in some nameless danger that she couldn't remember, but Mathilde had just given her a sleeping draught, and she was drifting on the edge of dreams. She heard his all-too familiar voice as he spoke to her attendant; then he came over to her bed to gaze at her. She felt his strange silver-grey eyes burning into her, and she struggled to clear her throat and speak. But he touched her hand, and shook his head slightly almost as if in warning, and turned to leave. She watched him go, her heart aching.

Soon after that she was sitting up, and drinking the thin but nourishing broth that the old dame brought her. She still felt weak and light-headed, but she wanted to get up. The woman would not let her.

'In a few days,' she said when Elena asked her again one evening. 'You're better off in here, lass, away from it all. 'Tis all talk of warfare and weapons out there, from dawn till dusk. And crammed to the rooftops with soldiers. Lord Aimery has archers mounted on the battlements, and horses and soldiers drilling constantly in the courtyard. They've all been crowded in here top to tail ever since the siege started.'

Elena frowned. 'Siege? The castle of Morency is under siege?'

'Aye! Of course you don't know, with being so sick. But those soldiers who attacked you as you were riding through the woods – those whom the lord Aimery drove off, thank God – they were outriders of Fulk of Anjou's army. Lord Aimery and his men got you and Isobel and all the rest of you here just in time to slam the gates in Fulk's arrogant face. So the Count of Anjou has set up his army all around the castle – just beyond bowshot range – and there he sits. The count will wait all summer, they say, till we give up or starve.'

Elena pulled herself up against her pillows. Suddenly it had all come back to her. Alys's whispered warning of Isobel's treachery pounded at her temples almost as fiercely as the blow that had felled her from her horse. *'Tell the lord Aimery. Isobel's in league with Count Fulk, and has been making plans with him all winter . . .'*

Desperately she tried to swing her legs from the bed, but her limbs were still weak and heavy. 'Aimery,' she breathed. 'I must see Aimery.'

But the old crone Mathilde wasn't listening to her. Instead, she was busy crushing some dried herbs, and pouring them into a warm honey-sweetened tisane.

'Here,' she said. 'Drink this, my pretty one. It will ease your aching head, and help you sleep. Don't worry yourself about the lord Aimery. He'll keep us all safe, that one will.'

'No! You don't understand. I must tell him something – he might be in terrible danger . . .'

'He's a soldier,' said the woman dryly, bringing the

182

tisane towards her. 'Aren't they always in danger? Here, my lady. Drink.'

Elena took it. But the moment Mathilde's back was turned, she emptied it quickly into the ewer of water on the floor beside her bed. The crone was fussing to herself gently, gathering her dishes together. 'Now,' Mathilde was saying, 'I'll just be off down to the kitchens, to check they've remembered to save some ewe's milk for you. Rest, my lady. Almost everyone is abed except for the soldiers on guard. 'Tis well past compline. Rest – I'll be back with you shortly.'

The moment she had gone, Elena pulled herself out of the little bed. She felt, suddenly, as if she was being kept here on purpose. As if the herbal medicines the old woman kept giving her were to stupefy her, to keep her in a state of somnolence. She had to see Aimery. It sounded as if danger was gathering, all around.

She was dressed only in her chemise, but the gown in which she'd been travelling when they were ambushed lay laundered and folded on the small wooden chest in the corner. She pulled it on, smoothing the soft skirt of fine blue wool over her hips, and fastened the silk corded girdle with trembling fingers. Then she eased her feet into her buttoned shoes of calfskin which lay beside the chest. Her hair was long and loose, but there was no time now to braid it. Frantically she searched for a tortoiseshell comb, and dragged it through her pale golden tresses until they shone like a halo around her fragile face.

Aimery. She must find Aimery, to tell him that he faced some sort of treachery, from Isobel and Fulk of Anjou.

Stepping out of the door, she found that she had been sequestered in a small, isolated outbuilding, set between the granaries and a thatched stable where she could hear horses champing restlessly at their straw. Darkness had already fallen; pitch torches were thrust into iron holders on the stable walls, casting a dim, smoky light around the yard. At intervals around the palisade, she could see watchposts, rearing up into the black night; there were soldiers at each one, their helms gleaming in the moonlight as they gazed out into the darkness beyond. Somewhere out there, encircling them, was Fulk of Anjou's army.

She turned round. Behind her, the foursquare donjon, a miniature version of Rouen, dominated the stronghold of Morency. Thatched and wattled outbuildings clung to its lower walls; the donjon itself was stark and bare, with slitted windows and high ramparts. She could see the flicker of candles at the windows. In there somewhere would be Aimery. And Isobel, her enemy.

Praying that she would not encounter Isobel, she hurried to the stout wooden doorway. A soldier barred her way, then recognised her.

'My lady Elena,' he said, bowing his head deferentially.

'I seek Aimery le Sabrenn,' she said in an urgent voice.

Was it her imagination, or did his face twist with a hint of pity? 'He is in his chamber on the second floor, my lady,' he said slowly. 'But he has company. You'd be advised not to trouble him.'

'I must see him,' she said desperately, but he shook his head.

Then someone called to him, from the other side of the courtyard, and he went grumpily outside. Elena, seeing the curving stone staircase leading up into the tower, seized her chance and hurried to climb it.

This was no Rouen, with its maze of guest rooms and passages. On the second floor there was only one chamber of any size, and the heavy door was closed. Elena had half expected a guard outside if this was Aimery's room, but there was no-one. From within, she thought she heard the murmur of voices, and a low laugh.

She opened the door impulsively, desperate to see Aimery again and tell him her fears. But there was no sign of him yet, because she was in a dark little anteroom, bare except for a pallet in one corner. Perhaps Hamet slept here, guarding his master as always. A heavy curtain of rich tapestry hung on the far wall from the raftered ceiling to floor, guarding the way to the next room; from beneath it she could see the bright gleam of candlelight. She heard more soft voices, then what sounded like a woman, moaning softly, not in pain, but in some extremity of pleasure.

Elena's skin tingled in warning. Perhaps the guard was wrong, and Aimery was not here after all. But before she could think of retreating, she heard soft footsteps behind her. Someone had followed her up here. She whirled round. *Isobel.*

Her enemy looked dangerous, sleek, cat-like. Her slanting green eyes gleamed with malice; her cheeks were flushed with pleasure.

'Well, Elena,' she breathed softly. 'So you are better. Up out of your solitary bed at last. And you have decided to come and join us, have you? Or have you come simply to spy?'

Elena clenched her hands at her sides. Isobel, her old antagonist, was smiling with some unknown triumph, and the sight of that smile made her blood run cold. 'I have come to see Aimery,' she said as steadily as she could. 'I have no particular desire to talk to you, Isobel.'

'You want to see Aimery? Well, you shall see him,' grinned Isobel. 'But prepare yourself gently, my dear. We don't want any sudden surprises to upset your delicate state of health again, do we? Look, here. If I draw this curtain back, just a little way, we can spy on them from the shelter of the darkness. They will never see us. Believe me, they are far too engrossed in what they are doing.'

Then Elena knew. She knew with a sickening, blinding

185

certainty what she was going to see. The murmuring voices, the soft sighs, should have warned her. As Isobel touched the curtain, she was aware of the heated warmth that came from the inner chamber, the scent of rich wine, the unmistakable musk of sexual arousal.

Isobel pulled the curtain back, just enough for her to see, and stayed beside her, her green eyes gleaming raptly. The chamber now revealed to Elena's view was lavishly furnished, with rush matting on the floor, and rich tapestries on the walls, and wax candles gleaming in iron sconces. A log fire burned dully in the grate, adding to the flickering shadows that danced on the walls. Several carved couches, draped with wolf pelts and pillowed with feathers of goose down, lined the walls. Jugs of wine and dishes of sugared quinces lay on small oak tables around the room.

Aimery reclined on one of the couches, a silver goblet of wine in his hand. His face was in shadow. A pretty girl with flowing black hair, dressed in a gown of long blue silk, was kneeling at his side. She had eased apart his tunic, which was slit deep at the neck, and was stroking the smooth muscles of his chest with lascivious fingers. Her eyes were hazed, as if she had already consumed a good deal of wine. Elena saw Hamet leaning forward from another couch, gazing with rapt black eyes at the unfolding scene over at the far end of the big room.

A young man, standing upright, had been secured with his face to the wall, his spread-eagled arms tied with leather thongs to the iron candle holders set deep in the solid stone walls. He was naked except for the deerskin boots and linen hose that clung sinuously to the taut muscles of his narrow hips and strong thighs. The powerful sinews of his back were stretched painfully by the thongs; his head was bowed with degradation. Another lovely serving girl dressed only in a long white chemise that slipped from her bare shoulders stood

186

behind him with a leather whip in her hands. Even as Elena watched, hardly able to breathe, the girl raised her arm and the thong of the quirt curled heavily across the man's muscled shoulders, striping his sunbronzed skin. He shivered, lifting his head in despair, and Elena saw his face.

It was Gilles. She should have known, from his long brown hair, and his magnificent physique. She felt dizzy, as if her sickness had returned. She saw the laughing girl raise the plaited whip again, and say, 'You have been wicked, master Gilles. And now you will be punished properly.'

'No,' breathed Elena, and started to move forwards, to stop this mockery, but Isobel's hand gripped her shoulder in warning. 'Stay where you are, Saxon slut. Say nothing,' she hissed in a cold voice. 'Or your young squire's punishment will be even worse.'

Elena realised then that there were other girls in the room, gathered in the shadows. All hand-picked by Isobel, no doubt, for their looks and their lasciviousness. Isobel, as if reading her stunned thoughts, whispered, 'They are lovely, are they not? I knew Aimery would enjoy them. He is familiar with some of them already, because they were with me at Aumale, where Aimery stayed with me after his imprisonment. Oh, we passed the time in many pleasurable games there, as I believe I have told you. Little Marie, who is with him now, is a particular favourite of his.'

Elena wanted to put her hands over her ears to shut out the sights, the sounds. But at the same time, she felt the sweet, shameful surging of her own desire. Several of the girls were gathering around the handsome Gilles now, murmuring in soft, excited voices, like fluttering birds. Together, they untethered one of Gilles's wrists, then swung his tormented body round, re-fastening his free wrist swiftly to another iron sconce on the wall so that this time he was forced to face the breathless

187

company. Then they were ripping at his taut leggings, and Elena saw how Gilles shut his eyes in despair, because his exposed phallus was in a state of throbbing erection. The girls fought to touch it, rubbing it with heavy fingers, laughing aloud as it stiffened yet further. Gilles groaned with humiliation.

Elena shivered with forbidden lust as she remembered how deliciously the young squire's lengthy penis had pleasured her that night in the stables. At the same time, rebellion burned within her. Gilles was Aimery's squire. He was honourable, and faithful to his master. Oh, why did not Aimery stop this degrading torment? She cold hear Isobel's rapid, excited breathing beside her.

'Isn't he beautiful?' Isobel was murmuring. 'Look at his lovely youthful body, his heavy balls, his long, hard cock. But of course, you know all about him, don't you, Elena? He has consoled you sweetly with his lusty shaft, has he not? Tell me – is he good with his tongue as well? I should like to straddle his handsome young face with my thighs, and let him give me pleasure with his mouth, licking at my sweet juices as I squirm around over his face.'

Elena said in a low voice, 'I must go in. Aimery must stop this torment.'

But Isobel grabbed her wrist this time. 'Little fool,' she hissed. 'Don't you realise that Gilles is being punished because of you? If you go in now, and take the young squire's side, Aimery will only think of something worse for him!'

Elena felt unsteady, as if her sickness were returning. 'Aimery ordered this because of me?'

'Oh, yes, it was all Aimery's idea, from the very beginning. He actually hand-picked Gilles as an attendant for you on our journey here from Rouen, because he anticipated you would be tempted by the handsome young squire, and realised that your dalliance would give him an excuse for this diversion.'

'*No . . .*' Elena was shaking her head slowly.

'Oh, yes. After all, Aimery and I used to enjoy many similar entertainments when he was with me at Aumale. He has missed it all, as I knew he would. He has settled so well into life here in my castle. As you would too, if you gave yourself the chance.'

'*No.* He does not love you. He did not want to come here, to Morency . . .'

'Oh, my dear,' said Isobel silkily. 'You surely still don't think that he could love a Saxon? I tried to warn you, so many times. But you wouldn't listen to me, would you?'

A girl was rubbing hard now at Gilles's swollen shaft. Someone had handed her a phial of scented oil; she had spilled a little in her palm, and was running her hand lasciviously up and down the rigid stem. The squire's face was hot with despair. Hamet was leaning forward from his couch, breathing hard as he watched. A serving girl wriggled to his side, and quickly freed his erect penis from his clothing, gasping in delight at it, and dipping her head to run her flickering tongue along the massive rod of dusky flesh. Hamet shuddered, his hands twining in the girl's loose hair, his penis jerking up from his lap as he gazed at Gilles.

Aimery was very still. The girl beside him was still fondling his chest longingly, but he restrained her. 'Finish it,' he said curtly to the girls who clustered round his tormented esquire.

By now, Gilles's leggings had been ripped down to his hard-muscled thighs. They loosened his bonds, and pushed him to his knees. The girl with the whip fondled his tight buttocks briefly, then she raised the lash again and struck hard, three, four times. Elena, aching with despair, could see the red marks striping his bottom cheeks. Beneath his helplessly arching body, she could see Gilles's throbbing penis straining for release, could see his balls clenching tightly between his thighs, ready to spurt their seed. Then the girl dropped the whip and sank suddenly to her knees behind the squire. As the others drew back with bated breath, she slowly began to fondle Gilles's buttocks with her oil-smeared hands, stroking and parting the tight globes. Her fingers lingered over the whorl of dark hair that encircled his puckered anus. She stroked it lovingly and eased her forefinger in, pushing gently to stimulate his pulsing bottom hole as Gilles writhed beneath her. Carefully she tried to slide a second finger in, but his little ring of tight muscles resisted the extra thickness.

'Relax, my handsome lad, and enjoy it,' she whispered enticingly. 'Pretend it's some stalwart soldier sticking his brawny cock up you. Close your eyes, and pretend . . .'

Her fingers slipped in, and Gilles shut his eyes with an expression of despair, his engorged penis throbbing wildly as the girl's fingers penetrated him deeper and deeper. Another girl knelt quickly to take his phallus in her hand, rubbing the glossily oiled foreskin up and down so the glans swelled, purple and plum-like. The girl crouching behind him ravished him more strongly, thrusting three fingers deep between his clenched bottom cheeks, harder and harder. Gilles cried out, and his penis jetted out his sperm in great, hot gouts across the rush matting of the floor.

Tenderly the girl milked him, while the convulsions shook his strong body. Elena watched, hating herself because her own secret parts pulsed with shameful desire. The girl with Hamet was sucking furiously now at the Saracen's mighty cock; Elena could see the dark, rigid shaft pumping into her mouth as she struggled to take him all in. Frantically she cupped his smooth, velvety balls as he jerked his hips and spurted over and over into her greedily swallowing throat. His sperm trickled out at the corners of her mouth, and she licked it up, determined to take all he offered.

Aimery watched, impassive. Elena hated him for what he was doing to Gilles, but at the same time she wanted the Breton, so much. Her breasts ached with need, and her nipples hardened, pressing treacherously against her bodice. Isobel saw it, and whispered wickedly in her ear, 'Delightful, is it not? Aimery is capable of devising so many delicious diversions. Of course, his own self-control is formidable. He can keep his passions in check, right till the end. And tonight, to make up for our many weeks spent apart, he is saving himself for me.'

Elena shook her head slowly, still not able to believe her enemy. 'No. This cannot be. I must be dreaming still. The castle is under siege. Aimery must be crazed, or enchanted by you, Isobel. He would not spend his time willingly in such debauchery when his men are in such danger. What spell have you laid on him?'

Isobel laughed. 'No spell. Merely the promise of great power and riches, more than he has ever dreamt of. The siege, you see, is all a pretence. It is a clever ruse, to draw yet more of Duke William's soldiers towards Morency. Then, when the time is right, Aimery will lead his own men forth from the gates, to join with Count Fulk and destroy William's army. A cunning ploy, is it not? And meanwhile, as the siege that is not a siege draws on, we pass the time in merry diversions.'

Elena felt sickened, revulsed. 'No. You lie to me again. I must find Ralf. He will tell me the truth.'

Isobel smiled. 'Your husband, my dear, is as deep in debauchery as the rest of them. He will not appreciate your efforts to interfere. He's enjoying himself thoroughly, but his tastes are rather less refined than Aimery's. No doubt he's down in the stables, rutting with a couple of doxies – any he can find. Why, he even tongued and then ravished my poor, ugly Alys. A sign of genuine wantonness, I would say – wouldn't you?'

Elena stared at her. Ralf and Alys. It was so degrading

that it had to be true. Isobel would not dare to make up such an outrageous lie.

Then all the rest must be true as well. Aimery was in league with Fulk of Anjou. She had been desperate to warn him that Isobel was secretly scheming with Fulk. How he would have laughed at her if she had succeeded in warning him, because it seemed he knew of it all the time. He himself was as deep in treachery as Isobel.

She drew back, her face white, towards the door, her fists clenched at her sides as if she would fight Isobel off. 'Then I shall tell Aimery's soldiers. They are loyal to Duke William. Gilles and his companions would never permit such a terrible betrayal. They would never, ever join with Fulk of Anjou and turn on their fellow soldiers. They would throw you out of your vile castle first!'

Isobel laughed. 'Aimery was afraid you might do exactly that if you found out our little scheme. That's why he's been paying that old crone to drug you with herbs, to keep you slumbering on in your little chamber. Something went wrong tonight, though, didn't it? Mathilde must have forgotten to give you the correct dose. Aimery will have her flogged for that.'

The tisane. She had been meant to drink it tonight, to sleep through everything. Aimery was keeping her drugged and out of the way, in case she discovered what was going on. And she had been fool enough to think that he cared for her. Feeling sick, she turned to run, but before she got to the door, a pair of strong, brawny arms caught at her shoulders. Hamet, quickly summoned by Isobel, had captured her. He dragged her kicking and struggling into the firelit chamber, where the exhausted Gilles crouched on the floor with despairing eyes.

Aimery got to his feet, brushing aside the girl who still clung to him as Hamet brought Elena in and held her tightly from behind. He gazed at Elena, his scarred face expressionless. Then the Breton dismissed the serving wenches abruptly, telling them to release Gilles as well and take him with them.

'Your punishment is over, Gilles,' he said curtly to the young squire, whose shoulders sagged with humiliation as he silently pulled on his clothing. 'But I will arrange with the sergeant of the watch for your duties to be doubled. Now leave.'

They all left except Hamet and Isobel. Aimery turned to Elena, assessing her slowly with those hypnotic silver-grey eyes. 'Elena,' he said. 'Well, well. What brings you to join our company?'

Elena was shivering in Hamet's strong grip. This was like some cruel dream. Last time she was with him, that night at the monastery, his eyes had been tender with love. Now they were harsh, and mocking. She tossed back her loose blonde hair from her face and gazed up at him with scorn.

'You are mistaken in thinking I wished to join you, my lord,' she said. 'I wish, more than anything, to leave this vile place.'

Isobel broke in tauntingly, 'She knows, Aimery, that you have sworn secret fealty to Fulk. She wanted to run and tell your soldiers, and spoil our game. She would lose you Morency, and all the wealth that the Count of Anjou has promised you.'

Aimery slowly shook his head. 'We cannot have that, can we? Where did you find her, Isobel?'

'She was spying, my lord! Spying from behind the curtain. Watching her precious young squire, Gilles, in his degrading pleasure – no doubt longing to feel his lusty cock up her yet again. Or perhaps you're tired of that, are you, Elena? Perhaps you fancy some other sluttish pleasures. See, my lord Aimery, how her eyes are hazed with desire, how her pink little nipples push through her modest gown, betraying her secret lewdness.'

Aimery reached lazily to touch Elena's breasts. She

193

gasped with longing, and shame. He said, lazily, 'Contrary to your husband's belief, you always were a hot little wench, weren't you, Elena? Like all Saxons, you would rut with anyone. You should have come in earlier. We could all have watched while Gilles demonstrated what pleased you most.'

She struggled against Hamet's strong grip, feeling the despair wash through her. Up till this moment, she had tried to hope that Isobel had once more told her lies. But now she knew that Isobel was right. It all fitted into place. Aimery had seduced her effortlessly, cruelly reawakening her desperate passion for him, only to destroy her anew. It was all part of the games that he and Isobel had played, for so long. He hated women of the Saxon race with a deep, abiding hatred, for killing his brother, and scarring his own face. He had vowed revenge, on all of them. What had made her think that she was different?

Yet even now, as he gazed down at her with such cold scorn, she still could not believe that he would betray Duke William. She had thought him, in spite of all else, to be a man of honour, loyal to his liege lord. She gazed up at him, her blue eyes dark with resistance.

'My lord Aimery,' she said slowly. 'That you will always be Isobel's minion, I have long suspected. And I pity you for it.' She saw a muscle flickering in his lean jaw; his mouth thinned, but he said nothing. She went on, steadily, 'But that you plan to betray the lord to whom you have sworn fealty, Duke William of Normandy, I still find impossible to believe.'

He smiled, a cruel, dangerous smile, as the seamed scar that the Saxon girl Madelin had inflicted on him all those years ago lifted the corner of his mouth. 'Then you must start believing, Elena,' he said. 'And admit that your own sweet body betrays you even as you talk. Because, in spite of your self-righteous scorn, you still want me, do you not?'

Again, he touched her breasts, gently tugging at her nipples with his finger and thumb, and she leapt back against Hamet's hard body as if she had been burned. The Saracen tightened his grip on her wrists, pulling them back so that her tingling breasts were thrust high against Aimery's sword-calloused palms. The Breton laughed scornfully. 'How these sweet little buds of desire swell and burn beneath your gown. Did you enjoy watching just now as your passionate lover Gilles suffered such exquisite torment? Wouldn't you have liked to join in, perhaps to crouch beneath him and take his long, throbbing penis in your soft little mouth? You are rather good at that, as I recall.'

Elena closed her eyes in despair as Aimery's powerful frame towered over her captive body. Dear God, but it was the Breton she longed for, even now that she knew the very depths of his deliberate cruelty. And he was well aware of her longing. That was why he had been so adamant that she accompany him here, to Morency, to inflict this final degradation, to destroy her utterly, just as he had sworn to destroy all Saxon women since Madelin had killed his brother and slashed his face with her sword. And scarred his bitter soul for life.

He knew her helpless need for him. With strong, purposeful fingers, as Isobel looked on with breathless glee, he ripped her gown apart. He palmed her small, high breasts as Hamet tightened his grip on her from behind, pushing the creamy mounds together, his cool fingers rubbing her burning teats to and fro. If it were not for Hamet holding her wrists so firmly behind her back, she would have fallen, such was the dizzying yearning that assailed her at his touch. She realised now that Aimery was intent on destroying her. But, oh, she wanted the Breton so much. She longed to feel his hard mouth on her lips and on her swollen breasts, soothing them with his kisses; she yearned to feel his magnificent shaft sliding up into her hungry sex, ravishing her tortured inner flesh with its powerful length until she soared into sweet release.

Isobel was watching all the time, her green eyes glittering as Aimery continued to slowly caress Elena's full, blue-veined breasts. 'Get someone to pleasure her now, my lord,' she whispered. 'See how aroused she is. She will be all wet and melting down below, and would take anyone, would even beg to feel a man's lusty cock up her – she would give us much entertainment in her degradation. We could summon one or two of your burly men-at-arms, and watch as they slowly ravished her. Oh, they would enjoy sliding their hard shafts up into her sweet Saxon flesh.'

Aimery said calmly, 'No. Perhaps we can try such tricks another day, Isobel. Tonight, I am feeling a little sated with your diversions.'

He was pulling almost tenderly at Elena's rosy crests as he talked. She gasped and bit her lip, feeling the sweet pleasure-pain spreading like fire from her breasts to her loins, gathering there in molten longing. Her sex lips were plump and slippery with her inner juices, longing for the love of Aimery, her lord. Her dark, cruelly treacherous lord.

Isobel pressed on urgently. 'Then let her watch you and me together, Aimery. See how excited she is, how she yearns for further stimulation. My lord, take your pleasure with me, here, while the Saxon wench watches. She will squirm in her longing, and burn with jealousy as she watches you ravish me openly. What greater torment could you devise for her?'

As she spoke, Isobel was pawing Aimery hungrily, her eyes glittering with lust. Elena could feel Hamet, whose burly body was pressed against her as he held her, breathing hotly on her neck in his excitement. She suddenly felt the surge of his aroused phallus as it nudged hungrily against the crease of her buttocks. She felt on fire with longing, as though a fever consumed her, swept along in this hot tide of debauchery that had engulfed her since she entered this secret room. Hamet was moving his hips silently, rubbing his huge erection against her; she thought of its thick, dark length, thought of it sliding into her own pulsing inner flesh, and shut her eyes, dizzy with shameful lust.

Isobel lifted her hands to Aimery's wide shoulders. Then, glancing triumphantly at the captive Elena, she reached up to kiss the Breton, driving her tongue deep into his mouth; Elena could see it, darting hungrily between his lips. In bitter despair, still Hamet's captive, Elena watched helplessly as Aimery took Isobel in his heavily-muscled arms, pressing her sinuous body close to his as their mouths joined voluptuously, running his strong hands over her hips, her waist, her breasts. Then he drew her with him towards the fur-covered couch beside the fire, still kissing her deeply. Lithe as a cat, Isobel dropped eagerly back on to it to face him, spreading her legs, her feet just touching the floor. Then she pulled up her long gown to her thighs, and smiled lazily at the Breton.

'Pleasure me, my lord,' she whispered silkily.

Elena cold see between her white-stockinged thighs, to where her pouting sex lips were spread wide beneath the furry covering of dark hair. Isobel saw her watching, and grinned as she ran her finger lewdly down her glistening crevice. Elena felt her own body arch despairingly against Hamet's hold as Aimery carefully positioned himself between Isobel's welcoming thighs and drew out his rampant phallus. Isobel made little moaning noises when she saw its pulsing length, and wriggled her hips towards him, like an animal on heat. Aimery steadied his heavy erection with his hand, positioning the blunt head at her juicy entrance, then drove it in deeply.

Isobel cried aloud, her face flushed with delight, and wrapped her supple calves around his narrow hips. To her torment, Elena could see it all, as Aimery's darkly powerful penis pleasured Isobel, ravishing her again and again with endless cool strength. Elena watched, tortured by her need, desperately aroused as her clitoris burned and throbbed. Oh, just one touch of that rigid shaft would send her into a despairing vortex of pleasure. She could hear Isobel's whimpers rising higher and higher as Aimery toyed with her, dipping his phallus into her just an inch or so, as she writhed and begged for more, driving her into realms of excruciating torment. 'Oh, God,' Isobel was moaning. 'Oh, my lord Aimery. Drive all of your hard cock into me, I beg you.'

Sweet heaven. Elena could not bear to watch, and yet she could not drag her eyes from the lewd sight of the Breton's massive phallus, driving so relentlessly in and out of Isobel's molten flesh. Isobel had torn apart her gown, and was thrusting her breasts at Aimery's face, demanding his mouth on them. Elena shuddered with despair, feeling her own juices running down her thighs.

Suddenly, she realised she was not alone in her torment. Hamet was behind her, still gripping her by her arms, but instead of watching the others, he was starting to kiss the nape of her neck with fierce, strong kisses, as his darting tongue stabbed hotly against her white skin. She moaned softly, and suddenly his hands were round her naked breasts, cupping them, soothing their agony, yet at the same time sending fresh shafts of longing down to her churning loins as she glanced down to see his strong black fingers squeezing the stems of her nipples. She closed her eyes. Her clitoris pulsed hotly. If she could not have Aimery, then she would have Hamet. She wanted him so badly that her loins were melting for him, her thighs sliding apart as he pressed his urgent erection repeatedly against her hips.

The big Saracen knew exactly what she needed. Still fondling her breasts deliciously with one skilful hand, he slowly bent her over, away from him, still supporting her with his other big hand that pinioned her wrists behind her back. And then, as she sank to her knees, she almost swooned with longing as she felt the hot, hard length of his stiffened penis pressing against the backs of her thighs. He kept her captive, supporting her easily with his incredible muscular strength, and then he swiftly pulled up her woollen gown, and his massive phallus, hard and hot and velvety, was dipping eagerly in the honeyed softness between her trembling legs.

Elena gasped with desire as his big hand caressed her hardened nipples. She was on the very brink as she felt his penis rub against her open vulva. And then, her longing changed to shock as she felt the blunt head of his shaft draw back suddenly, and nudge its way up the cleft of her bottom cheeks, and push stubbornly for entry at the forbidden little hole of her anus.

Dear God, no. She could not take him in. He was so big.

But his member was so smooth, so slippery, and he worked with such skill, that steadily he stretched her tiny entrance and sank himself into her, filling her loins with such rich, heavy pleasure that she thought she would die of it. Inch by inch he eased himself in through the tight ring of muscles, fondling her breasts all the while. And soon she could feel nothing but the burning, shameful delight of that delicious rod of dark flesh so firmly impaling her backside. She heard her own little whimpers of ecstasy as he pulled at her turgid nipples. She threw back her head, driving her buttocks against him, wanting more of him, loving the feel of his bulky testicles swaying against her tender bottom cheeks.

All the time, even in the midst of her dazed pleasure, she was feverishly aware of Aimery and Isobel moving together on the couch, bucking towards mutual release as Isobel ground her sinuous hips frantically against the Breton's pounding shaft. The sight of them together pierced her like a knife blade. But then Hamet was thrusting his mighty black rod hard and deep into her secret place; and she began to sob her way to her own rapturous climax as he reached round her body to stroke at the ridged cleft of her clitoris. The degrading pleasure engulfed her. She felt his cock pulsing hotly inside her as he spent himself lingeringly between her bottom cheeks. His penis still felt huge and hard as the last of the waves of bliss melted lingeringly through her pliant body.

At last, still supporting her with strong but tender hands, he withdrew himself. So many times, Elena had seen his stalwart weapon in play during Isobel's dark games. She had thought his penis frighteningly big, with its lengthy shaft and swollen, bulbous end. Now she knew that it offered blissful relief. But he was not Aimery.

Aimery and Isobel had turned, replete from their own lovemaking, to watch as Hamet sighed out his release. They were gazing at Elena with cold scorn, and Elena felt the last of her pleasure suddenly die away. Isobel was saying, as she ran her delicate hand possessively down Aimery's strong thigh,

'Well, my lord Aimery. It looks as if the dainty Saxon wench is prepared to enjoy our games after all. Who would have thought it? How fortunate that the ever-willing Hamet was here to ravish her itching flesh in such an obscene way. What would her husband Ralf say? Just think, he imagines her to be frigid.'

'He would probably enjoy watching,' drawled Aimery, leaning back relaxed on the couch. 'Hamet, you are insatiable and bestial.'

Hamet hung his head. 'My lord,' he whispered, 'you heard her cries of pleasure. She was every bit as eager as I.'

Elena, still on her knees with Hamet's hands gripping her wrists behind her, heard it all with burning shame. She wanted to cover her breasts, but was afraid that any move would bring yet more of Isobel's, and, worse, Aimery's, scorn upon her.

Isobel drank from her glass of wine and said suddenly to Aimery, 'You say that her husband would have enjoyed watching. Now, there's an idea. Ralf might be persuaded to join in our games. He could devise torments for his wife, and enjoy watching her. He has certain tendencies, lord Aimery, which I could exploit to the full.'

Aimery got up, putting Isobel's hand aside, and went towards the flagon of wine on the table by the door. 'I'm sure you could, Isobel,' he said, refilling his own goblet. 'But I'm a little bored with the Saxon girl. As I've said before, she is too insipid for my liking.'

Isobel tried to conceal the sudden smirk of pleasure that lit up her beautiful features. 'You are sure, my lord? She is an unexpected source of entertainment, you must admit. First Gilles, and now Hamet. Think of her perhaps taking your stalwart men-at-arms, one by one, or perhaps writhing around on the end of Pierre's mighty weapon. Oh, she enjoyed Hamet so much – how she would cry out in pleasure when she felt all of Pierre inside her.'

'No,' said Aimery. 'She's more trouble than she's worth. We will find other diversions, Isobel.'

'But my lord, you can't let her go,' said Isobel, her voice suddenly urgent. 'She knows, about your pact with Fulk of Anjou. If she were to talk, to tell your men about your strategy before you've had a chance to prime them fully about the rich rewards that await them in Fulk's service, then our plans will be ruined. You must silence her.'

Elena felt Aimery's cold grey eyes assessing her. They lingered on her flushed cheeks and naked breasts with such scorn that she felt icy cold in spite of the warmth of the firelit room.

She knew now that Aimery felt nothing for her. All he

wanted to do was destroy her; and she feared he was very close to his achievement of that task. And the name Isobel had mentioned – Pierre – sent shivers of unknown fear through her as she struggled to place it in her memory.

'Is it necessary to silence her?' Aimery said. 'She is of little importance, after all.'

'Yes, she must be silenced, or she'll tell everyone,' emphasized Isobel.

His mouth curled cynically. 'My dear Isobel, I don't think that any of my men would believe the story of my plan to join with Fulk anyway.'

'Oh, they will believe you, Aimery, when you command them to ride out and join Fulk of Anjou in defeating William's army,' breathed Isobel excitedly. 'When do you think the relief you sent for will arrive, my lord?'

'An army on the march travels fast. Another few days, perhaps.'

Isobel's green eyes glittered. 'We cannot afford to take any risks when our triumph is so close. You must do something with Elena for those few days, to keep her from talking.'

Aimery was tracing the rim of his goblet with his forefinger. Never once did he look at Elena, who was still bowed with shame. He spoke to Isobel at last.

'Put her in a secure chamber with a guard outside her door,' he said. 'We can tell everyone that she is ill again of a fever, and needs to be isolated. Sickness spreads with devastating speed through a besieged castle. The word must be put around that no-one, not even Ralf, can visit her, on pain of death, or the fever will infect others.'

'My lord, it shall be done,' said Isobel delightedly.

After that, Aimery and Isobel continued to talk in low, urgent voices, but Elena wasn't even listening any more. Hamet led her silently to a tiny cell in the base of the stone donjon, with a bare pallet on the floor, and a grating set high in the wall, just to allow her a glimpse of the sky. She lay on the pallet in despair after the heavy bolt had been drawn outside her door. Her body still trembled with desire. If she closed her eyes, she could see again the hateful but enthralling lovemaking of Isobel and Aimery.

Isobel had won. How had she ever thought that she, Elena, could defeat her? Not only was Aimery as cruel and calculating as she had feared in her darkest dreams, but he was also plotting terrible treachery against his liege lord, William of Normandy. Yet she still wanted him.

Suddenly, she heard the bolt drawing back, and the door began to open. Isobel glided in, with a tall man hovering behind her in the shadows. Elena sprang to her feet, her back pressed against the rough stone wall of her cell, her blue eyes wide with resistance.

Isobel said silkily, 'Poor Elena. Things are not going well for you, are they? Don't worry. I have brought you a good, loyal attendant to see to your every need. You remember him?'

The big young man moved forward, his hungry gaze darting all the time over Elena's frozen figure. And Elena remembered.

It was Pierre. Pierre had been Isobel's manservant at Thoresfield three years ago, eager to do his mistress's bidding in every way. And Pierre was the shadowy figure she had seen ravishing old Mathilde in her sick-room several nights ago, when she had begun to return to consciousness. No wonder he had seemed so ominously familiar. She had thought it was a bad dream. But he was here, now, gazing at her with hot brown eyes.

'Yes, Pierre will look after you well,' continued Isobel. 'But don't even think of trying to get a message out through Pierre to one of your friends, or even to your weak husband. As you may remember, my Pierre can hear every word you say – but he is dumb, dumb as the beasts of the field. Every secret is completely safe with him. Isn't it, Pierre?'

She turned to the man behind her, and ran her fingers sinuously up his powerfully built shoulders. He gazed at Isobel with longing.

'We have many secrets, Pierre and I,' said Isobel softly. 'He has been my servant for many years. You may also remember, Elena, that he is magnificently endowed; are you not, my fine Pierre?'

Pierre nodded eagerly, his handsome but curiously blank face flushed with excitement. Elena pressed herself back against the wall of the cell, her heart thudding. She said, 'Aimery would not permit this. He would not allow me to be attended by such a man.'

'My dear Elena, I have just spoken to Aimery, and he heartily agrees that Pierre should be your servant. He is most anxious, you see, that you should not spread any rumours about his anticipated allegiance with Fulk of Anjou – and Pierre is the only one in the castle we can trust. You can beguile him, plead with him, seduce him even.' She let her hand slide lightly over Pierre's groin, and grinned at Elena's gasp of horror. 'But this man will never betray either Aimery or myself, because he cannot speak. You will no doubt remember, though, that he has many other outstanding talents, which you might employ to pass the time.'

She fondled the hardening bulge beneath Pierre's tunic with thoughtful appreciation, and the man shuddered with delight, his big hands clenching into fists at his sides.

Elena whispered, 'I still do not believe that Aimery knows of this. You must let me speak to him.'

Isobel smiled sadly. 'Oh, my poor Elena. You still don't understand, do you? Aimery knows exactly how Pierre's presence will humiliate you; and that is what he wants. You see, he's not forgotten what you did to him in the forest, three summers ago. How you humiliated him in the company of those other Saxon girls; how you ravished him with a thick bone phallus while he was a bound, helpless captive in the hands of the outlaws. You remember it well, don't you? So does Aimery. That is why he had Gilles punished in that way, knowing how shamefully such forbidden pleasure degrades a man. Oh, Elena. How many times have I told you that he hates all Saxon women, and his life is dedicated to revenge? And just to make sure that there is no way you can escape, you will be chained up, by Pierre, every night.'

'No!'

'Yes. See to it, Pierre.'

Elena looked wildly around the stone walls of her little cell, but she knew that for her, this time, there was no escape.

Chapter Twelve

*F*or the fourth time that day, Henriette climbed the sunbaked ramparts that surrounded the donjon of Morency and gazed down at the encircling tents and pennants of Count Fulk's army. She was bored and unhappy, and she was frightened too. How long would this hateful siege go on? The sight of the threatening soldiers all around the castle, their weapons shimmering ominously in the midday heat, made her shiver. Even if Duke William sent aid, as they all seemed to think he would, there was no guarantee at all that Fulk of Anjou would actually be defeated.

She'd tried to see Aimery le Sabrenn several times to seek his reassurance. But she was always told, by Hamet or whoever else was on guard, that the Breton was busy with the defence of the castle, and had no time to see her. Henriette was beginning to wish that she'd never embarked on her impulsive scheme to follow Aimery and make him hers. She was certainly no nearer on in her task.

She left the open ramparts to return to her little room in the donjon and impatiently paced the floor, listening to the sounds of soldiers at sword practice in the courtyard below and wishing she had someone she could talk to. Apart from Isobel, there were no suitable companions for her here. She ate alone in her room. Even the lady Elena, whom she was wary of anyway since she suspected her of betraying her to Aimery that night at the monastery, was out of her reach. She was still ill, they said, and locked away somewhere private until she recovered fully from her fever.

Henriette almost felt fevered herself. It was so hot in here, without a breath of air, and she had to push the shutters back wide for any hint of coolness. Yet she knew she had no cause for complaint about her chamber. It was small, but luxuriously furnished, with tapestry hangings on the walls and a bed covered with furs. Isobel herself had brought Henriette armfuls of her own clothes to wear, and a silver-backed brush for her hair. Isobel's own maid, Alys, had been instructed to attend the young heiress assiduously. And considering that they were under siege, thought Henriette rather bitterly, there seemed to be no shortage whatsoever of luxuries. Wine and sweetmeats were brought regularly to her room whenever she asked for them, and there was plentiful water for bathing. There only seemed to be one thing she couldn't have – Aimery. And he was all she wanted.

Even Hamet seemed to be ignoring her lately. This upset her, because she'd thought that the big Saracen was her friend, and she'd thoroughly enjoyed the vigorous pleasuring he'd given her when he saw through her boy's disguise. She remembered now that he'd rebuked her strongly after the episode at the monastery, telling her that she was putting them all in danger with her wanton ways. She'd wanted to confide in him that it was Isobel who had instructed her to indulge in such games, but Isobel had sworn her to secrecy.

'Please!' Henriette had begged Isobel the other day as she'd passed her in the hot sun of the courtyard. 'I need your help. How can I make Aimery invite me to his bed?'

Isobel of Morency had looked at her almost scornfully. Henriette suddenly realised that Isobel's green eyes could be dangerous, almost cruel. 'My dear Henriette,' she said smoothly, 'nobody makes the lord Aimery do anything. Hadn't you realised that yet?'

Henriette said sulkily, 'Sometimes I almost think you gave me false advice, lady Isobel. I have done exactly as you said, by trying to behave in a wanton manner, and telling Aimery all of my adventures. But it doesn't seem to work. In fact, now, it seems that he doesn't want to see me at all.'

'Dear me,' said Isobel scornfully. 'Well, then. You will have to try harder, won't you? Now excuse me. I have many things to attend to.'

The trouble was that Henriette herself was thoroughly bored with her own behaviour. She was homesick for Rouen, for her doting family and her friends and the delicious gossip of the town. This castle, leagues from anywhere, was hateful – filled with noisy soldiers, and the clash of weapons, and heat, and dust. She'd tried to liven things up, by summoning a couple of young squires and a soldier or two to her room and ordering them to pleasure her. But they were swift and inexpert, with no thought for her satisfaction; and although she loved to fondle their virile bodies, and enjoyed the feel of their stout members pounding away between her thighs as much as ever, all in all she was beginning to find these episodes distinctly unsatisfying.

The last soldier she'd called up, a man called Daner, had been particularly unpleasant. She'd dressed herself with care in a gown of rich cream wool that clung enticingly to her curvaceous figure, and impressed upon him when he entered her room that she was Henriette of Sizerne, future bride of the lord Aimery himself. But he'd only laughed at her.

'So the lord Aimery's had enough of you, and now you're turning to the likes of me for some real satisfaction. Is that it, lass?' He grinned, starting to unfasten his leather breeches. 'Here, take a look at this stout fellow of mine, and you'll soon forget the lord Aimery.'

Henriette was trying hard not to look at his big, half-swollen penis, which he was swiftly rubbing to erection. 'No,' she retorted. 'You've got it wrong. I am to marry the lord Aimery – he loves me.'

'Oh, aye?' he jeered. 'And he permits you to copulate with the likes of me, a common soldier? Never. He'd kill me for this if you were really to be his bride. Let's have a look at your lovely titties, now.'

'I am to marry him!' Henriette stamped her foot. 'He doesn't mind me entertaining myself like this, while he is so busy with the siege.'

The soldier laughed, stroking the stiffened length of his purple phallus lovingly. 'Busy with the siege? Busy fucking the lady Isobel night and day, more like. Mind, I wouldn't object to a taste of that particular lady myself. Here, lass, touch this fine cock of mine, will you? See how it's ready for you.'

'*Isobel?*' Henriette had gone white. 'No. No, you lie.'

'I don't, lass. The things that go in that chamber of hers, I wouldn't like to guess at, though we've all heard whispers of it. That green-eyed lady Isobel, she plans all kinds of tasty treats for her lord's entertainment, though she makes sure it's always her with him at the end. Can't get enough of him, she can't. Soldiers on guard at the door have heard her gasping and moaning as he drives his lusty cock into her – begging for it, she is. Though all the wenches seem to go mad for the lord Aimery. Had a session with him yourself, have you, lass? Is that why you spread these stories about marrying him? Never mind. Try a taste of this instead. You won't be disappointed, I assure you.'

And Daner was moving slowly across the room

towards her, his heavily erect penis swaying. Henriette said through white lips,

'No. Get out, please. I don't want you in here. Leave me alone.'

The man froze. 'You're jesting, aren't you? You invite a soldier up here, tell him to get on with it, and then you turn on him and order him to go? No, my lady Henriette. That's not how we do things round here. Now, you let me pleasure you, nice and slow, and I'll make you forget your fine lord Aimery pretty quickly, I promise you.'

He was rubbing himself while he spoke to sustain his erection, stroking meaningfully at the swollen shaft of his penis. His eyes were dark, and burning with lust. Henriette backed away, folding her hands across her breasts as if he could see through her gown.

'I told you, I don't want you. It was a mistake. Please, please, just go.'

His eyes narrowed into angry slits. He stopped fondling himself. 'All right, I'll go,' he growled. 'I wouldn't want to do it with you now if you paid me. They call you all sorts of names down there in the barracks, lady Henriette. Did you know that? Well, I'll have a few choice names to add to them now.'

Shoving his dwindling penis back into his leather breeches, he glared at her scornfully and strode from the room. Henriette sank back into her chair. Aimery. Aimery and Isobel. Isobel had given her such detailed, lecherous instructions as to how to win Aimery's love; and all this time, she had wanted him for herself.

When Alys brought her food up to her some time later, she was openly startled when the lady Henriette didn't fall on it eagerly, as she usually did, but instead stayed sunk in her chair in the corner and waved Alys listlessly away.

'Take it back, please, Alys. I'm not hungry.'

Alys froze in astonishment. 'Not hungry? Are you ill, lady Henriette? Should I fetch you some physic? There's an old wise woman in the castle called Mathilde, who has many powerful preparations.'

'No!' Henriette almost snapped. Then, her voice quieter, nearly indiscernible, she said, 'I'm just not hungry. Leave me alone, please.'

A day or two later, Henriette was wandering listlessly around the castle yard, because there was nothing else to do. No point in even trying to see Aimery any more, because he was Isobel's property. She had been tricked. A searing wave of homesickness for her father's big house in Rouen shook her so hard that a big lump rose in her throat.

Here, nobody cared for her. They all wished she wasn't here, because she was an extra mouth to feed, an extra person to draw water for. And she wished she wasn't here as well. All around, the castle was packed with soldiers busy with their tasks in the heat of the sun: knights schooling their horses as best they could in the confined quarters of the courtyard; squires polishing precious armour as if their lives depended on it; the burly blacksmith and his assistants forging molten iron into blades and arrow heads with fierce monotony. Nowhere was there a friendly face.

Henriette wondered suddenly if the lady Elena had known about Isobel and Aimery. Once Elena had said to her, almost sadly, 'You are your own worst enemy, lady Henriette.' Again, Henriette wished she could talk to the gentle Saxon lady, but she was still ill of a fever, they said, and her mind was wandering.

Clusters of flies tormented the sweat-sheened horses, and the air seemed hot and stale. All around the ramparts, Aimery's bowmen watched with straining eyes, their bowshafts as brittle as their tempers. There were rumours that Count Fulk's men would attack soon, before the relieving army could appear. Henriette swallowed hard on her mounting fear. They were probably

211

waiting until Aimery's men, whom they outnumbered hugely, started to weaken with the strain of the siege, and then they would pounce on the beleaguered fortress. Fulk's soldiers would crash across the moat and through the thin wooden palisade, killing all the soldiers in their way. And then . . .

Before her fevered imagination could run riot with terror, she pulled herself up quickly, because she'd wandered inadvertently behind the barracks, where a couple of soldiers were lounging, rolling dice on the dusty floor of the courtyard. She turned quickly to head back to the main thoroughfare, but one of the men had seen her, and swiftly jumped in front of her, barring her path. He was grinning down at her with insolent familiarity, and she realised, with a sickening jolt, that it was Daner, the coarse-mouthed soldier she'd dismissed from her room the other day.

She pretended not to recognise him. 'Let me past, please,' she said, rather faintly, because she realised suddenly how very much alone she was here, between the high walls of the barracks, her exit at either end barred by these two soldiers. She could hear the second one coming up slowly from behind, his boots thudding on the beaten earth.

'Well, well,' said Daner. 'It's the lady Henriette. The little whore who decided I wasn't good enough for her, because she has designs on the lord Aimery herself. Changed your mind, have you, and come for a taste of me after all?'

Henriette's heart was thudding in panic, because Daner was big and muscular, and already she could see the straining bulge at his groin. 'Let me pass,' she pleaded, and sprang to avoid him, but the other man had caught her from behind, and was holding her easily in his strong soldier's grip. She could feel his hot breath on her cheek as he laughed in triumph.

212

'Here she is, Daner,' he said. 'All ready for you now, eh?'

Daner was advancing slowly. He reached out to paw at her breasts, feeling for the nipples, rubbing each one until the delicate erectile tissue stiffened and pressed at her bodice. 'Hungry as ever, eh, sweetheart?' he said slowly. 'Well, so am I.'

Henriette said, 'I'll scream if you don't let me go.'

'Oh, yes? And what will you tell anyone who should come? I told you, sweetheart. The soldiers have got names for you. They know you. They'll just think you're up to more of your little games.'

As Henriette stood transfixed, he pulled at her gown, ripping the fabric, and then let out a great, low sigh as he gazed at her naked breasts. Her dark brown nipples were puckering tightly as the fresh air touched them. 'Well,' he breathed. 'These beauties were worth waiting for. Kneel down, lass. Kneel, I say!'

The man behind her pressed her down firmly by her shoulders, and she sank to the ground, gazing up at Daner mutely as her breasts tingled and throbbed. Swiftly Daner pulled his penis from his breeches. It was already rampant. He bent forward, gripping it hard, and rubbed the velvety glans across Henriette's straining crests, one by one; a glistening tear oozed from its little mouth to fall on her breast, and his phallus slipped about in the moisture, pushing her teats slowly to and fro. Henriette gasped and closed her eyes as the lascivious pleasure of it burned through her.

'Enjoying this, lass, aren't you?' gritted Daner. 'Just another minute or so, and I'll slide myself into you nice and slow. Just as I told you, me and my friend Guillaume here will soon make you forget your fine lord Aimery. My friend's got a thick, sturdy cock too. Between us, we'll keep you happy all afternoon –'

Henriette, hot and frightened, sprang to her feet, knocking him out of the way. 'You're a gross, lecherous fool!' she cried out. 'Leave me alone. If you dare to follow me, I'll have you whipped, I swear it.'

She plunged for the way out before they could catch her, desperately pulling her torn gown across her breasts. They were stumbling after her, their faces red with anger. And then, someone else caught hold of her: someone big and strong, with a deep, familiar voice. 'You are in trouble, lady Henriette?'

She leant weakly against his heavily muscled chest. *Hamet*. Oh, she was so glad to see him. She saw his dark eyes quickly assessing her torn gown, her frightened face. Then he turned his attention on the two angry men who had frozen in their tracks.

'Daner. Guillaume,' he said with soft menace. 'If you have assaulted this lady, I will have you strapped to the ramparts and flogged.'

Guillaume hesitated. Everyone was wary of the lord Aimery's powerful Saracen servant. But Daner, his blood still raging with unslaked lust, retorted scornfully, 'Assaulted her? No need, when she constantly begs for it!'

Hamet's big fist connected with the man's jaw even before he had finished speaking. Daner toppled to the floor; Guillaume shrank back, stuttering,

'A mistake, lord Hamet, I assure you. We meant the lady no harm.'

'For your sakes, I hope so,' said Hamet softly. Then he drew the shivering Henriette into his arm, hiding her torn bodice, and led her across the courtyard and up to her room.

It was cooler up there, out of the glare of the sun. He closed the shutters, to keep out the noise of the yard below. Then he ordered wine, and held it to her lips as she trembled and shook on the corner of her bed.

'I shall command those men to be flogged anyway,' he said, standing above her.

She gazed up at him, her brown eyes wide and

haunted. 'No. It was – it was my fault. I'd summoned the one called Daner to my room. I was bored, and unhappy. But, oh, he was vile. And he told me that – that Aimery and Isobel are *lovers* –'

She began to tremble again. Hamet sat on the bed beside her and put his arm round her shoulders; she could feel the warmth of his strong body.

'You did not already know that?' he said slowly.

'No! I even asked Isobel for advice on how to gain Aimery's love. She told me to be as wanton as possible, to display myself to Aimery in every way –'

'*Isobel* did?'

'Yes. That is why I behaved as I did, at the monastery. Oh, I can see now that she was mocking me, laughing at me. How they must both be laughing, together.' She bowed her head in misery.

Hamet stroked her rich chestnut hair gently. 'The lord Aimery will not be laughing at you. He will have had nothing to do with Isobel's cruel trickery of you, believe me. But he and Isobel have been lovers for many years. She possesses, I think, the dark side of his soul.'

'Oh,' cried Henriette, the tears filling her eyes. 'How can I ever face him again? How can I ever face *anyone* again?'

Hamet said calmly, 'You will face them all with courage and spirit, as you have always done. Pretend that nothing has happened. Those soldiers know that any vile stories of theirs about you will earn them a harsh flogging. The castle is under siege. In a day or two, everyone will have too much on their minds to even think of lecherous gossip.'

Henriette turned to him. Her tears were drying on her cheeks, streaking her soft skin. 'You think Count Fulk will attack so soon?' she whispered, afraid.

He hesitated, his black eyes suddenly shadowed as if he was hiding something from her. 'I think that the lord

Aimery will be making preparations for battle. He expects action very shortly.'

She tried to keep her voice steady as she said, 'Do you think that Count Fulk will kill us all?'

'No,' he said. 'I do not think that.'

She was silent for a few moments, absorbing it. He continued to stroke her softly, where his hand lay across her shoulders. He said at last, 'Are you all right, my lady Henriette? I must assure you of my devotion at all times. Is there anything I can get you, anything I can do for you?'

Henriette lifted her tear-stained eyes to his dark ones, and suddenly her piquant face lit up in a familiar, lascivious grin.

'Yes,' she said. 'I'm feeling rather desperate for you, Hamet. If you don't take me now, as you did in that rain-soaked shed at that horrible monastery, I shall – I shall tell the lord Aimery that you make a habit of spying through his keyhole, just as you did that first night in Rouen, when I hid myself in the lord Aimery's bed.'

Hamet grinned, his even white teeth lighting up his face. 'He knows that already,' he breathed. And greedily he pushed Henriette back on to the bed and bent to kiss her.

Henriette had never really forgotten just how delicious Hamet's mighty cock was, but she was rather anxious to refresh her memory. He growled with desire as she urgently stripped him of his tunic and his breeches, running her fingers over his powerful smooth chest and fingering the black beads of his taut nipples. He closed his eyes and shuddered as she cupped the velvety bulk of his heavy testicles. Then she lowered her head reverently to the long, snaking thickness of his phallus, tasting its strength as it stirred and grew along his ebony thighs.

'Oh, Hamet,' she breathed as it stiffened into wonderful erection. 'How do you like it best? What would you like me to do, most of all?'

216

His black eyes were brilliant with lust as he breathed, 'I want you to ride me, lady. Sit yourself astride me, facing me, and then I can play with your wonderful breasts as you lower yourself on to me.'

Happily she scrambled astride him, her tears all gone now, her face flushed and radiant. She threw her torn gown to the floor, so she was dressed just in her flimsy chemise and silken hose; her heavy breasts bobbed free as she bent over the Saracen, her brown nipples already stiffly erect. Swiftly she pulled up her skirt and splayed her thighs across his loins, so Hamet could see the ripe gleam of her pulsing sex beneath the curling chestnut hair. Henriette gazed lustfully at his rearing black cock. It was thick and rigid, its underside gnarled with veins, and his balls were big, dusky globes at its base.

'I can't believe,' she breathed, 'that I will ever get that massive creature inside me.'

He smiled, serenely relaxed, but she could see a pulse of excitement stirring in his strong throat. 'You will,' he said. 'You've managed it before. Lick it first, then ease it into yourself a little at a time.'

Obediently she did as he said, and Hamet's face tightened with bliss as she sucked the juicy end of his thick penis.

'Now,' he breathed. 'Lift yourself over me, push yourself down.'

She lifted herself as he said, her eyes narrowed with concentration, and she unfurled her own swollen sex folds with her fingers, shuddering as the exquisite sensations gathered in her loins. Then she gripped his glistening shaft, and glided its bulbous tip cautiously into her vagina. As she sank on to the first inch, feeling its girth stretching her deliciously, her eyes opened very wide.

'Oh, God,' she whispered. 'Dear God, I must have more of that.'

Steadily, lifting and lowering her quivering hips, she

impaled herself on more and more of his mighty black penis. Hamet gazed entranced at her voluptuous creamy flesh, pulling and teasing with his big hands at her straining nipples. At last, she felt all of him inside her, throbbing away, filling her. Hamet began to thrust powerfully, unable to hold back; his thick cock ground against the soaking cleft where her clitoris protruded, dragging and pulling at it deliciously; she tugged urgently at her own nipples, rising and falling in passion on that glistening dark shaft, delirious with pleasure as it pounded into her.

'Dear God, Hamet,' she breathed. 'Keep on. Fuck me, oh fuck me . . .'

She pulled herself up from him, almost to his very extremity, so she could see his dusky black member penetrating her swollen vulva. And then she saw his broad black brow beading with sweat, and he was thrusting up into her dementedly as she clutched with her inner muscles at that shiny black thickness. Then she was over the brink, washed in wave after wave of ecstatic, melting pleasure. And the Saracen was at his extremity too, pounding into her, his lengthy penis spasming and leaping at her very heart, on and on, as he poured his copious rapture into her.

She sank at last on to his broad chest, sighing with happiness as his burly arms folded around her, his hands still caressing her voluptuous breasts. Hamet was not Aimery. But perhaps her feelings towards the lord Aimery had cooled somewhat. She wasn't at all sure she wanted to marry him now, if he was going to make a fool of her with the likes of the cruel, beautiful Isobel de Morency.

She sighed regretfully against Hamet's broad shoulder. Who was she trying to fool? She'd have the Breton now, if he was interested in her. He was easily the most attractive, most tantalising male she'd ever met in her life, and clearly she wasn't alone in her infatuation with him. But he wasn't interested in her, whereas Hamet clearly was. As she rubbed her naked legs comfortably along the Saracen's brawny black thighs, she could feel the silky thickness of his phallus, plainly ready to surge into life again at the slightest encouragement. She sighed again, with happiness this time.

Hamet was stroking her luxuriant hair. 'Are you all right, lady Henriette?'

'Much, much better,' she whispered, snuggling against him. 'But Hamet, I'm still afraid. What if Count Fulk's soldiers attack us in the night, and kill us all? There are so many of them, and Aimery's soldiers are so few.'

'They won't take Morency,' he said.

He spoke with such certainty that Henriette was startled. 'How can you be so sure?'

Hamet hesitated, and Henriette knew then that he was keeping something from her. At last he said, 'Because the lord Aimery knows exactly what he is doing. You must trust him.'

Henriette frowned at the mention of Aimery, still torn between desire and resentment. 'I thought he was too busy bedding Isobel to be thinking of our safety,' she said rather petulantly.

Hamet's grip on her tightened. 'Oh, no. Do not underestimate him,' he said.

Henriette still sulked, but then she felt the nudging of Hamet's freshly stirring phallus against her legs, and she sighed happily, readying herself for more.

It was late afternoon, and Ralf was polishing his sword in the relative coolness of the armoury when Isobel came in. He breathed her scent first, then he turned and saw her, outlined in the doorway against the bright sun. As ever, her beauty made his loins tighten with longing.

'Preparing for battle, my lord Ralf?' she enquired silkily.

'Of course,' he replied, somewhat shortly, because the

thought of the inevitable bloodshed made his stomach churn with fear. He wiped the sweat from his forehead with the back of his hand, and put down the soft leather cloth he'd been using on his sword. 'It cannot be long now. Fulk is bound to attack before the relieving army has time to arrive. And then what chance will we stand?'

'You sound,' she said, drawing closer to him, 'as if you wish you had never come to Morency.'

He stared at her, entranced as ever by her slanting green eyes. Even in this cursed, fly-ridden heat, she looked cool and unattainable in a clinging gown of dark rose silk, her hair covered by a fine veil. 'Oh, never that, my lady,' he breathed. 'How could I regret it?'

She turned her back on him teasingly, pretending to examine a coat of tarnished chain mail that some knight had left for his squire to burnish. 'Your wife, I think, might disagree,' she said softly.

Ralph put down his sword and ran his hand tiredly through his sweat-streaked blond hair. His wife. He felt guilty about her, and angry with her as well, because he didn't enjoy being made to feel guilty. He'd been told that in her weak state after her injury, she'd succumbed to a contagious fever, and needed to be tended in isolation to prevent it spreading. He was happy not to visit her. He couldn't bear any kind of sickness. 'Ah, yes. Elena,' he said stiffly. 'How is she? I trust she is recovering from her fever. I was told that not even I was allowed to visit her, in case the sickness spread.'

'Your wife is perfectly well, Ralf,' said Isobel softly. 'But she is being kept locked away at the lord Aimery's command, because she is making a nuisance of herself.'

Ralf froze. 'What did you say?'

'She isn't really ill, Ralf. But it seemed best, all things considered, to keep her in complete isolation.'

Ralf went white. 'Explain.'

'Oh, Ralf.' Isobel's exquisite face was full of pity. 'You had no idea, did you? Your innocent-looking wife has been cuckolding you with the lord Aimery. Several times, since they were reunited at Rouen, she has run to him in the night, panting with lust, and enticed him into her arms.'

Ralf felt the perspiration trickle from his armpits, dampening the long linen shirt he wore under his armour. 'Elena and Aimery. No.' He laughed shortly. 'This must be a jest. My wife is not interested in such sports, believe me.'

'Oh, she is, Ralf, I'm afraid. She's enjoyed herself with Aimery, and the young squire Gilles, and the formidable Hamet. Who knows who else? But don't worry – ' she put out a restraining hand as Ralf reached for his sword – 'she is being dealt with. Your best policy is to go along with Aimery's ploy that she is ill. Later, when all this is over, you can disown her completely. You do not want everyone to know that the lord Aimery was the young mercenary who first seduced her from her convent, and taught her the mysteries of love, do you?'

Aimery. Aimery and Elena . . .

Suddenly, for Ralf, it all fell sickeningly into place. His wife's avoidance, almost fear, of the Breton on his arrival in Rouen. The way Ralf had caught the two of them occasionally, talking in low, urgent voices, only to fall silent when he appeared. His helpless anger raged. He thought of challenging the Breton, but then remembered Aimery's prowess with the sword, and changed his mind. His anger transferred itself to Elena.

'The little slut,' he breathed. 'So it was Aimery, was it, who took her from the convent? How dare she make a fool of me? I'll have her beaten. I'll get rid of her, banish her to some convent where there are no men to satisfy her lustful cravings.'

'No.' Isobel put her hand on his arm, and her touch was cool and wildly enticing. 'Calm yourself. You can do nothing yet. We are all trapped in here together. Leave her be. She is suffering punishment enough, shut away as she is in seclusion. Put her from your mind for the moment. Come to my room later, lord Ralf, to take wine with me, and I will make you forget her.'

Ralf was still shaken and upset. 'No,' he said sulkily. 'Last time you tricked me with Alys. And anyway, I don't understand. There is all this wine, and apparently plentiful supplies of fresh food, even though we are under siege. No-one seems at all worried that Fulk of Anjou might attack us any day, any hour. Why doesn't Fulk attack? Why aren't you afraid of him?'

She put a finger to his lips, to silence him. 'Ah, sweet Ralf. You ask too many questions.' She pulled his head down, and kissed him. She tasted sweet and fragrant, and his loins tightened as her moist little tongue slid between his lips, teasing and tantalising. She pulled away at last.

'Soon, you'll get your reward,' she murmured. 'Very soon.'

Then, before the stunned Ralf could say anything, she glided out, her silk gown rustling on the cobbles, leaving him entranced. He imagined her sinking to her knees before him and caressing his hard cock, sucking its stiff length sweetly with her lips and tongue and eagerly swallowing his spurting seed.

He made his way quickly across the crowded court-yard towards the relative coolness of the disused granary, where the women gathered. These were the women who were half kitchen serfs, half sluts; some of them had accompanied Aimery's convoy, and worked hard for their keep. By day they laboured in the kitchens, scrubbing pots and tending ovens; they drew water from the precious well, and washed clothes, and swept out the soiled rushes from the main chamber. But their main business was to keep the soldiers happy, and after nightfall there was a steady stream of visitors to these secluded quarters.

Ralf found that some of the doxies were there already,

avoiding the keen eye of the steward, preparing themselves for a busy evening's trade on this hot, oppressive night. He found a dark-eyed woman with black hair like Isobel's, and led her just outside, to where the drop of the overhanging eaves gave them some privacy. He was in a hurry. Quickly he pulled up her ragged skirts and pressed her against the wall. She gasped and sighed as he sank his hard penis into her splayed wetness, murmuring, 'Such a mighty weapon, my lord. Oh, let me feel all of it inside me...' Ralf gritted his teeth against the impending pleasure and thrust hard, again and again, as his juices spilled from his body. He pulled out at last, panting with exertion, and the woman grinned and smoothed down her dishevelled skirts. 'Your denier, my lord?'

Ralf was just handing the coin to her, and wiping the sweat from his face, when he heard a sound that made his blood freeze in his veins. The sound of a distant trumpet, calling from afar through the sultry air. The alarm, the call to battle.

A moment of stunned silence seemed to hold the whole castle in its grip. Then suddenly, men were running everywhere, shouting, barking orders, calling to the squires for their weapons. Ralf felt quite sick. Fulk must be attacking. There was no way their small force would hold him off. They would all be slaughtered. There was nowhere to run.

A soldier he knew came hurrying past, the sweat running down his face in the suffocating heat. He stopped when he caught sight of Ralf standing there with the flushed doxy, and called out with glee, 'Plenty of time to finish your swiving, Ralf. The lookout on the tower has just spotted Duke William's army approaching from the north, a good league hence, led by the Count of Evreux. Just in time to take up their positions and set up camp before darkness falls – then, they say, we will join battle at dawn. By tomorrow, this cursed siege will be over.'

Ralf, wishing that he felt half as confident, thought of sharp blades, and blood, and pain. He swallowed the sudden bile from his throat, and went slowly to fetch his armour.

Chapter Thirteen

*E*lena was lying curled on the straw-filled palliasse in her tiny, airless cell when she heard the sudden sounds of shouting outside, accompanied by the shrill braying of the war horn from the ramparts. She pulled herself quickly to her feet and ran to the high, barred window. If she clung to the ledge, she could just see a corner of the courtyard, where it was confined by the timber palisade. Men were running past, calling out to one another; horses whinnied in the stables, and there was the jangle of armour as swords and shields were fetched from the donjon. She clasped the bars, knowing that one way or another, her imprisonment would soon be over. And what then?

She heard the heavy bolt being drawn back, and Pierre came in, bearing food and water. She whirled round to face him, her back to the wall.

'Fulk of Anjou is attacking the castle?' she rapped out sharply.

Pierre shook his head, never taking his eyes from her ragged figure as he put down the plate of cold food and the jug of water.

'Then – William's army is on its way?'

He nodded, carefully pouring some water into her beaker, and Elena leant back against the rough stone, knowing only too well what this must mean.

The army sent by Duke William of Normandy to relieve the siege of Morency must have been glimpsed in the distance. It was almost dusk now, too dark to fight, even if they were ready to after their long march. So tomorrow, at first light, she guessed, the battle would begin. Aimery would gather his loyal followers in the courtyard and tell them, at the last minute, that they were to ride out to join with Fulk of Anjou, and turn on the army that had come to their aid.

She still could not believe that it would really happen. But nor could she forget that terrible night in Isobel's room, when Isobel had told her all about the proposed treachery, and Aimery, watching Elena with cold scorn, had not troubled to deny it.

Her own vile imprisonment was proof enough of their base plan. For she was the only person in the castle – other than Isobel and Aimery, and Hamet – who knew of what they plotted. That was why she was locked away in here, with no-one but the dumb serf Pierre to attend to her. She'd thought, briefly, that Ralf might make enquiries and somehow come to her aid, but quickly dismissed the foolish hope.

Pierre was coming towards her now, holding out the chains. Every night, he secured her in them according to Isobel's instructions, his big hands trembling as they brushed against her captive flesh. That first night, she had recoiled from him with horror, refusing to submit to such degradation. But then Isobel, watching, had said coolly, 'Suit yourself, Elena. If you will not permit Pierre to secure you here, in the privacy of your cell, then I will have you shackled publicly in the courtyard, where everyone can watch your shame.'

Elena, knowing only too well that Isobel would carry out her threat with the greatest pleasure, submitted then to Pierre, trembling involuntarily as the big serf fastened the leather shackles to her wrists before securing her to the wall by the long iron chain that was looped between them.

She was frightened of Pierre. He had been Isobel's minion at Thoresfield, and she knew that Isobel employed him in many of her dark games. But he seemed to be under some kind of stern command from Isobel, and it soon became apparent that he would not dare to touch Elena any more than necessity ordained.

He had almost finished his task now. Moistening his fleshy lips with his big tongue, he fastened the long chain to the iron ring set high in the wall. She could see the bulge at his groin, betraying his simmering excitement at her helplessness, and she remembered suddenly how she had seen him ravishing the old crone Mathilde, remembered the size and strength of his gnarled penis as it plunged deep between the woman's thighs. She felt her throbbing clitoris strain agonisingly, and her juices gathered and seeped from her loins. Dear God, but her thoughts were shameful. Isobel knew exactly what she was doing, to imprison her thus. And so did Aimery. Did he too take pleasure in her exquisite humiliation?

At the thought of Aimery, a pang of searing longing knifed through her tethered body. She closed her eyes in anguish. Pierre, with one final, lingering look, turned at last to go, and she heard the heavy fall of his footsteps, the thudding of the door. Then she heard the bolt scraping across.

Her chains gave her room to move, to lie down, even to walk across to the window. But that was all. She sank to her knees on her straw pallet, her tethered hands resting in her lap. Gazing up at the high barred window, she saw that it was almost dark outside. But she could still hear the sounds of preparation in the courtyard outside: the muffled orders of the sergeants, the soft jangle of armour, the whickering of restless horses.

Tomorrow, it would all be over. The battle would be fought. Morency would be in the hands of Fulk of Anjou. Isobel and Aimery would be triumphant in their treachery. She did not dare to even think what would happen to her then.

Exhausted with thinking, she lay down on her pallet, struggling to make herself comfortable as the leather shackles tightened around her wrists. For a moment, she wondered what would happen if Aimery's men defied his orders the next morning, and refused to obey his command to join with Count Fulk. But reality replaced hope. She knew that the steward, Hugh de Brosny, would do whatever Isobel commanded. And most of the soldiers in Aimery's company, like Aimery himself, sold their swords to the highest bidder. His knights were gathered from all parts: Poitou; Maine; Gascony; Flanders. They would be just as happy to serve Fulk of Anjou as Normandy, provided they were rewarded with sufficient land and riches.

Yet there must be some men here who were still loyal to their liege lord, Duke William. There must be! Oh, if only she could speak to Gilles. He had seen what Isobel and Aimery were capable of. He would believe her story; he would rally those who would refuse to obey Aimery's terrible orders. She had to get out of here, before dawn brought the terrible battle. She had to.

She stumbled to her feet and tried the door again with her pitifully tethered hands, knowing it would be heavily bolted on the outside. She sagged back, crouching on her pallet. She was trapped like an animal here. And it seemed to grow hotter, not cooler, as darkness fell; the close air stifled her. Outside, she could hear the low, steady sounds of armourers at work by the light of gleaming lanterns. She thought, too, that she heard the ominous rumble of approaching thunder curling around the beleaguered castle.

She lay on the pallet, the leather straps tormenting her.

She moved to ease herself, and realised how desperately aroused she was. The moisture trickled between her puffy labia, and her breasts ached, while her nipples were like burning brands as they thrust hungrily against her bodice.

Aimery had willed this torment for her. She had thought, in her innocence, that he had forgiven her for his grim imprisonment three summers ago in the forest, when she had lived with the Saxon rebels and joined in, with apparent willingness, to rouse and humiliate his magnificent body. She had ravished him, as Isobel reminded her, with the thick bone phallus offered to her by one of the gleeful Saxon girls, and had driven it into his tethered body as he groaned with despair. She shut her eyes desperately as she remembered the feel of his tight anus gripping at the bone shaft. Her own pleasure had been excruciating as she stroked its thick length in and out, deep within him, until his narrow hips clenched so hard that he almost pulled it from her grip, and he spurted hotly, shamefully on to the leafy floor of the forest.

She had told him the truth of it afterwards, that she had pretended to be with the rebels in order to secure his escape. But she could not deny the voracious excitement that had gripped her own secret flesh at seeing his degradation. He had not forgotten it either, apparently, nor had he forgiven. Instead he had told Isobel about it, and she had connived at this subtle, hateful revenge.

But dear God, she still loved the Breton, still wanted him. She would never be free of his dark, brutal hold on her soul. In a torment of despair, Elena arched her hips and stroked the heated ridge of her clitoris with her tethered hands, imagining Aimery's strong penis pressing against her vulva. She imagined him finding her lush entrance and driving the long, thick shaft deep within her, over and over, as his hot mouth fastened round her burning breasts.

She groaned aloud as the silken walls of her passage clenched and throbbed around emptiness, caressing herself into an excruciating, silent climax.

Her body wet with perspiration, she lay there listening as the muffled sounds of preparation for battle continued in the courtyard outside. She knew that Isobel and Aimery would never let her go, even after all this was over. She had to escape. She had to warn someone of Aimery's treachery before the attack, or she would be their prisoner for ever.

She tossed and turned on her pallet all through the hot summer night, her sweat-sheened body in a torment of arousal as she heard the thunder rumbling ominously closer. Slowly, she forced herself to accept that there was only one person who could possibly help her to escape from this hateful cell.

And that person was Pierre.

That night, Isobel too could not sleep. Tomorrow, Aimery would be hers, bound to her for ever by mutual ties of treachery, stronger by far than any vow of loyalty.

During the last few days, Aimery had come rarely to her luxurious chamber, and that disappointed her. But when he did, it was wonderful. Admittedly, he'd visited her only briefly, and not indulged in the exquisite feasts of pleasure she'd hoped for. But she knew that he was busy, abstracted with his plans, keeping a tight rein on his men – who could easily simmer into insurrection within the confines of a summer siege such as this – and preparing them for the forthcoming battle.

They did not know yet, of course, that they would be fighting the army from Normandy, not Fulk. Isobel had wanted Aimery to warn them earlier, and explain the rewards that were on offer, but he refused. He insisted that an element of surprise was essential. 'If we give them time to brood on it,' he said, 'they might ask for more money. And it would give any troublemakers plenty of time to stir up dissent.' He told her that he would inform them at just the right time, when battle was imminent. Isobel agreed. The offer of a purse of gold and a good war horse to each knight, paid for by Fulk, should steer their battle-heated ardour in just the right direction.

And the battle was imminent at last. Isobel's blood tingled in her veins at the thought. Tomorrow, at dawn, she would be able to see the fruition of all her scheming. Then Aimery, the victor, would be all hers.

She was growing tired of waiting by herself, night after night, in her chamber. She imagined some pleasurable diversions, involving her favourite girls, and perhaps Pierre, who was in a perpetual state of arousal over Elena. Isobel grinned. She hadn't told Aimery about Pierre, or about the chains that secured the Saxon girl during the hours of darkness. But then, he hadn't asked.

Isobel still worried, just a little bit, about Elena. The Saxon girl had an undeniable hold over Aimery. What should she do with her after tomorrow? It was no good just sending her away: she knew too much. Perhaps Isobel should arrange for her somehow to be debauched in public. There would be much feasting and licentiousness after the forthcoming battle, and Elena was deliciously wanton beneath that virginal facade. Perhaps Isobel should arrange for a few stout soldiers to ravish her heated body, and ensure that she was grovelling for them desperately. That would put Aimery off her for good.

Pleased and pleasantly aroused at the thought of the virginal Saxon girl giving pleasure to four, perhaps five rampant men, using her mouth and fingers as well as her body, Isobel wandered out into the courtyard to find Aimery.

There was a storm coming. It was still unbearably hot, but there was a curious sense of expectancy in the night air, and she could see lightning flickering in the distance, on the western horizon, vivid against the blackness of the heavy sky. The castle itself was in a tight, dangerous state of expectancy. Even at this hour, long after compline, the blacksmith was still labouring, his burly torso gleaming with sweat as he hammered lance tips over the glowing furnace. Armourers were counting swords, and arranging for shields to be mended by the light of flickering lanterns. Those soldiers who weren't on watch had been told to rest, but rest was impossible on this night. They gathered in corners, tense with excitement in the hot night air, talking in low voices or rolling dice absently to pass the time.

She wondered, briefly, where Ralf was. He was probably inside, drinking himself senseless in some doxy's arms to drown his fear. She dismissed him with a scornful smile. What about Henriette? She was more of a puzzle, that one. She seemed calmer, quieter, as if she'd given up at last on Aimery. Isobel had seen her the other afternoon playing chess with Hamet in the shade, laughing like a happy child as the big Saracen let her win. Did she let him swive her? Longing to find out, she'd sent Alys to spy on them. Alys had come back shortly afterwards, her ugly face flushed with arousal, to tell Isobel that they were together in an empty barn. Isobel had rushed to see them, and was just in time to glimpse Hamet's huge, glistening penis rising and sinking between Henriette's open thighs as the young heiress gasped and moaned in pleasure. This wasn't the first time they'd coupled, judging by the way Henriette shuddered out her crisis, then familiarly pulled Hamet's incredibly erect cock out from her body and towards her naked breasts. Isobel watched dry-mouthed as the girl milked his huge shaft with loving fingers until his juices poured out over her stiffened brown teats, rubbing the twitching glans across them with sighs of pleasure as her orgasm lingered on and on.

Isobel felt a stirring of acute envy, but was distracted

and displeased by Alys's sulkiness. The woman was worse than ever, since that beating she'd given her on the journey here. If Alys wasn't so useful – so inquisitive, always knowing about things like *this* – Isobel would have got rid of her years ago.

Hamet, she saw, was down in the lantern-lit courtyard now, busy about more serious business. He was talking to one of the sergeants, and she saw his dark face gleaming in the flickering light as he gesticulated earnestly. Discussing tactics for the morning, no doubt. She watched him approvingly. He and Aimery had certainly kept up an excellent pretence of resistance to Fulk, and now their apparent preparations for sallying forth to attack the Count of Anjou and join Normandy's men were excellently done. No-one would suspect for one moment what was really going to happen.

Smiling to herself, she mounted the steps to the planked walkway that ran around the inner girth of the ramparts, and gazed out into the breathless darkness. It was no fresher up here – there was not a hint of cooling air. But a storm was coming. She could hear the distant rumble of thunder now, and the eerie lightning was playing over the forest that stretched all around.

Duke William's army had encamped at the edge of the forest. Aimery had studied the distant pennants as dusk fell, his keen grey eyes narrowing as he assessed the drooping emblems. 'The Count of Evreux leads them,' he said quietly. 'A seasoned warrior. The Duke of Normandy is taking no chances.'

Isobel had caught her breath. 'But you – together with Fulk – will beat this Count of Evreux?'

He gazed down at her. 'Apart from Bavinchove, I have never been beaten,' he said.

Isobel had sighed happily.

From the ramparts, she gazed down now at the ring of Fulk's army that still surrounded them in outward menace. She could just make out the dim shapes of the tents clustered beyond the flat meadows that immediately encircled the castle. Lanterns twinkled, and she could see the shadowy shapes of men, still awake, still alert. Like Aimery, and the Count of Evreux, Fulk would not indulge in sleep either that night – of that she was sure. He was a wily fox, like his friend and ally, Philip of France. He would be discussing tactics with his commanders, planning how best to destroy Evreux's army when Aimery le Sabrenn and his horsemen rode out to join the army of Anjou.

The loss of Morency to Anjou would be a grave blow for Duke William. Morency itself was not of great importance, but the ignominious defeat, the open treachery from within his own ranks, would be a severe setback to Normandy's duke in his constant battle against his neighbouring rivals.

The thought of what tomorrow would bring made Isobel's skin tingle with excitement. A little pulse of desire was throbbing deep in her loins. Dear God, but she wanted Aimery. She knew, from the way the soldiers on watch cast their eyes longingly at her slender figure as she stood there on the ramparts, that she was as vibrantly lovely as ever. She would have the Breton, and soon.

Suddenly she saw him down in the courtyard, talking to Hamet. His tall, commanding figure was unmistakable. She saw, with a pang of excitement, that he was already clad in the chain-mail hauberk that clung so sinuously to his magnificent physique, though he was not yet wearing his helmet. His thick hair with its distinctive russet colour gleamed in the lantern light; his chiselled features seemed stern and harsh as he spoke in a low voice to his Saracen servant. Isobel felt her pliant body melt in longing for him. There would never be anyone but the Breton for her. To have come so close to losing him in the past merely heightened the delicious victory of making him hers again, for good. After tomorrow, they would not be parted.

Glancing up as if aware of the longing in her gaze, he saw her alone on the ramparts. He moved towards her, taking the stairs with long strides, his hauberk rippling across his wide shoulders. Her pulse raced as he drew near her in the darkness. Lightning flickered close by, accompanied by a low growl of thunder, and she saw the white ridge of his terrible scar, the steely gleam of his silver-grey eyes.

'Isobel,' he said. 'You should be resting.'

'I could not sleep,' she said huskily. 'I want to be with you, my lord. You have sent someone out secretly to Fulk, to give him details of your plans?'

'Yes,' he said. 'I have sent Ralf. He slipped over the palisade while the watch was being changed. He will stay there overnight. It's too risky for us to attempt to get him back inside here again.'

Isobel laughed. 'At last someone has found a use for him,' she said. 'He must have been most surprised to learn of your secret plans, my lord.'

'I told him there was a fine reward in it for him. And I think he was glad to get away from here. Presumably he thinks he will stand more chance of survival, surrounded by Fulk's army. If the day goes well, he might not even have to lift his sword.'

She stretched out one hand to touch his shoulders, loving the feel of the cold metal rings that protected the hard, muscled warmth of his body. 'Of course the day will go well. Oh, Aimery. Take me. Take me, now.'

She could not see his face in the shadows, but she could hear his slow, steady breathing. 'I must be with my men during the night watch,' he said. 'There is much to prepare before dawn.'

'But surely, you are confident enough of victory?' She pouted, lifting her hand to stroke his lean jaw. The sight of him in his armour always excited her, reminding her of his power over other men, his ruthlessness and strength.

'Oh, yes,' the Breton said. 'I am confident.'

'Then we have plenty of time, my lord. For – *this*.'

She dropped to her knees in one supple movement, and reached beneath his long hauberk to run her hands up his knee-high deerskin boots to stroke at the smooth linen breeches that clung to his powerfully muscled thighs. She felt him tense and go still as she found the opening at his loins, and ran her palms with mounting excitement over the heavy, somnolent length of his penis. It began to stir thickly beneath her fingers. Above her, Aimery rasped, 'Isobel. I must go.'

'Of course,' she murmured, her hands still working busily. 'Whatever you say, my lord.'

Then she heard him gasp for breath between his gritted teeth, and she felt his strong fingers bite suddenly into her thinly clad shoulders as she stuck out her tongue and began to lick along the swelling shaft of his phallus. As it grew inexorably, she gripped it in one velvety hand and leant forward to take his heavy testicles in her mouth, sucking at the rough, hair-covered globes one by one, circling the coarse flesh with her darting tongue. She could hear him breathing harshly above her, his strong thigh muscles bracing against the delicious torment.

In one smooth movement, she took the whole of his rigid member into her mouth. Still gripping her shoulders tightly, he began to pump himself into her, his velvety glans rhythmically stroking the back of her throat. Feverish with excitement, Isobel cupped his tightening scrotum with her hand and swirled her tongue eagerly round his thick, veined shaft. He tasted salty and hot. Ah, he would not take long. Her power over the Breton was still great. Dizzy with triumph, she ran her moist, encircling mouth hungrily up and down the stunning length of his throbbing penis. He went very still for a moment, then began to thrust hard, pouring the hot, salty liquid down her welcoming throat. She swallowed eagerly, her tongue coiling round his pulsing shaft. He spurted again and again, his powerful body quite rigid with the force of his emission.

At last, he was finished. His grip on her shoulders slackened, but she could still hear his strenuous breathing as he recovered from his climax.

She licked the long, softening shaft of his velvety phallus tenderly one last time. Then she got slowly to her feet, her eyes like a cat's, emerald slits in the heavy darkness. Her lips were still moist with his copious seed. Across the distant forest, the thunder rolled nearer, and the lightning split the night sky. She rose to her feet and gazed up at the Breton, as sated as if he had spent himself in her body.

'My lord,' she whispered, lifting her slender, jewelled hands up to his strong shoulders. 'After tomorrow, nothing will part us.'

She still could not see his face properly in the darkness, and that disappointed her. But she knew that after tomorrow, she would be able to gaze on him to her heart's content.

He put his hands lightly round her narrow waist. 'Isobel,' he said, his eyes a strange silvery-black in the shadow of his face. 'One thing you did not tell me. If I had refused to join in with this plan of yours and Fulk's, what would have happened to me?'

She laughed, because, after all, what did it matter now if he knew everything of the cynical bargain she had made with the scheming Count of Anjou? 'If you had refused,' she said silkily as she fingered the taut muscles of his upper arms, 'Fulk would have attacked Morency weeks ago, of course, and taken it easily. He would have been forced to kill or imprison all of your men – though you yourself, of course, would have been held safe, and open to offers of ransom, or other negotiations. So it is fortunate, my lord, that you agreed to the plan.'

'Indeed it is,' he replied evenly.

Down in the courtyard below, a troop of foot soldiers were being marshalled to the commands of a tense sergeant at arms. It was time for the changing of the watch – the last watch before dawn. Smoking pine torches had been set in brackets around the donjon's ward, casting flickering shadows across the soldiers' tense, expectant faces. Aimery said, 'Forgive me, my lady, but now I must go.'

Isobel watched him descend purposefully to the yard to speak to his soldiers, happy in the knowledge that by this time tomorrow, he would be hers for good. In the meantime, she went to satisfy the cravings of her deliciously aroused flesh with the soldier Moldo, whom she'd assigned to her own personal service after her pleasant encounters with him on the journey here. Moldo was swarthily handsome, and he had a big, sturdy penis, which was always ready for service.

That night, she got him to take her roughly, holding her up against the wall while he thrust and grunted into her, and she clenched herself around him as her sweet orgasm enveloped her, letting him rasp at her breasts with his long tongue as his shaft spasmed vigorously in her womb.

He wasn't Aimery. But he would suffice until she had the Breton permanently at her side.

Elena stirred restlessly, tormented by disturbing dreams as the first grey shafts of dawn glimmered through the high barred window of her cell. Her body was hot and heavy, unrefreshed by her brief slumbers. Her woollen gown, clinging uncomfortably to her legs, seemed to press intrusively against the warm, swollen flesh between her thighs. Her dreams still enveloped her, even as she struggled to force her eyes open. For a moment, she thought that Aimery was with her, as he had been in her dreams. His strong hands were cupping her tethered body, moving slowly over her naked, thrusting nipples. She could hear his steady breathing, could feel his warm breath on her cheek. Her body throbbed with arousal, and with a little cry, she opened herself to him.

Then she realised. It was not Aimery, but Pierre. The big house serf had crept in while she slept and was crouching over her, gazing at her, his eyes hot with lust. He'd carefully unlaced the bodice of her gown, and his hands were gently stroking her naked breasts. That was why the swollen, creamy globes of flesh were tingling so in her sleep; why her nipples were dark and stiff, sending tormenting shafts of pleasure arrowing down to her secret parts. Sweet heaven. His strong, stubby fingers moved greedily to her crimson teats, teasing and pulling at them as he crooned wordless endearments. She could see where the massive outline of his sturdy penis pushed up against his short woollen tunic as he crouched over her. She opened her mouth in readiness to shout her protest, knowing his fear of Isobel would keep him at bay.

But then, she saw that he had left the door ajar. She quailed, just for a moment, but she knew all the time what she must do.

'Free me, Pierre,' she whispered huskily against his stubbled cheek. 'Oh, Pierre, how I long for you. Free my wrists, so I can caress your fine body properly.'

He backed away, his dread of Isobel's anger written across his broad peasant's face.

'Pierre,' she whispered. 'Pierre.' She shifted her slender thighs beneath her gown, feeling the trickle of her own secret moisture laving the puffy folds of her labia. She moistened her lips. Dear God, but her dreams of Aimery had left her open and wildly aroused. 'Touch me, please.'

Pierre's big hand pushed her skirt up tentatively

towards her thighs, and she moaned and parted her legs, no longer knowing if her lust was a pretence or for real, no longer even caring. All she knew was that she could not bear the torment of her arousal any longer. She needed the sweet bliss of a man's hard phallus thrusting inside her.

Pierre was hungrily smoothing his palms over her turgid nipples now, driving her into a paroxysm of need. She gasped out his name again, and his eyes were alight with greed as he bent his big body to kiss her, his tongue plunging into her mouth, devouring her sweet softness.

'Free me,' she whispered again, pulling with her tethered wrists at the chain that held her taut, but he shook his head, and the sweat beaded his downy upper lip as he pulled away from her. She gave a little whimper of disappointment, afraid that his fear of Isobel had got the better of him and he was leaving her; but then she realised that he was scrabbling at his tunic, hitching it up to reveal a huge, meaty erection. She remembered it all too well, from Isobel's games. His penis was stupendously long, and curved enticingly at the tip – enough to make any woman faint with desire. Slowly he circled its massive girth with his folded fist and began to pump at it, his eyes fastened on Elena's naked breasts all the time. She felt her vulva throb and quiver as she gazed at his jutting member, and moved her hips silently with need as her legs fell apart to expose her moistly swollen sex lips. Eagerly Pierre reached with his other hand to caress her there, the blunt tips of his fingers sliding about exquisitely in her juicy wetness. The extra pressure almost sent her over the edge; he sensed it and slowed his stimulation, while still rubbing at himself with increasing fervour, pulling the foreskin up and down his incredible shaft as he gazed at her secret parts.

The bulbous tip of his phallus was glossy and swollen, and his big balls, almost naked of hair, looked plump and obscene as they gathered tightly at the base of his shaft. Elena gazed at them greedily.

'Unchain me, Pierre, and I'll touch you there, just as you like.'

With a feral growl, he jumped to his feet to free the chain from the wall, and unlooped the shackles from her wrists. Free. At last she was free, and the door was open. But before she could even think of moving, he was flinging himself astride her, supporting his heavy weight with his brawny arms, nudging his hips between Elena's spread thighs as his massive member sought blindly for entrance.

She could have fought him off even now, with one whisper of Isobel's name. But she wanted him, craved him with every inch of her body. Desperately she reached for his massive cock with trembling fingers, and eased him between the liquid petals of her labia. The blunt head of his penis thrust hungrily as he rammed into her silken entrance, heavy and hard and blissfully satisfying.

Elena shuddered beneath him as he drove his thick length into her, again and again. She clenched herself desperately around him, almost ready for her hot, melting release. He watched her expressive face with fierce possessiveness, ravishing her with long, pulsing strokes of his mighty penis until the sweetness overwhelmed her and the tiny cries of rapture started to escape from her parted lips. Then he pulled his glistening shaft out of her, and rubbed himself hungrily, his face contorted with ecstasy as his seed spurted time and time again over her swollen breasts. Elena felt the convulsive jerking of his powerful body as he feverishly tugged his mighty member.

At last, he was finished. He slumped beside her, utterly spent; his big, muscled body replete; his eyes closed. Elena stayed beside him, just for a moment. Then she quickly, silently eased herself away from him and smoothed down her gown. The door was still ajar. Her chains were unlocked. She was free. Pierre, Isobel's dumb minion, had both freed her from her desperate, feverish lust, and had also given her the chance to escape from her prison. Her body still trembling from the force of her climax, she stepped quietly through the door, listening all the time for sounds of danger, but there were none. The courtyard was empty; there were no signs of life, except for the soldiers who watched from the ramparts, gazing out at the enemy. She was safe, until Isobel discovered her release. She stepped out into the courtyard, and realised that it was raining; the storm had passed by overnight, and rain still fell from the dull, leaden skies, cooling her heated skin, which still burned from Pierre's caresses.

It was dawn. She must find Gilles, because any moment now, the men of Normandy would launch their assault on Fulk of Anjou's soldiers, and Aimery's horsemen would ride out, in treachery, to attack them. Aimery. A sudden blinding flash of longing for the Breton smote her with such force that she had to shut her eyes against it, but she thought of him spending this past night with Isobel, perhaps laughing at her own captivity, and, biting back her pain, she pressed onwards. She must find Gilles. Aimery was only going to divulge his plans to his men at the very last minute. Pray God Gilles would have time to listen to her, and then to forewarn those still loyal to Duke William of the Breton's treachery. All was quiet and still. There must be time.

Then, as she rounded the corner into the main courtyard, she smothered a gasp and pressed herself back against the wall. The sight of row upon row of armed knights mounted on ranked destriers all but dazzled her, even in the cold, damp light of dawn; their ominous silence overwhelmed her with menace. She had underestimated the Breton yet again. They were all ready to

242

ride forth, mighty fighting machines, gathering in chilling quiet before bursting through the palisade's gates to fight for Fulk of Anjou. Even the horses were still, held under icy control. The courtyard was flanked by bowmen, and foot soldiers bearing swords and shields, their faces set and grim. She was too late. Aimery must already have told them. Desperately she scanned their lines for Gilles, but the long nasals of their helmets made them featureless. They were ready to move, awaiting only a single word to set them in deadly motion, like a bow-string awaiting release. She could see the men by the great gates, waiting to draw back the heavy beams of wood that held them shut.

And then she saw Aimery le Sabrenn. Mounted on his great black charger, he was riding to the forefront of the rain-soaked, silent ranks, ready to lead them into treachery. Elena stumbled blindly forward. 'No,' she cried out to the nearest soldiers. 'You must not listen to him. He is bewitched by Isobel. You must not do as he says.'

Faces turned towards the shivering, thinly clad girl, her gown already drenched in the chill morning rain. Some were blank with surprise; others were twisted in scorn. Aimery wheeled his mount towards her and sprang from his horse. He caught her by the shoulders, overwhelming her with his nearness, his strength; his lean jaw was darkened with stubble, and his steel-grey eyes glittered ominously beneath his helmet. 'Elena. Are you mad?' he hissed.

'No! I was only trying to save them from your treachery. Where is Gilles? He will help me.'

Aimery shook her. 'For the love of Christ. Are you trying to ruin us all? Gilles is not here.'

'He – he is dead?'

'No, he is safe.'

'I don't believe you. You have killed him . . .'

'Get back inside, Elena. The gates are opening.'

She could hear it now, the ominous grating of metal

and wood as the heavy barricades were slowly drawn back. She twisted herself in Aimery's rain-soaked grip and called out to the nearest ranks of his men, 'You must not do it. You must not join with Fulk of Anjou, as he has ordered –'

The men who heard her started to glance at one another uneasily, muttering as they gentled their big horses. Aimery seized her tighter, and turned to face his men.

'Take no notice of the girl,' he said abruptly. 'She has been sick with a fever, and does not know what she is saying. Those who were supposed to tend her will be severely punished for letting her escape from their care. You, Robert, and you, Warin –' he spoke sharply to two of the ranked men-at-arms – 'you will take the girl to the ramparts, and guard her for the duration of the battle. Give her your cloak, Warin, to shield her from the rain. I charge you to look after her well.'

They nodded, swiftly moving forward to take Elena from Aimery. Elena struggled, but Aimery's hands were wrapped relentlessly round her arms, and his body was braced against hers with all-too familiar strength. Gazing up into his harsh, rain-streaked features, she felt the despair overwhelm her, because she still longed for him. Even now, his nearness melted her with desire. She would never be free of him. 'Aimery,' she whispered. 'Dear God, Aimery, but I still cannot believe this of you, even now.'

'Go,' he whispered harshly, his steely eyes burning into her. 'For the love of Christ, Elena, for your own safety, get away from here.'

And then he pushed her towards his men, and turned to face a newcomer – Isobel.

'Isobel,' he said. 'I thought I told you to stay in your chamber.'

She moved close to Aimery's side, wrapped in a fine woollen cloak that hooded her hair and protected her from the persistent rain, though it still sparkled on her cheeks and her dark lashes. She glanced scornfully at Elena, who was held firm by the two men-at-arms.

'I came to warn you that the little Saxon slut had escaped, Aimery,' she said in a low voice. 'But I see you've already found her. She seduced the imbecile Pierre, let him defile her. She is fevered with lust. Get her out of the way while you explain our plans to your men, or she will cause trouble.'

Aimery replied harshly, 'I have already informed them of our plans. They are ready.' He turned to Elena's two guards. 'Take her away.' Then he turned back to Isobel. 'They are going to watch the battle from the ramparts. I suggest that you accompany her, lady, to see that she causes no more mischief.'

Isobel laughed. 'And then I can make sure that she doesn't try to seduce these two wretches, you mean? I hardly think that is a danger, my lord. Look at her. A pitiful sight.' She gestured scornfully at Elena, laughing at her bedraggled hair, her haunted eyes, her white face. 'But I shall do as you say, Aimery, just in case.' She turned to go with Elena, and the light of imminent triumph glittered in her green gaze. A distant cacophony of battle trumpets split the cold, sullen air: the horses pranced restlessly on the beaten earth of the courtyard. The gates were drawn back.

Aimery waited for the trumpets to cease their call. Then he said softly, 'Fulk of Anjou is ready for battle.' With one long, last look at Elena, he turned to spring into the saddle of his black horse, and rode towards the gateway, Hamet just behind him, while his men following in silent ranks.

Elena shivered despairingly as the two soldiers half led, half dragged her up the stairs to the ramparts. The thin cloak offered her little protection from the torrential rain. From the palisaded heights of the castle, she could see Fulk's army circling in battle array, his knights mounted and ready. Beyond, through the grey curtain of drizzle, she could just see the men of Normandy, under the Count of Evreux – Duke William's loyal veteran warrior. They would have seen, by now, that the gates of Morency were open. They would be waiting for Aimery's men to ride forth and hurl themselves on Fulk's rear, while they attacked him from the front. Little did they know of the treachery that was about to assail them.

The rain streamed down her hair and face, but she didn't care. She didn't even care about Isobel, standing near to her in her warm cloak and gazing out with proud, happy excitement shining in her hateful green eyes. Elena gazed down at the distant figure of Aimery, who had halted his horsemen just a little way beyond the gates, waiting for them to fall into line while he gave them their last instructions. No sign of Gilles. She feared very much that he was dead, that Isobel had contrived the ultimate punishment for the valiant young squire. She felt sick. Yet surely, even now, some of the other soldiers would refuse to obey Aimery's traitorous command? But then she remembered Hamet saying, 'The Breton's men worship him. They would follow him to hell and back, without question . . .'

They began to move again, with lances raised, their horses gathering into a slow, steady canter. She was aware of Isobel watching her triumphantly, and she knew that the battle was as good as over.

She knew the plan, because Isobel had told her of it, gloatingly. Fulk's army, just as they were about to engage with the men of Normandy, would draw apart at the centre as Aimery approached, allowing the Breton's knights to thunder on through and fall upon their supposed rescuers. Elena gazed blindly as Aimery's men gathered pace, still in formation, with their deadly lances levelled. The knights of Anjou and Normandy were clashing already, horse against horse, sword against sword, sending shock waves reverberating across the rain-swept meadows. All around her, the bowmen on the battlements whom Aimery had left to guard the donjon tensed and tightened their grip on their weapons. Aimery's men had almost reached the battle line. She watched despairingly as Fulk's men, hearing them approach, started to draw apart even as they fought, to make room for them to ride through and wreak havoc on the Norman ranks.

And then, just as a fresh curtain of rain swooped across the ramparts, stinging her eyes and momentarily blinding her, Elena saw that something was wrong. As Fulk's lines parted, Aimery's horsemen did not appear to be sweeping through the open space. Instead, they wheeled at the last moment, spreading along the rear of Fulk's ranks in both directions, their swords raised as they began to hack and slice at the men of Anjou. Elena heard Isobel beside her give a harsh gasp of dismay. 'No,' she gasped. 'No. This is wrong. Dear Christ, what is he at?'

The soldiers who held Elena looked at Isobel questioningly. One of them, Warin, said flatly, 'Looks good enough to me, my lady. That was the battle plan, wasn't it? The lord Aimery to ride out as soon as the men of Normandy gave the signal, then both of them to fall on that rat Fulk of Anjou from both sides. Aimery sent out young Gilles secretly last night to inform the Count of Evreux of his intentions. And it's worked perfectly; the Breton couldn't have timed it better. It all looks sound enough to me. But then, what do you expect of Aimery le Sabrenn? Duke William hasn't a finer soldier in the land.'

Isobel, her face quite drained of colour, said no more. But Elena saw how she began to tremble, and saw how her jewelled, nerveless fingers clutched the edge of the palisade as the rain poured from the leaden skies. Elena too gazed in disbelief, her exhausted mind a turmoil of confused thoughts as she saw Aimery's men hew their

247

way through the battle lines of the men of Anjou, who did not know which way to turn, trapped as they were between the horsemen of Morency and the army of Normandy under the battle-hardened Count of Evreux. Elena suddenly knew that Aimery had not ordered his men to turn traitor. Gilles was safe, sent out at night as a secret messenger to the Count of Evreux. Aimery had never, ever intended to carry out Isobel's vile plan.

Fulk's men fought with increasing desperation, their faces grimed and bloodied as their leaders tried to rally them. The air was filled with the terrible squealing of horses, the screams of broken men, the crash of shattering shields. Then a wavering cohort turned to flee, and it was the beginning of the end. Soon Fulk's soldiers were riding or running from the field, abandoning their tents and proud pennants, leaving their wounded strewn across the battlefield. Ringing cheers of jubilation rose from the watching soldiers on the ramparts of the stronghold of Morency, and only Elena saw Isobel, her face as white as death, slipping silently away. Elena continued to gaze across the ramparts, stunned, as the victors joined ranks, then turned to ride triumphantly back towards the donjon, arraying themselves in some sort of order as they moved. Elena could see Hamet in their midst, his helmet pushed back on its coif, his dark face gaunt with weariness as he fondled the curved sword that nestled against his thigh. As they drew closer she recognised many more of Aimery's soldiers, the men who had accompanied them here from Rouen, their expressions stern, their bodies exhausted after the fray. But where was Aimery? She could not see him. Desperately she strained her eyes for his familiar proud figure on his great black horse, but she could see no sign.

Then the shouts of triumph from the ramparts seemed to die away suddenly, and as the silence fell all around, Elena heard the words, 'Aimery le Sabrenn has fallen in battle.'

Chapter Fourteen

*I*t was Hamet who found Elena some time later, by herself up on the battlements. The big Saracen came wearily up the steps to her, still in his armour, and went towards her in silence. Then he said,

'Lady Elena. Your clothing is wet through. You should go inside, and change, and get yourself warm before a fire.'

She spun round to face him then, her blue eyes dark and haunted. 'Oh, Hamet. Aimery – he will live?'

Hamet bowed his dark head. 'They do not know yet,' he said gently. 'His old wound, the wound he got at Bavinchove, has opened up again. He has lost a lot of blood. The Count of Evreux has ordered him to be tended in his own tent, well away from the noise of the castle.'

She bowed her head in silence. Then she said, 'He never intended to join with Fulk of Anjou, did he? Never intended to betray his duke.'

'No,' said Hamet. 'Aimery the Breton is a man of honour.'

'Then why?' Elena's voice was husky with pain. 'Why pretend to Isobel, and to me, that he was preparing to be a traitor?'

'He had no choice, lady Elena. He was brought here into the middle of a trap, many leagues from any ally who could help him. He had fifty men, Fulk five hundred, and more, if he chose to summon them. If Aimery had refused Isobel's plan of treachery, Fulk's army would simply have overwhelmed Morency and killed us all.'

'Why did he not tell me all this? Why did he have me locked away? Why did he make poor Gilles suffer so?'

'It was Isobel who demanded Gilles's punishment. She had a fancy for him herself, and was jealous of his love for you, lady Elena. Aimery agreed to her request, for the sake of appearance, but he was careful that Gilles was not really hurt. Afterwards he explained everything fully to Gilles in confidence, and Gilles agreed to steal through the enemy lines last night as Aimery's secret messenger to the Count of Evreux.'

Elena gazed at him, absorbing it. Then she said quietly, 'So much for Gilles. But why did Aimery make *me* endure so much, Hamet?'

Hamet was silent for a moment. Perhaps he, too, was remembering how Elena had despairingly allowed the big Saracen to ravish her as she watched Isobel and Aimery together. Hamet said at last,

'Aimery was afraid for you. He had no proof, but he suspected that your injury on the way here was inflicted by one of Isobel's men. So he tried to keep you shut away, out of further danger, while you recovered in peace. But you evaded the old woman who tended you, and Isobel, out of sheer malice, decided to tell you about her scheme. From then on, you were a danger both to yourself and to the lord Aimery. Up till then, he had convinced Isobel that he would go along with her evil strategy, and would tell his men of it when the time was right. Of course, he never intended to tell them at all, because his plan was still to attack Fulk of Anjou. But you challenged him about his treachery, in front of

Isobel. He knew that if you told any of his soldiers about Isobel's plan, they would rebel against it, and he would be in an impossibly dangerous position. Isobel wanted Aimery to kill you, lady Elena. She has always hated you, as you know. To satisfy her, and to keep you out of harm's way, he himself suggested that you be imprisoned, in an isolated cell.'

'Where I was humiliated, and taunted by Isobel, who sent her servant Pierre to attend to me,' broke in Elena bitterly.

Hamet's face darkened. 'Pierre? I did not know that. Nor did Aimery, I swear.'

'That cannot be true, for Isobel told me that my degradation was at his orders.'

'Never! Remember that in many ways the lord Aimery was a prisoner here himself. But he was always desperately aware of the need to keep you safe.'

'Safe?' Elena leant back against the wall, suddenly aware of how exhausted she was. 'But why would he want me safe, when Isobel told me that he hated me?'

His dark eyes burned into her. 'Oh, he never hated you. Never that, my lady.'

She gazed at him despairingly. 'But you hate me, Hamet, don't you? You believe that I betrayed him. You have been so cold to me, ever since we set out from Rouen.'

Hamet said in a careful voice, 'You married Ralf, lady Elena. When my master was imprisoned, and afterwards sick for many months, you did not wait for him.'

'But he was with Isobel. Oh, Hamet. How do you think I felt, to know that he had gone back to her?'

Hamet shook his dark head. 'No. He was Isobel's prisoner, as much as if he were still a captive of war. He was ill, and fevered from his wound and the deprivations of prison. As soon as he was strong enough, he rejected Isobel and set out to find you, Elena. He was waiting for a passage to England when he learnt that you were married. I was with him when he heard of it. He was still weak from his sickness, and the blow of that news was worse than anything he'd suffered on the battlefield. Can you blame me, for not being glad that you had come back into his life?'

Elena shook her head, stunned. 'But I heard news that he was well and happy, and carousing with Isobel at her castle of Aumale. That he would never, ever come back to England.' She put her hands to her face. 'Isobel's work again. Oh, I understand all too well now why he would not trust me. Why he could not tell me of his plans, even while he did his best to keep me safe.'

'I believe he always loved you, lady Elena,' said Hamet gravely. 'And still does, even though Isobel has always done her best to poison your feelings for him, and his for you.'

Elena drew herself up, her blue eyes brilliant with unshed tears, the pain knifing her heart. 'Isobel,' she breathed. 'Where is she? She was here, watching it all, with me. I saw her face when Aimery turned on Fulk of Anjou's men. She looked – stricken. And then – Hamet, I don't remember any more about her. She must have slipped away.'

Hamet was suddenly alert, his hand on the hilt of his curved sword. 'We must find her,' he said. 'I should have thought of it before. She could still be a danger to us. I will set soldiers to search the castle.'

'I will look too,' said Elena. Silently, she added, 'And oh, Hamet, I pray that I find her before you do.'

'See that wench over there? The one with black hair and green eyes? Now she looks promising.'

The soldier pointed, grinning, to a dark corner of the disused granary where the kitchen sluts gathered when they wanted to earn some extra deniers from the men of the castle. Isobel, seeing his hot eyes searching her out, shrank back even further into the shadows.

252

In the chaos that followed the ending of the battle, she'd tried to conceal her identity by running to her room to pull off her fine clothes and dressing hastily in one of Alys's rough serge gowns instead. Then, desperate for somewhere to hide until her chance came to escape completely, she'd thought of this place, where the women gathered in the near darkness and nobody asked any questions.

The victorious soldiers, a mixture of the garrison of Morency and the Count of Evreux's men, had been busy feasting all night in the hall above, and drinking their fill. The steward had the scullions and kitchen girls hurrying frantically to and fro from the kitchens, plying them with food and wine. And, ever a realist, Hugh de Brosny had turned a blind eye to the fact that quite a number of the livelier wenches had sneaked away to the old granary, where the triumphant soldiers who had taken their fill of the feast were now set on enjoying other kinds of fleshly pleasures. Isobel shrank into the background as the women clustered and grouped in open invitation. It had been easy so far, in the crowded granary, to avoid attention. She kept quiet, and looked on in scorn as the soldiers picked their women to take outside, or even swived them in some dark corner down here, lying on grain sacks, with just a ragged, dusty blanket to conceal what they were up to. While there were so many here, and the place was in darkness, Isobel felt she was safe. Aimery would not come down here; and it was Aimery she was afraid of.

He had tricked her. She was still trembling with rage and pain at the realisation of it. Dear God, he had tricked her all along, made a fool of her. He might be laughing about her even now, up in the hall – *her* hall – with the Count of Evreux and his men. And she could not hide from him for ever, not even down here.

'There she is. The wench with green eyes I caught sight of a moment ago. Isn't she a beauty?'

Damn. Isobel cursed him under her breath. It was that same drunken man, pushing his way stubbornly through the shifting groups of soldiers and wenches, almost knocking over a couple who were twined in a lascivious kiss. Two of his square-shouldered comrades followed right behind. Isobel's face and figure had caught their fancy. They'd sensed that there was something intriguingly different about her, in spite of her shabby clothes. She twisted behind a stone pillar, almost falling over a couple that were copulating on the floor in the darkness. She cursed them and pulled herself upright, only to find that she was trapped.

The man stood in front of her, his hands on his hips, grinning. His two companions stood on either side of him. She looked wildly around for escape. He said softly,

'Not trying to run away from me, were you, lass?'

Isobel said scornfully, 'Get away from me, you boor.'

He laughed then. 'This one likes to play games,' he said to his companions. 'What kind of welcome is that for a poor soldier who's ridden all this way and fought against Fulk of Anjou to save her pretty skin?' He caught Isobel round her slender waist, and pulled her against his hard body, and kissed her.

He was strong, and heavily muscled, and smelled of male sweat. As his tongue probed hungrily between her lips, Isobel couldn't help but be aroused. Dark fingers of need clawed suddenly at her lower abdomen as her wanton body betrayed her.

'A hot wench,' he whispered, pulling away a little, though his big hands were still tight round her tiny waist. 'How about letting me and my two friends here fuck you for five deniers, hey?'

He thought she was a whore. Somehow she wrested herself free, and struck him hard across one cheek. 'Let me go,' she said in a low, vehement voice. 'How dare you speak to me like that? I am Isobel of Morency!'

The man, his palm pressed to his stinging cheek,

backed away uncertainly, as did his companions. Isobel held her breath, waiting her chance to flee. He was one of the Count of Evreux's men, so he could be excused for not recognising her. But surely he could tell from her voice, her bearing, that she was not for the likes of him.

The soldiers moved aside reluctantly to let her pass, because it was too big a risk to doubt her, although their eyes still burned with lust. Isobel, with a little sigh of relief, hurried past them towards the door, suddenly desperate to get out of this degrading place and find some safer hideaway until she could escape.

But then a familiar female voice said clearly from close by, 'What are you waiting for, soldiers? You don't really believe that slut is Isobel de Morency, do you? It's just a game of hers. She is slightly crazed, you see. Someone once told her she bears a slight resemblance to the lady Isobel, and it has preyed on her mind. She wants you to treat her like a fine lady, then pleasure her with your strong bodies one at a time until she's demented with lust. Go ahead, take her. But I warn you – she'll want ten deniers, not five.'

Isobel hissed aloud. It was Elena who spoke. Elena, who was standing in the shadows by the doorway, her lovely oval face perfectly framed by her long, pale gold hair, which gleamed in the light of the horn lantern she was carrying. This corner of the granary seemed suddenly still and quiet, but it was not empty. She realised, with a sickening jolt, that there were faces all around, gathering, watching in the ring of shadows that surrounded her.

The men glanced questioningly at Elena, then moved forward again. They were still uncertain, but hungry for their prey. Elena was gazing at Isobel, her blue eyes calm and purposeful. Isobel wheeled to face the soldiers. 'Don't come near me, you scum. I am Isobel de Morency, I tell you.'

Elena laughed. Then she said, 'If you are really Isobel

de Morency, then what are you doing skulking down here, dressed as a servant?'

Isobel struggled to reply, hating the Saxon girl with all her heart. Damn her. Elena knew very well who she was. What deadly game was she playing? The men were grinning now, moving closer with more confidence.

Elena gave them all time to acknowledge Isobel's silence, then went on softly, 'I have an idea. Hamet the Saracen knows the real lady Isobel well. Perhaps I should fetch him down here, to prove her false or otherwise –'

'No,' Isobel broke in with a cry of desperation. Hamet she feared almost as much as Aimery. He knew just as much about her treachery as his master did. He would put her in chains, and take her to Aimery to await the Breton's punishment. 'No,' she repeated, through dry lips. 'There is no need to fetch the Saracen. I – I am not the lady of Morency. It was nothing but a jest.'

'Perhaps, then, you would like to explain what you are doing down here,' said Elena sweetly. 'Not to spy, I hope? These soldiers have earnt their pleasure. They don't like people who come merely to watch.'

Isobel gazed at her with bitter hatred in her eyes. How she had underestimated the Saxon girl. She lowered her gaze to the floor. 'I came here in hope of pleasure, like everyone else,' she muttered sullenly.

Elena seemed to let out a little sigh. She said to the waiting men, 'There. You heard her. It was but a game of hers, to feign reluctance. Take her – she's yours. Oh, by the way, her greatest pleasure is to suck at a soldier's penis, while another takes her from behind. Try her; you won't be disappointed.'

The soldiers fell on Isobel, clawing at her shabby clothes, stroking her glossy black hair, exclaiming over her soft, scented skin. As their fingers caressed her ripe breasts and white thighs, lust overwhelmed her. She forgot about Elena standing there, forgot about the silent onlookers who had stopped their furtive drinking and carousing to watch, forgot about her own imminent danger at the hands of the Breton. Already the first soldier was down on his knees before her, and she bent naked on all fours, reaching for his surging cock as he pulled it out of his breeches. She grabbed it, and sucked hungrily on the swelling shaft as he eased himself with a groan into her luscious mouth. Another soldier was behind her, gripping her buttocks, pulling up her skirts. She could feel his hard member prodding between her thighs, dipping in her juices, thrusting into her melting vagina with hungry, solid strokes. Oh, dear God. Isobel felt the remorseless excitement gripping her shuddering body, felt her burning clitoris, pulled two and fro by the giant shaft that impaled her from behind, throbbing on the edge of explosion. The other soldier was continuing to slide his big penis rapturously in and out of her mouth, groaning with delight as her fervent tongue caressed him. She was suddenly aware that the third man was crouching down beside her, reaching to fondle her aching breasts, pulling at her stiffened teats with his fingers until she was quivering with delight. Then he grabbed her hand, and pushed his own hotly erect member into it, and she gripped eagerly with her fingers as he drove himself to and fro. 'That's it, my beautiful wench,' he groaned. 'Hold me harder. Oh, yes – that's it –'

The man behind her was gripping her bottom cheeks and pumping away furiously, his massive length sliding deliciously in and out. The cock in her throat was leaping, bursting with seed. A huge shudder ran through Isobel as they all began to spend themselves within her. Her loins clenched around the rampant penis that ravished her so stalwartly, and the overwhelming release rolled through her exquisitely sensitised body. Her mouth was filled with the hot seed of the man whose phallus thrust between her lips; and the man whose cock she gripped in her hand pushed rapturously against her silky palm, spilling out his sperm over her fingers in quivering bliss. The shadowy lair was filled with the soft animal sounds of their satisfaction. At last Isobel rolled over, sated, on to the floor. She closed her eyes, her whole body still tingling with passion.

'Was she worth ten deniers, soldiers?' called Elena softly from the shadows. 'Let me tell you that the lord Aimery does not think so.'

Isobel pulled herself up, clutching for her discarded robe. 'Damn you,' she whispered furiously. 'Oh, damn you –'

But Elena had gone.

Elena went quickly to look for Hamet, to tell him where to find his prisoner. She should have felt elated at the downfall of Isobel, her enemy. But instead she felt cold and empty.

After all, in a way, Isobel had won, even now. She had kept Elena and Aimery apart, and manipulated them both with subtle cunning, bringing them to the brink of utmost danger. As Elena made her way swiftly across the courtyard towards the hall, hoping that Hamet would be there, she found herself filled with increasing fear. Aimery had been badly wounded. Hamet had said little, but his face had been taut with concern. Elena resolved that she would see that Isobel was suitably restrained, so she could do no further harm. And then she, Elena, defying Hamet's orders if need be, would go to the place where Aimery was being tended, and stay by his side. If he was unconscious, she would wait for him. She needed to tell him how much she loved him, how she had always loved him. Her heart felt overburdened with her desperate need to be with her lord.

The hall was still crowded with men, but somehow to Elena it seemed their voices were subdued, and they ate and drank with less fervour, as if it were a necessity rather than a celebration. Elena felt a curious chill of warning.

She could see the grizzled Count of Evreux sitting at the high table, talking earnestly to his commanders. Of Hamet, she could se no sign. But Henriette was there, and she came hurrying towards Elena as she stood uncertainly by the door. Henriette's face was flushed, and there seemed to be recent tears on her cheeks.

Fighting down the sickening fear that somehow gripped her heart, Elena said, 'Henriette. I am looking for Hamet. Have you seen him?'

Henriette bit her lip. 'Oh, lady Elena! He has gone to the tent where they were tending the lord Aimery.'

'*Were* tending him?'

'Have you not heard? He – he is dead.'

'You will come inside, lady Elena, to share our repast? It is but humble fare. Bread, and cheese, and a little watered wine. But you are most welcome to it.'

The nun's gentle voice was kindly and concerned. She twined her fingers together eagerly as she waited for Elena's reply.

Elena turned to smile up at her. She was sitting on a stone bench in the little courtyard, where the late evening sun still poured warmly into the sweet scented herb garden of the convent. Doves murmured in the eaves, and a pale yellow rose bush clambered over the grey stone walls, a haven for droning bees. She felt almost content here, because it reminded her of the convent where she had spent her girlhood. Of the time before she met Aimery.

'Thank you, sister Fleurette,' she said gently. 'But I am really not hungry. And I fear I would be poor company for you all.'

'Oh, never!' said the young nun quickly. 'You know you are most welcome to stay here for as long as you wish. My brother Luc spoke most highly of you to the lady abbess.' She blushed suddenly. 'He enjoyed your company, lady Elena, on your journey to Rouen.'

'And I enjoyed his,' said Elena quietly. 'Your brother has been a good friend to me.'

Sister Fleurette hesitated, as if about to say more, but then she blushed furiously and said, 'Well, then. I will leave you in peace.'

Elena watched her go, thinking that she was indeed fortunate to have found such a refuge here, at this peaceful convent just outside the walls of Rouen, even if it was only for a while. It gave her time, and privacy; time to think what to do next – to bring herself to even care about her future was the first task.

When she'd heard from Henriette that Aimery was dead, she'd been desperate to get away from Morency, from the hateful place that was still filled with Isobel's presence. Stunned by the news, she'd taken refuge in action. Hamet himself did not come back to the stronghold that night. As Aimery's servant and closest companion, he would be grieving, in his own way, as deeply as Elena. She knew that, and respected him for it.

She'd asked, not really caring, about Ralf. One of the Count of Evreux's commanders, who knew her husband, told her that they'd been puzzled to see Ralf in the company of Fulk of Anjou during the battle. A little later he had fled, it seemed, with Fulk's men. Elena bowed her head. So Ralf, ever Isobel's minion, had played the traitor. She hoped Fulk would reward him for his pains, because he would never be able to return to Normandy or England again.

The Count of Evreux took rapid command of the garrison of Morency, and Elena learnt that he had arranged for a party of his soldiers to set out for Rouen the following morning, with requests for vital supplies in case Anjou should attack again. Elena was filled with the vague aim of returning to England, for that was her home, if she had any home now. She pleaded with the

Count of Evreux to let her travel with the convoy bound for Rouen, for she knew that from there, she would be able to take a ship to England. Evreux, abstracted with his responsibilities, was reluctant at first, telling her that his men would be setting a hard pace, but she persisted stubbornly, and he agreed in the end, impressed by her quiet courage. He had no idea that the beautiful Saxon girl had been involved with Aimery le Sabrenn, but just saw a young woman who was alone and far from home. He finally weakened to her request, but told her that she, a gently born lady, could not possibly travel alone amongst a band of soldiers. It was not seemly, he said. Had she not got some female friend, or attendant, who would travel with her?

Elena was about to shake her head, when suddenly Alys was there at her side.

'I will go with the lady Elena,' she said. 'If she will have me.'

Elena turned in surprise to face Isobel's servant. 'Alys,' she said. 'You are sure you want to leave? I can offer you no money, no reward.'

Alys said in a low voice, 'I hated Isobel, and now she is gone. I am free of her at last. If I can be of any use to you, my lady, then I will gladly travel with you.'

So Elena had departed on horseback at dawn, with Alys just a little way behind, both of them looking their last on the isolated fortress of Morency.

Isobel had eluded capture in the confusion that followed the news of Aimery's death, but Elena did not care. She found that she didn't care about anything very much now, though she was glad when Henriette told her shyly, just before she left, that she and Hamet were to be married. Elena was surprised, and pleased for them both. It would give Hamet a new purpose after the loss of his master.

The journey to Rouen passed swiftly, much more swiftly than the journey south, because the Count of

261

Evreux's soldiers were determined to make good time. Nevertheless, even in their haste, they were full of solicitous respect towards Elena, always finding her gentle but speedy mounts, and making sure that she had everything she needed, and bringing the choicest pieces of the food whenever they stopped to eat. Alys found the riding hard, and was jolted about on her plump rouncey, her bones stiff and aching, but she did not grumble, and as her riding skills improved, she even appeared to be enjoying herself, especially when one of the soldiers, a gruff, bearded veteran, started to pay her some flattering attention.

The captain of the soldiers, Luc de Rosnan, spent much time with Elena, talking to her courteously about his travels, and the time he had spent in England. It was he who suggested the convent to her. One of his sisters, Fleurette, was there, he told her. He was sure they would take good care of her until she could find a passage to England. He asked her, suddenly shy, if he could visit her occasionally while he was in Rouen, and asked her many leading questions about her home, and whether there was anyone there waiting for her.

Elena did not tell the kindly soldier Luc, did not tell anyone, that she had no home to go to.

And now, she sat in the courtyard, alone, as the sun started to sink and the shadows spread across the thyme-scented flagstones. The chapel bell tolled for compline, the last service of the day. Oh, if only she could have told Aimery how much she loved him.

She went at last to her room, a tiny chamber furnished with a wooden coffer and a narrow bed, where she prepared herself to sleep. Alys came to see her, bringing water for washing, and a plate of food and a beaker of ewe's milk to tempt Elena's appetite. But Elena dismissed her gently.

At last, clad only in her white chemise, and discarding the coarse woollen blankets because the night was so warm, she lay down on her little bed, feeling unbearably alone. It was still almost light outside. She could see the fading silvery dusk glimmering through her high little window, could hear the murmuring of the doves. She thought she heard the muffled clatter of horses' hooves, somewhere beyond the refectory, where visitors were received. It was late for callers to the little convent. She opened her eyes, suddenly alert. But then silence fell again, and she drifted into sleep.

She dreamt about Aimery, as she always did, even in her sleep dreading the pang of loss that would come when she awoke and knew he was gone. She dreamt that he was lying with her, holding her in his strong arms, kissing her tears away, and when someone touched her shoulder softly, trying to stir her from sleep, she moaned in protest, clinging desperately to her dream.

'Elena,' a voice said. 'Elena.'

She opened her eyes dazedly and saw a man standing over her little wooden bed, a tall, wide-shouldered man, with a scarred face and heartbreakingly tender eyes. Aimery. Elena whispered his name in soft disbelief. Her dream was so real, she felt she could almost touch him. She reached up to stroke his lips, to linger over the cruel scar that split his cheek, and she cried out with a low cry of need.

He sat beside her on the small bed, drawing her up close to him, covering her face with kisses. His lips were warm, and sweet as wine, and his tongue was strong and searching as he explored the inner softness of her mouth. She lifted her hands to clasp his strong shoulders, feeling the warm muscles and sinews beneath his tunic. Such an exquisite dream. As she raised her arms, her chemise fell open, revealing her soft white breasts, and his mouth travelled down the slender column of her throat to catch each rose-tipped nipple in his mouth, sucking and teasing. She lay back in his arms, her body

263

throbbing with need, and the longing tugged painfully at the pit of her stomach. Her dreams of Aimery had never been so strong, so clear. She never wanted to wake. His fingers slowly reached to push up the crumpled skirt of her chemise; then his hand slipped between her thighs and gently traced the lips of her wet, swollen sex. The muscles of her vagina clenched tight with aching desire, and she cried out in the desperation of loss as he moved away. But then she saw that he was removing his dusty, travel-stained tunic. She watched from her pillow, dry throated.

In the soft light that crept through her little window, his naked body was powerful, and thickly clad with strong muscle. His tautly ridged abdomen tapered down to narrow hips, and from the seductive contours of his loins, she saw his pulsing phallus rearing upwards from its cradle of hair, proudly virile, and full of dark promise.

With a little cry, she reached out to him, and he lay down beside her on the little bed, raising himself on one elbow so he could gaze down at her.

And that was when she saw the freshly healed scar, still red and ugly, that sliced down from his ribs; and she knew that this was no dream.

'Aimery,' she breathed. 'They told me you were dead.'

His silver-grey eyes burned into her. 'They expected me to die, *caran*. But I lived. And I have followed you, come for you . . .'

He kissed her again, his tongue plunging slowly into her soft mouth. Then he reached between her thighs again, and guided the hot, swollen head of his penis into the moist folds of her labia. Elena cried out, again and again, as he penetrated her with his thick phallus, the sweetness of his possession filling her, ravishing her. Her blood was on fire as he gathered her taut nipples in his mouth. She grasped at his penis fiercely with her fluttering inner muscles as her senses began to tighten into a spiralling cascade of bliss. She arched her hips feverishly against him as he drove himself slowly, deeply into her. 'Aimery. Ah, dear God. Aimery.' The ecstasy billowed through her. He continued to pleasure her steadily, prolonging her bliss as she clung to him, crying out his name, her body sheened in sweat. At last he permitted his own release to overwhelm him, his strong shaft pulsing deep within her. She held him tightly in her arms, stroking the silken muscles of his back, still dazed with rapture.

'I still think I'm dreaming,' she said.

'No dream, *caran*.' His finger caressed her cheek. 'There were rumours of my death, admittedly, and some of my men chose to let them persist, for my own safety. Hamet came to find you, to tell you that I was safe and would recover, but you had already left Morency.'

'I couldn't bear to stay there,' she whispered. 'The memories were too hateful.'

'I understand,' he said quietly. 'I set out to find you as soon as I was well enough. Luc de Rosnan told me you were here. But I wasn't at all sure that you would want to see me again.'

'You have your answer now?' she murmured, running her finger down his cheek, stopping at the curve of his beautiful, sensual mouth.

He smiled, and his smile turned her heart over. 'Oh, yes. But I was so afraid you would hate me after Morency.'

She considered it, her eyes dark and full. 'I didn't understand what was happening,' she said slowly. 'I didn't realise the danger you were in, and how you were trying your hardest to keep me safe. To see you in that room, with Isobel, was like the worst of my dreams coming true.'

'You understand now? Why I had to do what I did?'

She nodded gravely. 'Hamet explained to me that all the garrison would have been killed if you had not gone along with Fulk and Isobel's plan. And he explained how you tried to keep me safe from it all.' She shivered. 'She is evil, Aimery, so evil.'

He held her tightly, soothing her. 'Hush, little one. Isobel has fled. She will never dare to show herself within Normandy's borders again.'

She was still trembling. 'She wanted you so badly, Aimery. She will stop at nothing, even now.'

'Hush. She has failed, and she knows it. She lost her power over me when I first met you, *caran*. Did Hamet tell you that when she arranged my release from that prison in Flanders, I was too sick to know what was happening?'

She nodded fiercely. 'But Isobel spread rumours that you were living happily with her, were settled with her for good. So I married Ralf. Oh, Aimery. It has been the worst of nightmares.'

He was stroking her, soothing her. 'For me too, little one. But it is all over now.'

She nestled against him. 'Truly over. Ralf has gone. Isobel has gone. We will never be parted again.'

She moved in the darkness to let her chemise fall from her shoulders, then knelt up beside him. His breath caught raggedly in his throat at the sight of her perfect naked breasts. She bent to kiss his mouth, then moved downwards, deliberately caressing his silken chest with her tongue, taking first one hard nipple in her mouth, then the other.

He tangled his hands fiercely in her golden hair, his body already leaping with desire. 'Ah, *caran*. See what you do to me. They will throw us out of the convent when they find us here at daybreak.'

Her mouth continued to journey slowly down his body until it reached his rearing phallus. 'It is a long time till dawn, my lord,' she murmured.

He laughed huskily, then the sound died away abruptly as she took the swollen head of his shaft between her moistly parted lips. 'Mercy, my little Saxon warrior,' he breathed.

She lifted her head and smiled back, her heart brimming with love, her eyes shining with fire. Aimery, her destiny. 'No mercy, ever, my lord,' she replied, and passionately took possession of him once more.

Visit the Black Lace website at
www.blacklace-books.co.uk

LOOK OUT FOR THE ALL-NEW BLACK LACE BOOKS – AVAILABLE NOW!

All books priced £7.99 in the UK. Please note publication dates apply to the UK only. For other territories, please contact your retailer.

CIRCUS EXCITE
Nikki Magennis
ISBN 0 352 34033 9

Julia Spark is a professional dancer, newly graduated. Jobs are hard to find and after a curious audition she finds herself running away with the circus. It's not what she expected – the circus is an adult show full of bizarre performers forbidden from sex yet trained to turn people on. The ringmaster exerts a powerful influence over the performers, and seems to have taken a special interest in Julia. As the circus tours the UK, Julia plays the power games with Robert, finding herself drawn into his world of erotic fantasy. He dares her to experiment, playing with her desires and encouraging Julia to explore the darker side of her own sexuality.

Coming in June

WILD CARD
Madeline Moore
ISBN O 352 34038 X

When Victoria Ashe lures an ex-lover to her London hotel room, their passion is reignited with startling intensity. She's out to prove to Ray that intimacy can be just as exciting as the thrill of the chase. Ray Torrington might actually agree if it weren't for Kinky Bai Lon, a Hong Kong bombshell who doles herself out one delicate morsel at a time, always in public. And Penny, a champion poker player known as 'The Flame of London', also has her sights on the saucy jackpot. The scene is set for a high stakes game of sexual exploration. When the wild card keeps changing it's difficult for even the most accomplished player to know who's bluffing and who is telling the truth. In this lusty tournament of champions, the winner takes all.

SAUCE FOR THE GOOSE
Mary Rose Maxwell
ISBN O 352 33492 4

Sauce for the goose is a riotous and sometimes humorous celebration of the rich variety of human sexuality. Imaginative and colourful, each story explores a different theme or fantasy, and the result is a fabulously bawdy mélange of cheeky sensuality and hot thrills. A lively array of characters display an uninhibited and lusty energy for boundary breaking pleasure. This is a decidedly x-rated collection of stories designed to be enjoyed and indulged in.

Coming in July

THE ANGELS' SHARE
Maya Hess
ISBN 0 352 34043 6

A derelict cottage on the rugged Manx coast is no place for a young woman to hide out in the middle of winter. But Ailey Callister is on a mission – to find and overthrow the man who has stolen her inheritance. Battling against the elements and her own desire for sexual freedom, she fights ghosts from her past to discover the true identity of Ethan Kinrade, the elusive new owner of the vast, whiskey-producing estate that by rights should be hers.

THE DEVIL INSIDE
Portia Da Costa
ISBN 0 352 32993 9

This is exactly what happens to the usually conventional Alexa Lavelle after a minor head injury whilst holidaying in the Caribbean. And in order to satisfy her strange and voluptuous new appetites, she is compelled to seek the enigmatic and sophisticated doctors at an exclusive medical practice in London. Their specialist knowledge of psycho-sexual medicine takes Alexa into a world of bizarre fetishism and erotic indulgence. And one particularly attractive doctor has concocted a plan which will prove to be the ultimate test of her senses, and to unleash the devil inside.

Black Lace Booklist

Information is correct at time of printing. To avoid disappointment, check availability before ordering. Go to www.blacklace-books.co.uk. All books are priced £6.99 unless another price is given.

BLACK LACE BOOKS WITH A CONTEMPORARY SETTING

☐ ON THE EDGE Laura Hamilton	ISBN 0 352 33534 3	£5.99
☐ THE TRANSFORMATION Natasha Rostova	ISBN 0 352 33311 1	
☐ SIN.NET Helena Ravenscroft	ISBN 0 352 33598 X	
☐ TWO WEEKS IN TANGIER Annabel Lee	ISBN 0 352 33599 8	
☐ SYMPHONY X Jasmine Stone	ISBN 0 352 33629 3	
☐ A SECRET PLACE Ella Broussard	ISBN 0 352 33307 3	
☐ GOING TOO FAR Laura Hamilton	ISBN 0 352 33657 9	
☐ RELEASE ME Suki Cunningham	ISBN 0 352 33671 4	
☐ SLAVE TO SUCCESS Kimberley Raines	ISBN 0 352 33687 0	
☐ SHADOWPLAY Portia Da Costa	ISBN 0 352 33313 8	
☐ ARIA APPASSIONATA Julie Hastings	ISBN 0 352 33056 2	
☐ A MULTITUDE OF SINS Kit Mason	ISBN 0 352 33737 0	
☐ COMING ROUND THE MOUNTAIN Tabitha Flyte	ISBN 0 352 33873 3	
☐ FEMININE WILES Karina Moore	ISBN 0 352 33235 2	
☐ MIXED SIGNALS Anna Clare	ISBN 0 352 33889 X	
☐ BLACK LIPSTICK KISSES Monica Belle	ISBN 0 352 33885 7	
☐ GOING DEEP Kimberly Dean	ISBN 0 352 33876 8	
☐ PACKING HEAT Karina Moore	ISBN 0 352 33356 1	
☐ MIXED DOUBLES Zoe le Verdier	ISBN 0 352 33312 X	
☐ UP TO NO GOOD Karen S. Smith	ISBN 0 352 33589 0	
☐ CLUB CRÈME Primula Bond	ISBN 0 352 33907 1	
☐ BONDED Fleur Reynolds	ISBN 0 352 33192 5	
☐ SWITCHING HANDS Alaine Hood	ISBN 0 352 33896 2	
☐ EDEN'S FLESH Robyn Russell	ISBN 0 352 33923 3	
☐ PEEP SHOW Mathilde Madden	ISBN 0 352 33924 1	£7.99
☐ RISKY BUSINESS Lisette Allen	ISBN 0 352 33280 8	£7.99
☐ CAMPAIGN HEAT Gabrielle Marcola	ISBN 0 352 33941 1	£7.99
☐ MS BEHAVIOUR Mini Lee	ISBN 0 352 33962 4	£7.99

❏ FIRE AND ICE Laura Hamilton	ISBN 0 352 33486 X £7.99
❏ UNNATURAL SELECTION Alaine Hood	ISBN 0 352 33963 2 £7.99
❏ SLEAZY RIDER Karen S. Smith	ISBN 0 352 33964 0 £7.99
❏ VILLAGE OF SECRETS Mercedes Kelly	ISBN 0 352 33344 8 £7.99
❏ PAGAN HEAT Monica Belle	ISBN 0 352 33974 8 £7.99
❏ THE POWER GAME Carrera Devonshire	ISBN 0 352 33990 X £7.99
❏ PASSION OF ISIS Madelynne Ellis	ISBN 0 352 33993 4 £7.99
❏ CONFESSIONAL Judith Roycroft	ISBN 0 352 33421 5 £7.99
❏ THE PRIDE Edie Bingham	ISBN 0 352 33997 7 £7.99
❏ GONE WILD Maria Eppie	ISBN 0 352 33670 6 £7.99
❏ MAKE YOU A MAN Anna Clare	ISBN 0 352 34006 1 £7.99
❏ TONGUE IN CHEEK Tabitha Flyte	ISBN 0 352 33484 3 £7.99
❏ MAD ABOUT THE BOY Mathilde Madden	ISBN 0 352 34001 0 £7.99
❏ CRUEL ENCHANTMENT Janine Ashbless	ISBN 0 352 33483 5 £7.99
❏ BOUND IN BLUE Monica Belle	ISBN 0 352 34012 6 £7.99
❏ MANHUNT Cathleen Ross	ISBN 0 352 33583 1 £7.99
❏ THE STRANGER Portia Da Costa	ISBN 0 352 33211 5 £7.99
❏ ENTERTAINING MR STONE Portia Da Costa	ISBN 0 352 34029 0 £7.99
❏ RUDE AWAKENING Pamela Kyle	ISBN 0 352 33036 8 £7.99
❏ CAT SCRATCH FEVER Sophie Mouette	ISBN 0 352 34021 5 £7.99
❏ DANGEROUS CONSEQUENCES Pamela Rochford	ISBN 0 352 33185 2 £7.99
❏ CIRCUS EXCITE Nikki Magennis	ISBN 0 352 34033 9 £7.99

BLACK LACE BOOKS WITH AN HISTORICAL SETTING

❏ MINX Megan Blythe	ISBN 0 352 33638 2
❏ THE AMULET Lisette Allen	ISBN 0 352 33019 8
❏ WHITE ROSE ENSNARED Juliet Hastings	ISBN 0 352 33052 X
❏ THE HAND OF AMUN Juliet Hastings	ISBN 0 352 33144 5
❏ THE SENSES BEJEWELLED Cleo Cordell	ISBN 0 352 32904 1
❏ UNDRESSING THE DEVIL Angel Strand	ISBN 0 352 33938 1 £7.99
❏ FRENCH MANNERS Olivia Christie	ISBN 0 352 33214 X £7.99
❏ LORD WRAXALL'S FANCY Anna Lieff Saxby	ISBN 0 352 33080 5 £7.99
❏ NICOLE'S REVENGE Lisette Allen	ISBN 0 352 32984 X £7.99
❏ BARBARIAN PRIZE Deanna Ashford	ISBN 0 352 34017 7 £7.99
❏ THE BARBARIAN GEISHA Charlotte Royal	ISBN 0 352 33267 0 £7.99

To find out the latest information about Black Lace titles, check out the website: www.blacklace-books.co.uk or send for a booklist with complete synopses by writing to:

Black Lace Booklist, Virgin Books Ltd
Thames Wharf Studios
Rainville Road
London W6 9HA

Please include an SAE of decent size. Please note only British stamps are valid.

Our privacy policy
We will not disclose information you supply us to any other parties. We will not disclose any information which identifies you personally to any person without your express consent.

From time to time we may send out information about Black Lace books and special offers. Please tick here if you do _not_ wish to receive Black Lace information. ❏

Please send me the books I have ticked above.

Name ....

Address ....

....

....

....

Post Code ....

Send to: Virgin Books Cash Sales, Thames Wharf Studios, Rainville Road, London W6 9HA.

US customers: for prices and details of how to order books for delivery by mail, call 1-800-343-4499.

Please enclose a cheque or postal order, made payable to Virgin Books Ltd, to the value of the books you have ordered plus postage and packing costs as follows:

UK and BFPO – £1.00 for the first book, 50p for each subsequent book.

Overseas (including Republic of Ireland) – £2.00 for the first book, £1.00 for each subsequent book.

If you would prefer to pay by VISA, ACCESS/MASTERCARD, DINERS CLUB, AMEX or SWITCH, please write your card number and expiry date here:

....

Signature ....

Please allow up to 28 days for delivery.